Reginald Fitz-Roy Stanley

Passages from the Auto-Biography of a Men of Kent

Reginald Fitz-Roy Stanley

Passages from the Auto-Biography of a Men of Kent

ISBN/EAN: 9783337013554

Printed in Europe, USA, Canada, Australia, Japan

Cover: Foto ©Raphael Reischuk / pixelio.de

More available books at **www.hansebooks.com**

PASSAGES FROM

THE AUTO-BIOGRAPHY OF A
"MAN OF KENT."

TOGETHER WITH A FEW ROUGH PEN-AND-INK

SKETCHES, BY THE SAME HAND,

OF SOME OF THE PEOPLE HE HAS MET, THE

CHANGES HE HAS SEEN, AND THE

PLACES HE HAS VISITED.

1817—1865.

EDITED BY

REGINALD FITZ-ROY STANLEY, M.A.

LONDON:

PRINTED BY WHITTINGHAM AND WILKINS.

1866.

RESPECTFULLY AND AFFECTIONATELY

DEDICATED TO

MY MANY FRIENDS,

BY A

" MAN OF KENT."

CONTENTS.

INTRODUCTION BY THE EDITOR.

HESE " Passages from the Auto-bio-graphy of a ' Man of Kent ' " were written at the request of a large circle of friends, and in the brief intervals of leisure, extending over a period of seven years, which the writer could snatch from an increasingly active life.

The manuscript has been placed in my hands, as an old friend, with a request that I should say something by way of introduction. I have yielded most willingly to the request, and in looking over the pages have done little more than occasionally draw my pen through a few passages, which, from family allusions, or otherwise, would not be understood by the general reader.

Some account of the writer, in addition to that which he has himself supplied, may not be out of place here, and will moreover enable the reader to form a better conception of the idiosyncrasies of the " Man of Kent."

My friend has been known to me for more than a quarter of a century, and scarcely a day has passed during the greater part of that period without my meeting him either in business, or at the fire-side.

The " Man of Kent" is a Nonconformist; not by birth and education, but upon principle and deliberate choice, as he has told us in the following pages; and although he is one of the noble few who

" Reverence his conscience as his King,"

he is nevertheless ready at all times, where compromise of principle is not expected, to co-operate with all denominations of Christians in everything calculated to benefit the commonweal.

In politics he was, in early life, what is termed an out-and-out Radical; but thought and observation have in a great measure corrected and modified the theories of his younger days, and he has become in what may be called the afternoon, if not the evening, of life, a moderate and progressive Reformer. I remember hearing him upon one occasion at a Debating Society, stand out most determinately for the " People's Charter;" but though he believes the leading principles laid down in that able document to be the natural right of every well-conducted citizen, he sees also that education and moral training must prepare the millions of our still unenfranchised countrymen for that which undoubtedly must shortly be conceded to them.

The "Man of Kent" is distinguished by a love of justice, and is a thorough hater of everything mean and dishonourable. I have sometimes thought that my friend must have been born under the influence of the planet Mars, as he has a fiery disposition, ready in an instant to meet an opponent. He is a bold, resolute, and fearless man, and would have made a good soldier, had not a hesitation in his speech have been the means of turning his early career into another channel. He is rather choleric and hasty, with a dash of sarcastic humour, and a certain impetuousness of temperament, that not unfrequently make him in danger of being misunderstood. I fear he has sometimes given offence to those who do not know him well, by his vehement manner, and the strong language he makes use of when excited. He is an *intense man*, and possesses an unconquerable will that sometimes appears to defy all opposing forces. He is rather impatient of reproof; but gentle remonstrances from a friend of whose intention and kindness he is assured, and whose judgment he approves, have often great weight with him. He is always ready for the arena of conflict, and when he is thoroughly convinced of the injustice of any wrong, he will advance

again, and again, and yet again, until he has con-
quered.

There is a marked individuality in the "Man
of Kent;" he can, when the occasion requires it,
say the most bitter and withering things; he has,
however, a good deal that is genial and tender in
his nature, and can comfort the sorrowful, as well
as encourage the timid. As a visitor of the sick,
in the later years of his life, he has always been
welcome, having himself suffered repeatedly from
illness. Before ill-health had told upon him he
was a man of great energy and quickness.

My friend would have been an orator, but for
the defect in his speech acquired in his youth;
which, however, he so far corrected in his riper
years as to be able to address a public assembly,
when it would have been difficult to detect a
vestige of what he calls his " old enemy." The
" Man of Kent" never gets up to speak without
being thoroughly in earnest, and, as he feels his
subject intensely himself, is an effective speaker.
We recollect once hearing him deliver a lecture
" On Public Speaking and Reading Aloud, with
Illustrations from the Throne, the Senate, the
Pulpit, the Poets, and the Bar," before a large
gathering, when he succeeded beyond the expectations of his friends.

The " Man of Kent" is endowed with considerable powers of persuasion; is witty and piquant in

conversation; and possesses no small amount of acuteness and discrimination: he has a keen appreciation of the beautiful in nature and art, and has a cultivated taste. He is quickly moved by objects of sorrow and distress, and is always readily induced to acts of kindness; many a bereaved family circle has been soothed and comforted by his brotherly sympathy, and cheered and encouraged by his kindly counsels. No man had ever a kinder heart for sympathy, or a more open hand for the relief of distress; and no mind was ever more formed for the enthusiastic admiration of noble actions.

My friend delights in jovial society, has a good ear for music, though no musician; can sing a good song, and is passionately fond of poetry, music, and dancing, though this latter accomplishment was more freely indulged in the dawn and exuberance of his early life. He is active and enterprising in everything that he takes in hand; the things he most excels in are the labours which he undertakes voluntarily. My friend is not altogether indifferent to applause, and he is rather ambitious of renown.

I scarcely like to touch upon the domestic characteristics of the " Man of Kent," though, from a long and uninterrupted friendship, extending over many years, I have had ample and frequent opportunities of knowing what he is in the home circle. I may say, however, that he is a kind and indulgent husband, and the father-love in his heart is deep and unfailing.

As a friend he is faithful, frank, and true-hearted, as many of those who read the following pages will be reminded; and I trust that the day is very far distant when his genial company and hearty laugh will be no more heard in our social gatherings. I am sure I shall be borne out by the willing testimony of those who know him, in saying that he never grudges any amount of labour that his numerous friends exact from him. His correspondence is very voluminous; and since the introduction of the " penny postage " it must have cost him a small fortune for " Queen's heads." Few private men have a larger circle of correspondents; and this, combined with his every-day work, leaves him but little leisure for recreation. His kind and playful intercourse with children has made him a special favourite with them, while his natural gallantry always secures him a hearty welcome from the mothers and maidens. His manly qualities have endeared him to the fathers and brothers, so that he is always greeted with a hearty welcome by his many friends.

In personal appearance the " Man of Kent " is rather above the average height, with brown hair, moustache, and ample beard. These latter appendages he adopted some years before they became so generally worn. He is of open visage, quick, penetrating dark eyes, and of highly nervous temperament.

In conclusion, I may say that the "Man of Kent" has no pretensions to literary talent beyond throwing off an occasional letter or article for some of our London and provincial journals. It is, however, believed that these rough-and-ready reminiscences of what my friend has denominated "an ordinary every-day life," told as they are with freedom and faithfulness, will not be an unwelcome contribution to the light literature of the day.

I must regret that the failing health of my friend should have compelled him to retire from some of the more active duties of his busy life; and trust that, as he is relieved from these exacting labours, he may, in a well-earned and happy retirement, be spared to his family and friends for many years.

REGINALD FITZ-ROY STANLEY.

Maitland Park,
London, N.W.

Christmas, 1865.

AUTO-BIOGRAPHY OF A "MAN OF KENT."

INTRODUCTORY.

N sitting down to write some particulars of what may be termed an ordinary and every-day life and history, I have not the vanity to believe that I can record anything new or startling, much less that which is deep and profound. Neither is it my intention to discuss the question whether a man should, or should not, be his own biographer, as that has already been done by far abler pens, and among others by no less a writer than the late John Foster, in his justly celebrated " Essays."

We all revert with an affectionate interest to our past life, " the days that are no more," and I am not without the hope that perhaps by committing to writing some of the incidents in my own history, and the mental and moral revolutions that have taken place in connection with them, I may influence some who are just entering the great arena of conflict. At all events it shall be my endeavour to point out, to our young men especially, a few of the shoals and quicksands that I have met with in my own career; and in recording these I may retrace—

> " Footprints, that perhaps another,
>   Sailing o'er life's solemn main,
> A forlorn and shipwreck'd brother,
>   Seeing, shall take heart again."

B

Biography has been aptly said to be " Philosophy teaching by example." A distinguished American writer tells us that " all things are engaged in writing their history. The planet, the pebble, goes attended by its shadow. The rolling rock leaves its scratches on the mountain ; the river, its channel in the soil ; the animal, its bones in the stratum ; the fern and leaf, their modest epitaph in the coal ; the falling drop makes its sculpture in the sand or the stone. Not a foot steps into the snow or along the ground, but prints, in characters more or less lasting, a map of its march. Every act of the man inscribes itself in the memory of his fellows, and in his own manners and face. The air is full of sounds, the sky of tokens, the ground is all memoranda and signatures, and every object covered over with hints which speak to the intelligent." Another equally distinguished man of our own time, and our fatherland, tells us, in words that I am glad to transfer to my humble page—" Think of ' living !' Thy life, wert thou the ' pitifulest of all the sons of earth,' is no idle dream, but a solemn reality. It is thy own; *it is all thou hast to front eternity with.* Work then, like a star, unhasting, yet unresting."

I.

PARENTAGE, INFANCY, AND CHILDHOOD.

"My boast is not that I derive my birth
  From loins enthroned, or rulers of the earth:
But higher far my proud pretensions rise,
  The child of parents pass'd into the skies."

 MAN is rarely or seldom asked in the present age about his parentage; but if from any cause he comes before the world, the question is at once put to him "Who are *you?*"

Nevertheless, it is interesting, to those more immediately concerned, to know something of the origin and family of such as we are daily coming in contact with, and therefore I shall, for their information, record that my father was the son of a farmer, and was born at Boughten-under-Blean, a small village on the old London road, about six miles from Canterbury.

From a family register, most religiously chronicled, and preserved in an old Bible, I find that my grandfather was born in 1739, and was twice married. Two children were the result of the first marriage; and thirteen of the second, nine sons and four daughters. My father was the third son of the second marriage, and was born in 1782.

I have often heard him speak with admiration of my grandfather as one of the best-looking men in that part of the county, "standing six feet two in height." He ap-

pears to have been a man of kindly disposition, but rather
a severe disciplinarian in his family.

At meal times they mustered rather a large party, and
it was the custom at that time for the children to stand at
the table. My grandfather kept within convenient reach
a long osier stick to correct any juvenile indiscretions.
The offender was spoken to once, but the second offence
was sure to bring down upon him a rap from the long
stick. He was quite an oracle in the little village, and
was accustomed to frequent the parlour of " The Squirrel"
in the evening, to read the newspaper aloud, and to discuss
the political questions of the day. My grandfather's death
is duly recorded in the family registry, "aged 72 years,
5 months, and 20 days."

I have a vivid recollection of my grandmother, who, at
the death of her husband, came to reside at Canterbury,
and died there when I was nine years old. Well do I
remember her kind and benevolent countenance: she was
rather below the average height, a well-proportioned handsome old lady, and in her youthful days must have been
very pretty. I return, however, from this little digression,
to my father. After receiving a plain commercial education, at the best school in the neighbourhood, he was ap-
prenticed to a bookseller at Canterbury, who combined with
that business an extensive printing establishment. Several
local publications were printed and published by his master,
and amongst others that might be named are " Hasted's
History of Canterbury," and the second edition in octavo
of that writer's famous " History of Kent."* Both these
valuable county histories have been long out of print. The
first edition of the latter work has now become so rare that
whenever it is found in the market, book collectors and
bibliographers will give a large sum for the handsome

---

* The author's beautiful copy of the first edition of this work is
in the Grenville Library at the British Museum, and contains
some additional plates, which are very scarce, with a list of them
in Hasted's handwriting, and his signature attached.

volumes. This gentleman was also the printer and pub-
lisher, for many years, of the " Kentish Chronicle," and
was a member of the corporation.

The young apprentice applied himself so industriously
and sedulously to his duties that he soon gained the special
notice and esteem of his master, who kindly encouraged his
persevering endeavours to become thoroughly acquainted
with every branch of the business, and who was much
pleased with his amiable and respectful demeanour.

At the expiration of his term of apprenticeship, my father
had become so valuable to his master that he took him at
once into partnership. Shortly after this, the young trades-
man was chosen a member of the Corporation, and so popular was he as a citizen that he was elected Mayor the same
year; an incident, I believe, without precedent in the corporate annals of that ancient city.

On the death of his partner he succeeded to the business,
and for many years conducted the editorial department of
the weekly journal printed and published at the establishment, of which newspaper he was one of the proprietors.
He was subsequently a second time elevated to the office
of chief magistrate, and continued an active member of
the Corporation till his removal from Canterbury.

It is not too much to say of my father, with reference
to his official career as a magistrate, that he gained the
respect and esteem of all classes by his frankness and
amiable manners, nor less by his desire at all times to
temper justice with mercy. As a master, I may quote
from one who served his apprenticeship to him, and who
afterwards became editor of one of the most influential
and popular of our metropolitan weekly journals,* in his
obituary notice, says, " It might be truly affirmed that
to his numerous workmen he was indulgent to a fault,
and those who were reared by him to the business of a
printer, loved him as a parent and a friend."

---

* The " Weekly Dispatch."

In my early years we saw very little of my father, save on Sundays, when he gave himself entirely up to his family. Business, and his official duties, absorbed his time and attention during the week. My mother always made it a rule that the children should be in bed by the time he left business, as it was his custom every day to go somewhat carefully through the London papers.

As we grew up he took a loving interest in all that concerned his family, and was especially delighted on the fine Sunday afternoons to take us boys for a long walk. Those of my readers who are acquainted with Canterbury know that the neighbourhood abounds in picturesque scenery; and well do I now remember many of the beautiful walks with my father and brothers on those happy Sundays. My youngest brother would generally contrive to call my father's attention to what is now known as " a sweet-stuff shop," and a packet of sweeties was always readily given to add to the enjoyment of our walk. We all loved our father very much, and while I pen these brief recollections of him the beautiful words of the Poet Laureate come instinctively to my mind :—

> " His memory long will live alone
> In all our hearts, as mournful light
> That broods above the fallen sun,
> And dwells in heaven half the night."

How shall I speak of my mother? It seems but yesterday that her gentle face was shining on me, and I almost hear now her soft and loving voice. Oh! there is nothing like a mother's love. Years can never efface thy memory from my heart. I loved my father, but as I write my bowels are moved at the recollection of my mother. How much do I owe to the thousand gentle influences that were showered upon me from thy self-forgetting daily and hourly ministrations? Much, very much, do I owe thee, thou sweet guardian of my early days; would that I had followed the advice of thy loving voice in the morning of my life: how many sorrows I should have thereby escaped. I, alas! could not boast of being

> " A son that never did amiss,
>   That never shamed his mother's kiss,
>   Nor cross'd her fondest prayer."

My mother was born at Ostend in 1785, and was an only daughter.

My grandmother, on my mother's side, was, from all accounts, a very beautiful woman; and this is fully borne out by a portrait in possession of one of the family, painted by a distinguished Flemish artist of that day. She did not however live happily with her husband, who appears to have been a man of harsh and severe manners, wanting all those gentle and tender qualities that make a good husband and an endeared father. My grandmother died at the early age of thirty-eight, and at her death, my mother, then only eight years old, came to reside with some relatives in London, and afterwards at Exeter; but not being happy with these relatives, she ultimately lived with a family at Margate, and found there a comfortable and happy home.

During her residence at Margate my mother was an occasional visitor at Canterbury, having a relative living in that city; and it was on one of these visits that she was introduced to my father, then a handsome young bachelor with a thriving business, a member of the Corporation, and one who had already filled the important office of chief magistrate of the city. A mutual attachment grew out of these occasional visits to Canterbury, ending in that " consummation most devoutly to be wished;" and in 1811 they were married.

INFANCY.

" Our birth is but a sleep and a forgetting :
The soul that rises with us, our life's star,
Hath had elsewhere its setting,
And cometh from afar :
Not in entire forgetfulness,
And not in utter nakedness,
But trailing clouds of glory do we come
From God, who is our home :
Heaven lies about us in our infancy."

Having said thus much of my parentage and pedigree,
I come now to speak of myself.   I was born at Canterbury
in 1817, and am a " Man of Kent."   It is scarcely necessary to remind my readers that in what are called " the
good old times," that city was the metropolis of the kings
of Kent.   The learned tell us that Canterbury is derived
from *Durwhern* (Dur-Gwern, river of marshes, mead, or
alders), latinised *Durovernum ;* and it was also denominated in the ancient British language, *Caer Cient*, or City
of Kent ; and in Anglo-Saxon, *Cant-wara-byrig*, City of
the Men of Kent.

The Civic Government of Canterbury is very ancient,
as the city archives testify : those documents, so carefully
preserved by our forefathers, offer a rich field for the antiquarian.   Not long since some highly interesting particulars relating to the manners and customs of the early
Canterburians were brought to light by a very competent
hand, Mr. Thomas Wright ; and good service has also
been rendered in this respect by an accomplished citizen
of Canterbury, Mr. John Brent, the younger.

Much has been said, and not a little written, by those
interested in matters of this nature, as to the origin of, and
distinction between, " Men of Kent," and " Kentish Men."
Having taken some pains to examine the question, I sus-
pect the real origin of the terms to have been to distinguish
any man, whose family had long been settled in the
county, from time immemorial it may be, from new settlers ;

the former being genuine " Men of Kent," the latter only
" Kentish Men." The West Kent men, according to
tradition, are styled " Kentish Men ;" while those of East
Kent are more emphatically denominated " Men of Kent."*

Believing that nothing is trivial in the formation of character, I may mention that my parents were members of
the Church of England, and that my mother was particularly careful to bring me up in the religious observance of
all the ceremonials of that communion. While she was
ever mindful to instil into me from my earliest days, in
common with my brothers and sisters, the love of God and
of goodness, all this was done in connection with, what I
may call, the domestic requirements of the Established
Church. We were all in our infancy duly taken to the
baptismal font, and as soon as we could be taught anything
formally, the catechism of that Church was most assiduously
inculcated upon us.

As soon as we were able to walk we were taken to the
parish church; and well do I now remember the high boxed-
up pews that hid from us altogether the surrounding congregation, and only when we were lifted up to stand upon
the seats, could we get a glimpse of the parson. The
peculiar close and fusty smell of that old church I have
never thoroughly got rid of. The morning service of the
Church of England is very long and tedious even to an
adult, and how little children are kept at all quiet during
its performance is to me a wonder. Many a time, as the
communion service and the sermon came, have I begged
leave to sit down upon the reed hassock that I might lay
my head down upon the comfortably stuffed green-baise
seat and take a little nap. I was always sure to wake in

---

* Should the reader be desirous of pursuing this question any
further, he will find some particulars in " Notes and Queries,"
Vol. v. p. 615 ; and also, in a work by the late Charles Sandys,
Esq., of Canterbury, entitled, " Consuetudines Kantiæ ;" see also a
highly interesting little volume lately published, " Canterbury in
the Olden Time," by John Brent, junior

time, as I had a great horror of being left in the church.
When from any cause I could not get my accustomed nap,
I was much amused in looking up at the hatchments that
adorned the white-washed walls of the sacred building. I
recollect very often spelling out that rather long word
" RESURGAM," wondering what in the world it could
mean ; and when I whispered my wonderment to my
mother she would put her finger to her mouth, and with
a reverend shake of the head, place her hand gently
on my shoulder and bid me sit still, and be a good boy.
Altogether the service at church was a very slow affair :
there was no " high embowed roof," no " storied windows
richly dight, casting a dim religious light," no " pealing
organ," no " anthems clear :" the service was tediously
long, bald, and cold ; and the attempts at psalmody were
such as did not endear good old Tate and Brady to my
juvenile recollections.   Right glad was I always when the
vicar wound up his dry and unimpassioned sermon of forty
minutes with the welcome words, " Now to God the Father,"
&c, which was a signal for us to get ourselves into marching order, and once more breathe the pure sweet air of
the bright and cheerful street.

The Sunday afternoons were generally spent in reading
aloud the Scriptures, learning the collect for the day, and
never omitting the catechism, every part of which is fresh
in my recollection to this day. Sometimes my dear mother
would read to us a chapter from " The Whole Duty of
Man," a well-bound volume, frequently found in those
days in close proximity to the Bible in most families connected with the Church of England. I do most cheerfully
bear my willing testimony to the constant and unremitting
care of my father and mother to bring us up in the faith
and practice of the Church of our forefathers, and also to
illustrate their teaching by consistent example.

II.

BOYHOOD: SCHOOL-DAYS, AND YOUTHFUL FOLLIES.

> "Shades of the prison-house begin to close
>   Upon the growing boy,
> But he beholds the light, and whence it flows
>   He sees it in his joy;
> The youth who daily farther from the East
>   Must travel, still is nature's priest,
>   And by the vision splendid
>   Is on his way attended;
> At length the man perceives it die·away
> And fade into the light of common day."

N looking back upon the home of my childhood and early school life, I cannot but be struck with the inseparable connection existing between these two important periods in the history of a child; and yet they are for the most part spoken of and treated separately. Home itself must be a school; and the school, if it is to be of salutary use in forming the moral, as well as the mental man, must be a home.

The education of a child begins on the mother's bosom, or upon her knees, as it prattles around the household hearth, and is daily and hourly influenced by all that it hears and sees. It begins with the earliest dawning of the intellectual powers, before we perceive the difference between looks, and words, and actions. How responsible then is the position of parents for the first impressions made upon the young. Streams of influence flow in upon the child, every one of which will work its own result in moulding the future character. Happy is the child that is born into a family where the parents are distinguished by culture and intelligence; and where tenderness, high moral feeling, and good sense is the atmosphere breathed around.

Parents are very properly careful about the food that their children partake of, but how much more careful should they be of the example placed before them; of the books they read; and also of the companions they associate with.

I think also that children should from their earliest days have "no place like home:" suitable amusements should ever be combined with early teaching, as much of the restlessness which characterizes children is attributable mainly to their not being wisely instructed and entertained in the home circle.

I was allowed to run about pretty much as I liked till I was five or six years old, when I was sent to what was then called a Dame's School. I have a most affectionate remembrance of the kind and patient treatment of the lady to whose care I was entrusted for my early education. She quite won my young heart by her gentle manners and loving disposition, and was the first out of my own family to call forth that desire to please, which I have cultivated in after life, especially in reference to those whom Burns denominates "the blood-royal of life." I feel it to be strictly true in my own case, that

> "The earliest wish I ever knew
> Was woman's kind regard to win;
> I felt it long ere passion grew,
> Ere such a wish could be a sin."

Parents are not careful enough in ascertaining the character and disposition of those to whom they confide their children. Some people have an idea that the child must be treated harshly and rudely, to develope a rough manliness or hard womanliness, but observation will convince us that this is a great mistake. There is in all of us a yearning to be loved, and gentle influences tell most effectively on the springs of action. The little child has this longing to be loved; it is that désire which prompts the tiny infant to put out the little chubby rounded arms to the mother, and purse up its rosy mouth for the sweet and tender kiss. If "every flower enjoys the air it breathes," so does the babe enjoy and rejoice in the love that is poured out upon it; and it is my belief that every loving caress of the mother goes down deep into the heart of the child, and sounds a latent depth of feeling there, which will be developed in after years. The love that the mother lavishes upon her babe is not lost; it goes flowing through that little form, touching the tender and infantile spirit with sweetness, and we may hope waking the most exquisite pleasure there.

It is my firm conviction that harsh and severe treatment on the part of parents, or instructors of youth, will never succeed in education; and that it is love and gentleness that will call out the best qualities of the child.

I remember somewhere to have read that "if you want your children to meet the world manfully and womanfully, fill them with love till they overflow. Begin in the cradle; rock them into love: sing love into them. Let all things pure and beautiful speak to them from the pictures on your walls, if you can afford pictures; let love play out upon them in the music of harp and piano, if you can afford harp and piano; and every mother ought to know how to sing, and the child's cradle should be rocked, and the little one lulled to sleep, by snatches of melody wafted down from the very gate of heaven."

But to return from this digression on early educational influences to myself. On leaving my first school, and my kind instructress, I was sent to a "Commercial Academy" at Canterbury, presided over by a man of impulsive and hasty temper, with very little aptitude for teaching. It was a large school of about sixty boarders, and more than that number of day-scholars.

The course of study at this school included all the branches of a sound English and commercial education: the scholars were mainly composed of tradesmen's sons in the city, and the rough and ruddy scions of the surrounding farmers. We attended at the Dancing Academy of a late celebrated and well-known professor, one afternoon in the week, and always looked forward with much pleasure to those cheerful exercises, as the girls from several boarding schools in the neighbourhood were accustomed to meet us on those occasions for the practice of that healthful and exhilarating accomplishment. I look back upon those dancing meetings as among the pleasantest and purest of my boyish days, and regret much that there exists any prudential reasons why parents should deny their children the great pleasure of learning, in the morning of life, how to " trip it on the light fantastic toe."

I was not so fortunate as my eldest brother in the matter of education. He was sent to the " King's School" at Canterbury, where some of the most distinguished men of the county were educated. Among them may be mentioned Lords Thurlow and Tenterden, who have received their due from the ready pen of Lord Campbell, the able biographer of the Chancellors and Chief Justices of England. Sir Egerton Brydges, of Lee Priory, was also educated at the King's School, and a host of others too numerous to mention.*

The master was assisted by three ushers; and there was scarcely a day passed without my witnessing corporal punishment, in the shape of a good caning, inflicted upon some of my schoolfellows, and not unfrequently coming in for a share of it myself.

---

* See "Memorials of the King's School, Canterbury, by Rev. J. S. Sidebotham, M.A." A most interesting little volume that every "man of Kent" should possess.

The master of the school to which I was sent appeared to love flogging for its own sake, rather than as an unpleasant, but in some instances necessary, auxiliary to teaching. Never shall I forget the intense feeling of indignation with which I witnessed, what may be called, in school parlance, the ultimatum of corporal punishment. The poor culprit was a boy about thirteen years of age, and had been guilty of some petty theft in the school, as well as having been a constant trouble to the master and his assistants by frequent misbehaviour. The poor trembling fellow was led by the master to a double desk, upon which he was placed. He commenced the flagellation with cruel earnestness, and proceeded for some minutes to use a new birch made for the occasion, in spite of the shrieks and writhing agony of the helpless boy. The punishment did not end till the strong arm of the master was tired with his savage work, and the poor degraded lad was led out of school to his bed-room, amid the half suppressed groans of the boys; not so much for the crime for which the poor fellow had suffered this degrading punishment, but with a feeling of horror and disgust at the malicious and brutal manner in which this infliction had been conducted. The boy ever after had a stricken look, and even in play hours, as well as in the school, appeared always conscious of the scene he had been the unhappy occasion of. I ceased from that day to have any respect or regard for the master; and this feeling was intensified not long after, when, for some trivial offence, he struck my younger brother a violent blow on the side of the face, which brought blood from his ear, and obliged him to remain at home under medical treatment for more than a fortnight.

This tyrant of a master lost so many of his pupils by his harsh and severe treatment that he was obliged to give up the school. He was succeeded by a man who, though rather fond of using his cane, never proceeded to the more degrading and disgusting exhibitions which I have felt it to be my duty to record.

The new master was in many respects a more estimable man than his predecessor, but was deficient in firmness, and wanted that controlling and administrative talent that should characterize the head of a large school. He found out in a short time his unsuitableness, and gave up the scholastic profession for the more quiet and unobtrusive pursuits of a country clergyman.

About this time I acquired a habit of stammering, which was not only a great annoyance to me at school, and frequently a subject of some merriment to the boys, but has also been a source of bitter mortification and grief to me all through life.

It was, however, as I shall hereafter relate, the cause of altering very materially my subsequent history.

Physiologists and medical men have ascribed this distressing malady to various causes; but in my case the habit arose from being occasionally in the company of a relative who stammered badly, and being rather a quick and imitative lad, I unhappily became a most inveterate stammerer. The subject has been one that I have necessarily thought much about, and I have carefully read everything that came within my reach relating to it, and hope in a future part of the story of my life to say something further of stammering and stammering-curers.

My new school-master took rather a liking to me; and as my impediment of speech prevented me at times from taking my usual place in the classes, he kindly allowed me to sit at a vacant desk by his side, on an elevated platform, that I might have the benefit of hearing the lessons without subjecting me to the pain of making an exhibition of myself to the other boys. It is however rather singular that my stammering never kept me from taking part in the elocution classes. I could always read, or recite, any composition that ran on flowingly and continuously; I only failed in dialogue.

I had always a great fondness for reading aloud and reciting poetry, and gained several prizes during my school-days for elocution. I remember upon one occasion so far forgetting myself, as in the temporary absence of the master, to rise from the raised desk, and with a grave look, and loud voice, give out in true clerical style—" Let us sing, to the praise and glory of God, the one hundredth psalm." I commenced the well-known words,

"All people that on earth do dwell."

* * * * *

The thing was so suddenly done, and the consternation of the under-masters so great, that I got fairly through the first verse before they had time to hush me into becoming silence. A severe but kindly reprimand from the master, on returning to the school, rewarded me for this my maiden attempt at public speaking.

My connection with this school was shortly interrupted by an incident that induced the master to beg that my father would remove me from his establishment. I was one day leaning over the desk at which I was at work, speaking to a boy on the opposite side, with my back to the master, when he came softly and silently behind me and gave me two sharp cuts with the cane below my jacket. I was so stung by the cowardice of the thing, and indignant at what I considered an unmerited punishment, that I instantly snatched up a slate before me and hurled it with all my might at the master's head. Fortunately it did not hit him, but it gave him to understand most unmistakably that I was not a boy to be trifled with, or that would quietly submit to any punishment that mere caprice would prompt him to inflict. He very properly felt that some serious castigation must follow such an offence as that of which I had been guilty, or that, for the sake of example, I must leave the school; and I cannot but think that he acted wisely in preferring the latter alternative.

On my leaving this school my father sent me to a " select academy" in Guildhall-street, Canterbury, presided over by rather a superior man in point of education; but from his

c

bad temper totally unfit to have the care and management of boys. I took a dislike to him from the first, and an event occurred, shortly after my being placed under his care, that rendered my removal from his influence necessary.

He was a tall, thin, red-haired man, with a vinegar aspect, and very passionate. He resided at some short distance from the school, and one favourite mode of punishment with him was, on leaving in the afternoon, to give a boy some hundred lines to learn, and lock him up in the school for two or three hours.

Three of us one afternoon had misconducted ourselves so as to come under his displeasure, and at five o'clock we were duly locked in with "a hundred lines" from "Enfield's Speaker" to commit to memory. It so happened on this afternoon that a large party of us had determined to go for a swim in the Stour at the close of the school, and we three poor unfortunates felt the disappointment very much. After thinking a little upon the hardness of our fate, I suggested that we should give the old gentleman the slip, and join our companions at the river. One of the fellows who was locked up with me consented to go, providing I could devise a way for our escape from the durance vile, and would lead the van; but the other fellow, a boy of phlegmatic temperament, and who afterwards became a lawyer, and practised for many years at Canterbury, thought very naturally what we should catch in the morning, and therefore prudentially declined to join us in our flight.

I was determined not to be disappointed in our promised bathe, and a glance at the fan-light over the school door convinced me at once that we had only to remove one of the squares of glass, and we could get out as comfortably as possible. We collected the boxes and placed them against the door, and having raised a platform of the requisite height, I set to work to remove the putty with my pocket-knife, and in a few minutes the glass was out, and I was down on the other side. My plucky companion soon followed, and in twenty minutes we had joined our schoolfellows at the bathing place. We were received with three hearty cheers, and as "stolen waters are sweet," I never enjoyed a bath more in my life.

However, matters wore a very different aspect in the morning. The master had come to the school at seven in the evening to hear our tasks and to let us out; and no small stir was made when he found that two of the birds had flown. The boy who had remained behind told the infuriated master all about how it happened, and that I had been the instigator of this unwarrantable breach of school discipline.

As soon as the school was assembled on the following morning, and the customary prayers had been duly gone through, we were summoned to the desk; and after the case had been fully gone into, and the daring character of our misconduct pointed out and dilated upon, I was adjudged as the principal delinquent to be flogged: and the other fellow, who was my junior by a year, was let off with a good caning and a severe lecturing. This being over, I was led out of the school by the master with birch in hand into the adjoining lobby, and ordered at once to prepare for a flagellation; I told him promptly, and with a most defiant look, that I had never made an exhibition of myself yet, and that I should not do so then. A deadly paleness came over the master's face, and he saw at once that it would not do to lay violent hands upon me; so I was conducted back to the school, and the old gentleman having announced that I had refused to undergo the punishment awarded, I was dismissed from the school. I very soon bundled my books into my box and placed it on my head, wished the master good morning, and made my appearance at home, much to the astonishment of my father and the regret of my poor mother. However, when I came to explain the nature of my offence, and had told them of the penalty that was to have been inflicted, they neither of them blamed me for refusing to submit to the brutal and degrading punishment.

My father was obliged once more to look about for another school for me; but finding none that were at all suitable at Canterbury, I was sent to an old established boarding school at Ashford, presided over by a clergyman.

As I had never been away from home before I found a boarding school presented some new phases of life to me, and I was not long before I sadly missed the constant and tender care of my dear mother. The school was pleasantly situated in the outskirts of the town, and at the bottom of the playground stood one of the most noble windmills I have ever seen. Many an hour have I spent in looking out from the fantail of that mill upon the beautiful surrounding country, and the mysteries of milling were always interesting to me as a boy.

The master, as I have said, was a clergyman, and was a tall well-proportioned man of about fifty-five, with a kindly benevolent face and highly attractive manners. He was assisted in the school by two ushers, one of whom was his eldest son. The school consisted of about fifty boarders and half-a-dozen day scholars. The mistress was a regular termagant, and when in a passion was a complete fury. She was a short stout woman of about fifty, a large white face, small nose, and very ugly red hair. She was an object of fear and hatred to the whole establishment, and I was often half inclined to believe that this feeling was shared to a great extent even by the master himself. There was an only daughter, who very much resembled her mother, only that she had the redeeming quality of being young. I used to admire the golden tresses that hung around her white neck and fell upon her plump shoulders. An usher from the adjoining grammar school was paying his addresses to this young lady during the time of my remaining at the school, and I only hope that if she ever became his wife that she has turned out better than her mamma. There was a younger son, a lad of about eight years old, who took a great liking to me, which I was glad at times to turn to good account. Boarding schools in those days were all famous, or rather infamous, for keeping the boys short of food, and I regret to say that that at Ashford was not an exception. I soon found that the change of diet and the limited allowance began to tell upon me. I was a strong growing boy of twelve, and at no one of the three meals a day which were allowed did I get enough to eat. Many a time have I played the monkey to amuse the master's little son, who, as a reward for the fun I occasioned, gave me some slices of thin bread-and-butter, or an extra piece of bread-and-cheese, which he had got for himself.

We were rung up in the morning at six, and expected to be in our places in the school by half-past ; and studied till eight. Breakfast consisted of a buttered roll, (not by any means large,) and half-a-pint of milk and water, which we denominated "sky blue." Some of the boys, from a love of money, would sell half their roll; and many a time, when the funds would allow of it, have I given a halfpenny a day for weeks together for the half of some poor fellow's allowance.

School re-opened at nine and continued till twelve. An hour was allowed to play, and dinner at one. This meal generally consisted of joints and puddings, except on Saturday, when the fragments of meat were collected together, and made into an immense pie, served up with a plentiful supply of gravy. Saturday's dinner was a general favourite with us, except you happened to light upon a bit of meat in the pie a little too gamy. No boy was expected to send up his plate for a second supply of either meat or pudding, though the invitation to do so was always politely put by the master and mistress at each end of the long table. We used to get a good deal of boiled rice, rendered very palatable by being served up with hot milk and sugar. The bread puddings were always dreaded ; as they consisted of all the stale pieces that had accumulated during the week : it went by the name of "stick-jaw," from the fact that it clung so tenaciously to the mouth. The favourite puddings were currant, and baked plum; the former was denominated "cat's tail," from its being made in long rolls; and I must mention rather an amusing little incident that occurred one day with reference to the latter, which was a favourite dish with me.

These puddings were made in large round flat dairy tins, and came to the table always hot from the oven. The boys had been served all round, and an extra slice or two remained in the dish. Being rather an unruly fellow, I sat always at the top of the table (the post of honour!) next the master; his back was turned away for a moment, and in an instant I dexterously seized upon one of the tempting pieces of pudding, and slipped into my pocket. The boys on the opposite side were not a little amused at the movement. It was, however, so terribly hot in my pocket, that I could not possibly endure it, and began to be very uneasy in my seat, and to hold the bottom of my stomach, as if I had been suddenly attacked with spasms or cramp. I tried in vain to shift the stolen morsel from place to place. The master, seeing my restlessness, inquired if I was unwell, and this remark produced a burst of laughter from the boys, which led him to insist upon knowing the cause, and I was obliged very reluctantly to produce the precious morsel. Never shall I forget the look of the mistress; she did not speak, but her worthy husband saw in a moment that it must not be passed over as a joke, so I was desired to leave the table. I beat a retreat, sadly mortified, not only at losing the pudding, but I knew that I should get a regular roasting from the boys, as well as being punished for the offence.

When school assembled in the afternoon I was called up to the master's desk, and seriously talked to on this breach of decorum; the lecture ended in my being awarded four strokes from the "flapper."

This instrument of juvenile correction consisted of a piece of thickish leather, about six inches long, rounded off at the top, and attached to an old ruler. It very much resembled the flappers seen in butchers' shops for destroying blow-flies. When applied rather sharply to the palm of the hand, it produced not an altogether unpleasant tingling feeling, and would, I should imagine, be a good thing to promote a sluggish circulation of the blood in those who are troubled with chilblains. When I had duly received the appointed number of strokes, I held out my hand for another and another; the master saw at once that this mode of punishment would not succeed with me. It was the first time since my arrival at the school that he had administered corporal punishment upon me, and it was the last. He led me into his study, took me by the hand and spoke kindly, and reminded me in gentle words how grieved my mother would be should he be obliged to inform my father of my bad behaviour. Tears flowed freely down my cheeks, and from that afternoon I was an altered boy. The good man had found out what others might have done before him, that gentleness and kindness will generally succeed, where severity and harshness totally fail. This was the turning-point in my school life; the kindness and confidence thus wisely manifested wrought so powerfully upon my better nature, that I began to love the master, who told my father at the end of the quarter that I was the most manageable boy in the school, and that he had not the smallest trouble with me.

I soon became a special favourite with the little son; but I was not so fortunate as to get into the good graces of the mistress: she was a cruel and passionate woman; she had none of the qualities, either of mind or person, that were at all likely to tell upon such a nature as mine. I may just mention one instance, among many that come to my recollection, of her cruelty and spitefulness. Our heads were carefully inspected once a week with a small-tooth comb; and this not at all agreeable operation was always performed by the mistress, assisted by the housekeeper, a good, kind creature, by the name of Rachel, and one who was beloved by every boy in the school.

The boys who had for any reason fallen under the displeasure of the old lady during the week were selected and told off for a combing, and upon them she would scrape away so unmercifully that many a time have I been ready to scream out at the pain inflicted.

Numerous are the tales of fun and frolic that recur to my memory while thinking of this period in my history, and the time would fail me to tell of the usual gambols which boys at school indulge in. We were always sent off to bed early, and the apartment I slept in contained about twenty boys. We used to hold concerts with an orchestra constructed with our boxes piled up, and frequent were the spouting meetings held in that room upon all sorts of subjects, to say nothing of leap-frog, blind-man's-buff, and other games.

I was often called upon to mount the rostrum, consisting of boxes, and hold forth upon some given subject, and it was not a little singular that at these oratorical displays at our " midnight meetings," I never found my stammering an impediment. I used to hang fire most of all when I stood up in class, and had not spent overmuch time upon my lessons.

I must, however, now take leave of this period of my history, and I do so with the feeling that the last two years of my school-days spent at Ashford were among the pleasantest of my early life.

III.

LEAVING SCHOOL, CHOICE OF A PROFESSION, AND EVIL INFLUENCES.

" Look not mournfully into the Past; it comes not back again. Wisely improve the Present; it is thine own. Go forth to meet the shadowy Future, without fear and with a manly heart."

 COME now to speak of one of the most important periods in my life and history— that of leaving school, and before entering upon any employment.

It would, I think, be well if parents thought more carefully of what they intended doing with their sons on leaving school. I have often found, on conversing with fathers on the subject, that there has been no decision arrived at as to the future destination of their boys; but in many cases they have imagined that something would turn up when the time for their leaving school arrived. Surely it is a subject of very great importance, that a youth should have selected for him some trade or profession that he may enter upon at once on leaving school, and for which his previous education shall have prepared him. Although the taste and predilections of a youth should be considered in a matter so deeply affecting his future welfare, and care should be taken not to make a boy a tailor or a tinker, if he is better qualified for an architect or a civil engineer; yet it is, I think, desirable that a father should thoughtfully and wisely select that oc-

cupation for his son that he deems most in accordance with
the leading tendencies and characteristics of the boy, and in
the pursuit of which he would be most likely to succeed.

I fear in my own case that my father was so absorbed in
his large business, together with his public and official en-
gagements, as to have had little time for observation to study
the individual character and tendencies of my brothers and
myself, and to select the occupation most suitable for us.

I was accustomed to spend a good deal of my time in
my father's printing-office, and had rather a liking for
some branches of that business. My sympathies, however, were more with the pressman than with the more
quiet and sedentary work of the compositor. I have many
an hour when a boy stood and watched the snowy sheet
laid carefully upon the block of type, and envied the man
who, with the turn of a handle, and a hearty pull, could
produce the ample printed page. I greatly admired the
pressman, whose work in those days of printing was very
different to that which obtains in the present day, when
machinery has almost superseded manual labour. I remember that the person referred to was a tall, thin, wiry
man, with shirt sleeves turned up above the elbow, showing an arm with unusual muscular development. He
sometimes would allow me to pull an occasional sheet; but
these were generally cast aside as waste, for though I was
a strong and sturdy boy, there was needed the length of
arm, and the firm footing to produce the good impression.

My mother had a very strong objection to my becoming
a printer, as the language and habits of those employed in
that business were not such as to improve the moral status
of a boy who had a decided leaning to imitate whatever he
deemed manly in those around him.

I was very partial to the bookselling and stationery
branches of my father's business, and many an hour did
I spend in looking carefully through the new books, particularly the "Annuals" that were so numerous at that
period. My father dealt largely also in patent medicines,

and I was very fond of going through the long series of
drawers containing these certain and infallible cures and
remedies for all the ills that flesh is heir to.

My eldest brother was in the shop acting as an assistant, together with a young man who had served his apprenticeship to my father, so that my services were not
much needed in the business. I was, however, useful on
" Magazine days" in tying up and delivering the monthlies
and quarterlies which were distributed among my father's
numerous customers.

When not engaged in the shop I used to visit the estab-
lishments of our neighbours, and so got an insight into
" the art, trade, and mystery" of a good many businesses.
Among these was a pastrycook's, where there were three
very pretty daughters; and I have stood by the hour together to watch them make up the tarts and puffs, and
" three-corners," &c, until I got quite to like, not only
the pastry, and the company of the young ladies, but could
also roll out the paste and manipulate some of the fancy
articles manufactured pretty well.

There was also a large drapery business directly opposite to my father's, and I was allowed to have the full range
of that establishment, and used not unfrequently to assist
them in " taking stock." The haberdashery and the glove
departments were the favourite branches with me.

I was a frequent visitor also at the shop of a chemist
and druggist near us, who allowed me to gum the labels
on the perfumery bottles, and sometimes to roll up the pills
into swallowing order.

A butcher who lived within a few doors of us came in
for a share of my help, for I thought chopping sausage-
meat and filling the skins a very pleasant diversion, and I
soon became quite an adept at the work. The slaughter-
house adjoining was not an uninteresting place to me, and
I have for many an hour looked on at the operations taking place there. To see an ox led to the slaughter, and
the noble beast felled to the ground by a single blow of

the pole-axe, has often inspired me with awe and fear.
These sanguinary exhibitions were, however, always repulsive to me, and I could not help regarding the man
who killed the poor beasts, and dressed the carcases, with
a kind of instinctive feeling of horror.　I have sometimes
gone into the pen where ten or a dozen sheep have been
awaiting the knife, and watched with tender interest the
affrighted look and beseeching eye of those gentle creatures, who would " lick the hand just raised to shed their
blood."　Some members of my family proposed that I
should become a butcher; but though I was often a visitor
at this place of death, it was for the most part because I
had nothing else to do.

At the back of my father's house was a large gin dis-
tillery, and as I was well known to the proprietor I was
often there, and have witnessed many a time the process
of converting the juniper-berry into " Old Tom."　The
fragrant smell of the pure and unadulterated liquor was to
me far more agreeable than the taste.

There was also a wholesale wine and porter establishment hard by, and I have for days together helped to
bottle off many a pipe of sherry and hogshead of London
porter.　The owner of the business, an old bachelor,
dealt largely also in ginger beer and lemonade.　A nephew
lived with him as chief assistant, and for whom I formed a
strong attachment.　He was a fine young fellow of about
two-and-twenty, and under his tuition I became quite
a first-rate hand at bottling off, corking, and tying down
the ginger beer and lemonade.　Poor fellow, it would have
been well for him had he confined himself to these cooling
and refreshing beverages, but the temptation was too strong,
and he became at length an habitual drunkard.　His end
was very painful and tragical.　He had taken upon one
occasion more than his usual quantity and became up-
roariously intoxicated, he was seized with an attack of
delirium tremens, and died in the greatest possible agony.

The death of this young man made a great impression

upon me. His uncle, a most kind-hearted man, was very fond of him, and was deeply grieved at the sad event. Knowing the intimacy that subsisted between his nephew and myself, he was desirous that I should take warning by his dreadful death. The day before the funeral he took me into the room in which the body was laid, and never shall I forget the sight when he slowly removed the lid of the coffin, and revealed to me the disfigured, almost un-recognizable countenance of him who had been my friend. When in health he was a noble fellow, with an open, frank, and manly face; but the fearful disease from which he died had so disfigured that countenance that I could hardly discern the well-known features. That sight, and the look of his poor weeping uncle, I have never forgotten. We stood silently gazing upon the now repulsive form that lay before us for some minutes, not a word was spoken. The broken-hearted uncle took my hand with a gentle pressure, and I retired with a sorrowful and a heavy heart. I was among those the next day who followed him to his early grave, and I never now think of him without lifting up my heart to God that I may be preserved from that damning habit which destroys body and soul, and in the present instance removed from a wide circle of friends one of the noblest young men I have ever met with.

In leaving this sad story the words of the poet recur to me—

"When cold in the earth lies the friend thou hast loved,
    Be his faults and his follies forgot by thee then ;
Or if from their slumber the veil be removed,
    Weep o'er them in silence, and close it again."

I must here digress a little from my personal history to speak of my native city as it was at the time I refer to.

Canterbury in my youthful days was the principal city in the high road from London to the Continent, and a stream of private carriages and post-chaises, containing the gentry and great celebrities of the day, were continually rolling through the narrow streets of the old city, on their way to Dover and the Continent.

The " Fountain Hotel," kept at that time by one that was always spoken of as "Sam Wright"—peace to his memory—was almost a little town in itself, and that worthy gentleman made a large and well-earned fortune from his business. He was well known and highly respected by all the distinguished personages who visited his establishment *en route* to the Continent, as well as by the gentry of the surrounding neighbourhood. I was very intimate with this gentleman and his family, so that I could run in at any time. I was a special favourite with Mrs. Wright, and her only daughter presented me with my first watch and chain. I recollect watching with much admiration the graceful manner in which this " fine old English gentleman " would lift his hat, and bow to the inmates of the carriages as they left his hotel. I don't think that Simpson, of Vauxhall notoriety, could have performed this salutation with more ease and grace.

The stage coaches at this time running between London and Dover were as well horsed as, or better than, any in the kingdom; and the coachmen were famed both for their intelligence and gentlemanly bearing. It will occur to many of my readers who were acquainted with Canterbury some thirty-five years since, that the Tally Ho! coaches, corresponding in coaching to " express trains " on the rail, were among the finest sights of the kind to be seen in all England. The vehicles themselves were smart and elegant, built by a first-rate London coach-maker: the horses were selected from a large and well-chosen stud, and caparisoned in such a manner as to give the turn-out more the appearance of private carriages than of public conveyances.

These two splendid four-horse coaches,—alas! now among the things of the past,—were driven by gentlemen who are even now well known and most highly respected all through from London to Dover, and therefore I shall be guilty of no impropriety in mentioning their names in my humble pages; I shall do so in the terms they were spoken of when I was a boy. " Ned Clements " and " Tom Bolton," of the " Rose Inn," Canterbury, are names that will not soon be forgotten, at least by the generation in which they lived, though the iron horse and the hissing rattling train have long since taken the place of the Tally Ho! coaches.

With both these gentlemen it was my happiness to be well acquainted when a boy, and hundreds of times have I stood opposite the " Rose Inn " to see the horses changed, and have admired the masterly manner in which those noble animals were led off and managed by these accomplished whips.

The father of Mr. Edward Clements kept the " Rose Inn " for very many years; and I do not forget, even at this distant period, that Tom Bolton married one of the daughters, who was moreover one of the prettiest of all the pretty girls in Canterbury.

Canterbury, at this time, was anything but a place to improve the moral and intellectual status of a youth of ardent temperament just fresh from school. Of what was going on in the upper classes I know but little, but the state of society among those of my own rank at that period was most deplorable.

The tradesmen, for the most part, spent their evenings away from their families, at the parlour of some inn, where the newspapers of the day were read aloud by the best reader that could be selected; and the scandal and talk of the city formed the topics of conversation over their grog and pipes. No provision whatever was made to find suitable evening amusement for the young men.

At the time referred to there were no " Young Men's Associations," or " Societies for Mutual Improvement," at least not of the character which obtains at the present day. A young man has only himself to blame now if he gets into bad society, and forms improper connections. Everything is done now-a-days to benefit this deeply interesting class, and to bring them under good influences. Associations are to be found in all our provincial towns, as well as

in London, to provide entertainment, and furnish opportunities for mental culture, that were never thought of in
the days of my youth.

Let any one glance at the handsome series of volumes
of lectures issued under the auspices of the Christian
Young Men's Association in London for proof of what I
say. Among the lectures in that series are to be found
some of the foremost literary men in the country; as well
as not a few of the most distinguished preachers of the
day; and each successive session does but show the desire
on the part of the Committee, and the zealous and intelligent Secretary of that most admirable association, to give
the young men of the metropolis ample opportunities of
improving their minds.

The Dublin Young Men's Christian Association is not
so well known on this side the Channel; but the Committee of that Association have also issued an annual series of
volumes, not so handsome in point of typography and get-
ting-up, but numbering among its lecturers some of Ireland's noblest sons, and most accomplished scholars, with
the late revered Archbishop Whately at their head.

Leeds, Manchester, Birmingham, Liverpool, Norwich,
Sheffield, and many other of our large provincial towns,
have also noble institutions, where young men engaged in
business may find a home for their leisure hours, and
opportunities of improving their minds, which, alas! in my
younger days, never existed.

We young fellows at Canterbury were allowed to find
any amusements that offered, and I was very soon drawn
into a circle of acquaintance and companionship, the boast
of which was that one should outstrip the other in ribaldry
and licentiousness.

At the period I am writing of harlotry and concubinage
obtained to a fearful extent at Canterbury. Few, indeed,
I fear, were the married men who did not indulge in
licentious habits; and as for the young men of that day it
was a reproach not to have gone to " the same excess of riot."

Just at this very critical time I formed an acquaintance with a man of fascinating manners and good address, who took a great liking to me. He was a man old enough to be my father, and obtained great influence over me. His conversation chiefly turned upon women, of which he professed to be a great admirer. He put into my hands some filthy and abominable books, profusely illustrated, and calculated to excite within me, and prematurely to develope, all that was bad in the nature of such a temperament as mine. Oh! the injury, the irreparable injury done by' this man. I curse his memory down deep in my heart of hearts even now. He was the means of inflicting upon me one of the greatest curses that can be borne by a thinking being,—that of an unhallowed imagination. Those pictures of wickedness have never passed away. They haunt me like ghosts wherever I may be, and beckon me often into forbidden paths. The inflaming and damnable letterpress accompanying those illustrations has been so imprinted in letters of living fire upon my mental being that the foul, filthy, and blasting characters will never be erased from my mind. Would that I could put upon these pages the bitter bitter grief these abominable books have occasioned me in after years. Oh, my young brothers, guard most jealously your moral purity, for if you lose it once, it is gone for ever! You may, by God's grace, be rescued and delivered from the terrible abyss, and become a husband and a father; but you can never hope to enjoy the pure and blissful pleasures which those have who have kept their garments white. Believe me when I tell you that the man who in his youth has indulged in forbidden and licentious pleasures never can have the enjoyment of him who is innocent of " the great transgression."

Should these pages meet the eye of some youth just entering upon life, full of hope, and with "a heart as merry as a marriage bell," and should he be tempted to purchase for himself, or borrow from another, books of this

D

character, oh ! I would say to him, I entreat you, I pray
you, as you value your immortal soul, and that body which
has been given you for far nobler ends, shun these books
as you would an accursed and damnable thing. Do not
look at them ; fly from them as you would from a deadly
serpent; turn away from them as you would from one
covered with a foul and loathsome disease. No defilement
is so bad ; no physical evil that can come upon our poor
fallen humanity is at all comparable to this leprosy of the
soul, this defilement of the inner-man, this that will follow
you like a horrid ghost wherever you may be,—into the
family circle with all the domestic sanctities of life ; into
the fair and beautiful scenery of nature, which can never
be thoroughly enjoyed by a polluted mind.

An impure imagination I feel to be, even now that " my
days are in the yellow leaf," my greatest curse. I hope
and believe that I am a forgiven man, yet I cannot rid
myself from it. If it was intolerably loathsome to be
tied and bound to a putrid and stinking corpse ; oh ! my
young brothers, believe me, when I say that an impure
mind is a far greater curse. No words of mine can ever
adequately convey the intense grief that those books have
occasioned me ; and no greater and more terrible damna-
tion in a future world could, I think, be endured than that
of being compelled to carry such a mind through the endless ages of eternity.

I never see books of this character (though those that I
more particularly refer to are not allowed to be sold in
public) exposed in the shop windows of some well-known
localities, made justly infamous by this vile traffic, without
feeling a very strong inclination to smash the window, and
tear the accursed thing into a thousand fragments, and
crush it beneath my feet as I would an adder's egg.

Pardon me, my gentle reader, if I have spoken strongly
upon this unwelcome subject ; but if you are a father or a
mother, your son could not be warned against anything
that could do him so great an injury as that of which I

have been speaking. If you are a sister, oh! pray that those noble brothers of yours, whom you love so much, and are so proud. of, may be preserved from this great evil;—and if you are a youth just opening into manhood's prime, oh! my young brother, turn away and flee from this damnable and accursed thing as you would from the gulf of hell.

I was introduced to many places by the man I have just referred to, and among others to a house where were held the meetings of what was called " The Mountain-Pecker Club."

The members of this association, chiefly composed of tradesmen and young men of the city, held their meetings weekly at a well-known inn at Canterbury. The meetings commenced at eight o'clock in the evening, and any member had the privilege of introducing a friend. It was a kind of free-and-easy debating society, interspersed with a little singing, and concluded with a supper consisting of sheep's heads (from whence its name) baked and boiled, with sausages (for which Kent is famous), and mashed potatoes.

The members of this club were a set of jolly fellows, and I was the youngest among them, and as happy as a king. The subjects discussed were chiefly political and social; but occasionally a religious question came before us, and I remember on one occasion standing up, with all the effrontery and boldness of a young precocious youth of fifteen, and delivered an oration, which was much applauded, against Christianity as a thing not at all in harmony with a fellow enjoying life in any and every way he pleases. The songs at these meetings were for the most part of a questionable character, as songs almost always are where women are excluded from the company.

I thought, even then as a youth, that there was something extremely disgusting and revolting in a number of men, some of them hoary-headed, meeting together to excite each other by loose conversation, *double-entendres*,

and lewd and licentious songs, to all sorts of wickedness.

It may readily be imagined what an effect such meetings as these produced upon a youth of my age and temperament—full of life, and buoyancy, and health—and
ready to indulge in anything and everything which would
minister pleasure and gratification.

It was proposed, after some little time, that I should be
admitted a regular member of this club; but my eldest
brother, who was also a member, objected to my admission
on account of my extreme youth, and also because he did
not like my being a witness to scenes and society which I
might at any time enlighten the home circle about.

The landlord of this inn, a very kind-hearted and benevolent man, took a great fancy to me, as also did his wife;
he invited me one evening to take a walk with him, and I
found it was for the purpose of having some conversation
with me upon the subject of my becoming a member of
the " Mountain-Pecker Club." He put the fact of my
being so young, and the grief that it would occasion to my
father and mother (he had lived with my father as a news-
man in his early life) at my associating with men so much
older than myself at an inn, together with the injurious influence it would have upon my morals. All this was laid
before me so kindly and wisely, that I was induced to give
up the desire I had so readily expressed of becoming a
member. I never think of this kind-hearted man but with
gratitude and thankfulness, and always make a point of
calling upon him whenever I visit my native city. He
has retired from public life for many years, and lives now
in one of the pretty little cottages in the beautiful neighbourhood of Harbledown.

The annual return of the fair at Canterbury, held in the
Cattle Market, was an event always looked forward to with
much expectation.

I need not remind any of my Kentish readers, acquainted
with Canterbury at this period, that there were at this fair

many attractions for both old men and maidens, as well as for young men and children; perhaps foremost among them was Madame Tussaud's unrivalled collection of wax figures, in which were depicted, with life-like faithfulness, the great and illustrious men and women of ancient story.

With me the favourite group of the collection was that of Cleopatra and Marc Antony. I remember to have gazed admiringly at these figures as a boy, and to have almost envied the great Roman warrior as he reclined by the side of Egypt's beauteous queen.

Now my country-cousins may, on visiting the great metropolis, gain the *entrée* not only to the general collection, where will be found the all-but breathing effigies of the mighty and illustrious dead, but also obtain an introduction to men and women that you have perhaps for the most part only read and heard of, yet whose names are as "familiar as household words." Men and women of whom England may be justly proud. Then there is the hall of kings, where you may study at your leisure the countenances, and forms, and costumes of all the monarchs that have reigned over our beloved country.

Those who are interested about the great Napoleon— and where is the Englishman who is not?—may here see an unrivalled collection relating to that name, at which once "the world grew pale;" and such as are fond of studying humanity in some of its less attractive forms may have their taste gratified to the full in the "Chamber of Horrors."

But it was not my intention to have dwelt so long upon Madame Tussaud; and lest I should be open to the charge of puffing, let me assure my readers that I have no connection with that establishment further than occasionally visiting the collection with my family, and paying my shilling as other people do.

To return, however, from this digression to Canterbury fair; there was Wombwell's menagerie with "the famous lion Wallace," and the "real Bengal tigers," leopards, laughing hyænas, monkeys, together with birds of gay and gorgeous plumage; the never-tiring elephant picking up the sixpences dropped by the delighted spectators, and which were carefully handed by the noble creature to the keeper, to find him in tobacco and beer.

In addition to Madame Tussaud's and Wombwell's menagerie, must be included " Richardson's theatre" and " Middleton's puppets;" the last-named has I believe of late years passed off the scene, while Richardson still flourishes at our country fairs in all the bloom and freshness of his early fame. To these must be added the "Pig-faced Lady," and dwarfs before Tom Thumb and his sweet little wife of Barnum reputation were even heard of; the " Real Mermaid " and the " Learned Pig " came in for a share of the patronage; and then lastly, but by no means the least attractive, were the "peepshows," where for a penny you might see the battles of Waterloo, the Nile, and Trafalgar, with the " dreadful tragedy of Maria Martin and the Red Barn."

Though in common with my young fellow-citizens I was not a little delighted at the annual returns of the long-looked-for fair, yet the thing of all others that charmed me most was "Algar's Crown and Anchor dancing booth." There, as soon as the shades of evening came down, was a blaze of variegated lamps in every conceivable device and form ; and about nine o'clock might be seen pouring into this attractive place almost all the (I was going to say respectable) well-to-do male population of my native city: to the honour of the matrons and maidens of Canterbury, no woman with any regard to propriety and decency would be seen at such a gathering ; and so my readers may well imagine the character of those of the other sex that frequented this fascinating place. Here indeed

> ·　·　" was a sound of revelry by night,
> ·　·　·　·　·　·　· and bright
> The lamps shone o'er fair women and brave men;
> A thousand hearts beat happily; and when

Music arose, with its voluptuous swell,
Soft eyes look'd love to eyes which spoke again,
And all went merry as a marriage bell."

The moral atmosphere of such a gathering was not one
for the matrons and maidens of Kent, and would ill accord with the sanctities of domestic life. At the Crown
and Anchor dancing booth there was no restraint ; and
every one seemed for the time to be forgetful of all the
decencies and proprieties of life, and bent only upon plung-
ing into the whirlpool of pleasure.

It was at such a scene as this, which I have been attempting to reproduce and to describe, that I first met with
a girl that afterwards exerted a great influence upon me.
I was introduced to her by one of my boon companions
far older than myself. She was a fair and frail young
creature of seventeen, with well-formed figure, a face not
remarkable for beauty, though what may be called good-
looking.

"She was not pretty, many said,
To me she was far more—
One of those women women' dread,
Men fatally adore."

She danced like a Taglioni, and it was long after the
hour of midnight ere we gave over that fascinating and
dangerous amusement.

At the time referred to I had only just turned fourteen,
but was far older in appearance and manners : it was not
a little flattering to my vanity that a good-looking girl,
some years older than myself, should take a liking to me.

Oh ! it is a dangerous, and sometimes a damning thing
for a woman to look approvingly into your eyes. It needed a
strength of virtue, and a control of self that, alas, did not belong to me then,—and even in late years such a temptation
must not be tampered with,—there is safety only in flight.

This fair young creature had fallen into the hands of
an officer belonging to one of the infantry regiments at
that time stationed at Canterbury. He was a very handsome man of about forty, and he allured his victim from

school to his base and lustful purposes. He kept her
away from her home with him in his quarters in the barracks for more than a week before he could break down
her virtue, and effect his wicked and selfish ends. He only
succeeded then, as many other villains have done, and are
now doing, by promising to make her his wife. Is it to
be wondered at that young girls fall victims to such wiles?
Here was a man in the meridian of life, handsome and
fascinating, a soldier, an officer, using all the artifices of a
pretended affection to allure this young maiden to yield
herself to his lustful embraces. Oh! my readers let your
indignation and scorn rest upon the man who looked into
those eyes, and gazed upon that soft cheek, mantling in eloquent blushes, and as he breathed out what she, alas, believed
to be his heart's love, in tender and tremulous words, gained
the heart and the person of that innocent and unsuspecting
girl. Blame her not, ye matrons and sisters,—she was
once as pure as any of yourselves, and but for this designing
man might have been a faithful loving wife and a happy
mother. My readers! these are the men that help to fill our
streets with poor unfortunates, and then tax our pockets
to provide " homes " and " refuges " for such as we can
persuade to avail themselves of them.

Should any maiden read these pages, and I trust there is
nothing in them that shall really defile any pure mind, may
she take warning from the fall I have just adverted to; and if
any man assures her, either in burning words, or in eloquent letters, with protestations that he will love her for
ever, to obtain possession of that priceless thing which, in a
woman, when once lost *can never be repaired*, oh, believe
him not—let her not say in her heart, he cannot betray me!
Believe me, my dear young fair reader, that such tender
words, such burning words, such melting words, have been
uttered in every generation since the first bad man be-
trayed, and since the first unsuspecting victim fell. These
lines may reach the man who effected the ruin of the young
creature that has given occasion to these remarks,—for he

yet lives, and is now honourably married, is the father of
children, and is a clergyman holding a dignified position
in a well-known and memorable parish in the west of England. What must be that man's reflections when he thinks,
as he must do occasionally, of the pain and misery he has
inflicted not only upon those whom he drew away from the
home circle to gratify his base and grovelling appetite, but
also upon the families involved in their ruin. I know from
the best authority, himself, that this was by no means a
single instance of his seductive power. Let him think of
the broken-hearted fathers who through his infamy have
hung their heads for very shame, and upon the mother's
curse that rests upon the man who has ruthlessly torn from
her heart and home the child she so tenderly and lovingly
reared. What terrible revelations of this nature will the
world to come make known !

But to return to the narrative. She lived with this
officer, as his mistress, for a few weeks only, when he embarked for India with his regiment, leaving this young
trusting creature to mourn his absence, a ruined and degraded girl.

The result of this cruel amour was the birth of a child
before the poor girl was sixteen years of age, and for
which no provision whatever had been made by the man
who had so basely allured her from the path of rectitude.
For anything he knew to the contrary, she might have
been turned out of doors, as many are, to find a home for
herself and his child in the wide wide world, shunned by
her own sex, who, in their desire to show their abhorrence
of such a fall from innocence, too often forget to denounce
the scoundrel who has brought about the ruin of their
fallen sister.

I became well acquainted with the father and mother
of this girl afterwards, and was a welcome and frequent
visitor at their fireside. The father was a horse-breaker,
and I was a special favourite with the mother, who looked
upon me almost as her own son.

It is not to be wondered at that this intimacy with the daughter led to that which should have been avoided. To the honour of her father and mother be it recorded that no countenance was given by them to anything of an improper nature ; they looked upon me as a young man fond of their daughter, and were pleased with my genial company.

*　　　　　　*　　　　　　*

*　　　　　　*

I fell, as thousands had done before me ; and who could wonder that I did so ?　Just imagine for a moment an ardent youth, full of life and lusty vigour, with an imagination inflamed by those blasting and pernicious books and prints to which I have before referred, and coming in daily contact with one very attractive in person and in address, older than myself, and you will, my gentle reader, I think come to the conclusion that had I escaped it would have been almost a miracle.

Oh ! that I could make this fall of mine a lesson of warning to others :—true indeed that " stolen waters are sweet"—and there are " pleasures of sin for a season :"— yes, the gratifications of illicit love snatched in this way are intoxicating to a fearfully dangerous degree ; yet in after life the recollections will be sad and the results irremediable.　Young man, keep yourself, or ask God to keep you, pure, if you would be really happy and truly manly. Yield not to the voice of the charmer, charm she never so enchantingly.　Hear, my young brother, the voice of Wisdom, "Attend to my words—incline thine ear unto my sayings.　Let them not depart from thine eyes ; keep them in the midst of thine heart.　For they are life unto those that find them, and health unto all their flesh. . . . . For the lips of a strange woman drop as an honeycomb, and her mouth is smoother than oil : but her end is bitter as wormwood, sharp as a two-edged sword.　Her feet go down to death ; her steps take hold on hell. . . . . Remove thy way far from her, and come not nigh to the door of her house: . . . . . and now mourn at the last, when thy flesh and thy body are consumed, and say, How have I hated instruction, and my heart despised reproof; and have not obeyed the voice of my teachers, nor inclined mine ear to them that instructed me."—*Prov.* iv. 20, &c.

Let these weighty words be pondered by you, my dear young brother—and "*Flee* youthful lusts:" for there is only safety in flight; parley not with them, or you will be overcome: to listen to solicitations from without, or to yield your heart to the more subtle and dangerous promptings from within, is to be overcome—is to fall. Unlawful gratification of those instincts, which God has endowed us with for nobler purposes, are and may be for the time most intoxicating and pleasurable, but in after life they will " sting like a viper and bite like a serpent."

One who had his fill of all this, and who died in the flower of his manhood, said mournfully at its close—

> " My days are in the yellow leaf,
> The flowers and fruit are gone ;
> The worm, the canker, and the grief
> Are mine alone."

Oh! what would I have given to have been preserved pure in the days of my youth. The moment you yield to these unhallowed pleasures you lose your self-respect. Self-respect is one of the noblest virtues that a man can cultivate, and to cherish it heartily will inspire you with the most elevated feelings. The man, or the youth, who *habitually* keeps this in exercise will not defile his body by sensuality, nor his mind by low and servile thoughts. This noble sentiment carried into daily life will foster all other virtues. To think meanly of one's self is to sink in one's own estimation, as well as in the estimation of those by whom we are surrounded, for " as a man thinketh in his heart, so is he." The feeblest among us may be sustained by the proper indulgence of this feeling, and there is no condition of life in which we may find ourselves that may not be lighted up by self-respect. Oh! my brothers, it

is a truly noble sight to see a young man hold on in a
course of purity and integrity amidst all the allurements
around him of the world, the flesh, and the devil, and resolutely refuse to demean himself by low and unworthy
actions.

My father now began to see the immediate necessity of
my being employed, for

> " Satan finds some mischief still
>   For idle hands to do."

As I wrote a tolerably good hand, he made an arrangement with a conveyancer in the city, who was also well
known to him, and who wanted a clerk, to take me as his
scribe.

The gentleman with whom I was placed was a little
dark handsome man of about forty-five, and lived in one
of the quiet lanes in my native city, the like of which is to
be found in all our cathedral towns. Although he kept
but one clerk, he had a good business, for most of the engrossing was put out to a law-stationer to be copied. The
drafts of the leases and conveyances were drawn up by
himself, as were also the long abstracts of title. The fair
copying of these last-named documents was given to me;
and I was much delighted with the work, as they had to
be written upon nice smooth rolled paper ; the pen used
to glide over the broad and ample page so quickly and
pleasantly, and the phraseology of these necessary accompaniments to a conveyance was so similar that I
soon learned it by heart, and had only to take a glance at
the leading word of a sentence to know all that was to
follow. I was glad when we had a conveyance in hand, as
it made the little master very good-tempered, and it was a
kind of work that one could do almost mechanically.

I was always particularly fond of writing, and furbished
up my German text that I had learned at school. I soon
did so well in my German text as to be entrusted to engross
a deed of conveyance with a heavy stamp affixed. I was

a little nervous at starting; but I dashed into it, and gained the commendation of my master for this my first attempt at engrossing. I was allowed to attach the skins of parchment together with the green ribbon, and append the seals myself, and also to fold the skins and endorse the outside title, and was not a little proud to lay it before my master in its finished state as my own " act and deed."

The salary I was to receive was £10 a-year, and never shall I forget the first quarterly payment. My master gave me a cheque for the amount, and I ran home all the way to present it to my father. I think I now see his quiet smile as he congratulated me on the event. I duly presented it at the Canterbury Bank for cash; and as it was the first money I had ever earned, I felt that I had a stake in the country.

I was my master's only clerk, and he had an only daughter, a fair-haired girl of nineteen. She had just returned from Boulogne, where she had been sent for two years to complete her studies. This young lady's return was not only welcomed by her father and mother, but helped very much to gladden some of the dull afternoons when there was not much business in hand. She used to look in at the office occasionally to see how I was going on, and her presence always filled the room with gladness. She was rather below the average height, but was well proportioned, and had the prettiest little feet I ever saw; they remind me, even at this distant period, of Wordsworth's lines—

> " Her feet beneath her petticoat,
> Like little mice stole in and out,
> As if they fear'd the light."

Oh ! there is something very beautiful in a fair young girl of nineteen, with

> " Rosy cheeks and lips of coral,
> Snowy neck and rounded arms."

And that man is not to be envied who, whatever else he

may possess, has no appreciation of maidenly beauty. What is more beautiful in this world of ours than to look upon a young and innocent girl in the early morning of life, " a graceful maiden with a thoughtful brow ?" There is a distinctiveness of character which cannot be mistaken, arising from a natural ingenuousness, mental repose, and the absence of everything which gives to more advanced age the impress of influences unfavourable to beauty of character, and also beauty of form.

Some one has said,—I quote from memory,—that " character is more visibly impressed on the faces of women than of men ; the former rarely wear a mask ; the latter, from the struggles, and toils, and anxieties of life, are often compelled to assume a countenance totally foreign to their feelings and nature, till it becomes almost habitual. Youth has this advantage over both ; time and care have graven no furrows on the cheek nor lines on the brow ; passion has not given a false lustre to the eye, nor grief a rigid and angular expression to the play of the mouth."

Another writer upon this subject says truly, " It is not the smile of her pretty face, nor the tint of her complexion, nor the beauty and the symmetry of her person, nor the costly dress and decorations, that compose woman's loveliness ; nor is it in the enchanting glance of her eye, with which she darts such lustre on the man she deems worthy of her friendship, that constitute her beauty. It is her pleasing deportment, her chaste conversation, the sensibility and the purity of her thoughts, her affability and open disposition, her sympathy with those in adversity, her comforting and relieving the poor in distress, and, above all, the humbleness of her soul, that constitute true loveliness."

Jean Paul Richter, a high authority on matters of this nature (for I confess I love to linger over the theme), says, " We do not discriminate sufficiently, when we imagine that the source of woman's power arises principally from the beauty of her countenance. For, although it may begin there, yet the charm and fascination is also manifested in a whole kingdom of gentle influences, distinguishing her from the other sex—such as the soft and graceful movements of her person, the tones of her voice, the loving moderation evinced in every action and expression, her yielding courtesy, her serene repose, the complete suppression and concealment of her own independent wishes and will, where they would clash with those of others. All these and such like qualities inspire us with that love and admiration which we wrongly suppose to be excited alone by the more tangible and unvarying charms of feature and face."

But to return from this rather lengthened digression to the conveyancer's pretty little daughter. Sometimes when her father was out, and her mother engaged in her domestic duties, and business did not particularly press in the office, she would give me lessons in singing. She had a soft and melodious voice and could play skilfully upon the piano. I was always fond of music, and with such an instructress it is not to be wondered at, that, in her estimation at least, I made some progress in my singing. She taught me, among other ballads and songs of that day, " The beautiful maid of my soul," " Love's young dream," " Meet me by moonlight alone," " I've been roaming," " Bid me discourse," &c, &c, and many others of a kindred character. We were accustomed not unfrequently to sing the favourite duet, " My pretty page," and she was particularly pleased with one óf Braham's noble songs, " The sea!"

My little instructress was a quick and sensitive girl, and would sometimes give expression to her feelings in silent tears as I tried " The last rose of summer," and " The meeting of the waters." Those tears richly rewarded me for all my pleasing toil ; for the poet sings—

> "So bright the tear in beauty's eye,
> Love half regrets to kiss it dry :
> So sweet the blush of bashfulness,
> Even pity scarce can wish it less."

Sometimes these pleasant diversions from "Now this indenture witnesseth," &c, were suddenly interrupted by the return of her father; and as I well knew his rat-a-tat at the street-door, I was always back in the office at my work when he returned.

I spent eighteen very pleasant months at these duties and pleasures, and, although I have long since forgotten much that took place in the office, the recollections of this fair girl and her lessons in singing have never been forgotten, and still linger lovingly in my memory as "a joy for ever."

The disparity in our relative ages, and the purity of heart of this gentle creature, were such as to restrain me, in those days of lawless gratification, from yielding to anything which would at this time embitter the recollection of these truly halcyon days.

The society and companionship of virtuous women are among the most ennobling influences that can be brought to bear upon man, and these little episodes in my early history tended to make me a better youth. I went back to my work with more zest and pleasure.

Happy would it have been for me had these influences been all that I was subjected to. On leaving the office at night, I came at once into contact with other and less holy influences: and all the poetry and music of the day past only helped to make the maddening cup of intoxicating pleasure, presented to me in the evening by the siren hand of her of whom I have before spoken, the more dangerous.

There was one advantage, however, in the attachment I had unfortunately formed, inasmuch as I spent all the time not occupied in the office either at her home, or in the long walks we had together; and this was the means of taking me away from the companions of my own sex, whose time was almost wholly given up to cards and gambling, and less exceptional excesses.

At the time I am writing of, St. Augustine's monastery

at Canterbury was desecrated to the purposes of a brewery
—such are the base uses to which some of the noblest
buildings which man can erect are subject to—and the
gardens adjoining, once the resting-place of the nuns and
monks of the holy order instituted by their illustrious
founder, were used as a bowling-green and tea-drinking
place for the plebeians of Canterbury. A part of the
original building was used as a fives-court, or racket-
ground, and I have seen in my early days some good
matches played there between the citizens of Canterbury
and some crack players from London.

I am happy to be able to record, for the information of
such of my readers as may not be aware of the fact, that
this grand old monastery of ancient story, and its beautiful
ruins have been rescued from these base purposes by the
munificent liberality of Mr. Beresford Hope, a gentleman
well known and very highly respected by all lovers of art.
That which was used as a brewery has long since given
place to a missionary college, under the able presidency of
the Rev. Henry Bailey, B.D., the successor of the lamented Bishop Coleridge, the first warden of the college ;
and the chamber over the fine old gateway that was once
devoted to cock-fighting—this is a veritable fact—is, I
believe, restored as much as possible to its original appearance, and is now used as a council-chamber by the heads
of the college.

The tea-gardens connected with the public-house adjoining the brewery, and part of the sacred building of St.
Augustine, on Lady Wootton's Green, presented, at the
time I am referring to, a kind of Cremorne on a small
scale. Fireworks, balloons, and the Blondin of those days,
attracted crowds of Canterbury lads and lasses, and the
old people as well—for it is most observable that at all our
places of amusement devoted almost exclusively to young
persons, there will be found not a few venerable-looking
men and women, who appear to be quite as much delighted
with what is going on as the young people.

E

St. Augustine's brewery!—(for so it was designated; what would the grand old saint have said to such a degradation?)—was at this time rented by the father of a schoolfellow of mine of the name of Beer,—a somewhat singular coincidence, and will afford a hint to Mr. Lower, in a new edition of his interesting work on " Surnames."

I can say with very much pleasure that having enjoyed the *entrée* to this establishment at all times, I can record the many happy hours spent in the fine old building, often climbing its lofty towers, which are even now in a fine state of preservation, to look out upon the splendid view to be obtained from the summit; and many a draught have I had of the good home-brewed, wholesome beverage manufactured under its sacred roof.

The brewery has been removed, and the building reclaimed from its odour of malt and hops to some of its primal sanctities. The brewer, who heartily welcomed me within its sacred walls, is dead; his son, my schoolfellow, carries on the business at a short distance from the original spot: he hardly recognized me a few years since, when I called to renew the acquaintance of our early days, and to remind me of some of my juvenile reminiscences.

What changes do a few short years make—how strange and altered Canterbury appears to me now! There is a mournful pleasure in revisiting old haunts when we can

> " Review the scene,
> And summon from the shadowy past
> The forms that once have been."

A new generation has now sprung up in the place of those who were seen in the shops and streets of the old city; and as I have loitered amid the scenes of my youth, I have been reminded of the reflections of one on going back to the scenes of his childhood:—

" I remember, I remember, the house where I was born,
The little window where the sun came peeping in with morn:
He never came a wink too soon, nor brought too long a day,
But now I often wish the night had ta'en my breath away.

I remember, I remember, when I was used to swing,
And thought the air would rush as fresh to swallows on the wing ;
My spirit flew in feathers then, that is so heavy now,
And summer pools could hardly cool the fever on my brow.

I remember, I remember, the fir trees dark and high ;
I used to think their slender tops went close against the sky ;
It was a childish ignorance, but now 'tis little joy
To know I'm further off from Heaven than when I was a boy."

I have many a time of late years walked through the
streets of my native city, a stranger to those who are moving up and down its now quiet thoroughfares—have looked
into the windows of shops where I once knew every one,
and now know no one—have gone to the playground of
the " Dane John Academy," and heard the merry laugh of
happy boys, the sons of those who were once my school-
fellows—have called upon the master of that school, who
was an assistant there when I was a boy, and had to introduce myself to one whom I had known almost as intimately
as my own brother. These remind one of " the days that
are no more." One who has felt all this has said—and
they have often been my own feelings—

" I love to linger on my track,
    Wherever I have dwelt—
In after years to loiter back,
    And feel as once I felt.

*   *   *   *

Old places have a charm for me
    The new can ne'er attain :
Old faces—how I long to see
    Their kindly looks again !"

I was much shocked not long since, on revisiting Canterbury, in company with a friend who had never seen our
magnificent Cathedral, to find, on inquiring at the old house
on the Parade in which I was born—the shop and reading-
room of which remain even to this day exactly as they were
when I was a boy—that the gentleman for many years in
partnership with my father, and who carried on the book-

selling business there as aforetime, died only a few days before my visit. He was my sponsor at the baptismal font, and was a quiet, kindly man—one of the old school. To the last he wore the blue dress-coat, buff waistcoat, white cravat, and the frilled shirt of former days.

Peace to his memory! The name of Robert Colegate will not soon be forgotten by those who have known Canterbury for the last half century. Though a singularly reserved and undemonstrative man, and a bachelor withal, he always greeted me with a kindly smile in my visits to my native city.

" World of sorrow, care, and change,
　　Even to myself I seem,
As adown thy vale I range,
　　Wandering in a dream :
　　　All things are so strange.

For the dead who died this day,
　　Fair and young, or great and good,
Though we mourn them, where are they?
　　—With those before the flood :
　　　Equally pass'd away !"

To those who knew Canterbury in the bustling days of posting and coaching it must now appear extremely dull; but should any of my readers have been acquainted with the place thirty years ago, they will be glad to be reminded of the state of things there at that time, and also of some of the local events that transpired at the period.

I remember very well being present at the opening of the Canterbury and Whitstable Railway, an event which ought not to be forgotten, inasmuch as this was the first commercial and passenger railway in England. That undertaking was sneered at by the wiseacres of the day, and not a few were the derisive jeers that greeted those who saw further than their neighbours, and took their seats in the uncovered square carriages of those early days of railway travelling. This railway is now, I believe, the property of the directors of the South-Eastern line; and is, moreover, one of the best paying lines in the three kingdoms.

I was also present as a boy at the ceremony of driving the first pile of the noble pier at Herne Bay, now a magnificent structure, erected from a design furnished by the great engineer Telford.

For the information of any of my readers who may not be acquainted with this quiet and retired little watering-place of summer resort, I may say that it is situated between Whitstable and Reculver, and is about six or seven miles from Canterbury. The salubrity of the air at Herne Bay has become almost proverbial, and now forms one of its chief sources of attraction. All the steamboats that leave London during the summer for Ramsgate and Margate call at Herne Bay, and a branch line now connects it with London, from the London and Chatham Railway; so that this beautiful little watering-place will become better known to those who are in quest of health and quiet.

East Kent, about the time I am writing of (1830), was the scene of some terrible incendiary fires. Scarcely a night passed without the citizens of Canterbury being startled by messengers riding into the place at full speed to summon the assistance of the fire-engines, which were kept in constant readiness, manned and horsed, for immediately proceeding to the scene of action. I have gone up after dark to the Mount of the Dane John, for several nights in succession, and have seen three and four, and sometimes five, farms blazing away at one time, in different directions.

Machine-breaking was also very common at the time, and detachments of dragoons were constantly being sent to disperse large bodies of agricultural labourers, who were bent upon mischief.

In 1832, the Reform Bill came into operation, and I was present as a spectator at a grand banquet held to commemorate that memorable event in a large tent erected in a field near the Dane John. Party feeling had at all times run very high in Canterbury, and the rejoicings of the people on this occasion were very general and enthusiastic.

I must be permitted here to digress a little from my personal history, to mention an incident in the life of my father, which will illustrate the state of political parties at this time.

In 1832, the late Dr. Howley, a man of singular meekness and gentleness, visited Canterbury in his official capacity as archbishop, and preparations were made, as usual, by the mayor and corporation to pay him all the respect due to his high station and character. It was customary to invite his Grace on these occasions to a banquet prepared in the Guildhall by the corporation, at which were present the clergy and their families, and the wives and daughters of the several members of the corporation. Popular feeling at the time was very strong at Canterbury against those who had in any way opposed the passing of the Reform Bill, and it was known that the venerable archbishop was by no means favourable to that great measure. The feeling of what may be termed, without intending to be offensive, the lower orders, was decidedly against the clergy, and the people were determined to make this apparent in their reception of "the metropolitan of all England" on his arrival among them.

Long before the amiable and venerable Prelate was expected on the day in question, the streets were crowded by those who called themselves Reformers, though the state of excitement and intoxication in which many of them were found would seem to indicate, whatever their zeal might be to extend the rights of citizenship, that they were not the best specimens to recommend an extension of the suffrage. Although a goodly number started for Harbledown, a small village just out of Canterbury on the London Road, to meet the good old man, and give him some foretaste of what he might expect to receive on his arrival, the great mass of the people had congregated in the High Street in the immediate vicinity of the Guild-hall. As soon as his Grace's carriage drew up in front of that building he was greeted by a torrent of hissing and howling and groans, and these were followed by mud, rotten eggs, and stones, which fell around the carriage as thick as blackberries. The few constables that were on duty at the time were entirely unable to hold the mob in check, or put down the disturbance, and matters began to look very serious, inasmuch as there was a cry raised to drag the venerable Prelate from his carriage.

My father was one of the magistrates present on the occasion, and seeing the great danger of the Archbishop, went at once from the steps of the Guildhall, with head uncovered, to the door of his Grace's carriage. This pro-ceeding on the part of my father rather increased the tumult and incensed the mob, who were determined to inflict summary vengeance on the person of the aged Prelate. My fears were awakened for the safety of my father, but he was cool and self-possessed. He grasped the handle of the carriage-door, and called to many by name, who were immediately around, to desist from such cowardly and disgraceful conduct. The coolness and courage dis-played by my father had the effect of keeping back some of the ring-leaders, and he persuaded his Grace not to think of alighting, but to drive at once to the Deanery in the Cathedral precincts, where he had arranged to spend the night. The coachman was instructed to do so, and the outriders, by the aid of their horses and long whips, managed to cut a passage through the mob for the car-riage. Unfortunately, both the outriders and coachman were alike unacquainted with the locality of the Deanery, and in the confusion turned up a street, St. Margaret's, directly opposite to that which they should have made for, namely Mercery Lane, which was the direct route for the Deanery. The mob ran pell-mell after the carriage, but one of his Grace's footmen, born near Canterbury, and who knew something of the neighbourhood, directed the coachman to make a *détour*, and his Grace reached the Deanery in safety.

The Archbishop sent a messenger immediately to thank my father for his conduct on the occasion, and on the following day the Dean was instructed to call upon him to say that his Grace would have come in person to have thanked him but for fear of exposing both himself and my father to the insults and abuse of a low and brutalised mob.

Some correspondence appeared in the Canterbury papers at the time relating to this shameful outrage, and unkindly reflections were made upon my father having taken upon himself to interfere in his individual capacity as a magistrate. A correspondent of the " Globe" newspaper made some remarks condemnatory of my father. This induced him to vindicate his conduct, on the occasion, from the aspersions cast upon him by the writer in that journal, and those who are interested in the matter may see that letter in the impression for August 11, 1832.

An address, signed by nearly all the respectable inhabitants of Canterbury, repudiating in very strong terms the conduct of the mob upon this disgraceful occasion, was presented to the Archbishop, in which his Grace was assured that he held a high place in the estimation of the citizens and gentry of the city, and the reply of his Grace was all that could be desired, and so the matter ended.

No account of myself would be complete which did not include the influence exerted upon my early days by the Cathedral of my native city. Born almost beneath its great shadow, I had been wont from my childhood's days to look up to its noble towers, black with the age of many centuries, as to the loved countenance of some near relative. I was taken within its sacred walls as a child, and loved

> " The high embowed roof,
> With antique pillars massy proof,

And storied windows richly dight,
Casting a dim religious light."

Even then the language of my soul was—

" There let the pealing organ blow,
To the full-voiced choir below,
In service high, and anthems clear,
As may with sweetness, through mine ear,
Dissolve me into ecstasies,
And bring all heav'n before mine eyes."

As soon as I grew up to be a boy of nine or ten I regularly attended the morning and afternoon service on the Sunday, and used to slip in in the afternoons sometimes during the week in time to hear the Anthem. I was well known to most of the lay-clerks and choristers, and used to get a seat as near them as I could, in order that I might follow them in the performance of the service. I was always an ardent admirer of the Cathedral service, and think now in my later years that it is the nearest approximation to the service of heaven to be found in this sin-stricken world.

The preaching, at the time I refer to, was for the most part of a very ordinary and uninteresting character. Among those who held prebendal stalls there at that time, were Drs. Welfit, Russell, and Spry, the Hon. and Rev. Wm. Boscawen, and Dean Pellew, Lord Nelson, and the Rev. John Peel. The last-named, a brother of the late Sir Robert Peel, was by far the best preacher. I remember even now some of his earnest and solemn sermons. One on the parable of the Prodigal Son made a deep impression upon me at the time, but passed away " as the morning cloud and the early dew." Lord Nelson, the brother of the hero of the Nile and Trafalgar, was quite a character. He was rather short and stout, wore a long black frock coat nearly to his ankles, Hessian boots, and a large shovel hat.

I was accustomed to see him daily at my father's library, where he used regularly to attend to read the daily papers, and have many a time held open the door for him, and

made him one of my best bows. He was a kindly old
gentleman, and would often put his hand upon my head,
and pat me gently on the cheek with a pleasant smile.
He took the trouble once to go to the Bank to get me a
new shilling for a Christmas-box. He was very deaf, and
this unfortunate infirmity led him into some rather strange
practices. The prebendal stalls in the Cathedral were nice
comfortable places, where you might take a nap without
being seen. The venerable Prebendary referred to used
occasionally to take the provincial newspaper in his pocket
to church on the week-day afternoons, and sometimes in
turning it over he forgot that others could hear better than
himself, and I have often seen a significant look, and a
suppressed titter among those who sat near enough to hear
the rumpling of the paper.

Lord Nelson used to take his turn at preaching, but he
rarely exceeded a quarter of an hour, or twenty minutes
at the utmost.

The services at the time I am speaking of were not of
that popular character that they now are since the days of
Dean Alford, whose appointment there every right-minded
man in the kingdom must heartily approve; and whose
influence will be felt for many years. I regret to learn
that he has met with much opposition on the part of those
who should have seconded his praiseworthy endeavours to
popularize the services of the Cathedral ; but this has ever
been the lot of those who have set themselves to remove
evils that have grown up for many generations. The increased accommodation afforded to the general public, is,
I believe, mainly to be attributed to him, as well as the
sermon on Sunday afternoon. This last-named innovation
was most stoutly opposed by his brethren of the Chapter,
and it was only conceded upon the understanding that he
should preach the sermon himself. I have heard with
great pleasure some of these afternoon sermons of the
erudite and learned Dean, and trust that his example will
not be lost upon his clerical brethren.

But to return from this digression to the services as they existed in my early days. All the families connected with the Cathedral were present at the Sunday-morning service, and consequently the attendance was more select than numerous. The afternoon service was always looked forward to as a treat; there was no sermon, and the anthem was the great attraction. The Cathedral on Sunday afternoons was mostly crowded; it was the fashionable meeting-place for the Canterbury belles and their admirers. At the time referred to the officers of the various regiments stationed at Canterbury were accustomed to appear in full dress, and their handsome uniforms added not a little to the *tout ensemble* of the scene.

I have many a time at the close of the service stood at the bottom of the steps—

> " To watch the moving scene,
> And recognize the slow, retiring fair."

There was one family never absent from the service; the father, a very handsome man, who, was legal adviser to the Dean and Chapter, and four daughters, all of them pretty; but one, the youngest, whom they called Baby, was "beautiful exceedingly." She was a charming graceful creature, and even as a boy " her beauty made me glad," and I have lingered about her and looked admiringly after her as a something from which I could not withdraw my gaze. These visions of youth have passed away, and this once beautiful maiden has long since grown into womanhood, and is now probably a portly matron in some happy home; but still the recollection of those days gone by are pleasant even now.

Naught on earth abideth, " the fashion of the world passeth away," and yet the grand old Cathedral remains the same, a " dwelling-place for all generations," a sacred home where the devout and thoughtful may find a hallowed resting-place in the journey of life.

An eloquent writer of the present day, who now worthily

fills one of its prebendal stalls, says of Canterbury Cathedral,—" There is no church, no place in the kingdom,
with the exception of Westminster Abbey, that is so closely
connected with the history of our country."

I have often thought, in my occasional visits to the
Cathedral in riper years, of the many royal and illustrious
personages that have entered its sacred portals, and of the
memorable events that have taken place within its walls.

The author of the interesting work before referred to, in
his " Canterbury in the Olden Time," reminds us of some
of the great and distinguished names in our national
history that have been connected with our ancient city and
its cathedral.   He talks to us of " Cæsar with his legions;
the Jute, the Angle, and the Saxon; the Danes in their
marauding excursions;   Augustine bringing Christ and
Christianity;   the superstitious Ethelbert and the gentle
Bertha, his queen;   the noble Godwin proclaiming his
descent from the Norse Sea-kings;   Harold came oft to
Canterbury, and, but for that chance arrow at Hastings,
might have been the father of our kings to this day.
William the Conqueror and his sons frequently passed
through the city to and from their Norman provinces;
hither came the four assassin knights to confront and slay
Archbishop Becket; hither, not long after, came the very
king in whose name they committed the murder, pacing,
as a penitent, with bare feet the Cathedral pavement.

" Through Canterbury passed Richard, the lion-hearted
king, on his way to the Holy Land, and here came he on
his return to give thanks to ' God and to St. Thomas.'
The restless and profligate John was often at Canterbury.
In the Cathedral Edward I. celebrated his marriage with
Margaret of Anjou.   To Canterbury came the gallant
Black Prince from the victories of Crecy and Poictiers, and
from his doubtful but not less dangerous encounters in
Castile and Arragon;   his brass gauntlets, the casque,
whose plume never bowed in submission to earthly foe, the
leathern covered shield of wood, the surcoat emblazoned

with the arms of France and England, are still suspended
in the Cathedral over his tomb. Henry the Fourth's remains rest within the walls of the Cathedral. Henry V.
came here on his return from Agincourt. Time would
fail me to tell of Margaret of Anjou, paying her devotions
there at the shrine of the Martyr; of Richard the Third's
visit; and, some years later, Elizabeth the queen, his successor, is presented with a piece of plate by the corporation.
In 1520, Henry VIII, Charles V, and Cardinal Wolsey
were entertained at Canterbury by the Archbishop.
Eighteen years later the shrine of Becket is despoiled. In
1573, Queen Mary visits the city, and the great Elizabeth
is entertained by Archbishop Parker at his palace. In
1628, Charles I. conducts hither from Dover his bride, and
not long afterwards the city is visited by Cromwell's
soldiers, if not by the Protector himself. And 1660 witnessed the arrival there of Charles II. from the continent,
and a few years later the Prince of Orange, afterwards
William III, passed through the city." Kings, Queens,
and Prelates have all gone to return no more, for—

> " The boast of heraldry, the pomp of power,
> And all that beauty, all wealth e'er gave,
> Await alike the inevitable hour;
> The paths of glory lead but to the grave."

The chiefs of rival creeds are for ever silent, and their
dust mingles side by side. The magnificent old Cathedral
in stately grandeur remains, " a poem in stone," while
those who raised it in all its spiritual beauty, and those who
successively worshipped beneath its glorious roof, have long
since passed away. Canterbury pilgrims, in search of the
beautiful, still linger within its sacred precincts, charmed
with its architectural beauties, connected as they are with
rich historical associations; and I have often, when lingering in its sacred precincts, found myself repeating the
poet's lines,—

> " Daily the tide of life goes ebbing and flowing beside them,
> Thousands of throbbing hearts, where theirs are at rest for ever;

> Thousands of aching brains, where theirs no longer are busy;
> Thousands of toiling hands, where theirs have ceased from
>   labour;
> Thousands of weary feet, where theirs have completed their
>   journey."

While its daily service reminds one of that " Temple not
made with hands," where the Lord God Almighty and the
Lamb are the Light thereof, and where those who are once
admitted to its glories " go no more out for ever."   But
here—

> " Naught on earth abideth! Morn hastes away,
>   And all its orient pomp expires in day;
>   Day's glories fade, and beauty
>   Veils her head with evening's shade.
> The shadows deepen, gloom on gloom descends,
>   And evening ends.
> Calm night, that comest down in sable guise,
>   Broider'd with galaxy, and star, and orb,
> And with thy fingers shuttest up the
>   Eyes of half the world—fadeth away!
>   The morning star comes forth,
> Dims and dissolves, and day again hath birth.
> Naught on earth abideth! Youth and beauty fade,
>   The morn of joy yields to the night of sorrow;
> And hopes to-day, on firmest pillars stay'd,
>   Are laid in ruin'd heaps before to-morrow.
> All flesh is grass, and, like the flower
> That withers on its sod, its comeliness doth pass;
> Death comes anon the silver cord to sever:
> Naught is abiding save the Word of God,
>   God's Word abideth ever!"

Just about this time the celebrated Courtenay visit to
Canterbury took place, and I was an eyewitness to most
of that gentleman's public eccentricities.

It may be interesting to some of my readers, though
not the most creditable to the intelligence of my fellow-
citizens of Canterbury, if I briefly recall a few recollections
of that extraordinary individual, and of the still more extraordinary manner in which he succeeded in imposing upon
my fellow-citizens and the people in the neighbourhood.

Towards the close of 1832, it was rumoured at Canterbury that a gentleman was staying at the Rose Inn who passed under the name of Count Rothschild. His costume and countenance denoted foreign extraction, while his language and conversation showed that he was well acquainted with almost every part of the kingdom. He was said to live with singular frugality, notwithstanding abundant samples of wealth, and professions of an almost unlimited command of money. He appeared to study retirement, if not concealment, although subsequent events demonstrated that society of every grade beneath the middle class was the element in which he most freely breathed.

Such was the eccentric individual who surprised the city by proposing himself as a third candidate for its representation, and who created an entertaining contest for the honour, long after the candidates had composed themselves to the delightful vision of an unexpensive and unopposed return.

In an address to the citizens, soliciting their support, he condemned in turn all parties in the State, and all the leading politics of modern governments. He spoke with a high regard for the authority of the Christian faith, but condemned the clergy most unmercifully for taking the tithes, which he asserted were the property of the poor. In that address the law of primogeniture, chartered and corporate bodies, sinecure and placemen, the Episcopal bench, and even the Throne itself, were treated with as little ceremony as they would meet with from the veriest radical scribe of the London Press.

This address, strange as it may appear, immediately gave the man a place in the confidence and hearts of hundreds, and some of these generally passing for men of sense in the city.

It may well be asked, how did this mysterious personage acquire the astonishing popularity in the ancient and enlightened city of Canterbury? That venerable city, once the capital of the kingdom, and always the capital of the Church, has ever been eager in its boast of having left the towns of Kent and its kindred counties greatly in the rear of civilization and science. The Canterburians, however, on the present occasion were in some way or other outwitted, for they thought they discovered in this impudent pretender almost the attributes of Divinity: they verily thought they discerned much of the moral, as well as the personal image of the great Founder of Christianity in this bold adventurer.

The citizens of Canterbury placed the aspiring chieftain among the city candidates for a seat in the first Reformed Parliament of the nation, and assigned to him nearly four hundred votes.

Not contented with having been rejected for the city, he was put in nomination for the eastern division of the county, but obtained only three votes.

Having failed in his electioneering projects, he tried to ingratiate himself with the lower orders. He made it known that his condescension was as great as his rank and wealth, and that he would be willing to accept the invitations to visit the humblest families, and to eat and drink at the peasant's and the labourer's table.

This, as it might be easily imagined, charmed a thousand hearts, and he became almost an object of worship among the lower class. For a man who had announced himself as Sir William Percy Honeywood Courtenay, knight of Malta, king of Jerusalem, &c, &c, to be the guest of the poor peasant was an act of condescension that won the love and confidence of all hearts, and he knew how to turn all this to further his ambitious ends.

It will be remembered that he closed his remarkable career in an affray with the military at a place called Bosenden Wood, Boughton, near Canterbury. He had gathered together several hundred peasants and labourers and armed them with bludgeons and any weapons at hand; nine of these poor infatuated men were slain by the military: but the officer commanding the detachment, a lieutenant Bennett, was unhappily killed in the affray, and several of the soldiers were severely wounded.

The real name of this remarkable pretender was John Nicholls Thom, a spirit merchant and maltster, of Truro, in Cornwall.

I must return, however, to my personal history. The little conveyancer with whom I had been living for about eighteen months was a very choleric and hot-tempered man, and some error in copying one day so upset him that he poured out such a torrent of abuse upon me that I determined to leave his employ. I did so in a month from that day, according to our agreement, and I scarcely believe that Adam left the Garden of Eden with much more regret than did I the conveyancer's office and its surroundings. I was fond of the work, and the occasional interviews with the pretty daughter, together with the music lessons, all made me very much regret the separation; but I was rather a high-spirited young fellow, and would not intimate to the father any desire to stay, and so we parted.

The elections for the city and county, which I have just adverted to, were about to take place, and my father succeeded in obtaining for me a clerkship in the committee-room of Sir Edward Knatchbull, the well-known Tory candidate for the eastern division of the county.

The central committee of Sir Edward sat in a large room over my father's shop. The work apportioned to me mainly consisted in copying letters, issuing summonses for meetings, &c; and as the remuneration was good, my regret was that it would be so soon over.

I was, however, a little uneasy at the thought of sailing under false colours, for all my predilections were decidedly in favour of liberalism, and I confess that I should have felt far more comfortable had I acted in the same capacity on the Radical side of the question.

Fortunately for public safety, as well as for private purses, the election for the counties under the Reform Bill was confined to two days only. The scenes at Canterbury, and Barham Downs, the place of nomination, will not soon be forgotten by those who were present on the occasion. Party feeling at the time was at its height, and the scenes which took place daily during the canvassing of the candidates, and at the nomination and subsequent election, were of the most exciting and alarming character.

A man well known at that time in Canterbury, and indeed, all through East Kent, by the name of Bill Elliott, a post-boy at the Fountain Hotel, but better known as *Boar Shields*, a name given to him on account of his strength and toughness, played a somewhat conspicuous part during this election. This man was a Tory to the back-bone, and was a great favourite with all the county gentlemen of that party. I knew this character well, and received from him some lessons in the art of self-defence. He was famed for fighting, and took a special delight in me for my daring, and was wont to speak of me as a pluckish fellow. An anecdote or two of this man will not be uninteresting, and will exhibit the characteristics of the individual better than any description of mine.

Just before the election, he was driving Mr. Deedes, the chairman of Sir Edward Knatchbull, afterwards member for the county, to Margate, for the purpose of canvassing the electors on behalf of Sir Edward. It was known at Margate that Mr. Deedes was expected, and a large number of the Radicals had assembled at the entrance of the town, who, as soon as he made his appearance, greeted him with a tremendous volley of groans and hisses, and shouted, "Bullock's liver and barley bread!" a saying which had arisen in consequence of one of the Tory party having said that such fare was good enough for poor people. Bill Elliott, finding the crowd increased, and the pressure upon the horses not at all agreeable, immediately dismounted, turned up his sleeves, and laid into four or five of the foremost in such a manner as to inspire the mob with terror, and then, quietly mounting, drove Mr. Deedes into the town, very much to the amusement of that gentleman.

On another occasion, he was driving Mr. Plumptre, the M.P. for East Kent, to Mersham Hatch, the county-seat of Sir Edward Knatchbull. He had been told to use all expedition, as the interview was an urgent one. On arriving in front of Sir Edward's mansion, Boar Shields saw some one on the lawn in his shirt sleeves. He shouted out to him with his stentorian voice, " Holloa ! you chap in the shirt sleeves, pull the fore-door bell !" Mr. Plump-tre saw at once that the party addressed was a son of Sir Edward, who was fond of gardening, and tried to make the post-boy understand this ; but it was all in vain, as Elliott had enlisted him in his service, and he very good-naturedly did as he was instructed.

On the day of nomination, at Barham Downs, there was a terrific uproar, and Elliott, who was there in all his glory, offered to fight any man on the Radical side that might be brought against him ; but no one had pluck enough to confront this redoubtable combatant.

The procession of Sir Edward Knatchbull at that election was preceded by a very handsome banner, which was reported to have cost £500, presented by the ladies of the county for the occasion. That procession was headed by five hundred men, selected from the farm-servants of the neighbourhood, who were paid 5*s.* a day, with an ample supply of food, and an almost unlimited quantity of beer, marched at the head of the procession to protect this flag, which had been threatened by the Radical party. These men were all arrayed in clean white gaberdines, and armed with a stout bludgeon. No attempt was made on the part of the Radicals, however, to injure the flag.

I acted as one of the Poll Clerks during the two days the election lasted, and in about ten days my duties ter-minated.

All the officials connected with the election were not only well paid, but there was a handsome dinner given them at the close. I was present at that dinner, and am bound in truthfulness to record that those around me put the port wine so prominently forward, and I was induced to par-take of it so freely, that, after singing one song, I have no further recollection of anything that transpired. I awoke the next morning with a splitting headache, and was informed by my mother that I was brought home in a state of insensibility. Though humbled at this confession of my folly, I am glad to be able to record that this was the only instance in my life of my being "the worse for liquor."

My having no regular employment, and the excitement occasioned by the late elections, had made me feel very unsettled. There is nothing much more unfavourable for a youth at sixteen, and especially with such a temperament as mine, than to be casting about for something to do ; and the few months of my life spent in this way are among the worst of my history. Idleness and listlessness are dangerous for any one to indulge in, and therefore it cannot be wondered at that I spent much of this time in the company of those not calculated to improve my morals, or help me on in a course of rectitude.

Some of my acquaintances induced me to keep late hours at night, which led me into painful and annoying altercations with my father and mother, and obliged me to invent all sorts of excuses for not being home at suitable hours. My dear mother sat up for me many a weary night, long after all the household were asleep, and I dreaded her kind reproachful look on my return far more than the angry words that fell from my father's lips in the morning. However, I had fairly plunged into all the gaieties and dissipations within my reach at Canterbury at that period.

I was a favourite with the manager of the theatre, and had the privilege of being admitted behind the scenes, where I formed an acquaintance with some of the actors and actresses. One of the latter, wife to the principal tragedian, was a particularly handsome woman. I recollect on one occasion, when her husband had been playing Macbeth, he was so exhausted with the last scene, that when the curtain fell it was with difficulty we could rouse him, so great was his prostration from entering so heartily into the combat that closes that grand play. His pretty wife hung over him, chafing his hands, and fanning his face, and looking most beautiful. I was not a little proud of acting as a young knight to so distinguished a chieftain and his lady fair.

The manager of the theatre at this time was a celebrated comic singer, and he and I became quite cronies. It was well for me that the dramatic season did not last very long, or I should have become so enamoured of plays and play actors as to be inclined to have tried my hand at histrionic exhibitions. I have many times envied this famous comic singer as he drew down upon him the applause of a crowded house. My impediment of speech would have stood in the way of my becoming an actor; but I could always sing, and few things are more gratifying than popular applause, though so much has been affectedly said against it.

About this time a strong desire arose within me to go into the army. I had become thoroughly weary of a life of listlessness and want of purpose and—

> "I had heard of battles, and I long'd
> To follow to the field some warlike lord."

I expressed this military predilection at home, but never met with any encouragement from my parents, and my mother trembled at the thought of a boy of hers

> "Seeking the bubble reputation at the cannon's mouth."

The desire, however, strengthened, and as I had expressed to my father a preference for the Royal Artillery, he spoke to a gentleman living at Canterbury who attended our Reading Room daily, and who was moreover officially connected with that regiment.

This gentleman held the rank of Major-General in this regiment, and promised to do everything in his power to help me if I persisted in my determination, and get me sent out to India or one of the other colonies.

My mother was opposed to my going into the army, and

did all she could to dissuade me from the project ; but the
more I thought of it the more I longed to be engaged in
some pursuit where my energies would be called forth,
and where I should be released from the dull monotony of
my unemployed life at Canterbury.

My mother, seeing my determination for soldiering, took
an early opportunity of calling upon the wife of the Major-
General, and urged all a mother's reasons for dissuading
me from my resolution.   This kind-hearted lady, who had
known me from my infancy, desired me to call upon her.
She spoke to me with the gentleness of a true lady, and tried
all her persuasiveness to induce me to give up my military
schemes.

After talking with me for some time, she rang the bell,
which was answered by a youth of my own age, in a green
suit and brass bell buttons : she gave him some instructions
as to calling on tradesmen for certain little commissions,
and when he left the room she turned to me with a smile,
and asked me whether I should not rather be a page to her
than to be a soldier : that it was a quiet occupation, with nothing of a menial or arduous kind to do, and that her page
was the son of very respectable parents.   I verily thought
the old lady was joking with me, as the idea of being
rigged out as " a boy in buttons" had never for a moment
entered my mind.   I thanked her very sincerely for all
her good intentions ; but this interview only tended to
strengthen my desire to become a soldier, and I determined
to carry out this resolution as soon as a favourable opportunity occurred.

Shortly after this I was induced by some of my boon
companions to join them in a carousal that lasted through
the night, and I was not home until long after

" The grey morn had dappled into day."

I found that my mother had been sitting up for me, and
I was ashamed to look at her tired and grief-worn countenance as she gently and tearfully upbraided me for my

unkind behaviour. My father was exceedingly angry with me, and told me in plain terms that I should not remain under his roof any longer than I conformed to the law of the household. I found that matters were growing more and more serious at home, and that the breach was widening every day. Under these circumstances, I gained my father's reluctant consent to my leaving for the army, and having obtained a letter of introduction and recommendation from the Major-General to the Adjutant of the Royal Artillery at Woolwich, my little wardrobe was packed up, and I was started to London to see my eldest brother and sister, who were residing there, before entering the army.

I remember how grieved my father and mother were at my going out to breakfast, on the morning I left home, with the family that I had been accustomed to spend the greater part of my time with, when not engaged in other pursuits with my juvenile companions.

I distributed the few knick-knacks I possessed among my younger brothers and sisters, and gave my "Church-Service," a scrap-book, and a favourite canary bird with a nightingale note, to her who had obtained great influence over me, and who, I verily believe, was not a little concerned at my leaving Canterbury. I received in return for these a small ring with a heart tied to it by a true-lover's knot.

The parting on this occasion was such as might have been expected; mutual promises were given and responded to, and fair visions of future happiness were indulged on both sides that were never to be realized.

The leave-taking at home was a far more serious affair. I kept up my courage as best I could, till I heard the door closed behind me, and then my choked feelings found expression in a flood of tears, which were only interrupted by my taking my seat on the top of the "Eagle" coach for London.

III.

MANHOOD: ITS STRUGGLES, DUTIES, TRIALS, RECREATIONS, AND RESPONSIBILITIES.

" In carrying out any work of improvement, or of reformation in your character, you must begin by *acting* in such a way as conscience tells you is right. You must not wait till you are completely in a proper frame of mind; and defer doing what a virtuous man would do till you have the dispositions and inclinations of a virtuous man. It is only by practising virtue that you can bring yourself to delight in virtue."

ONDON had always been in my youthful imaginings the place of all places in the world which I had a strong desire to see; and to feel that I was actually on my way there was almost more than I could believe. The journey in those days was a very different thing to what it is now, when a couple of hours by the rail puts you down within a stone's throw of London Bridge. The coaches, a continuous stream running to and from Dover to London, were well horsed, and a ride on one of them, as an outside passenger, was perhaps as pleasant a one as any to be found in all England.

I remember that it was a bright cloudless autumn day, " bathed in rich amber-glowing floods of light," with the foliage of orange, and brown and red, more beautiful than any painter, save Turner, who dared to be natural, could put on canvass, lest he should be scouted as extravagant and unnatural. The undulations of the country all through the journey made the views at every turn of the road new and interesting. The road from Canterbury to London winds through an extremely beautiful variety of hill and dale, rosy orchards, golden cornfields and hop gardens ; and as I had never before been further on the London road than Boughton, my father's native village, it had the additional interest of being entirely new to me.

Chatham, Rochester, and Stroud were passed in succession ; the former place, teeming with soldiers, made my young blood tingle as I thought fondly of what I might one day do in defence of my country. As we neared London my feeling of wondrous expectation scarcely allowed of my remaining in my seat. I was at the back of the coach, and ever and anon I rose from my seat to look ahead for the first glimpse of St. Paul's, or some visible indication of being in reality within reach of the great metropolis. No young Israelite, on his first pilgrimage to "the City of the Great King," felt more intensely anxious than I did to stand within the City of London and walk about its streets. All that I had ever read, and heard from others, came welling up from my full heart, and my excitement increased as Blackheath was crossed, and the great city lay spread out beneath us dimly in the distance.

At last we entered the streets, and London Bridge, which had been opened a few months before, was the first object of attraction. I had never at Canterbury seen any river wider than the Stour, on whose banks I had wandered many a time as a boy, and in whose limpid waters I had so often bathed and frolicked. The noble Thames was therefore to me a magnificent sight, and as the coach slowly made its way over the bridge, the shipping, with its tall masts, and the steamers, with their variegated and smoky funnels, all impressed me with the greatness and importance of the city I was just entering. I caught a glimpse of St. Paul's, with its golden cross glittering in the afternoon sun, and on the opposite side the Tower of London ; a few minutes more brought me abreast of the monument.

The " Spread Eagle " in Gracechurch-street was then

the terminus of the Canterbury " Eagle " coaches, and as
the coach slowly turned into the narrow gateway of the
hotel, I saw my eldest brother looking out for me, and it
was quite a relief to hear his well-known voice greeting
me in the midst of the noise and bustle of that great
thoroughfare.

My brother was an assistant in the establishment of a
wholesale stationery and account-book business in Gracechurch-street, and boarded and lodged with an uncle in
the neighbourhood, who had for many years been chief
superintendent of the city police, but had recently retired
from that very difficult and responsible office to a less arduous post connected with London Bridge, and the parish
in which it stands.

I was to be the guest of my uncle, and I much enjoyed
the few weeks spent with him.   The house was situate in
St. Benet's-place, rather a dingy-looking court, leading
out of Gracechurch-street to nowhere.   There were but
few houses in the place, and I remember that a bookbinder
lived immediately opposite my uncle's, and as the space
between the two houses was rather narrow, we could look
from my uncle's rooms almost into those of our opposite
neighbours.   The dull and monotonous prospect was often
gladdened by the bright eyes, and happy smiling faces, of
three daughters of the worthy bookbinder, who were seen
occasionally at the windows.

My uncle was a remarkably tall and well-proportioned
man, though he stooped a little from age, and long active
service.   He told me that, as superintendent of the police,
he had for a great many years perambulated the City of
London twice every day, and entered his name, and time
of calling, at every police-station within the city bound-
aries.   His duties, in his new position, required him to be
out pretty nearly all the day on London Bridge, and about
the Ward, to look after the police, and see that everybody
connected with the bridge was at his duty.   I was his
constant companion in these rambles, and he used to point

out to me the pickpockets and thieves that infested that great thoroughfare. It used to amuse me to see the members of the swell-mob lift their hats as they passed my uncle in the streets, and to observe how these light-fingered gentry glided away out of his sight as he would sometimes shake his head at them.

I was very fond of my uncle, and he was exceedingly kind to me; he would have done almost anything to have dissuaded me from soldiering, but the desire for the army still burned steadily within me.

An old copy in manuscript of the "Rules and Regulations of the Bridge Ward," was suspended over the fireplace in the watch-house, and my uncle proposed that I should make a fair transcript of this document. He was so pleased with this specimen of my penmanship, that he submitted it to the Alderman of the Ward, Sir Chapman Marshall, as the work of his nephew. Sir Chapman made some kind inquiries about me, and gave my uncle a sovereign to reward the youth who could turn out such a piece of ornamental penmanship, and remarked that I was fit for something better than soldiering.

My visit to my uncle was unhappily interrupted by a misunderstanding between my brother and himself as to late hours at night. My uncle would insist upon every one being in by ten o'clock, and this early hour was not at all agreeable to my brother. Angry words ensued, and it ended in my brother leaving, and going to board and lodge with a friend, who kept an inn in Smithfield Market. My uncle was so hurt and annoyed at my brother leaving him, and spoke out so strongly against him, that the friends with whom he lived prevailed upon me to transfer my quarters to them, for the few weeks that intervened before leaving for the army.

It was with real regret that I left my uncle, whose genial society I very much delighted in; his narrations of London life, and what he had seen, and taken part in, quite charmed and captivated me.

I heard, moreover, afterwards, from my aunt, that he
was quite hurt at my yielding to the persuasions of my
friends to go with my brother to Smithfield.

In my new quarters I found, however, that I had more
freedom, and liberty of action, and my peregrinations ex-
tended to the different parts of London. All through the
day I had nothing to do but to walk about, as every one
was too much engaged to give me their company; and this
being the case, I visited the parks, the Bank, the Royal
Exchange, the Tower, with all its wonders and strange
legends, the docks, the principal churches, the bridges, the
Thames-tunnel, the British Museum, the Horse Guards,
Westminster Hall, and the Courts of Law, the Houses
of Parliament, then very different structures to what
they are now. The old Abbey, which I often visited,
and re-visited, and was never weary of wandering about
its sacred pavement, and reading the many inscriptions
recorded there of men whose names had long been as
familiar to me as "household words," and whose dust
lay mouldering beneath my feet. I never lost an opportunity, when going west, of looking in at the old Minster,
and "Poets' Corner" had a charm for me beyond most
places in London. But the place that most of all attracted
me was St. Paul's, that king among the architectural
structures of London. I have stood for the hour beneath
its dome, looking up in dreamy wonderment at the dim
and glorious summit, and then leisurely let the eye wander
around at its growingly beautiful proportions. As a building, Westminster Abbey fell very short of my expectations, as I contrasted it with the Cathedral under whose
shadow I had spent my early days; but St. Paul's more
than realized all my most sanguine expectations. I used
to walk around its exterior, and from different stand-points
look up with silent admiration as I gazed at its magnificent dome, and golden cross, with the blue heavens as a
back-ground. It is indeed a noble and enduring monument to the great architect who conceived its vast and

beautiful design, and mapped out all its wondrous details; and is a sanctuary worthy in all respects of the great and illustrious saint whose name it bears. Oh! it is something that speaks well for England to have erected such an edifice in the heart of its great metropolis, and to have dedicated it to a man who towers as far above his fellows as the vast dome does the buildings with which it is surrounded.

My attention was not, however, confined to these buildings, but I was naturally enough attracted to the theatres. Drury Lane, Covent Garden, the Adelphi, Astley's, and the Italian Opera, were names that awoke within me the most stirring thoughts and extravagant expectations. I gained frequent and free admission to all these theatres from a gentleman who was editor of one of the most popular weekly journals, and had served his apprenticeship to my father, and who had, moreover, known me from my infancy. I had seen at Canterbury some of the chief actors, who occasionally visited the provincial towns; but a London theatre, with its superior accompaniments, in the minor characters, and also in the scenery, fully realized my highest expectations.

The chief actors on the London stage, at the time I am writing of, were Charles Kemble, (his brother John and the elder Kean had passed away), Macready, Doughton, Charles Kean, Harley, Buckstone, Keeley, Farran, and Jack Reeve; and the actresses were, Madame Vestris, the Misses Tree, (afterwards Mrs. Charles Kean and Mrs. Bradshaw), Mrs. Yates, Mrs. Keeley, Madame Celeste, Mrs. Nisbett, Mrs. Honey, Mrs. Humby, Mrs. Waylett, Miss Paton, and Miss Grattan, with a host of minor names long since forgotten.

The theatres at which these then distinguished actors and actresses were to be seen and heard were visited by me not unfrequently, but the place that had the foremost attractions was the Italian opera. The tall grenadiers at the entrance, the vast dimensions of the interior, with its gorgeous embellishments, the stage and its splendid scenery

and decorations, the first-rate instrumental and vocal music,
the audience composed chiefly of England's fairest women,
and some of her noblest sons, had a wondrous effect upon
me.   All 'this was crowned by the *ballet*, with its inflam-
mable attractiveness.

· It is not to be wondered that this fascinating theatre
had a charm to a youth of my age beyond all the rest, and
many a night did I drink in the intoxicating draughts,
until I could scarcely tolerate the tame and insipid attractions of every-day life.

Knowing in my own case the effects produced by such
exhibitions as these, I confess that I am at a loss to imagine how it is that fathers and mothers take their sons and
daughters to witness such sights.   I cannot believe that a
right-minded father would willingly introduce his sons to
such scenes as I have often witnessed, where there is
everything to call forth and develope the strongest passions
of our nature ; and how any mother, with any pretensions
to modesty and propriety herself, can allow her young and
innocent daughters to be contaminated by such exhibitions,
is to me a marvel.

Men and women are selected for the *ballet* who are
formed in nature's fairest mould, and they are attired in
such a costume as to display to the greatest advantage
their beautiful proportions, and well-turned limbs.   The
dancing, it is true, is perfection, the very poetry of motion,
but it is terribly dangerous, I think, to both sexes; not
only to those who are engaged in it, but also to the spectators.

A caustic anonymous writer of the day, speaking of such
an audience, says :—" A word to you, young fashionable
ladies, and your foolish mothers, who frequent the Italian
Opera, and gaze with looks unquailed on a spectacle that
makes the veteran who has 'braved the battle and the
breeze' throw up his hands in amazement as he takes a
survey of the house from the stage to the five tiers, from
the dress circle up to Mount Olympus, where sit the

'gods and goddesses.' Many a night have you proved, while gazing on the *ballet*, with all the men around you, how little you cared for morality, or decency either. The *ballet-girl* is the living representative of the 'social evil' in full force—'tis her vocation ; you see it, and you know it. She spares you the trouble of going behind the scenes; she comes forward with lascivious mien and gesture to invite you with her *désir valse* to follow her example. *She* may be vicious, but *you* are the lady patronesses of vice."

It is well known that the Italian Opera is the favourite resort of the English aristocracy, and those among them who would exclude the *ballet* as objectionable, and would retain only the operatic entertainments, would do well to consider that the operas most popular of late years are not at all such as to exert a salutary influence upon our young aristocratic scions, male and female. The immorality and profligacy set forth, in the most alluring and attractive manner, in *Don Giovanni, Lucrezia Borgia, Rigoletto, La Sonnambula, Norma,* and *La Traviata,* are too notorious to need any further reference to them, and I should hope that no sober-minded father would be found to give his deliberate consent to his sons and daughters witnessing, night after night, either the indecent exhibition of the *ballet*, or the not less dangerous and pernicious tendency of the operas.

During my stay in Smithfield I formed an acquaintance with some medical students, who lodged in the same house as myself, and who were attending the lectures at St. Bartholomew's Hospital. I spent a good deal of my time with these young gentlemen about town, and visited Vauxhall Gardens, and other places of less exceptional character. Most of these young fellows were from the country, and their parents could have had but little idea of the kind of life they led in London. I found that, for the most part, they were allowed to procure lodgings for themselves, somewhere in the vicinity of the hospital ; and there being little or no restraint upon their movements, they were often out at all hours of the night. It is not surprising that young men at this very critical age, left so much to themselves, should in many unhappy instances form habits of dissipation and profligacy which cling to them all through their after-life.

While I was living in Smithfield the anniversary of St. Bartholomew's Fair came round. The fair at that time was rather on the wane, but it attracted large multitudes of people, and lasted, I think, three days. Such an assemblage as that, in the very heart of London, could but be interesting to " a young man from the country." I very much enjoyed my rambles among the crowds of sightseers, and paid my threepence more than once to have a place on Richardson's outside stage, for the purpose of looking round upon the sea of upturned faces. I had a few narrow escapes of getting into some rather awkward scrapes with my medical friends from our larkish pranks. Peter Crawley, the celebrated pugilist, kept a tavern in Little Britain, and most of the medical students were frequent visitors at this establishment, not only to be instructed in the art of self-defence, but to play at skittles, bagatelle, and other kindred amusements.

Having spent about two months at Smithfield, and seen a good deal of London, I began to think seriously again of my long-cherished purpose of becoming a soldier. My brother and an elder sister, staying in London at the time, were both anxious to divert me from my military predilection, and proposed my seeking a situation in some house of business, or look out for an appointment in the civil service. I could not, however, think of settling down to anything short of soldiering; and the idle and dissipated life I had been leading for some months past only tended to strengthen the resolution I had formed to enter upon a career that would call forth my energies, and give me some purpose in life.

It was on a fine, bright, frosty morning, in the winter of 1833, that I left my kind friends in Smithfield for the head-quarters of the Royal Artillery at Woolwich. I got up on the outside of an omnibus in Gracechurch-street, and enjoyed the pleasant ride through Greenwich, and in due time was put down at the nearest point to the Artillery Barracks. I inquired of the sentry at the outside gate for the adjutant's quarters, and having found them, sought an interview with that gentleman, and presented my letter of introduction from the major-general at Canterbury. The adjutant was a tall, soldierly looking man of about forty, who received me very kindly. He told me that he had already heard of me from the major-general, and that he had been expecting me for some weeks. He appeared to be pleased with my appearance, but was fearful that the impediment in my speech would be an objection on the part of the medical officers. Having given me some good advice as to what to do and what to avoid, as a soldier, he encouraged me to hope that, by good conduct and careful attention to my duties, I should soon be made a non-commissioned officer, as I had a very influential friend and patron in the major-general.

I was then handed over to the orderly corporal, with the adjutant's instructions that I was to be taken to the medical officers for their examination. The major-general's letter, and also one from the adjutant, were enclosed to the doctors, and my heart beat high with anxious expectation as I marched off to the inspection-room. On arriving there, I was ushered into a large apartment, with three gentlemen seated at a table in the middle of the room. The corporal presented the letters and withdrew, and I was left alone with this formidable conclave. I was in a state of no small nervous excitement; and after reading the letters, the doctors carefully looked me up and down. One of them, an elderly gentleman with white hair, inquired of me my name. Now, my own name had always been a great difficulty with me, as it began with a consonant, and I made several ineffectual attempts to get it out. My stammering tongue, however, would not obey;

my lips were sealed as with lead, and a cold weight
pressed on my heart. Again and again did I summon
my resolution to conquer the mocking demon, but failed,
and after many abortive efforts I was obliged to spell out
my name to them. Unfortunately the next question was,
" Where do you come from ?" Canterbury was another
difficult word with me, and the nervous dread and sensitive shame so common to stammerers increased upon me,
and I was foiled again in attempting to enunciate the
dreaded word.

In the meanwhile the doctors looked at me with patient
and kindly eyes, and at each other with gravity. The
president glanced at the major-general's letter that lay on
the table before him. I saw at once the critical position
in which I stood, and bitter was my mortification. I felt
that I could have uttered any but my *own name*, and I
wished that I had been born anywhere rather than *Canterbury*. Seeing the dilemma in which these gentlemen were
placed, to break the silence I volunteered some remarks
upon my stammering, and told them how I had acquired
the habit. This explanation was given with little or no
hesitation, and I began to hope that I should pass muster.
They made inquiries then as to my age, and the healthi-
ness and longevity of my family. My replies to these
questions appeared to be satisfactory.

I was requested to withdraw, that they might consult
upon the matter; and never shall I forget the dreadful
suspense I endured during the quarter of an hour that
deliberation lasted. My whole future life depended upon
their decision, and when the bell rang which was to summon me again into their presence, my heart sank within
me.

On re-entering the room I could see at once that my
doom was fixed. The president told me that they had
every desire to pass me, but that the Articles of War were
so strict that they could not consistently with their duty to
the service overlook the impediment in my speech, and

therefore they must reluctantly reject my application. One of the other doctors told me that my age, and personal appearance, were just such as they could desire, and that I should have made a good soldier; while the third remarked that I should no doubt succeed in obtaining some appointment as a clerk, where my stammering would not be an obstacle, either in my work, or to my advancement in life.

A note to the adjutant was duly written, indicating their decision; and having thanked them for their kind feeling towards me, I was marched back to the adjutant's quarters.

That gentleman expressed great regret at my not being able to pass the medical ordeal, and sympathized with me in my bitter disappointment. He said he would write to my patron at Canterbury, and tell him the cause of my rejection, and hoped I should be successful in procuring a situation in the Civil Service.

I thanked the adjutant for his kindness, and left his quarters with a feeling of dreary disappointment, known only to those who have been thwarted in the thing of all others that they had set their heart upon.

The corporal, in whose care I had been, was quite moved at my downcast looks, and I left him with a hearty shake of the hand, and with a feeling something akin to envy, as I glanced at his uniform with the double stripes on his jacket indicating his first promotion.

I took up my carpet-bag, and slowly retraced my steps to the outer gate of the barracks. I strolled on into Woolwich churchyard, which commands a fine view of the Thames, and sat me down on one of the tomb-stones to give vent to my feelings, and decide upon my future course.

One thing was quite certain, that I would never return to Canterbury "for scorn to point the slow and moving finger" at one who had boasted that he would be a soldier, and was rejected. No; I felt that I would rather sweep a crossing, or take the most menial office among strangers, than subject myself to the sneers and ridicule of some I should meet at Canterbury. And then, I felt that all my bright hopes of "battles, sieges, fortunes, moving accidents by flood and field, and hair-breadth escapes in the imminent deadly breach," were all dashed away, and gone for ever—and that I must bid "farewell to the neighing steed, and the shrill trump, the spirit-stirring drum, the ear-piercing fife, the royal banner, and all the pride, pomp, and circumstance of glorious war." How bitterly did I lament the habit of stammering I had formed, and began to feel it to be indeed true, that it is the fate of the stammerer "to be mortified in every point, baffled at every turn of life, for want of that most common privilege of man,

> 'The merest drug of gorged society,
> Words,—windy words.'"

I sat musing and meditating in this quiet churchyard for some time. At length my disappointed hopes and wounded pride found relief in tears; and as I looked down upon the river, and saw the outward-bound merchantmen slowly wending their course along the silent highway of the Thames, I thought if I could work my way out in one of those gallant vessels to a far-off land, some El Dorado, where, if I did not make a fortune, I should at all events get away from companions and connections that I knew would bring about the ruin of my body and soul.

It was no small mortification to be obliged to return to Smithfield crestfallen and rejected; but I was young, strong, and healthy, and was, moreover, determined no longer to live an idle and listless life.

I took my carpet-bag, and made up my mind to return to Smithfield, tell them of my rejection at Woolwich, and at once set about in right earnest to get something to do. My friends kindly sympathized with me in my disappointment; and as my host at the inn at which I had been staying as a guest, was once in the drapery business, he suggested that I should call upon some of his acquaintances in the trade, and endeavour to obtain employment.

I knew nothing of the drapery business, further than the smattering gained in my early days by frequently visiting a large establishment of a neighbour of my father's at Canterbury; but I had a mind to work, and a determination to do anything rather than continue to lead an idle life.

Accordingly, the next morning I started for the Strand to call on a gentleman known to mine host at Smithfield, and while there a town-traveller in the glove trade called. I was introduced to this gentleman, and he was informed of my disappointment at Woolwich, and of my desire for employment. He said it was a shame that a young fellow should be drifting away to nobody knows what, and asked what I was willing to do. I told him *anything*. He was pleased with my desire for employment, said he was going west, and should be calling upon all the large drapery firms in that direction, and proposed that I should accompany him.

I was delighted with his benevolent and frank behaviour towards me, and I felt an honest pride in carrying his neatly-packed parcel of sample gloves by his side, as we trudged on up the Strand. I found he was a man that I could speak to without any fear or reserve, and my stammering was scarcely recognizable. I gave him some brief account of my family and previous history, that made him the more desirous to be the means of serving me.

The first large establishment we called at was " Waterloo House," in Cockspur-street. I was introduced to one of the principals of the firm, who seemed inclined to engage me, though he demurred rather at the fact that I knew so little of the business. He appointed me to call the next day to hear his decision.

On leaving Waterloo House my good friend called upon many of the principal houses in Waterloo Place and Regent-street, but without any success so far as I was concerned. We pursued our course into Oxford-street, and at a large house a few doors from Marylebone-lane—now the celebrated firm of Marshall and Snelgrove—they wanted a ticket-writer, and some one who would make himself generally useful in the establishment. As I wrote a tolerably good hand, and was rather clever with my pen, I thought I could soon learn how to write the tickets that are attached to "splendid shawls" and "rich gros de nap," &c, exposed for sale in the window.

The proprietor of this establishment was pleased with my appearance, and engaged me at once. The terms were that I was to board and lodge in the house, and to receive a salary of £10 a-year. The engagement was to commence on the following day.

My kind friend and patron, the town traveller, to whom I was indebted for this truly disinterested service, was as much delighted as myself, and I was determined that my conduct should be such in every way as to justify, in some measure, the very kind interest he had taken in my welfare.

I parted with him at the door of the shop, and he left me with a few brief words of kindly counsel, and told me that he should always call and see me whenever he came west.

I was rejoiced on returning to Smithfield to tell my friends there of my success. They were a little amused at the thought of my becoming "a counter-jumper" so soon after my military adventure; but at the same time they were glad to find that I had succeeded in getting something to do, as they were becoming rather anxious about my restlessness, and they feared, moreover, that my intimacy with the medical students would not tend in any way to improve my morals.

I entered upon my new engagement on the following morning, and after a little practice found myself quite at home in the art of ticket-making. I was informed by some of my fellow-assistants in the shop that a person

who worked for the trade made sometimes as much as
fifteen shillings or a pound per day in going round from
shop to shop writing these tickets, and was advised to pay
particular attention to this branch of the business, in case
of my not excelling as a salesman.

When not occupied in ticket-making and in duties connected with the counting-house, I gained some practical
knowledge of the haberdashery branches of the trade, and
was soon able to serve customers very creditably. I found,
however, that my stammering often prevented me from
expatiating as eloquently as could be desired on the qualities of more expensive articles, such as a shawl, or a silk
dress, so that I was glad to make myself as proficient as
possible in the branches of the business where my pen and
pencil were brought into practice.

I was fortunate in gaining the good opinion of my employer, and still more happy in getting into the good books
of his better-half, an agreeable lady in the meridian of
life, with a numerous family, the younger members of
which took a special liking to me. Being rather a handy
fellow, my services were often called into requisition in
various ways by this lady, from whom I received many
little acknowledgments of my attempts to please.

The domestic arrangements of this establishment were
most excellent. Everything was done to make the young
persons in their employ comfortable and happy after the
hours of business, and the food provided for us was of the
best description. Family worship was regularly conducted
by the head of the establishment, and the young men from
the shop were invited, but not compelled, to attend these
services.

I was so pleased with the cheerful disposition of my
governor, and also by the consistent manner of conducting
his business, that I determined to attend one of these services. It was the first thing of the kind I had ever seen, as
nothing of this nature obtained in my father's family. I had
always the impression that only methodistical people in-

troduced such practices into their week-day domestic arrangements, and I always had a great horror of, and thorough contempt for, anything bordering upon Methodism.

I found, however, that there was an attractiveness about the service that very much won upon me. The family, consisting of the heads of the household, their children, the servants, and porters, and about ten or a dozen of the young men from the shop, were regularly assembled after breakfast in the morning, and also in the evening as often as circumstances would permit. The governor read a suitable chapter from the bible, and afterwards offered an extempore prayer of about eight or ten minutes. There was nothing wearisome about the service, and I could not help remarking that the young men who attended these meetings for Divine worship were for the most part among the best assistants in the shop.

I was struck, not only by the natural and becoming manner in which my employer conducted these services, but also I could not fail to see that his business was conducted in such a way as to recommend the sacred subjects dilated upon in his prayers and praises. It requires no small amount of moral courage for an employer, who is a religious man, in these cutting and trimming times, to maintain a becoming consistency between services such as these that I advert to, and his daily dealings with his customers, and those who are in his employ.

I am happy, however, to be able to record that few indeed were the inconsistencies I observed in the profession and practice of this good man during the eighteen months I remained in his employment.

My employer remarked one day at dinner, a few Sundays after I entered his establishment, that there was a pew at the chapel that he attended quite free to any of the young men who might desire to make use of it.

I had never attended a Dissenting meeting-house in my life; but my curiosity was a little excited to see and hear what sort of a preacher he could be who had such a consistent and cheerful man for a hearer.

I made up my mind to go on the following Sunday, and judge for myself, both as to the preacher and the services; and I accordingly accompanied one of the young men from the shop, who I found was accustomed to attend this place of worship.

The chapel was situated in the New Road, and was a large oblong, plain brick building, destitute of any architectural pretensions, and capable of holding 1200 or 1400 people. It is one of the commodious chapels that were erected in populous districts of the metropolis by the late Thomas Wilson, of Highbury, a man who deserves honourable mention by every Congregational Dissenter, as one who laid out a large fortune to promote the interests of that denomination, and who devoted a long and useful life to benevolent and philanthropic measures to benefit his less favoured countrymen.

The interior of the chapel was of the plainest and most unadorned description. We were there early; the place was comfortably filled some minutes before the hour of service, by a remarkably well-dressed and intelligent-looking congregation. At the hour of Divine service, a tall, dark, majestic looking man, between thirty and forty years of age, walked rather hurriedly from the vestry, and ascended the pulpit; he was attired in a black flowing gown and clerical bands. The clerk, or precentor, occupied what a Churchman would denominate the reading-desk. A hymn, from Dr. Watts's collection, was given out by the precentor, and each verse was read by him successively as they were sung; a practice, I believe, generally discontinued now in Congregational churches. The hymn being finished, the minister arose, and read selections from the Scriptures, consisting of a Psalm, and a chapter from the Prophecies of Isaiah. This reading was remarkably good and impressive. This was followed by an extempore prayer of about twenty minutes, in language alike devout and simple, and with a solemnity that very much struck me. The prayer being ended, another hymn was sung, and at the close came the sermon.

I have the most vivid and distinct recollection of the whole scene, as it was entirely new to me, and differed so materially from the Church of England services, with which I had been familiar from my childhood. The text was taken from Isaiah vi. 1-4; and it was a sermon on the memorable vision of the Prophet in the Temple. I can recollect even now, at a distance of more than thirty years, the opening sentences of that discourse, and the marked attention of the great congregation made a deep and lasting impression upon me. After reading the text very deliberately, the preacher looked up from the Bible, and with rather low and chastened voice said, " ' In the year that King Uzziah died,' which, according to chronology, was the year in which Romulus, the founder of the Roman Empire, was born. ' In the year that King Uzziah *died:* ' for kings must die. ' All flesh is grass, and the goodliness thereof is as the flower of grass.' The boast of heraldry, the pomp of power, all the beauty, and all the wealth of the world, await alike the inevitable hour.

> ' The path of glory leads but to the grave.'

' Cease ye from man, whose breath is in his nostrils; for wherein is he to be accounted of?' But God lives; He is the everlasting King; His throne endureth to all generations; His dominion does not pass away, and He revealed Himself in unwonted splendour and majesty to the mind of His Prophet when King Uzziah died."

The preacher then directed attention to two points from the passage selected. 1. The glory of God as manifested in Christ Jesus to the Prophet's mind: and 2. The manner in which the Seraphim witnessed the deed. The sermon was a full hour in its delivery, and was one of great beauty and power. The preacher had no notes before

him, and I was astonished at his ready eloquence, as sentence after sentence came from his lips in the most natural
and unaffected manner. The language was chaste and
elegant, his elocution the best I had ever heard, even on
the stage, and his gesture such as would have done honour
to John Kemble in his best days.

I went away from that chapel with a very different opinion
of Dissenters and their services to that which I had entertained all my life. I had always associated Dissent and
Dissenters with ignorance and vulgarity, and imagined,
as many other Churchmen do in the present day, that their
religion was made up mainly of cant and hypocrisy. Here,
however, was a scholar and a gentleman ; a man endowed
with the great natural talents and acquirements that make
up an orator; and exhibiting moreover, as I was informed, in
his daily life, the virtues that should ever characterize and
distinguish the minister of Christ.

I gathered from my employer, on returning from the
morning service, some few particulars relating to the preacher, and found that he had originally studied with a view
of becoming a clergyman in the Established Church ; but,
upon more mature inquiry and deliberation, he saw that he
could not honestly subscribe to the formularies and tests of
that community, and therefore became a Nonconformist minister. He commenced his ministry at Dublin in 1814, and
removed to London in 1817, and at the time referred to
was in the zenith of his fame as a pastor of the flock of
Christ, and a preacher of the everlasting Gospel.

I returned again to the services in the evening; and such
was my admiration of the preacher, and the earnest reality
there appeared to be in the mode of conducting Divine
worship, that I soon began to look forward to the Sunday
services as both an intellectual treat, as well as a becoming
acknowledgment of the sacredness of the day.

The opportunities I have had for the last thirty years
of making myself better acquainted with the ministers of
our Congregational and Baptist Churches, have produced

in me the conviction, that, beyond all question, there are men among them who in general learning, and scholastic attainments, are not a whit behind any of their more favoured brethren in the Establishment.

The literature of the Nonconformists, published during the last half century, will, I am sure, bear a fair comparison with anything that has been issued from those ancient and honoured seats of learning at Oxford, Cambridge, and Dublin, from which they have been excluded.

That I may not be deemed presumptuous in what I have stated of the learning and literature of the pastors of Baptist and Congregational Churches, I am glad to find that my humble opinion is fully justified and confirmed, by the deliberate judgment of a man in all respects qualified to be heard upon such a question. The late Josiah Conder, in his able and interesting account of the life and writings of Dr. Watts, entitled "The Poet of the Sanctuary," speaking of the pastors of Congregational and Baptist Churches, says, "Whatever there may be in the present aspect of our churches to moderate a boastful estimate, or to excite anxiety or humiliation before God, this may be safely and soberly affirmed; that, in no country in the world, at any former period, has there existed a body of men equally numerous, consecrated to the service of the Christian Ministry, occupying a higher position in point of attainments and efficiency, or exhibiting so perfect an agreement in sound doctrine, unshackled by articles or tests, with more exemplariness of character."

Surely such a testimony as this, and others that might readily be quoted, should check the flippant and reckless assertions that are not unfrequently made by Churchmen, as to the intellectual and moral status of a body of noble-hearted and self-forgetting men, most of whom have been driven from the Establishment, as were their forefathers, because they could not conscientiously and honestly give their "assent and consent" to the articles and formularies of a Church many of whose doctrines and practices they believe so contrary to the word of God, and subversive of the supremacy of Christ.

To return, however, to my own personal history. I continued my duties in the shop, and soon became quite proficient in the art of ticket-making, as well as being fortunate enough to retain the good opinion of my employer, and to stand well with my colleagues in the establishment. Unfortunately the hours devoted to business were long and exhausting. I was expected to be in the shop by seven in the morning, and for some months during the season we did not leave business at night before eleven and twelve, so that there was little or no time for mental and social culture.

I gained, however, not only a tolerable knowledge of some branches of the business, but also an insight into some phases of human character, both as to the young people in houses of business and also as to the customers who frequented our shops, that has been of great service to me in my subsequent career.

I was now a regular attendant at the morning and evening family worship, and was never absent from the Sunday services. The sermons I heard opened up to me new and important subjects, and a state of moral thoughtfulness was produced in my mind, such as I had never before been conscious of.

Matters went on thus for several weeks, and I became more and more convinced that there was a reasonableness in personal religion, and in the claims of God upon me, that I could not gainsay, and also that the whole course of my former life had been at variance with what I saw to be the Divine requirements. I had been taught by my dear mother in very early life that I should love the Lord our God with all my heart, and soul, and mind, and strength, and my neighbour as myself; but although I had been religiously brought up, and had, moreover, been duly baptized and confirmed by those whose Apostolic authority in the Church had never been called in question, yet I knew well enough that I was living practically " without God in the world," and yielding willingly to my own inclinations, whenever they came in collision with any higher require- ment.

Such was the state of my mind when I heard a sermon addressed particularly to the young, from the words, " Wilt thou not from this time cry unto me, My Father, thou art the guide of my youth?" (Jeremiah iii. 4). The preacher dwelt long and lovingly on the paternal character of God, and that His love flowed out to us altogether in- dependent of any goodness in the creature, but had its foundation in the infinite depths of a Father's heart. That God is our own Father, and therefore in our perverseness and rebellion never thinks of casting us off, but His thoughts turn constantly and persistently to the means of our restoration to holiness and happiness. The preacher spoke affectionately of the young; their unsuspecting trustfulness, their moral feebleness, their peculiar circum- stances, their exposure to stronger temptations than usual, their ardent temperament, their strong desire of gratifica- tion; the youthful passions struggling for development, and unrestrained indulgence, and the readiness of the youth to plunge into all the gaieties and pleasures of the world, without thinking of consequences, or dreaming for a moment of the retribution that must inevitably follow such a course. He then spoke of the unsatisfactoriness of a life of lawless indulgence, and instanced Solomon ex- claiming mournfully in the prime of his manhood, when he had taken his fill of all these things—" Vanity of vanities, saith the preacher, all is vanity."

The sermon concluded with an expostulatory appeal to the young of both sexes, full of tenderness and earnest pathos, to seek Divine guidance; and instead of looking for happiness in selfishly and foolishly following the plea- sures of sin for a season, to come back to God, and rest with a child's confidence in a Father's heart.

Every word of that sermon came home to my heart;

and I felt as certain of its being a message of mercy from the Great Father to me, as did the Apostle Paul when he was stricken to the earth by the Divine glory on his way to Damascus.

I did not speak to my companion as we returned from the chapel, but sought my bedroom, and there for the first time in my life poured out my full heart " in strong crying and tears" at the feet of that Great and Loving God against whose goodness I had been sinning, and whose parental authority I had dared to call in question.

I arose from my knees that night an altered young man : it was the great crisis in my life ; and from that moment I recognized a relationship that I believe shall never be dissolved, either in life or death, and the consequences of which eternity alone can fully develope and reveal.

There was no friend near to whom I could open my mind, and tell all the new and deep feelings that I was the subject of. The young man who accompanied me to the chapel was, I believe, a Christian ; but he was of a cold, unsympathetic disposition, and I intuitively shrunk from making him acquainted with the altered state of my mind. I could not summon resolution enough to speak to my employer upon the subject, though, I believe, had I done so, he would gladly have counselled me, and would, moreover, have instructed me more fully in the great truths that were now agitating my bosom.

Having left home hurriedly, I did not bring a Bible with me, and I felt ashamed to let those around me know this. I wrote to my mother, told her of my visit to the Dissenting chapel, and of how pleased I was both with the minister and its services ; and also that I was desirous of leading a new life, and should be glad to have a Bible.

In a day or two I received a copy of the Scriptures, bound up with the Book of Common Prayer. The latter circumstance I thought rather a significant fact, as I well knew the great objection on the part of my parents to anything in religious matters tending to lessen my respect for, much less to supersede, that which was prescribed by the Church of England.

My mother wrote to me at the same time a long and loving letter, telling me how I had gladdened the hearts of my father and herself by sending for a Bible. Her letter was such as only a mother could write to a prodigal and repentant son, and had my altered feelings with reference to religion been brought about in connexion with services of the Established Church, all would have been well; but her letter concluded by hoping that, in attending a Dissenting place of worship, I should be careful not to forget the Church of my Fathers.

I was very glad to possess a Bible of my own; and as I had a small chamber to myself, was determined both night and morning to make myself acquainted with its sacred contents. I had never, as far as I could remember, from choice, opened the Bible to read; though I had been taught to look upon it with reverence and respect from my earliest days; and on Sunday afternoons we were, as children, always required to read a chapter aloud to my mother, as well as being examined as to our knowledge of the Church Catechism.

In the absence, however, of any friend with whom I could converse on the subject of personal religion, and of my state of mind in reference thereto, I turned lovingly to the grand old Book I had so long neglected, and practically disregarded, and literally made it the man of my counsel. I found in the Psalms of David that which my inner and better nature yearned for; and many a time did I open my Bible, and, on my knees, make the fifty-first Psalm my own prayer to the Great Father, against whom I had so grievously offended.

I now set myself in right earnest to become better acquainted with the Scriptures; and as I had always been an early riser, sometimes I was up " before the grey dawn dappled into day," poring over the sacred pages, and drinking deeply " of the water of the fountain of life."

The historical portions I left for the present; but the Psalms of David, the Proverbs of Solomon, and the Book of Ecclesiastes, together with the Prophets and the New Testament, were read and re-read many times; and I began to wonder how any one with the slightest pretensions to be thought well informed, could live in ignorance of the sacred writings, even as a literary production.

I began to be twitted a little by some of my colleagues in the establishment as to my altered views, and more serious demeanour; and one of them went as far as to impute it to a desire to please the governor, and to ingratiate myself with his wife.

These little outward annoyances were, however, nothing in comparison with what was going on in my inner man. The terrible struggles there for the mastery of the new principle over the old and long-indulged nature were constant and severe. I began to find that habits, easily formed at the first, were not to be cast off in a day, or to be uprooted without a resolute, determined, and uninterrupted effort; and truthfulness compels me to acknowledge that, not unfrequently, have I been vanquished and overcome when I have fought hard, and struggled manfully to obtain the mastery over some evil habit formed in my early youth, and which had grown with my growth and strengthened with my strength.

The late Archbishop Whately, in one of his valuable and interesting lectures before the Dublin Young Men's Christian Association, entitled " Habits," remarks, " That the words custom and habit, though often carelessly used as if they were synonymous, are not so in reality, but denote, respectively, a cause and an effect. The frequent repetition of any act is a custom; and the state of mind, or of body thence resulting, is a habit. The custom is not the habit, but it forms the habit; and this habit, in

H

turn, helps to keep up the custom. For continued action is like a continued stream of water, which wears for itself a channel that it will not be easily turned from. The bed which the current had gradually scooped at first afterwards confines it. Any one for instance, who has long been accustomed to rise at a certain hour every morning, will have acquired the habit of waking and being ready to rise at that hour. And one who has been accustomed to drink to excess, will have fallen into the habit of craving for that stimulus, and of yielding to that craving. And so in other matters."

Now I found that what the accomplished prelate has thus laid down with his accustomed perspicuity and force was, indeed, terribly true in my own case. I had been wont, through many years, to yield willingly to the habit of profane swearing, partly from the assistance it gave me in surmounting my impediment in speech, as well as to render my speaking more emphatic; and also to indulge in other profligate and lawless habits at variance with the teaching of the Bible; and how to " cease to do evil, and learn to do well," was no small difficulty with me.

I began to read the Bible with a desire to make my daily life and thoughts conformable to its teaching; but it was one thing to read in the Book of the Lord what I should be and do, and quite another thing to bring out, and exemplify in my daily life, its sacred lessons.

" In vain the name of Christ we bear,
Unless the heart of Christ we share.
Through faith and charity alone
Is Christ received, and felt, and known.

In vain the name of Christ we bear,
Unless the faith of Christ we share;
Not words alone, but deeds shall prove
The living faith that works by love.

In vain the name of Christ we bear,
Unless the cross of Christ we share;
The path that leads us to the skies,
Demands love's perfect sacrifice.

In vain the name of Christ we bear,
Unless the love of Christ we share ;
That love that bids the dying live,
And whispers on the cross, Forgive ! "

These lines forcibly represent true Christianity; and
I found that the mere reading of the Bible, and listening to sermons, would do me no good, except I was resolutely determined to practise, and carry out, through
Divine help, the lessons of wisdom and instruction I was
gaining from a careful and diligent perusal of the Scriptures, and from attending the enlightened ministry of the
Word.

Here was the great difficulty with me; and I found
that successfully to overcome an evil habit, and to put in
its place the antagonistic virtue, was no easy task, but,
on the contrary, an Herculean labour, that called for my
most watchful and unwearied efforts. To correct an evil
habit of long standing is like rolling back a mountain
stream, after it has hollowed out a channel for itself; and
only deep and strong religious convictions of duty to God,
and to His kingdom in the world, will, with Divine help,
enable a man successfully to become the victor.

Still, my young brothers, let me tell you, for your
encouragement, that, hard and difficult as it is to get back
again in allegiance to God and duty, that it is not impossible, for " all things are possible to him that believeth " in
the power and sympathy of the Great Father to His weak
and erring children, and His readiness to help them in this
life-enduring struggle.

Let me assure you, my young readers, that there is no
joy to be compared with that of gaining a moral victory
over yourself; and also to remind you at the same time
that there is no feeling of shame, and self-loathing, and
contempt, comparable to that which is endured when we
wilfully and willingly yield ourselves to the gratification of
an evil habit, when all our better nature and higher
instincts rise up, and protest against its indulgence.

Recollect that—

> "Where'er an evil passion is subdued,
> Or virtue's feeble embers fann'd ; where'er
> A sin is heartily abjured, and left;
> There is a high and holy place, a spot
> Of sacred light, a most religious fane,
> Where happiness descending sits and smiles."

The greatest difficulty in fighting against, and over-coming, an evil habit, is in taking the first step to resist it ; but having done this, through Divine grace, keep steadily to the resolution, and though again and again you will be tempted by the syren charmer, and suffer much pain from the intense craving after the accustomed indulgence, yet the path will become less rugged, and smoother, and easier, the longer you continue to tread in it.

Do not be discouraged at finding bad thoughts, and forbidden desires, force themselves ever and anon into your mind, providing you do not cherish, and indulge, and retain them there. " *Resist* the Devil, and he will flee from you." Evil propensities will gradually become weaker, and lose their force, by being continually checked and restrained by right principle.

" To thine ownself be true," and you shall obtain the victory. " *Strive* to enter in at the strait gate," and re-member that the seven-fold blessing at the final goal is for him that overcometh.   Yes, it is " to him that overcom-eth will I grant to sit with Me in My throne, even as I also overcame, and am set down with My Father in His throne! "—Hold on my brother, bravely, and

> " Despair of nothing that you would attain,
> Unwearied diligence your point will gain."

The process will be slow and painful, but persevere and bear in mind that nothing great and durable has ever been produced with ease : labour is the parent of all the lasting wonders of the world, whether in verse or stone, poetry, or the pyramids ; and remember that the prize held out before you is great, and worth contending for; and also that—

> "Habitual evils change not on a sudden;
> But many days must pass, and many sorrows,
> Conscious remorse, and anguish must be felt,
> To curb desire,——to break the stubborn will,
> And work a second nature in the soul."

If you would obtain the mastery over yourself, and be pronounced the victor at the great day, you must not only be valiant for the truth; but you will have to grapple with deadly grasp the Devil in your own heart; but in so fighting, you are not alone. "No man, in this battle, goeth a warfare at his own cost." He who hath called you to enter upon this race set before you, is the Author, as well as the Finisher, of your faith; and He has promised, moreover, that He will "never leave you, and never forsake you." And when life's conflict shall be ended, and you have thrown away for ever the sword, as you did one day the scabbard, you will find yourself reposing under the branches of the tree of life, with all the truly wise, the holy, and the good, of every age and clime. Names, many of whom even here—in this dark world of sin and sorrow—

> .   .   .   "shall sink not in oblivion's flood,
> But with clear music, like a church-bell's chime,
> Sound through the rivers' sweep of onward rushing time."

And it is most true that—

> .   .   .   .   " there is but
> One great society alone on earth:
> The noble living, and the noble dead."

We are not told much, definitively, in the Bible, of what Heaven is; but we are informed that the "kings of the earth bring their glory and their honour into it." "Not only those born to royal estate, but as well the kings of mind and heart." The poet shall bring his crown of song; the orator, his crown of eloquence; the philosopher, his crown of thought; the scientific man, the crown

of his own magnificent inventions. These are crowns
that will last for ever, and shine upon the starry shore of
Heaven before our God. We hear, too, of the instru-
ments of God,—the music of harps fills the everlasting
hills with melody. And, above all, there is one instrument there—that divine instrument—the renewed nature
of man in its perfection. The affections with all their
beautiful strength, and their more beautiful weakness;
the imagination with

> . . . . . " the gleam,
> The light that never was on sea or land ;"

the conscience tuned to the music of God's eternal law :
these are the strings of that instrument that shall ring out
in Heaven's high arches for ever and ever. That instrument, my young brother, may be yours,—cultivate it,—
be it your ambition to present it to Him " upon whose head
are the many crowns," and you shall hear the thrilling
words, " Well done, thou good and faithful servant, enter
thou into the joy of thy Lord."

Now, while all this, and much more than any pen of
man can fully make known, may be yours, do not think
that it is to be obtained by listlessly yielding yourself to
dreamy reveries and wild imaginings. No; you must gird
up the loins of your mind, and remember, that, though
" the *gift* of God is eternal life," it is only so " through
our Lord Jesus Christ." That, while the Saviour has
triumphantly removed the great obstacles that stood in the
way of our reconciliation to God, by His spotless life and
sacrificial death, yet, we are to be " made meet for the
inheritance of the saints in light ; and this is a process
which is to be wrought in us, by the power and energy of
the Holy Ghost, in a daily and life-long struggle with
the evil that is in our own hearts, and with the habits we
have formed, that are contrary to the Divine requirements.
For although it is " the grace of God that bringeth salvation," yet it is ever found, in the Scriptures, in con-

nection with the practical subjugation of all our powers to God; or, as the great Apostle adds, in the verse I have quoted, "teaching us that, denying ungodliness and worldly lusts, we should live soberly, righteously, and godly, in this present world."

But I must again return to my personal history. I found more and more enjoyment in the sermons and services of the sanctuary; for it was my great privilege to be instructed in the divine things by a man who in his public ministrations was "a workman," in all respects, that "needed not to be ashamed, rightly dividing the word of truth." I subsequently found that in his personal intercourse with the people of his charge he was at once a faithful pastor, a discreet counsellor, and a sympathizing friend. He was far more than even this, and his worthiest and most enduring monument will be found in the book of God's remembrance.

The preacher brought under my notice the whole range of Christian doctrine and practice; and while my mind was becoming richly stored with sound theological teaching, the great change was slowly and silently going on within; and although daily failures in duty were not unfrequent, and humbled me in my own sight, yet I was fully conscious of being a new creature in Christ Jesus; because "old things were passing away, and all things were becoming new."

I recollect, just about this time, that some references were made from the pulpit to Doddridge's "Rise and Progress of Religion in the Soul;" and Wilberforce's "Practical View of Christianity;" and also to Thomas Scott's "Force of Truth." I procured these three works, and in my early mornings read them carefully. These justly memorable books shed a flood of light upon the moral relationship subsisting between my soul and God, and the duties arising out of this relationship, yet I many a time became thoroughly weary of them, and was glad to turn away from them to my Bible, where I found more real sympathy with

my heart struggles, and far greater help in overcoming
my moral difficulties. I saw plainly enough what I ought
to be, but how to perform that which was good was the
great difficulty.

My struggles after conformity of heart and life to the
Divine Image were not a little hindered and impeded by
my attempting to draw up written rules and regulations
for the guidance and governance of my daily conduct.
I have one of these papers now before me, extracted from
Doddridge's " Rise and Progress," in which I most cordially adopted every sentiment as my own ; and in witness
whereof attached my signature at the bottom of the sheet
of foolscap containing the directions.   I was vainly endeavouring to weave out for myself a garment of salvation
of my own providing, instead of trusting simply and entirely
in the blood and righteousness of the Lord Jesus Christ
for justification and acceptance in God's sight.

How men torture and afflict themselves in preparations
to receive the Grace of God, and many of the so-called
" guides" in matters of this nature, are calculated to lead
away the mind of an awakened man from accepting at
once the great Salvation as it is freely offered in the
Gospel ; for—

> "Oh, how unlike the complex works of man,
>   Heaven's easy, artless, unencumber'd plan;
>   No meretricious graces to beguile,
>   No clustering ornaments to clog the pile ;
>   From meanness, as from ostentation, free,
>   It stands, like the cerulean arch we see,
>   Majestic in its own simplicity.
>   Inscribed above the portal, from afar
>   Conspicuous as the brightness of a star ;
>   Legible only by the light they give,
>   Stand the soul-quickening words, *Believe and live.*"

Just about this time I saw advertised a work upon the
causes and cure of stammering, written by a gentleman
who had been an army surgeon, and who professed, in most

confident terms, to cure this irritating and annoying habit.
Although my means were very slender, having only ten
pounds a-year, and my clothes and washing to pay for out
of that sum, I purchased a copy of this work for three
shillings and sixpence, and read it with great avidity. The
author appeared to know something of stammering, and at
the end of the book was given a goodly number of testimonials from patients who had been benefited, and of some
that were cured by his treatment.

Now I felt that the impediment in my speech was not
only increasingly mortifying to me in the daily intercourse
of life; but it was also a serious obstacle to my making
any progress in the business. A stammerer, with ever so
good a knowledge of his business, (especially in one like
the drapery trade, where so much depends upon freedom
and readiness of speech,) would never be a successful salesman; and, consequently, I determined to seek this gentleman's professional assistance, if his terms were in any way
within my reach, and try if possible to overcome my inveterate enemy.

The work in question, like all similar productions, stated
that the author would see patients at certain hours as to
terms, &c, and I obtained easy permission from my employer to go and see this gentleman, and found that his
ordinary terms were entirely beyond my reach; but when
I told him of my circumstances, and the smallness of my
income, he agreed to give me his professional assistance for
an hour a day, until my impediment was cured, for five
pounds.

My employer was so anxious to fall in with my plans that
he not only gave me the permission to be absent from the
business daily for the purpose of attending to the instruction
of this gentleman; but he also, with great kindness, gave
me half-a-year's salary in advance, to enable me to avail
myself of the treatment.

Having paid my fee, the doctor explained to me the
physiological causes of my stammering; and with a view

of making this better understood he rang the bell for a
sheep's tongue to be brought up, from which he pointed
out the anatomy of the vocal organs, and causes of my
stammering, together with the means to be adopted for its
removal.

As there was no secresy imposed upon me by this
gentleman, I may mention that the mode of treatment
consisted mainly in speaking as much as possible from the
throat, or, as he called it, gutturally.

Although this produced an unpleasant indistinctness in
the voice, I found it gave me some relief, and after a few
lessons I could read from the " Times" a leading article
with very little hesitation.

I began to hope that I should be freed from my old
enemy, and found that I got on tolerably well with serving
customers, except they happened to be ladies of peculiar
temperament and disagreeable manners, when I sometimes
stuck fast, and was compelled to hand the customer over
to some more highly-favoured colleague who possessed a
fluent tongue.

I attended this gentleman's instructions daily for about
six weeks, and could read aloud not only to him, but also
to a room full of company, with very slight and occasional
hesitation. He considered the case to be so successful a
one, that I was shown as a specimen of the cure;
and remember reading before a Liverpool merchant, who
brought his daughter to the doctor for treatment, a beautiful girl of seventeen, who stammered fearfully. This young
lady, when attempting to speak, put both her hands to her
head, and made the most terrible grimaces, and after
several convulsive efforts to speak the words were ejected
with great force from her pretty mouth, and she was quite
exhausted. I took as much interest in this case as did the
doctor, who more than once hinted that she would make me
a suitable wife, and that her father was a man of considerable property.

I had no opportunity, however, of becoming better

acquainted with this young lady, and at the end of six weeks I left her still under the doctor's treatment, and have never heard whether she was the better for the instruction that she received or not.

In my own case the benefit derived was of a very transient and temporary nature, for in less than a couple of months from the time I discontinued the lessons my impediment returned, with all its terrible annoyances.

In 1834 my father, having failed in business, came to London. The Archbishop of Canterbury, hearing of his failure, presented him with an appointment in the National Library, where he remained till his death in 1847.

I continued in the drapery business for eighteen months, when I had some words with my employer, and gave him notice that I should leave his establishment. I never liked the business, and was moreover desirous of embarking in some occupation more in accordance with my taste than making attractive tickets for the window, and sometimes using my vocal powers in selling fidgety old ladies silks and satins, to say nothing of balls of cotton and pieces of tape.

I left my employer and his excellent lady with reciprocated regrets, and I shall never cease to remember with heartfelt gratitude not only the many kindnesses that I received from both of them, but also the great benefit I derived in a religious point of view during the time spent under their roof.

In the meanwhile I continued to attend the sanctuary, and on leaving my employer, engaged, with some difficulty, as the place was always crowded, a sitting at the chapel. I had now attended the services regularly for more than twelve months, and my attachment to the minister was increasing daily. The few weeks that I was out of employment gave me more time leisurely to take a retrospect of the change in my life and character that had taken place during the past year, and also to think more soberly as to what was to be my future course of action with reference to my again taking a situation.

My father and family had removed to London, and were living in the neighbourhood of Bedford Square. I had to put up with a good deal of bantering from my brothers and sisters in consequence of what they termed my Methodistical views ; and although my father and mother could not but be struck with the moral change that had been wrought in me, yet they both strongly objected to my going to a dissenting place of worship, and they were sadly afraid that I was becoming " righteous overmuch."

I am glad, however, to state that I was enabled to bear not only the taunts and jeers of my brothers and sisters, but also the more painful remarks of my father and mother as to chapel and chapel-goers, with a good measure of meekness and forbearance. I had no doubt or uncertainty as to the great change that had taken place within me, and was resolutely determined, as far as I could, to carry out to any extent, and in spite of all opposition, the religious convictions of duty that had been formed within me from a diligent and prayerful reading of the Scriptures, and the teaching I was listening to from the pulpit.

I could not help perceiving that the work of bringing about any change in my sentiments and inclinations, such as that which I had lately undergone, must be one of some considerable difficulty, and only to be effected gradually. I was painfully conscious of the labour and difficulty of forming good moral habits, especially as I had to *un*-learn so many evil habits of long standing and unrestrained indulgence. My age and ardent temperament were such as to render it necessary that I should exercise the greatest watchfulness, not only with reference to my outward deportment, but more especially as to the state of my heart. Oh, how often has that prayer of David gone up to the throne of the Eternal from my agonized bosom—" Create within me a clean heart, O God, and renew a right spirit within me." " Cleanse Thou me from secret faults, and keep back Thy servant also from presumptuous sins ; let them not have dominion over me."

I record it for the encouragement of those who may be similarly situated, that these two brief petitions were never unanswered. Moral and spiritual aid in answer to these heart cries has come quicker than the lightning's flash, and I have been strengthened with strength in my inner man. Whenever I have failed in duty, and yielded to temptation, it has ever been the result of infirmity of purpose and moral weakness. Those who know anything of their own hearts will, I am sure, bear me out in the assertion that no man is ever *compelled* to do anything that is evil ; but in a question of such vital importance the Word of the Lord puts the matter beyond all doubt, and says, in language that finds an echo in the heart of every thoughtful man, "Let no man say when he is tempted, I am tempted of God: for God cannot be tempted with evil, neither tempteth he any man ; but every man is tempted when he is drawn away of his own lust, and enticed. Then when lust hath conceived, it bringeth forth sin ; and sin, when it is finished, bringeth forth death." (James, i. 13-15.)

In this brief but pregnant quotation is contained the philosophy of temptation ; and the reading of many works on the subject of the freedom of the will, during the past thirty years, has only convinced me that the great Milton has summed up the whole controversy in one grand line of his immortal epic, when, in speaking of the fall of our first parents, he speaks of them as

"Sufficient to have stood, yet free to fall."

But, to return from this digression, and lest I should be wearisome, I must state that the great truths of Christianity were gradually and silently advancing in their influence upon my daily life. Many were the moral battles fought within my own bosom at that critical period of my life, and they have continued from those days of my early manhood to the present moment! And many of the practices learned in my youth will, I fear, have to be fought against, and resisted, until the " earthly house of this tabernacle" be taken down and laid aside for ever.

I have often been struck by the fact that almost all the great and mighty revolutions that are taking place around us in the material world are carried on in silence :—

> " In silence mighty things are wrought,—
> Silently builded, thought on thought,
>   Truth's temple greets the sky;
> And, like a citadel with towers,
> The soul with her subservient powers,
>   Is strengthen'd silently.
>
> Soundless, as chariots on the snow,
> The saplings of the forest grow
>   To trees of mighty girth;
> Each nightly star in silence burns,
> And every day in silence turns
>   The axle of the earth.
>
> The silent frost, with mighty hand,
> Fetters the rivers and the land,
>   With universal chain;
> And smitten by the silent sun,
> The chain is loosed, the rivers run,
>   The lands are free again.
>
> O, source unseen of life and light,
> Thy secresy of silent might
>   If we in bondage know,
> Our hearts, like seeds beneath the ground,
> By silent force of life unbound,
>   Move upward from below."*

So silently were the great moral transformations going on in my heart and mind. I found then, as I do now, " that in me (that is, in my flesh) dwelleth no good thing; for to will was present with me ; but how to perform that which was good I found not. For the good that I would I did not, but the evil which I would not, that I did." I found then, as I do, alas! now, " a law, that when I would

---

* From "The Rivulet," a contribution to sacred song. By the Rev. T. T. Lynch. A poetic gem.

have done good evil was present with me. And though I delighted in the law of God after the inward man, I saw another law in my members, warring against the law of my mind, and oftentimes bringing me into subjection to the law of sin which was in my members." (Romans vii. 18-23.)

" Progress is the law of life" in any form; and the life of God in the soul of man is not an exception to this general rule.

I began to think, now that I had more time for reflection, that I ought to connect myself outwardly with the people of God. The announcement was made every month from the pulpit that the preacher would be glad to see applicants for church membership, either at his own house or in the vestry of the chapel; and I was a little curious to know what was done at a " church meeting," which was announced to take place on the Friday evening preceding the first Sunday in the month.

I had never spoken to the minister, and was rather afraid to call upon him at his private residence, so I determined upon writing to him, stating the benefit I had derived from his ministry, and asking permission to be a partaker of the Lord's Supper.

Having presented my letter to the chapel-keeper, I waited in the chapel to know the result of my application. In a little while I was requested to go into the vestry, where I found the minister and two rather elderly gentlemen, who I afterwards learned were what are termed " deacons." The preacher received me very kindly, shook me by the hand with much friendliness, and requested me to take a seat.

I was a little taken aback by the presence of the other gentlemen, as there is a sacredness about communications such as I had made in my letter which we naturally shrink from making public. The preacher said that they were very pleased with my letter, and that the application should be submitted to a meeting of the Church which was to be held the same evening. The other gentlemen made a few kindly remarks, and I withdrew, greatly wondering what sort of an ordeal I should have to pass through at the church meeting.

This meeting took place in the chapel at seven o'clock, and I found myself with eight or ten more persons, who were also applicants for church membership, in a waiting-room adjoining the chapel.

We sat very silently in this waiting-room, and the voice of melody and the prayer that followed were distinctly heard by us. In a little while, to my great surprise, I heard the minister read out, in a low voice, my letter. Some remarks were made at the close in tones that I could not catch, and I waited patiently to know the result.

In a little while we were requested to enter the chapel, and the pew-opener led us to a seat exactly in front of the table, at which the minister sat. Immediately on our being seated, the minister arose and came to me; he said that my late employer, who was at the meeting, had corroborated all that I had stated in my letter, and had also furnished the meeting with some interesting particulars of the change that had taken place in my life and character.

It was customary for applicants for church membership to be proposed at one meeting, and, after inquiry had been made as to their moral character, &c, they were, if approved of, admitted to the fellowship of the Church on the following church meeting. Mine was, however, made an exceptional case, as my employer had supplied at once all the information that was needed. The minister therefore informed me that I was admitted as a member of the Church at once, and that he should be happy to see me at the Lord's table on the following Sunday morning.

I was so completely overcome by the strangeness of the proceedings, and the importance of the step I was taking, that my feelings obtained the mastery over me, and I gave vent to them in a flood of tears. At the close of the meeting the minister congratulated me on my admission to the

church, and gave me a very cordial invitation to call upon
him at his private residence, whenever I would like to converse with him upon any of the great subjects that had
brought us together.

I felt towards this good man more than any words
of mine can adequately express. He had been the means,
under God, of awakening within me a desire to lead a
new life; and I looked upon him with a filial reverence
and love that I had never felt towards any other person. My
affection for him increased daily, and I felt towards him a
deep and holy love, greater even than that I bore to my
natural parents. I accepted his kind invitation, and called
upon him several times, told him further particulars of my
early life, and of the jeers and persecutions I was subjected
to, from my parents and brothers and sisters, at my becoming a Methodist. He counselled me with words of wisdom
and tenderness; and, with a view of improving my mind,
offered me the free use of any books in his well-selected
and extensive library.

So annoying were the jeers and taunts I had to meet
with at home, that I asked my pastor to recommend me to
board and lodge in some religious family, however humble
their circumstances might be. He told me that I must
not think of leaving my home, but must bear with Christian meekness the reproach of the cross, and honour my
father and mother, by a willing obedience to their wishes
in all matters not relating to conscience and to God.

I shall never forget the memorable day that I first sat
down at the Lord's table; and for the information of many
of my old friends of the Church of England, I shall furnish a few particulars as to the mode of administering that
ordinance in the congregational church with which I was
connected.

At the close of the morning service, when the general
congregation had retired, the members of the Church, who
were communicants, occupied the complete area of the
chapel, to the number of seven or eight hundred. The

I

bread and wine were placed upon a table in front of the pulpit. The service commenced with an appropriate hymn, such, for example, as—

> " When I survey the wondrous cross
> On which the Prince of glory died,
> My richest gain I count but loss,
> And pour contempt on all my pride."

Then followed a short address on the sacrificial work of Christ, and his union with his people ; with his last request that they should do this in remembrance of Him.   This was followed by a short prayer, and the elements of the broken body and shed blood of the Lord Jesus were handed round to the members, who remained in their pews.   A hymn concluded the service ; and while memory holds her place in me I shall never forget the feelings with which I joined in the last verse of that sacred song—

> " Were the whole realm of nature mine,
> That were a present far too small :
> Love so amazing, so divine,
> Demands my soul, my life, my all."

A thousand hallowed recollections cluster around this happy period of my life ; and at a distance of more than thirty years I look back with devout gratitude to the step I was induced to take, as by far the most important event in my chequered history.

Being out of employment, and having no liking to the trade with which I had been recently connected, my father sought an interview with his Patron, the Archbishop of Canterbury, who was so kind as to give me an appointment in the National Library with my father.

I need not say that I found myself far more at home in my new occupation than in that which I had followed for the last eighteen months ; but for obvious reasons I shall not be expected at present to advert again to my official connection with a Library which has long since taken its high place among the foremost in Europe, and in which I shall ever esteem it a great privilege to have held, for the larger portion of my life, a very humble position.

My hours of attendance at the National Library gave me ample time for reading and mental culture, and I found in my good pastor a friend and adviser, ready at all times to give me not only the use of his library, but also the benefit of his own extensive reading.

My reading, up to the period of my coming to London, had been mostly confined to novels and romances, and books of far worse character; but I had a strong desire now to become acquainted with the literature of my own country, and as the impediment in my speech shut me out of society, to a great extent, I was glad to find in books the companionship that my heart yearned for.

I began to read some of the old Puritan Divines, and found a sound manly divinity in the works of Howe, Owen, Baxter, Brookes, Bunyan, and others, that enlarged and enlightened my mind in theological literature. I commenced also a course of reading from the poets, and cannot tell the rapture and delight I experienced at a first perusal of "Paradise Lost." I finished it at a couple of sittings, and committed large portions afterwards to memory. When I had thoroughly enjoyed the poetry of Milton, I turned to his English prose works with much pleasure and not a little profit. I find many young men who are fond of poetry, (and who is not? for it has been truly said that "poetry is the record of the best and happiest moments of the happiest and best minds"), and can quote long passages from Milton's Poems, while they know nothing of the incomparable energy and eloquence of his prose works. My good pastor called my attention to these writings of that great man. I recollect that Macaulay says of them: "Milton's prose writings deserve the devoted attention of every man who wishes to become acquainted with the full power of the English language. They abound with the noblest passages, and the style is stiff with gorgeous em-

broidery. . Not even in the ' Paradise Lost ' has the great
poet ever risen higher than in those parts of his contro-
versial works in which his feelings, excited by conflict, find
a vent in bursts of lyric and devotional rapture. It is—
to borrow his own majestic language—' a sevenfold chorus
of hallelujahs and harping symphonies.' "

Our Poet Laureate calls him, in one of his never-to-be-
forgotten lines, the

" God-gifted organ-voice of England."

These were followed by the works of Pope, Crabbe,
Butler, Goldsmith, Thomson, Gray, Cowper, Campbell,
Coleridge, Rogers, Byron, Wordsworth, Shelley, and
Moore. To these succeeded the plays and poems of the
great Shakespeare, which so enriched my mind and exercised my understanding that ever after their study I enjoyed
far more pleasure in my general reading. The Englishman who has never read the dramatic writings of our great
countryman is to be pitied: he little knows the mine of
wealth that he is neglecting, and the ever-widening fields
of thought that lie spread out before him in that marvellous writer. I would particularly impress upon our young
men, were there any necessity for its being done at the
present day, the desirableness of becoming thoroughly
acquainted with the writings of Shakespeare ; and any one
may do this now-a-days, inasmuch as there are not only
beautifully printed and splendidly illustrated editions of the
great poet, for those who can afford to purchase such
luxuries ; but there are also " penny " editions of his
separate plays, which you can purchase, and carry about
with you, as I have done ; and let them be the companions
of your solitary walks, as well as the delight of your fireside musings.

I remember somewhere to have read by an anonymous
writer that " Shakespeare was the profoundest thinker, the
wittiest, the airiest, the most fantastic spirit (reconciling
the extremes of ordinary natures) that ever condescended

to teach and amuse mankind. He plunged into the depths of speculation; he penetrated to the inner places of knowledge, plucking out 'the heart of the mystery;' he soared to the stars; he trod the earth, the air, the waters, with a kingly step. Every element yielded him rich tribute. He surveyed the substances, and the spirits of each; he saw their stature, their power, their quality, and reduced them without an effort to his own divine command."

My pastor and friend also recommended me to read the biographies of the great and good; and I thereby became acquainted not only with the leading men of our own denomination, as Robert Hall, Andrew Fuller, John Foster, the late Dr. M'All, of Manchester, Winter Hamilton, John Ely, of Leeds, Jay, of Bath, and a host of others, but also with the wise and good of other communions, such, for example, as Thomas Chalmers, Richard Watson, the Wesleys, Whitfield, Henry Martin, Leigh Richmond, Sir James Mackintosh, Lord Eldon, Wilberforce, Fowel Buxton, Southey's Life of Nelson, Boswell's Johnson, Stanley's Life of Arnold of Rugby, and many more whose memories are cherished by me with many grateful recollections. I also spent not a few of my early mornings upon the essayists of the Johnsonian period, as well as making myself tolerably acquainted with the best writers of fiction of that age.

My chief delight was, however, in theology and theological writers; and the preaching I was accustomed to attend led me not only to read writers of our own communion, but also made me desirous of becoming acquainted with the works of most of the great writers that have adorned the Church of England. The writings of Isaac Barrow, Jeremy Taylor, South, and the Venerable Hooker, could but exercise a beneficial effect upon me, and I am greatly indebted to these giants of the Church of my fathers for the intellectual and spiritual enjoyment I have derived from a careful perusal of their writings.

The two toughest books I ever read were, Jonathan

Edwards " On the Will," and Butler's " Analogy." The
former of these taxed my reasoning powers to the utmost,
and I have had to throw it aside altogether for a time, that
I might get my thoughts into another channel, and so
relieve my mind.   Butler's " Analogy " I have read again
and again : it is a dry, hard book ; but the man who will
take the pains to master it will be in little danger of having
his mind disturbed by the shallow, yet specious sophistries
of some of the semi-theological writings of our own day.

Having always had a love for oratory, I spent a good deal
of my spare time in reading the speeches of Burke, Pitt,
Fox, Sheridan, Curran, and others, as well as those of the
men of my own time, such as Canning, Brougham, O'Con-
nell, Shiel, Daniel Webster, and Macaulay.   I had always
a love for music ; but not even the harmonies of Handel,
or the melodies of Mozart, ever were so pleasurable to me
as a great speech or a good sermon from a living orator ;
and I have often felt, as I have been listening to a great
speaker, that I would rather be an orator than possess the
wealth of a Rothschild, or wield the destinies of a nation ;
for, after all, these are the true kings among men, and
they exert an influence upon the mental and moral condition
of their fellows, such as wealth could never purchase, and
despotic rule never command.

But, lest I should become wearisome to some of my
readers, in yielding to these rhapsodies, I would just say,
to my younger brothers in particular, that most of my
reading has been done before breakfast.   There is a freshness in the early morning that makes life a luxury ; and
those who indulge in long and late slumbers lose some of
the greatest enjoyments of which our nature is capable.

If you are a Christian, what is more fitting than early
rising and prayer?   It has been beautifully said by one of
our old poets that—

> " When first thy opening eyes receive
>   The glorious light of day ;
> Give thy awakening spirit leave
>   To be as blest as they.

Our outward organs well may teach
    Its duty to the soul;
And thoughts ascend, that need not speech,
    Unto their heavenly goal.

For hearts, whose love to God is true,
    Should open with the day,
As flowers, impearl'd with morning dew,
    Their tenderest tints display.

Give God thy waking thoughts, that He
    Throughout the day may keep
The spirit company, and be
    Its Guardian while asleep.

Yet sleep not when the sun has risen,
    For prayer with day should rise;
And holiest thoughts, set free from prison,
    Should soar above the skies.

There are appointed hours between
    Our souls and love divine;
Nothing of earth should intervene
    To mar their blest design.

The manna's heavenly charm was gone,
    With morning's stainless dews;
And flowers on which the sun has shone
    Their sweetest perfume lose!

Then let not needless slumber glut
    Morn's glories by its sin;
When this world's gates are closest shut,
    Heaven's open!—enter in!

Walk out beneath the roseate skies,
    Eye, ear, and heart awake;
List to the melodies that rise
    From tree, from bush, and brake.

Each fluttering leaf, each murmuring spring
    The great I AM doth own;
To *Him* the soaring sky-larks sing
    In music's sweetest tone.

Canst thou not sing? O! leave thy cares
    And follies; go thy way!
And morning's praises, morning's prayers,
    Go with thee through the day!

Serve God before the world below;
  Nor suffer, unimplored,
That blessing from thy path to go,
  He only can afford.

This done, to Him resign thy will,
  Who never will forsake
Those who, like Jacob, wrestle still,
  As day begins to break.

Mornings are emblems, shadowing forth,
  Unto the spirit's eye,
Man's resurrection, and the birth
  Of hopes that cannot die.

The glorious star which speaks them near,
  Like that of Bethlehem,
Is life and light! Its rise more dear
  Than crown or diadem.

But when the morning's prime is past,
  And worldly cares are rife,
May thy soul's harmony outlast
  The daily din of life!

Despatch whatever must be done;
  Life hath a load to bear,
Which may be borne; a path to run,
  Beset with many a care.   ·

Keep such without; and let thy heart
  Be still thy God's alone;
And He, thy spirit's better part,
  Shall bless thee as His own."

I offer no apology for adorning my humble pages with this exquisite poem of Henry Vaughan, modernized by Bernard Barton; as nothing I could say on the subject would induce the practice of such a custom, if a deaf ear be turned to such an invitation.

But I can truly say, that, in my own case, the habit of early rising has afforded me the quiet and undisturbed leisure for reading and meditation that has gone very far to allay that nervous irritability produced by my stammering, as well as given me an opportunity of reading many works that I should otherwise have neglected, and been ignorant of; and, I may add, that this rough-and-ready story of my life has been wholly written in the early mornings between four and eight.

Much has been said of books and mental culture to our young men of the present day; and I would add my humble testimony to the desirableness of giving attention to reading. Remember the words of England's greatest essayist, that should be written on your heart, " Read not to contradict and refute, nor to believe and take for granted, nor to find talk and discourse, *but to weigh and consider.*" Had I received better early training, I should have been a very different man to what I now am; and often do I mourn that I did not, in the days of my youth, possess the advantages for mental and moral culture that are now within reach of all our young men in our many " Christian Associations," and " Societies for Mutual Improvement."

Recollect, my young brothers, that—

" He who seeks the mind's improvement,
Aids the world in aiding mind;
Every great commanding movement
Serves not one, but all mankind."

The great Milton has told us that " a good book is the precious life-blood of a master-spirit, embalmed and treasured up on purpose to a life beyond life."

Old Richard de Bury, in " Philobiblon," written as early as the fourteenth century, says, in words that find an echo in many a lover of reading, " In books, we find the dead as if alive; in books, we foresee things to come; in books, warlike affairs are methodized; in books, the laws of peace are manifested. All things are corrupted and decay with time. Saturn ceaseth not to devour his offspring, and oblivion covereth the glory of the world. But God hath provided for us a remedy in books, without which all that were ever great would have been forgotten. To books, how easily, how secretly, how safely, may we expose the nakedness of human ignorance, without putting us to shame.

These are the masters who instruct us without rods, without anger, or without reward; if you approach them, they are not asleep; if you interrogate them, they do not hide themselves; if you mistake them, they never murmur; if you are ignorant, they do not laugh at you. Oh, books! alone liberal and making liberal, who give to all who ask, and emancipate all who serve you."

These golden words of the good old monk are confirmed by the testimony of one of the best men, and most elegant scholars of modern times; the late Dr. Channing, who says in his lecture on " Self-Culture," in eloquent language that every young man should remember,—" It is chiefly through books that we enjoy intercourse with superior minds, and these invaluable means of communication are in the reach of all. In the best books great men talk to us, give us their most precious thoughts, and pour their souls into ours. They are the voices of the distant and the dead, and make us heirs of the spiritual life of past ages. Books are the true levellers; they give to all who will faithfully use them, the society, the spiritual presence, of the best and greatest of our race. No matter how poor I am; no matter though the prosperous of my own time will not enter my obscure dwelling: if the sacred writers will enter, and take up their abode under my roof; if Milton will cross my threshold, to sing to me of Paradise; and Shakespeare, to open to me the worlds of imagination, and the workings of the human heart; and Franklin, to enrich me with his practical wisdom,—I shall not pine for want of intellectual companionship, and I may become a cultivated man, though excluded from what is called the best society in the place where I live. The great use of books is to rouse us to thought, to turn us to the questions which great men have been working on for ages, to furnish us with the materials for the exercise of judgment, imagination, and moral feeling, and breathe into us a moral life from spirits nobler than our own."

And lastly, as the preacher would say, let me refer my

young brothers to a work recently issued by one of our foremost living preachers, who, in speaking of the subject I am treating of, observes,*—" With what more than regal power do books invest us! The mightiest potentate cannot surround himself with a galaxy of more brilliant talent, or with wiser counsellors than they supply. I sit a king in my study, commanding the attendance, not of ordinary men, but of those who were princes in the realms of thought. I am instructed as I read their most matured thoughts on the loftiest themes which can occupy the attention of mankind; I am inspired by their fervid utterances. The masters of song strike their lyres at my bidding, and rouse me from my lethargy by their soul-stirring strains. On the wings of their lofty conceptions, I soar into the regions of the sublime, forgetting my corroding cares as I wander amid the glorious imagery which surrounds me there. The men of the past live before me as I pore over the historic page. I mingle in their gatherings; I listen to their talk; I share in their sorrows and their joys; I wrestle with them in their conflicts, and rejoice with them in their victories. I am cautioned by their mistakes; I am made better by their goodness; I profit by the experience of many generations."

Many a time before I was married, as I have sat in my own little room in the grey mornings, waiting for the day, and in the dusky evenings, before the lamp has been lighted, glancing at the few choice authors (who have been the companions of my solitary hours), as well as when I have been surrounded all day long in the National Library by—

> " The grand old masters,
>   And the bards sublime,
> Whose distant footsteps echo
>   Through the corridors of time,"

---

* "True Manhood: its Nature, Foundation, and Development. A book for young men. By William Landels, minister of Regents-park Chapel. 12mo. London, 1861."

have the beautiful lines of Southey, written in his library, come to my recollection :—

> " My days among the dead are pass'd;
>   Around me I behold,
> Where'er these casual eyes are cast,
>   The mighty minds of old;
> My never-failing friends are they
> With whom I converse night and day.
>
> With them I take delight in weal,
>   And seek relief in woe;
> And while I understand and feel
>   How much to them I owe,
> My cheeks have often been bedew'd
> With tears of thoughtful gratitude.
>
> My thoughts are with the dead: with them
>   I live in long past years,
> Their virtues love, their faults condemn,
>   Partake their griefs and fears;
> And from their sober lessons find
> Instruction with a humble mind.
>
> My hopes are with the dead; anon
>   With them my place will be;
> And I with them shall travel on
>   Through all futurity;
> Yet leaving here a name, I trust,
> Which will not perish in the dust."

I found, as many others have done, that while I gained strength and stability of character, as well as sympathy and aid in the Divine life, by my outward profession of Christianity, in connecting myself with a Christian Church; yet, after all, the great struggle was to maintain a right state of heart and mind, and to have subjugated within me those passions that were at variance with the Divine requirements, as well as antagonistic to my own happiness.

This is the battle-field where the Christian warrior must fight,—

> " His warfare is within. There he toils,
>   And there he wins fresh victories o'er himself,

> And never-withering wreaths; compared with which
> The laurels that a Cæsar wears are weeds."

Old habits had daily to be fought against, and criminal indulgences were not always successfully resisted, for—

> " Let but temptation touch the line
> Electrical within,
> That spark will spring the secret mine
> Of nature's ready sin."

But I struggled hard and prayerfully to eject the demon who had so long wielded his sceptre over my entire nature, and in the main I was the victor, and came off " more than conqueror through Him that loved me," for—

> " More things are wrought by prayer
> Than this world dreams of."

I was much struck with a sentence I met with in the life of Fowel Buxton, to the following effect : " The longer I live the more am I certain that the great difference between men,—between the feeble and the powerful, the great and the insignificant,—is *energy, invincible determination, a purpose once fixed,* and then *death* or *victory.* That talent can do anything that can be done in this world, and no one can be a man without it."

Just about this time I was appointed the London agent for two Universities, one in Ireland and the other in Scotland, entitled to certain privileges under the Copyright Act. The duties connected with these agencies occupied nearly my entire evenings during the week; but as my salary at this period was only £80 a-year, I was glad to increase my income from other sources, and the more especially as I was beginning to think of looking about me for some loving heart with whom I could share my joys and sorrows.

Some of my more serious readers will think it rather premature for a young man of nineteen to be thinking of marriage ; and, perhaps, under ordinary circumstances it is not well to be taking such a step at so early an age. But it will be remembered that I was a youth of ardent temperament, and that I had formed connections in my early days that were not of the most reputable character; and although I had long before this ceased to have any communication with these acquaintances, yet I nevertheless felt a yearning for some sister spirit; and a desire, also, to be settled in a home of my own, however humble that home might be.

I had many a time felt, in my own heart, as well as read in the well-known couplet, that even in Eden, with all its primæval beauty and loveliness,

> " The world was sad, the garden was a wild;
> And man, the hermit, sigh'd, till woman smiled."

Let philosophers, with Malthus at their head, and John Stuart Mill to bring up the rear, say what they will against early marriages, I am decidedly of opinion that a young man cannot do better, under certain circumstances, than form a virtuous attachment to some girl of suitable age; and, if his love be reciprocated, it will help to keep him from " the lips of a strange woman."

> " For, indeed, I know
> Of no more subtle master under Heaven
> Than is the maiden passion for a maid;
> Not only to keep down the base in man,
> But teach high thoughts, and amiable words,
> And courtliness, and the desire of fame,
> And love of truth, and all that makes a man."

It was not long before I saw among my new connections one that I thought in every respect would make me a good wife. I found, on our becoming better acquainted, that there was just that accordance of sentiment between us in matters of the greatest moment as to make our union likely to be a happy one. I made a full declaration of my love, and was accepted; and if the maiden I had selected was not " the idol of my youth," she was " my last love," and " the darling of my manhood."

She was as great an admirer of my pastor as I was;
and while we have listened to his sacred eloquence, the
services grew even more interesting and attractive, for
although sometimes it was true that—

> " Long was the good man's sermon;
> Yet it seem'd not long to me:
> For there sat by my side a maiden,
> Who was all the world to me."

Though our affection for each other grew exceedingly,
yet, as my income was a very slender one, there were
prudential reasons for putting off for awhile the " consummation so devoutly to be wished."

Though many years have passed since then, and some
of them dark and trying, yet I can even now say, in the
beautiful words of Scotland's greatest poet,—

> " O happy love! where love like this is found!
> O heart-felt raptures! bliss beyond compare!
> I've paced much this weary, mortal round,
> And sage experience bids me this declare—
> If Heaven a draught of heavenly pleasure spare,
> One cordial in this melancholy vale,
> 'Tis when a youthful, loving, modest pair,
> In other's arms breathe out the tender tale,
> Beneath the milk-white thorn that scents the evening gale."

I am glad to be able to record, for the information of
those of my readers who may have thought me a little
imprudent in my matrimonial anticipations, that we
waited in " the patience of hope" for four long years
before we were united in marriage.

These years of courtship were among the very happiest
of my life, and I look back upon them as truly halcyon
days. Frequently during that long season of joyful anticipation did I quote to her listening ear the well-known
lines,—

> " The fountain mingles with the river,
> And the rivers with the ocean;
> The winds of heaven mix together,
> With a sweet emotion.

Nothing in the world is single;
   All things by a law divine
In one another's being mingle,
   Why not I with thine?

See the mountains kiss high heaven,
   And the waves clasp one another;
No sister flower would be forgiven
   If it disdain'd its brother.
And the sunlight clasps the earth,
   And the moonbeams kiss the sea;
What are all these kissings worth,
   If thou kiss not me?"

With a view of still further increasing my income, in order that I might put by something to begin housekeeping with, I obtained some work of a literary character; and very frequently have I sat up after midnight, and begun again with the early morning, to complete work that I had undertaken to do by a certain time. These prolonged hours of hard work overtaxed my system, and brought on seasons of nervous exhaustion and depression that have caused me much suffering in later years.

In 1836 I made another attempt to get the better of my stammering, by attending the lectures of a professor of elocution from Scotland; but, I regret to say, with as little success as that which had preceded it. This gentleman was very desirous of effecting a cure, as it would have been of great service to him (as well as no small benefit to me) to have referred to the cure of a case so inveterate as mine was known to be. However, it was a failure, and I submitted to the renewed mortification and disappointment with as much Christian resignation as I could muster.

I found that reading aloud in my own room alone, and holding imaginary conversations with myself in the open fields, did more than anything else to remove many of my difficulties. The great thing to be attended to in stammering, providing there is no organic defect, is to understand clearly the right use of the vocal organs, and then to practise the voice in speaking and reading, as you would acquire the mastery over a musical instrument. There is no " royal road " to the cure of stammering any more than there is to any other art that we are desirous of becoming proficient in. Good speaking, under any circumstances, must be the result of quiet, persistent, indomitable, but patient labour; and these qualities are happily eminently characteristic

> " Of the Anglo-Saxon mind !
> That makes a man inherit
>   The glories of his kind:
> That scatters all around him
>   The conqueror of time.
> O mighty perseverance !
>   O courage stern and stout!
> That wills and works a clearance
>   Of every rabble rout,—
> That cannot brook denial,
>   And scarce allows delay,
> But wins from every trial
>   More strength for every day."

During our somewhat lengthened courtship we were accustomed to write long and loving epistles to each other, not only upon the usual topics that young people discourse upon in such circumstances, but also upon the subjects of our reading and thinkings, and upon the best way of bringing up a family, providing we had any.

I had acquired a great fondness for this interchange of thought from reading the beautiful letters of the poet Cowper; and I would advise any young man who is desirous to excel in letter-writing, to read, if he can, Southey's edition of the poet's writings, where he will find the most complete collection of these truly exquisite compositions. I was often reminded, while reading them again and again, of a passage I recollect from the writings of Robert Hall, the great Baptist preacher, wherein he says, that " the pleasures resulting from the mutual attachment of kindred spirits are by no means confined to the moments

K

of personal intercourse; they diffuse their odours, though more faintly, through the seasons of absence; refreshing and exhilarating the mind by the remembrance of the past, and the anticipation of the future. It is a treasure possessed, when it is not employed; a reserve of strength, ready to be called into action when most needed; a fountain of sweets, to which we may continually repair, whose waters are inexhaustible."

Having collected a little furniture, I selected apartments in the neighbourhood of St. John's-wood, that we might be near our chapel; and in the summer of 1840 we were married. Some one has said recently, in one of the public prints, that marriage is rapidly going out of fashion in England among certain classes. If this be true, it will be a fatal thing for our country, for it may still be affirmed that marriage is "honourable in *all;*" and no country in the world can flourish in the best sense where its sanctities are set at naught and made light of, or its sacred obligations neglected. Oh! that in moral, manly England it should ever be said that the flower of womanhood shall be allowed to blush in unappreciated beauty, and waste its priceless fragrance on things that are called men, who had lost the sense of so exalted an enjoyment. "Oh! woman, self-forgetting woman, poetry of human life," let it never be said of thee that the men of England desire to make thee only their paid mistresses, and degrade thee to the "hire of a harlot." Let my countrymen rather learn that—

> "Woman here, by wedded love, may be
> Nearest to divinity."

And come what will, poverty or riches, sickness or death, we may say—

> "I hold it true, whate'er befall,
>   I feel it when I sorrow most,
>   'Tis better to have loved and lost
> Than never to have loved at all."

Our marriage being over, we returned from a short

trip, and spent the greater part of our honeymoon in our own humble little home, happy as a king and queen, for—

> "There are as many lovely things,
> As many pleasant tones,
> For those who sit by cottage hearths
> As those who sit on thrones."

I soon found that a wife's influence in a dwelling was like the alabaster-box of ointment, whose fragrance filled the house; and I would fain persuade any young man, circumstanced as I was, to go and do likewise. The recollection of those happy evenings of my early married life oftentimes comes back upon me like a bright and beauteous vision; and after an interval of nearly a quarter of a century, during which period I have had great and terrible trials to pass through, the poet's words are true, that—

> "To lean our heart upon another heart
> In love that neither life nor death can part,
> So seek we still to end our life-long quest,
> For only in true love we find true rest.
>
> That love which makes another's life our own,
> And tunes our jarring natures to one tone;
> The filling up of all we've sought so long;
> For, leaning on itself, no strength is strong."

I found in her whom I had married not only a loving companion at my fireside, but she was also of great service in assisting me with my agency business. The books collected by me from the publishers, for the Universities I represented, were by her carefully sorted and arranged for marking off and invoicing; and when the cases were packed for their destination, she rendered me the greatest assistance.

Matters went on in this way, all merry as a marriage bell, for two years, when there was born to us a daughter. I shall never forget the first feeble cry of my own child. It opened a fountain of strange feeling in my being that I was hitherto unconscious of; and when I first gazed upon her little, round, and ruddy face, and imprinted upon her baby mouth the first long and loving kiss of a father, I felt as I had never felt before ; and glad indeed was my full heart to pour out its devout thanksgivings at the great Father's feet, who had so mercifully preserved my wife in this season of maternal solicitude, and given me a child of my own to give back to Him.

The day of a man's marriage is a memorable event in his history ; but the day when he becomes a father, if he be a Christian, awakens within him feelings the most sacred, and brings with it a responsibility that would be well-nigh overwhelming, did he not know that with the new relationship comes also the promise of the needful help rightly to discharge the important duties of a parent. I felt no small pleasure in writing a note on the Sunday-morning following the birth of our first child, to my dear pastor, announcing the happy event, and desiring to offer our united thanksgivings publicly for the great mercies we had received.

Many and hearty were the congratulations of my friends on the birth of our child, and the only drawback to our pleasure was in having a disagreeable old woman for a nurse. This venerable personage was a perfect nuisance ; she would never leave the bedside of my wife for a moment during the day, and at night she snored so loudly as not only to prevent her mistress from getting any sleep, but she awoke me in the adjoining room. And what annoyed us most was, that she denied that she ever snored, and was quite offended at me for giving her a little friendly advice how to counteract that unfortunate habit. However, she was attentive to my wife and careful of the baby, and in due time her month was up. This old lady's services were never engaged on any future occasion, and I threw up my cap and gave three hearty cheers as the cab drove away from my door with Mrs. Gamp and her box. I never could understand why young healthy women could not be trained to perform these necessary attentions, and I am glad to find that this is now being done ; for an ugly, old, gin-drinking woman to sleep with your wife and fondle your baby, and for the most part take her meals with you, is by no means a pleasant thing, and especially as there is no necessity for its being so.

The birth of our little one brought the subject of baptism to my notice; and it being the custom in the Independent Churches to administer this ordinance to infants, the rite was duly performed by my pastor at one of our public services. I never had my attention called particularly to this question until several years after this, when from associating with Baptists I was compelled to investigate the subject; but as I shall have to speak at a later period of my history of the alteration that subsequently took place in my views on baptism, I will not dwell upon the matter now.

Just about this period my three brothers left good mercantile situations for the army; and enlisted as private soldiers in a distinguished cavalry regiment at that time on foreign service in India. I was a good deal concerned at their taking such a step, as I fear it was my own example in the first instance that led them to think of the army. It was a great source of grief to my parents, as two of them were holding good situations in a large and old-established bookselling business in St. Paul's Church Yard, and the third was living at a wholesale stationer's establishment in the Strand.

They joined the depôt of the regiment at Maidstone, and after about six months' training there, were sent out to join the head-quarters of the regiment at Meerut. My eldest brother was a remarkably strong and healthy man, and was such an adept at the broad-sword exercise that his comrades at Maidstone frequently prevailed upon him, when not on duty, to go through the various cuts for their entertainment.

The climate of India, however, had such an effect upon him, that he had hardly joined the regiment at Meerut, before he was obliged to be sent away to the Military

Sanatorium at Landour, in the Himalaya Mountains, where he died a few months after of that Indian scourge dysentery. My surviving brothers being younger, were better able to endure the climate, and served with the regiment at the battle of Maharajpore, in 1843; and afterwards in the campaign of the Sutlej; and were fortunate enough to take part in the splendid action at Aliwal, under Sir Harry Smith; as well as being present at the battle of Sobraon.

The regiment was ordered home in 1846; and one of my brothers, after having gloriously sustained the character of a British soldier in the battles above referred to, died of cholera, at Berampore, near Calcutta, as the regiment was proceeding down the Ganges to embark for England.

Poor fellow, he was returning home after severe hardships, and many hair-breadth escapes, bringing with him several little relics of the battles he had taken part in. He had written to us on his birth-day, and only a few days before his death, full of joy and hope at the thought of coming home so soon. On the day he died he was walking with his comrades on the banks of the Ganges in his accustomed health and spirits; was taken ill at eleven, died at three in the afternoon, and was buried the same evening in the plains of Plassey, under the entrenchments thrown up by the enemy, where Lord Clive achieved his memorable victory, and, by a singular coincidence, on the anniversary of the day on which that great battle was fought.

He was a great favourite with the colonel, who had promoted him to be a sergeant, with the promise of a commission on his return to England. He died at the early age of 27. Three other men in the regiment died the same day of that dreadful disease.

How mournfully true it is that—

    "The path of glory leads but to the grave."

A young lady in one of the eastern counties of England,

who has published a volume of poems, made my brother's
death the subject of a short poem, from which I extract
the following two stanzas as no mean specimen of her
poetical powers :—

" He died not on the battle-field, where slaughter'd thousands bled,
Not in the ranks of ruthless war, his young life's blood was shed—
He fell not where the gleaming steel was flashing fiercely round,
When charging troops, and cannons' roar, mock'd e'en the thun-
    der's sound.

No ;—sword and bullet pass'd him by, amid that fated throng;
He rode erect, unharm'd, unscathed, in youthful vigour strong :
And he—the loved—the good, the brave—who 'scaped a soldier's
    death,
Beneath the stroke of sickness dread hath yielded up his breath."

My youngest brother returned to England, received a
commission in the regiment he had served in, and was made
adjutant; he remained in the regiment until he became
senior lieutenant, when he was obliged to sell out, his pay,
as an officer, being totally insufficient to enable him suit-
ably to maintain his position among his brother officers.

I cannot help remarking that it is a great fault in our
army, that, when deserving soldiers are promoted from the
ranks to be commissioned officers, their pay should be so
small, as either to involve them constantly in pecuniary
difficulties, or oblige them to sell their well-earned commission, and leave the service just when they are becoming
most valuable as soldiers, and could render the most efficient aid to their country.

A soldier who has gone through all the preparatory and
intermediate steps, as a private and non-commissioned
officer, before obtaining his cornetcy, ought to be too valuable to his country and his Queen, than to be obliged to
retire, because he has no private fortune to maintain his
position with his more favoured brother officers.

They manage matters of this nature far better in the
Continental armies, than we do in England; and our
authorities at " Horse Guards " would do well to take this

question into their serious consideration; every day's experience in modern warfare shows the necessity that those who are placed in command of brave men should be well trained and efficient soldiers. It will be remembered that the charge brought against us by our French allies in the Crimea was, that ours was " an army of lions commanded by asses ! "

If our country is to maintain her name and fame among the nations of the world, these manifest evils must be remedied, or the words of her greatest poet will cease to be verified, that—

> " This England never did—and never shall—
> Lie at the proud foot of a conqueror.
> Come the three corners of the world in arms,
> And we shall shock them !
>
> *Naught shall make us rue,*
> *If England, to herself, do rest but true.*"

I return once more to my personal history and experience. When first awakened to a concern about my spiritual state before God, I was too anxious to get that great matter settled to think very much about the subject of ecclesiastical polity. But as I continued to attend the service of a Nonconformist minister, and derived no small benefit from the same, the question as to whether I was right in leaving the Church of England came frequently before me.

The continued opposition also that I met with from my father and mother to my becoming a Dissenter, and the not unfrequent inquiries of friends as to my reasons for leaving the communion of the Established Church, led me carefully and thoughtfully to investigate this important subject.

As soon as I began to think upon the points in dispute, I saw clearly enough that it was not a question to be decided by those holding ecclesiastical position in the Church of England, and that, as a layman, I am equally responsible as the clergy for the views I hold, and for the system of Church polity I do my part to maintain.

If I am a Churchman, I am bound to accept all that the clergy are called upon to subscribe to. A noble earl, who is a distinguished member of the National Church,* says deliberately, in writing upon the subject: " I am not going to let it be assumed that in matters of this kind they [the clergy of the Church of England] are the only persons to be shot at, or take offence. I maintain that this is the cause of the laity just as much as it is the cause of the clergy. Why, if the clergy have been guilty of perjury, I—in supporting the clergy—have been guilty of subornation of perjury. I, too, have signed the Articles; I, too, am a subscriber to what is contained in the Prayer-book, just as much as the clergy are subscribers to it; I do, as a layman, everything that the clergy do, with the exception of the administration of the Sacraments; and I take my full share of responsibility with them."

Now, these words of truth and soberness come well from noble lips, and I endorse the sentiment contained in them most cordially. I have never been able to understand how laymen in the Church of England, or among other denominations, can excuse themselves from responsibility in questions of this nature, by stating that the formularies laid down as the ground of faith and practice are subscribed to and agreed upon by the clergy or ministers, but that the laity are not to be held responsible for what they contain.

It should always be borne in mind that the conforming to any ordained test is simply a response to law which peremptorily imposes it; and the Act of Uniformity, as every other statute of the realm, derives its force from the people as represented in Parliament. Every citizen in England who has a vote in electing members of the legislature is responsible, if not for the passing of that Act of

---

* Lord Shaftesbury.

Uniformity in 1662, yet assuredly for its continuance to
the present time; and therefore every layman is justly required to study both the propriety of the law as well as its
observance. The consequences of this act of the legislature concern every worshipper in the hierarchy and every
citizen of the empire. Feeling this to be the case, I
entered upon the consideration of the subject as a just and
legitimate act of inquiry, and in so doing, I took care to
consult the authoritative formularies of the Church, and
compared these with the standard of all appeal in matters
of this nature—the written Word of God.

I need hardly remind any of my readers that every
clergyman of the Church of England is required by law to
swear that he believes and adopts *ex animo* the Thirty-nine
Articles of that Church. If any one applying for ordination refuse a solemn declaration of consent to all that they
contain, he cannot be legally ordained; and if, after his
ordination, he learns from the Scriptures, or from any
other source, truths that may induce him to contravene
anything laid down in the Articles, his legal and ecclesiastical position and rights as a clergyman of the Church
of England are by that act forfeited. Now, the sixth
Article affirms that—" Holy Scripture containeth all
things necessary to salvation : so that whatsoever is not read
therein, nor may be proved thereby, is not to be required
of any man that it should be believed as an article of the
faith, or be thought requisite or necessary to salvation."

This appeal to the Scriptures is reiterated and confirmed
by the twentieth Article, which states, in language clear
as the light, that " it is not lawful for the Church to or-
dain anything that is contrary to God's word written,
neither may it expound one place of Scripture that it be
repugnant of another."

These being the authoritative affirmations of the National Church, no Englishman need fear being censured
for impertinence if he compares the formularies of this
Church with the Word of God as found in the Scriptures.
I felt, in investigating the matter, that as a layman I had

a great advantage over the clergy, inasmuch as they are bound to accept the teaching of the Church as defined by ecclesiastical law, while I was at liberty to reject any interpretation of the Articles, &c, that was not in harmony with the clear statements of God's word.

There is no term in the New Testament which has been so much abused and misunderstood as " the Church ;" and as I believed it to be of the first importance in the inquiry in which I was engaged, to have clear ideas upon that subject, I took more than ordinary pains to ascertain at the outset what is understood by " the Church."

The Roman Catholic talks of the church, and he means his own church, and affirms that there is no other church in the world except his own. The Episcopalian speaks of the church, meaning by that term what is called the Established Church of England in these realms ; many members of which, when they talk of the church, mean the building in which they worship. The Dissenter talks of the church, and he means the communicants of that chapel or congregation of which he is a member.

In order, however, to understand the peculiarities which distinguish the Church of Christ, we must make our appeal to the Scriptures, and whatever obtains among men that is antagonistic to, or not in harmony with, these sacred records, must be at once discarded. Institutions may exist professing to be the Church of Christ ; but if they cannot bear comparison with the teaching of Scripture they must be rejected, though they are built upon the edicts of councils, and come armed with regal authority and power. Since the foundation of the Church of Christ in the apostolic age, the battle for its corruption has been fought with an intensity of zeal and mental resource that are truly marvellous. Men have, unhappily, shown more hatred, malice, and uncharitableness, in discussing this question, than any other that has come under investigation ; and it is quite refreshing to turn from their angry writings to the calm and dignified teaching of the Word of God.

In the Scriptures we find that Jesus Christ is " the head

of the body, the church." (Col. i. 18). He is the fountain of its law, the author of its salvation, the responsible Head and centre of its movements, the source of its strength, and the security of all its hopes. The Church of Christ is " His body, the fulness of Him that filleth all in all." The " body " here spoken of appears to me to be that company of believers in the world which, filled with His life and guided by His will, are the representatives of His kingdom among men. They are subject to His rule and authority; a household designed for the nourishment of His children; an army to fight His battles in the world; the dwelling-place of God, glorious in the universality of its communion, its services, its privileges, and its destiny. Jesus Christ, and He alone, " is the Head of the body, the church; who is the beginning, the first-born from the dead; that in all things He might have the pre-eminence: for it pleased the Father that in Him should all fulness dwell." (Col. i. 18, 19). Now the terms His " body, the church," in this passage, cannot relate only to those to whom they were originally addressed; but I believe they include the saints and faithful in Christ in every age of the world, from that period. In accordance with this view we find that there have been bodies, or congregations, of men and women in the world, since the days of the apostles, guided and governed by the edicts of Christ, endowed by His gifts, filled with His Spirit, manifesting His life, bearing witness to His truth, and braving every danger rather than forfeit their love and allegiance to Him. These assemblies of the faithful may hold their meetings in many places at the same time. The Church of Christ, in the first century, had their assemblies at Rome, Colosse, Ephesus, Corinth, and many other places. They were separate and distinct from the world, and were constituted and built upon the foundation of the apostles and prophets, "Jesus Christ Himself being the chief corner-stone, in whom all the building, fitly framed together, groweth unto an holy temple in the Lord, an habitation of God through the

Spirit." Such, and such only, I believe to have been the Church of Christ in the first ages of Christianity; and wherever the Gospel has been preached since that period, there have been those who have, in the main, answered to these Christians of apostolic times. The one true Church of the living God, in the world, is made up of all true believers in the Lord Jesus Christ; those who have been brought, either by the preaching of the gospel or the reading of the scriptures, to trust in the love of God, through the blood and righteousness of Christ, as their only ground of acceptance in His sight.

Converted men and women in every place, all the world over, form the members of the Church; and wherever these are found there is a member of Christ's true and holy Church. They are "born, not of blood, nor of the will of the flesh, nor of the will of man, but of God." (John i. 12, 13). They are distinguished by holiness of life and conversation. They hate sin and love Christ. No power on earth can extinguish that Church; its members may be persecuted, oppressed, burned, cruelly treated, as they have been and may be again, but they can never be extinguished. The Pharaohs, the Herods, the Neros, the bloody Marys and their infernal bishops, and all the long black list of persecutors down to our own days, may do their best and their worst, but the Church of Christ will outlive them all. This is the only Church of which no member can perish. Once enrolled as a member of this Church, a man is safe for eternity. Its members may be few in comparison with the multitudes ,who despise them; but these are they who shake the universe and change the fortunes of kingdoms by their prayers; these are the life-blood of a country—the shield, the defence, the stay and support of any country they inhabit. A glorious Church, that shall one day be presented by Christ to the Father, "without spot or wrinkle, or any such thing," amid the wonder and acclamations of an assembled universe.

It would have been well if the kings and rulers of the

earth had left this sacred society alone, as its members would not interfere with any form of government that may obtain among men; but unhappily it has happened to the Church as its divine Founder had predicted—"In the world ye shall have tribulation;" and this is as true to-day as it was when that sentence fell from the lips of the Lord Jesus. Every reader of ecclesiastical history knows well enough that a power antagonistic to Christ and Christianity soon began to show itself. Pastors of Christian churches were found to have more influence than civil officers, and measures were adopted to make the churches comprehend the people. Papal Rome succeeded to heathen Rome, and men assumed the place of God. The Scriptures were laid aside for priestly dogmas, and canon law soon took the place of the laws of Christ and His kingdom. With the assumption of divine authority priestly power began to override all civil rule, subjecting it to its own use. Kings held the sword for popes, and the Church of Christ in England suffered from these innovations beyond all present calculation. England had not only to struggle against a power contending for authority with the throne; but the Church, under the same papal power and influence, suffered the far greater calamity which flows from a contest for supremacy with Christ.

History tells us plainly enough that ecclesiastical supremacy is never safe, but when vested in the great Head of the Church, Jesus Christ; and if monarchs, as well as their subjects, would only think at all upon the matter, they would shrink with instinctive horror from any human assumption of religious supremacy.

In subjecting the Church of Christ to the civil power, men have been guilty of the greatest sin against its Founder, as well as inflicting a deep injury upon the subjects of His kingdom. By placing the Church of Christ under human laws, that it may be national, has reduced it from its Catholic dignity and rights to a mere sectarian community, defined by civil law, used for civil purposes, and subject not to Jesus Christ its rightful Lord, but to the British Throne. In departing from the guidance, and forfeiting the support, of its Divine Head, it seems to me to cease to be the Church of Christ at the very moment, and by the very act which makes it the Church of England.

Lest I should be deemed uncharitable in what I have stated, I would remind my readers that the evidence which sustains this charge against the National Church is to be found in her own legal documents, in her oath of conformity, and in judgments recently passed in her Ecclesiastical Courts.

The Acts of Edward VI, Queen Elizabeth, and Charles II. are not merely declarative, but, as many have been made to feel, they are penal laws. They give the Church of England her national position and legal rights, and have placed dogmas, formularies for prayer and praise, with orders for absolution, and a host of other things that no one ever found authorized in Scripture, not only side by side with, but above, the authority of the Bible.

That it may be seen that I have not gone one whit beyond the facts of the case, I will quote the oath of conformity sworn by every clergyman in the following terms :—

" I do willingly and *ex animo* subscribe to these three articles above mentioned, and to all things contained therein."

These articles are as follows :—

First,—" That the King's Majesty, under God, is the only supreme governor of this realm, *as well in all spiritual or ecclesiastical things or causes, as temporal.*" Secondly, " That the Book of Common Prayer, etc. containeth in it nothing contrary to the Word of God," etc ; and thirdly, " That he alloweth the Book of Articles of Religion, agreed upon in Convocation, 1562: and that he acknowledgeth all and every the articles therein contained, being in number thirty-nine, besides the ratification, to be agreeable to the Word of God."

Now while admitting that there are two saving clauses in the above, viz. "*under God,*" and "*agreeable with the Word of God,*" two points are clear from these authoritative documents,—first, that "under God" the King is made by law to hold the place which God has given to our Lord Jesus Christ; and second, the term "*agreeable with the Word of God,*" affirms what is not true, inasmuch as the oath binding the clergyman to the use of the Book of Common Prayer, limits the use and interpretation of Scripture to that which is declared by law to be the matter which each clergyman is to teach and use. The clergyman is bound, not to his own conscientious belief of what Scripture teaches, but to that construction of Scripture teaching which has been beforehand defined for him by the English law, in the Articles, the Rubric, the Book of Common Prayer, and the Homilies.

This that I have stated is abundantly and conclusively confirmed by the late judgment delivered in the Ecclesiastical Court, by Dr. Lushington, in the recent prosecutions relating to a work entitled "Essays and Reviews." That distinguished judge is reported to have said that "he would not revert to Scripture as the test by which doctrine should be determined; and his decision was that all extracts from Scripture must be erased from the articles of the prosecutors." This authoritative declaration was confirmed by the following :—"As a Judge, he could not be guided by anything but judicial authority. Nor must he take for his guide the most learned and orthodox clergy of the Church; for all he had to do was to try to get the true construction of the Articles of Religion, according to the ordinary principles of law. If ever any great discoveries were made which were antagonistic to the Articles of the Church, a clergyman was not at liberty to avail himself of them in opposition to the articles: for the law must be obeyed, even to a degree of harshness, *and for a remedy application must be made to the legislature, by whom the Prayer Book was originally settled.*"

It has been truly said that by this judgment Dr. Lushington has made it clear to the British nation that the Church of England is no more subjected to the grammatical teaching of Scripture than she is to the supreme authority of Christ. Her head is the ruling monarch, whether he be Henry VIII, the second Charles, or George IV. Her doctrines and acts of discipline and worship are fixed by the legislature to which her clergy swear subjection ; and therefore by the Scripture, which she declares to be the Word of God, she is proved to be not in any just sense a Church of Christ at all. In the process of her nationalization she has departed from Christ, the Head, compromised His law for the law of England, forfeited His aid for that of national support, and become by her own acts, to all intents and purposes, a sect in separation from the body of Christ. The axiom that sustains the whole judgment of Dr. Lushington is, *the law of England must not be violated.* Discover what we may, therefore, in Scripture, or elsewhere, no truth from God or man can be used in the Church of England against her Articles and Prayer-book, which are fixed by law.

Now, lest I should weary my readers, these investigations into the Church of England, and my position as a Dissenter, led me, after mature thought and deliberation, to the determination never to be deterred by an obnoxious name (for I like not that of Dissenter) from an open avowal of the change that had taken place in my views relating to ecclesiastical matters. More than a quarter of a century has passed over me since I set myself to the examination of the claims of Church and Dissent ; and I am the more convinced every day of my life that while the clergy of the Church of England have enriched our literature with some of its choicest works, and the piety and moral worth of many among them are such as to command my admiration and respect, yet the system to which they belong is one of the greatest evils that has been inflicted upon our country ; and I will ever do the utmost in my power, by constitutional means, to remove so great an obstacle to the kingdom of Christ in the world.

I was perfectly sure, while going through the examination of the question of Church and Dissent, that I should retain many friends by remaining in the communion of the Church of England, and that it would be neither seemly nor wise to dissent from that Church if it could possibly be avoided. I could not but be aware, on the other hand, that by becoming a Dissenter I should bring upon myself a good deal of odium, and sink in the estimation of many whose good opinion I valued, and which would be of use to me as far as my worldly prospects were concerned. However, the *duty* of becoming a Dissenter was so pressed upon me, as the result of my reading and thinking upon the subject, that I was determined, come what might, to stand by my convictions, and openly avow myself as one who conscientiously and thoughtfully dissented from the Established Church. I think, at the same time, that no man ought to secede from the Church of England, if it can be avoided, as it is desirable on many accounts that Christians should not be divided, but should, if it were possible, constitute one united denomination, preserving the " unity of the spirit " and enjoying the " communion of saints." When this, however, is not possible, then I think it behoves a man to be able, with becoming meekness and firmness, to state boldly and unhesitatingly his reasons for seceding from the Established Church, and for casting in his lot with the Nonconformists. This I desired to do, with the feeling that all my early training and education, as well as my promotion in the world, very much inclined me to lean lovingly to the Church of my fathers ; but I had learnt from the reading of the Scriptures, as well as from the perusal of ecclesiastical history, that in matters of this nature inclination and interest must be laid aside, and a man must sternly and resolutely do his duty, come what may. A Christian man, it may be said—

" Holds no parley with unmanly fears,
  Where duty points, he resolutely steers,
  Facing a thousand dangers at its call,
  And, trusting in his God, surmounts them all."

In becoming a Nonconformist, I did not feel in doing so that it required any apology from me. I considered that I had an undoubted right to examine for myself the constitution and claims of the Church of England as one of the institutions of our country ; and, having done so, to discuss these claims with the same freedom as any other topic.

The Church of England I found to be of human constitution, the creature of the people ; and that which the people have created they surely have a right to examine, and, by legitimate means, to control. Churchmen sometimes look down from the high places of the Establishment upon Nonconformists as those who are chargeable with some weakness, or guilty of some wrong, and who need, therefore, to advance some extenuating plea for the purpose of evading reproof or of mitigating censure. As Nonconformists, we know that they are superior to us in many things that are indeed " highly esteemed among men," but at the same time we verily believe that we are superior to them in that " which is approved of God." No Nonconformist who has taken the pains to understand his principles need ever to be ashamed to avow them ; for although our brethren in the Establishment have undoubtedly the benefit of external distinction, we think we have the superiority of truth on our side.

The head and front of my objections to the Established Church consisted in its bold and undisguised assumption of a temporal headship, as not only being antagonistic to the supremacy of Christ, but also leading to evils of the greatest magnitude. In addition to this, the Book of Common Prayer contains in it formularies and services at variance with Scripture, and calculated, in my humble opinion, to do an amount of mischief by its false teaching that is appalling to think of. Recollecting as I do the influence of its teaching in early life upon my own mind, I am the more anxious to preserve my own children, as well as others, from its dangerous and pernicious tendencies.

Fearing that I have already trespassed too largely on the time and attention of my readers, by dwelling so long upon this vexed question of Church and Dissent, I would only say further, that I repudiate most heartily, as anti-scriptural and dangerous, many things in the baptismal services of the Church of England, where infants are made by a mechanical process "members of Christ, children of God, and inheritors of the Kingdom of Heaven;" and this in no limited sense, as is seen by the prayer offered by the officiating clergyman and congregation assembled, which states, in solemn and awful words: "Almighty and ever-lasting God, who hast vouchsafed to regenerate these thy servants by water *and the Holy Ghost,* and hast given unto them forgiveness of all their sins!"

There are also serious objections to the priestly assumption in the service for the visitation of the sick, where one sinful man thus addresses himself to another: "Our Lord Jesus Christ, who has left power to his Church to absolve all sinners who truly repent and believe in Him, of His great mercy forgive thee thine offences, and, *by His authority, committed to me, I absolve thee from all thy sins, in the name of the Father, and of the Son, and of the Holy Ghost.*"

Again, in the sublime service employed at the burial of the dead, what must we think of *invariably* hearing these solemn words pronounced over a most notoriously and profligate man, whose death-bed witnessed neither re-pentance for his past life, nor faith in the Saviour for the forgiveness of his sins: "Forasmuch as it hath pleased Almighty God of His great mercy to take unto Himself the soul of our dear brother here departed, we therefore com-mit his body to the ground . . . . *in sure and certain hope of the resurrection to eternal life,* through our Lord

Jesus Christ," &c? Then follows the prayer: " Almighty God . . . we give Thee hearty thanks, for that it hath pleased Thee to deliver this our brother out of the miseries of this sinful world," &c.

If words can be used and sentences can be framed to express error and to foster delusion, certainly these are such words, and they are acknowledged to be so by not a few even of the clergy, all of whom, nevertheless, express, in the presence of God, their unfeigned assent and consent to all and everything in the book which contains them, and every member of the Church sanctions the system of which it is a part.

Having stated as briefly as I can, consistently with the importance of the subject, my reasons for becoming a Dissenter, I shall be expected to say something for identifying myself with a denomination entitled Independents, or Congregationalists.

The distinctive and essential principles of the Congregational form of church government are, that a single congregation of believers, agreeing to walk together according to the faith and order of the Gospel, is a complete Church ; that every such congregation has (by necessary consequence) the entire power of government in itself. In support of the first great principle of Congregationalism, viz. that a single congregation of believers— and not a number of such congregations united together, and forming a denomination—is a Church, Congregationalists make appeal to the word " church" in the New Testament. There are unquestionable instances in the New Testament of the use of the word " church" in the Congregational sense. It is, indeed, the ordinary custom of the writers of the New Testament to call a single congregation of believers a Church. In support of the second great principle of Congregationalism, that every separate congregation of believers has the full power of government within itself—there being no higher authority upon earth to confirm or reverse its decisions—we may refer to Matt.

xviii. 15-17: " If thy brother offend thee," &c, "tell it to the church," i.e. to the body of communicants, whose decision is represented as final. As the last resort, the offence is to be told to the Church, and from its sentence there is no appeal; because, if they act according to the law of Christ, their sentence is confirmed by Christ. They refer, also, to 1 Cor. v. 1-7, compared with 2 Cor. ii. 1-5, where it will be found that both passages refer to the case of the incestuous person in the church at Corinth. These two Epistles to the Corinthians, it must be recollected, were addressed to the Church, i.e the society of believers in that city. Now let those of my readers who will take the pains to do so, remember that the Apostle censures that body for permitting the offender to remain among them, that he commands them to put him away, and that afterwards, when assured of his unfeigned repentance, he enjoins them to " confirm their love towards him," and they will see how powerfully this apostolic precedent supports the following great principles of Congregationalism,—that the private members of a church have a voice in, and some power over, the exclusion and restoration of offenders. The Apostle's command to put the offender in this case away was an intended test of their obedient spirit; but how could it have been so if they not only had no power over his expulsion, but if even their opinion in reference to it was not to be ascertained? And, again, it is evident that the decision of a separate Church, i.e. of the pastor and private members, is a final one.

We may appeal also, in support of both the great principles of Congregationalism, to the directions contained in the New Testament in relation to the reception of members into the Church. It will be seen, by those who will take the trouble to turn to the passages, that the reception of members into the Churches of the Apostolic age was the act of the Church, and not of the pastor and office-bearers only, as is the case in some Christian churches.

Those of my readers who defer to the teaching of Scripture on matters of this nature will find, by referring to Rom. xiv. 1, "receive you," i.e. the church; Acts ix. 26, "the *disciples* were afraid of him," and so they did not at first receive him. When Apollos was disposed to pass through Achaia, "the *brethren*" wrote recommendatory epistles, and sent them not to the office-bearers of the churches, but to *the churches*, "exhorting the disciples to receive him," (Acts xviii. 27). Such recommendatory epistles were common; they were attestations to the Christian character of the person who carried them, sent from the Church to which he had formerly belonged, to the *Christian body* existing in the place to which he was going. (See Phil. ii. 29; Col. iv. 10).

We may also appeal to the directions of the New Testament in regard to the exercise of discipline. These are all addressed to the Church at large. (See 1 Cor. v. 7; Gal. iv. 1, "Ye that are *spiritual* restore," &c.)

My apology, if one be needed, for entering thus rather minutely into particulars relating to the church government and order obtaining among the Congregationalists has been done to convince an unprejudiced reader (if such a personage can indeed be found) that we have scriptural ground and warrant for what is done in our Churches; and I would remark, that if errors are found amongst us, either in doctrine or practice, they can be rectified at once, without waiting either for an Act of Parliament on the one hand, or an edict from an ecclesiastical council or synod on the other.

I could also enter upon other matters relating to ecclesiastical polity obtaining among the Congregationalists, as, for example, the choice of a pastor or minister, the nature and extent of pastoral authority, the choice and election of elders or deacons, and other questions connected with the internal government and arrangement of our Churches; but it would perhaps be out of place in such a work as I am engaged upon, and some may also imagine that a layman should not intermeddle with subjects of this nature.

I trust, however, I have said enough upon the subject to convince my readers that I took some pains myself to understand the principles and practices obtaining in the communion to which I deemed it my honour and happiness to belong ; and that I had also good and sufficient reasons for leaving the Church of England, and becoming a Non-conformist.

I would only say further, in reference to what I have stated of the change that had taken place, not only in my religious views, but also in the estimate I formed of a Church establishment and Dissent, that while I hold decided and strong views upon these great questions, I nevertheless am most anxious to cultivate a spirit of real brotherliness towards all those who " love our Lord Jesus Christ in sincerity." I made up my mind upon this point while the subjects were under consideration, that I would never connect myself with any body of Christians where the terms of membership or communion were such as to exclude any who professed personal faith in Christ, and whose daily life was such as to justify the profession they had made.

I think that the union of Christians of all denomina-tions, where no compromise of principle is demanded, is most desirable ; and those who are like-minded with myself would do well to provide themselves with a most able discourse upon the subject, lately published, where they will find this deeply interesting question treated with the hand of a master, and in a truly Catholic spirit.* Christians of all denominations may read that sermon with profit.

I return from this somewhat lengthened digression upon

---

* " The Unity of the Church, a Discourse delivered at Greville-place Church, St. John's Wood, London. By the Rev. J. C. Gal-laway, A.M. Ward and Co. 1860. 12mo."

ecclesiastical polity to my own personal history again. In 1842, two years after my marriage, and shortly after the birth of my first child, I met with a serious diminution in my income. The amendment of the Copyright Act, passed in that year, disfranchised six of the Universities entitled to privileges under the Act, and made an alteration in the mode of delivery with reference to the libraries still entitled to publications under the statute. One of the libraries which I acted as agent for was disfranchised, and the alteration in the mode of delivery of the books rendered my service for the other no longer necessary. The diminution in my income caused by these alterations was a very severe loss to me, being no less a deduction than £100 a-year. I received the most flattering testimonials from the librarians of the colleges I had represented since 1835, expressive of their approbation as to the manner in which I had discharged my work for them, and regretting that my services would no longer be required.

This sudden decrease in my income led me at once to set about making up the deficiency in the best way I could. It grieved me to abridge some of the comforts of my little home, just when they appeared to be the most needed; but there was no help for it, and my wife cheerfully acquiesced in the arrangements we were obliged to make, and cheered me on like a true-hearted woman.

I obtained, through my official connections, a good deal of copying and work of a kindred nature, which occupied me fully during the hours I was not engaged in my regular employment. I sat up, sometimes, long after midnight, and rose again as soon as it was light, to work upon my manuscripts; and frequently the writing was so bad, and the interlineations so many, that it was with great difficulty I could make any way with them. However, I stuck to the work with a manly determination to do all in my power to make up in some degree the loss in my income; and for several successive years I appropriated my annual vacation to earning money to meet the increasing wants of home, instead of seeking the rest and recreation that should follow prolonged and unbroken toil. My Sabbaths during these years were priceless, and gave me some foretaste of "the rest that remaineth to the people of God." Oh! how refreshing was it to body and mind to lay aside the toils and labours of the week for the calm and tranquillising services of the sanctuary, and the quiet pleasures of my little home. How is that man to be pitied who, from any cause, robs his soul of the nourishment, and his body the rest and restorative influence of the Sabbath. The going with the multitude to keep holy day, the sacred songs of the house of God, the prayers and thanksgivings of my much-loved pastor, and his eloquent and heart-stirring sermons, helped mightily not only to preserve the life of God in my soul, but also to fit me better for returning to the poorly requited toils and labours of the week.

Well does an eloquent writer of our own denomination, lately deceased, Winter Hamilton, of Leeds, say, " Oh Sabbath! needed for a world of innocence, without thee what would be a world of sin! There would be no pause for consideration, no check to passion, no remission of toil, no balm of care! He who had withheld thee would have forsaken the earth! Without thee He had never given to us the Bible, the Gospel, the Spirit! We salute thee as thou comest to us in the name of the Lord— radiant in the sunshine of that dawn which broke over creation's achieved work ; marching downward in the track of time, a pillar of refreshing cloud and of guiding flame, interweaving with all thy light new beams of dis-covery and promise, until thou standest forth more fair than when reflected in the dews, and imbibed by the flowers of Eden ; more awful than when the trumpet rung of thee on Sinai. The Christain Sabbath! Like its Lord, it but rises again in Christianity, and henceforth records the rising day! And never since the tomb of Jesus was burst open by Him who revived and rose, has this day awakened but as the light of seven days, and

with healing in its wings ! Never has it unfolded without
some witness and welcome, some song and salutation ! It
has been the coronation day of martyrs, the feast day of
saints ! It has been from the first until now the sublime
custom of the Churches of God ! Still the outgoings of its
morning and its evening rejoice. It is a day of heaven
upon earth. Life's sweetest calm, poverty's best birthright, labour's only rest. Nothing has such a hoar of
antiquity on it ; nothing contains in it such a history ;
nothing draws along with it such a glory ! Nurse of
virtue, seal of truth ! the household's richest patrimony,
the nation's noblest safeguard, the pledge of peace, the
fountain of intelligence, the strength of law, the oracle of
instruction, the ark of mercy, the patent of our manhood's
spiritual greatness, the harbinger of our soul's sanctified
perfection, the glory of religion, the watch-tower of immortality, the ladder set up on the earth, and the top of it
reacheth to heaven, with the angels of God ascending and
descending on it ! "

There was not only an intellectual power of a high
order in the ministry I attended, but there was in every
sermon something that met the necessities of my spiritual
cravings, as well as affording me materials for thought
during the brief intervals of leisure I could command
during the week. The prayers of my pastor were such as
I have never heard equalled. He appeared on the Sunday
morning to come direct from the very presence of the
Eternal, and to breathe the atmosphere of Heaven.
Many a time have I been reminded, while kneeling with
him and the great congregation at the throne of the
heavenly grace, of the words of Cowper—

> " When one who holds communion with the skies,
> Has fill'd his urn where those pure waters rise ;
> And once more mingles with us meaner things,
> 'Tis e'en as if an angel shook its wings :
> Ambrosial fragrance fills the circuit wide,
> And tells us whence his treasure was supplied."

Oh! how much do I owe thee, thou kind-hearted and gifted man of God. I have sat delighted at thy feet for many years :—years marked by many sorrows, as well as hallowed by sacred joys, and grateful recollections. Never shall I fully know the greatness of my obligation to thee, till I find myself, through your instrumentality, safe and secure within the Father's house, to go no more out for ever!

My own troubles at this period were not a little increased by the pecuniary difficulties of my father; whose pecuniary embarrassments did not arise from his living beyond his income, but they were the result, in the first place, of old debts contracted at Canterbury, and these obligations were increased by the exorbitant interest charged by loan societies and bill discounters.

Justice to myself, and to my wife, obliges me to say, that I never on my own account incurred pecuniary obligations that I could not discharge; though often, through illness and unavoidable demands upon my slender finances, we have been put to the greatest possible shifts, and have been obliged to deny ourselves many little gratifications and indulgences which we otherwise should have enjoyed. However, I am glad to be able to say, for the encouragement of any of my readers who may be similarly circumstanced, that the discipline, though sometimes sharp and severe, has been salutary and useful; and also that I always found Divine help as well as human sympathy in all my difficulties of this nature.

In 1844 was born to us a second daughter, and shortly after this I was visited by my first serious illness. I had just before this time met with an advertisement in one of the papers that a lady, who had cured herself of a bad habit of stammering, offered her services for the removal of that affliction. I replied to the advertisement, saw the lady, and it was arranged that she should give me an hour's instruction daily until my impediment was removed.

As the lady referred to was both well-informed and

agreeable in her manners, these daily interviews were very delightful. Having explained to me the process she had herself adopted for the removal of the defect in her own speech, we carried on our lessons in a series of conversations upon almost every conceivable topic. Many were the hearty laughs we had in chatting over all sorts of things, subjects, and persons; and I looked forward to these daily exercises with great pleasure.

I profited so much by this lady's instructions as to be able to converse with both ease and fluency, and began to imagine that I should get rid of my old source of annoyance altogether. Every one who knew me was surprised at the alteration in my speaking, but unhappily the improvement was not of long duration..

One principal feature in this lady's treatment of stammering was to speak *with great force and energy.* In consequence of attending to this, and finding it so successful, I carried out these instructions to their fullest extent; but I regret to say nearly at the cost of my life. About two months from the time that I commenced this forced method of speaking, I was walking leisurely home from a weeknight service at our chapel, when I felt a peculiar sensation in my throat and chest, and immediately found my mouth filled with blood. Fortunately I was not far from home, and on arriving there my wife was very much alarmed, and went herself for our medical attendant, who lived in the immediate neighbourhood. The doctor told me I had ruptured a blood-vessel in connection with the lungs. He took from my right arm a large quantity of blood, and I was ordered to remain on the sofa through the night, and to be kept free from all excitement. The bleeding from the mouth continued at intervals through the night, and in the morning I was got to bed, though obliged to remain in a sitting posture, with bags of ice applied to my chest and kept as cool as possible, and almost starved. No one was allowed to see me but my wife, who

" Beside my couch of care an angel nurse she stood."

IIow true, beautifully true, are the poet's lines—

> " Oh ! woman, in our hours of ease
> Uncertain, coy, and hard to please,
> And variable as the shade
> By the light quivering aspen made:
> When pain and anguish wring the brow,
> A ministering angel now."

It is in sickness and trouble that we find out fully the gentle qualities of woman's nature.   Let a man be laid aside from his active employment and confined to a sick chamber, as I was, for many long and wearisome weeks, shut out from all his friends, and he will learn how to appreciate fully the gentle, thoughtful, and uninterrupted nursing of a loving wife.   Her quick eye, and attention to a thousand little things that minister to our ease and comfort, are then seen.   She intuitively discerns our wants almost before they are known to ourselves, and she ministers to them so lovingly as to conceal the extent of her obligation.   In the language of one * who has employed his eloquent pen upon this theme would we say, as a matter of experience, " How much better than man does a woman relieve the distressed mind, when, with a tact which would be artful were it not so natural, she diverts his thoughts from painful themes.   When she speaks words of comfort, how much more does she soothe us by her soft and musical accents than man by his sharp and ringing tones !   How effectually does her cheerful countenance and manner dispel our sadness !   And when to her natural qualities she has added the graces of religion, what so fitted as her quiet composure, amid difficulty and distress, to raise us from our despondency, and win us back to faith in God !   In the sick chamber, where man has neither the quiet manner nor the delicate touch, nor the assiduous attention, nor the sympathy and patience which are necessary, she moves with steps noiseless as falling snow-

---

* " Woman's Sphere and Work, considered in the Light of Scripture.   By W. Landels.   London, 1859.   8vo."

flakes, and speaks in a voice soft as an angel's whisper; though subdued, she feels no embarrassing restraint, nor does the softness of her manner interfere with the promptness or efficiency of her service.   Where man by rough handling would give pain, her touch is so gentle that it soothes the sufferer; and while everything is done for him which care or love can prompt, it is all done so quietly that, but for the offices she performs and the comfort which she ministers, he would be unconscious of her presence.   Man's sympathy is slow to move, and his patience is soon exhausted; woman's sympathy is not more prompt than it is enduring.   The sight of distress is sufficient to stir her deep womanly nature; and where she is brought much into contact with it, the constancy with which she ministers to it is marvellous.   On this account she is man's first and last solace.

> " 'O woman! woman! thou wert made,
> Like heaven's own pure and lovely light,
> To cheer life's dark and desert shade,
> And guide man's erring footsteps right.' "

The hemorrhage came on for several successive nights, and it was thought more than once that I must have sunk under the exhaustion.   The slightest movement brought on the bleeding, and my doctor strictly forbade me to make any attempt to speak, and directed me to make known my wants by writing on a slate.   For some weeks my life was despaired of; it hung tremblingly, as by a very slender thread; and I could plainly see, by the anxious looks of my medical attendant, who was frequently with me two and three times during the day, that matters were very serious. He told my wife, at the first, that had I been in an agitated and alarmed state of mind nothing could have saved me.   Happily, when it happened, I had been attending one of the quiet week-evening services of the sanctuary, and my friend and pastor had been preaching from the words, " He restoreth my soul."   My mind was kept in

perfect peace.   I had long ere this settled the great point,
and I could rely with deep and unwavering confidence upon
Him who had borne the penalty of all my sins,. and whose
obedience to the law that I had broken made me feel both
safe and happy.   The tranquil and blissful hours that I
enjoyed during that sickness will never be forgotten by me.
I was able, in quiet thought, to go down to the foundations of my faith and hope, and found them to be firmer
than the everlasting hills; yea, as immoveable as the
throne of the Eternal.

It has been said that "a sickness that leads the way to
everlasting life is better than the health of an antediluvian;"
and I found in these critical days and long wakeful nights
that only the strong consolation made known in the Gospel,
and cordially received into the soul, is sufficient to bear up
the mind when the great shadow of eternity falls fully upon
us.   Then it is that we see the meaning of life and the
sacredness of duty, and the utter helplessness and hope-
lessness of having nothing but one's own doings to put in
the place of God's requirements.   Often, as I lay awake
in those long nights, did I think of my past life and
history in connection with what Scripture reveals to us
of eternity, and the rewards and retributions of the future
world.   Any view of eternity is overwhelming, but more
especially so when we think that we shall exist for
ever.   I recollect reading, somewhere in one of Forster's
letters, that he was almost crushed under the idea of eternity, even apart from the idea of retribution.   The idea is
fearful !   How can I sustain an endless existence ?   How
can I prolong sentiment and action for ever and ever?
What may, or can become of me, in so stupendous a pre-
dicament?   What an accumulation of miracles will be
required to preserve my faculties, my being, from becoming exhausted and extinct !   How can there be an unde-
caying, ever new, and fresh vitality and animation, to go
powerfully along with an infinite series of objects, changes,
excitements, and activities ?

My mind was filled with such thoughts and inquiries, and then I found, as I had never to the same extent experienced before, the preciousness of Christ, and the blessedness of having a personal faith and trust in His great work of salvation. I saw then, as in letters of fire, that as " by one man's offence death reigned by one, much more they which receive abundance of grace, and of the gift of righteousness, shall reign in life by one, Jesus Christ:" that "as by the offence of one judgment came upon all men to condemnation, even so by the righteousness of One the free gift came upon all men to justification of life. For as by one man's disobedience many were made sinners, so by the obedience of One shall many be made righteous." That "where sin abounded grace did much more abound:" that "as sin hath reigned unto death, even so might grace reign through righteousness unto eternal life, through Jesus Christ our Lord."

A sick bed is not always the most favourable place to learn the way of salvation, because very often intense pain and anxiety about other matters so occupy the mind as to render it incapable of giving the attention that it deserves and demands; but it is the place to try the reality of a man's religion—whether it be a thing of mere sacraments and creeds, or a living principle in the heart and mind. Such being the case, I would press upon my readers the importance of settling this great question while they are in health, and have time and opportunity. Make your election now ; "now is the day of salvation, now is the accepted time ;" now settle the point in your own case, whether it shall be pleasure or duty ; your own will, or God's will ; the passions indulged, or kept down ; the maxims and customs of the world, or the convictions of conscience and the word of God ; Christ, or the devil ; heaven, or hell.

My illness was a very anxious one, and was also of long duration ; but the greatest possible kindness and consideration were exercised towards me by the gentleman at

M

the head of my department, who, although a severe disciplinarian, was a tender-hearted and sympathizing man, and in cases of illness particularly thoughtful and indulgent. As soon as I was well enough to be seen, my pastor came to my bedside, and in soft and loving tones spoke to me of my illness, and of the consolation I had enjoyed from the great truths he had been the means of introducing to my attention.

I became accustomed to look forward to these pastoral visits with much pleasure. I knew his well-known rap at the door, and "there was music in his very feet, as he came up the stairs." There was nothing exciting in his manner, and his visits always left behind a soothing influence upon me. He would tell me of the sermons he had been preaching during my absence, and talk to me of Heaven. His prayers, tender and low, that he offered up to the Great Father at my bedside, will never be forgotten either by my wife or myself. My eldest girl always ran to meet him, and there was something about his whole deportment that made him a favourite with every one in the house. He helped very much to allay the fears and apprehensions of my wife, and had always some cheering word of encouragement to say as to the future.

We were particularly happy also in the doctor that attended us. He was a gentleman of great skill and experience, and of large practice, yet he paid me as much attention as if I had been one of his most wealthy patients.

He took a particular interest in my case, having two others of a similar nature under his treatment at the same time, one of which proved fatal.

I have mentioned that I was almost starved under the treatment I experienced. I had no animal food of any kind for some weeks; cold water in abundance, and a very little rice, was all that I was allowed to take in the way of nourishment, as it was essentially necessary to keep me down to as low a point as possible consistent with being alive. I was obliged to sit in an upright posture in bed,

with the slightest possible covering upon me, and large bags
of ice kept incessantly applied to my chest. Often when my
wife brought me a little rice, almost cold, and hardly more
than would cover a crown-piece, have I asked if that was
all that I was to get for my dinner. She would look at
me with pity, and say cheerily that I should have more
the moment that the doctor ordered it. I used to implore
her to let me have another spoonful of rice ; but she was
inexorable, although I could see in her averted face the
tear stealing down the cheek that too clearly indicated
what it cost her to deny me this small request. The doctor told me at the close of my long illness that I had had
a most narrow escape, and that I owed quite as much to
the firm but tender treatment of my wife as to anything he
had done for me. I must mention an amusing incident
that occurred during my illness. When the hemorrhage
had ceased for about a week, the doctor told my wife that
I might have a little tripe for dinner. I was delighted at
the change of diet, though I had never tasted tripe in my
life, and had a peculiar aversion to it. However, the
article was procured and brought up to me. The joy
experienced by me at the sight of that savoury morsel can
only be adequately understood by those who have gone
almost without food, for I know not how many days I had
had nothing but a little rice and cold water. No tea,
coffee, chocolate, or cocoa—to say nothing of broth or
beef-tea—were allowed ; and to see and smell anything
that really looked like food was almost more than I could
endure. My wife left the tray for a moment on the bed, and
in a couple of minutes the plate was as clean as a cat could
have licked it. On returning to the room she was amazed
to see that it was gone, and almost thought that it had
slipped off the plate on to the floor. I told her, however,
what had become of it, and she gently chided me for eating
it so quickly.

The doctor came just as I had finished this banquet,
and was told that I had enjoyed my dinner very much.

He inquired the quantity I had taken, and was informed that it was about a quarter of a pound. He was quite angry at my having had so much, as he intended that I should only have had about two ounces. However, the result proved that the excess had done me no harm; but my wife was more careful in future not to let me have one iota more than the doctor prescribed, and all my coaxing solicitations were in vain.

After several weeks of careful nursing I was so far restored that the doctor said I might be removed to the country for change of air. My wife selected a snug little farm-house, belonging to one of her relatives, at East Rudham, a quiet little village in Norfolk, between Fakenham and Lynn, where she knew every care would be taken of me. My eldest little girl was sent with me, while my wife and the baby were left at home to keep house.

I enjoyed that visit amazingly, as the relatives were very kind, and I was allowed to do quite as I liked, and could wander about its green lanes and pleasant pastures with my little daughter " at our own sweet will."

The village of East Rudham is only about two miles from Houghton Hall,—a truly sumptuous pile,—built by Sir Robert Walpole, but now the property of the Marquis of Cholmondely. My brother-in-law, where I was staying, was very intimate with the head gamekeeper of this pala-tial domain, and an introduction to him gave me the free range at all times over the gardens, pleasure-grounds, and the magnificent park.

The park and pleasure-grounds that surround this princely edifice are laid out so as to give the greatest possible effect: they are so disposed as to appear one beyond the other, in different shades, and seem to stretch away to a very considerable extent. The Hall itself im-presses the mind with everything that magnificence can inspire, as well as presenting a fair specimen of the power, wealth, and grandeur of the illustrious Prime Minister who caused it to be erected. The large and celebrated collec-

tion of pictures that once adorned its walls are, alas! no
longer there: they were sold in 1779, by George, Earl of
Orford, to Catherine of Russia, for no less a sum than
£45,500; a sum that will in some way indicate their value,
but which was said to be far less than the great statesman
paid for them. There are a few good pictures there now;
there are also some choice specimens of sculpture, many of
them antiques, and some by the great artists of modern
times. The ceilings of some of the rooms are painted by
Kent, who also furnished designs for most of the furniture.
In one of the dining-parlours there is some beautiful pear-
tree carving by Grinling Gibbons.

Houghton Hall! how does thy name recall to me the
many pleasant weeks spent in wandering about thy beautiful scenes with my little daughter. I had for some years
been confined to London, and had worked with hands and
head incessantly. How grateful and gladsome were these
country scenes to me! One who had lived long in London
and had a keen relish for the country, says, in language
that I could make my own,—

> "As one who long in populous city pent,
> Where houses thick, and sewers annoy the air,
> Forth issuing on a summer's morn, to breathe
> Among the pleasant villages and farms
> Adjoin'd, from each thing met conceives delight;
> The smell of grain, or tedded grass, or kine,
> Or dairy, each rural sight, each rural sound."

I felt as free and frolicksome almost as the lambs that
disported themselves about me, and was as happy as the
little birds that sang among the branches. We used to
lie down under the large umbrageous trees, and watch the
squirrels in their gambols as they leaped from branch to
branch. While my little daughter would amuse herself
by the hour in gathering wild flowers, I enjoyed my book,
and gave myself up to dreamy reveries. The "lowing herd
winding slowly o'er the lea," the bleating sheep, the song
of birds, the rustling leaves, the hum of insects, and the

murmuring streams, are sounds fraught with exquisite melody to some minds.

I thoroughly enjoyed this holiday so long waited for, and my health very visibly improved. It could not be otherwise, for I seemed to drink in health with every breath, and all nature around appeared to sympathize in my gladness, so that the very trees of the wood clapped their hands with joy.

I had always been a lover of Nature, and my early life was spent among some of her most quiet beauties, so that my enjoyment of this change was very great, and I felt oftentimes—

> " O Nature, changeless as thou art,
>   Majestic in repose;
> The same, while kingdoms pass away
>   And generations close;
> The infant, in its hour of dread,
>   Will seek its mother's knee,
> And by a kindred instinct led,
>   I turn and fly to thee!"

These " quiet resting-places " in a world of toil are most grateful to an over-wrought brain and a debilitated body; and the weeks spent in this neighbourhood will ever be green spots in my memory. I have very often felt, when wandering alone amidst some of Nature's most beautiful scenes, that there is something more than sympathy in the works of God around us, for after all—

> " 'Tis not in outward loveliness
>   The spirit most delights;
> The landscape in its sunny dress,
>   Or starry pomp of nights;
> These are but silent witnesses
>   Of that which in them lies,
> A power pervading earth and seas,
>   And coming from the skies."

Some of my truest, deepest, and holiest feelings have been stirred within me as I have gone out alone at eventide to meditate in some pastoral scenery: the mind has seemed intuitively to turn to the Great Father in Heaven, and all the outward world around has appeared but one vast temple erected to His praise and filled with His worshippers. I have felt a seriousness of mind steal over me somewhat akin to what Moses must have experienced when he heard the Divine Voice say, in accents soft and tender, " Put off thy shoes from off thy feet, for the place whereon thou standest is holy ground ; " and then—

> " Transfigured in this glory fair,
> The whole earth stands, one house of prayer,
> One ante-room of Heaven ;
> For surely, though we know it not,
> God's presence is in every spot,
> To those who seek it given."

There are holy interviews between the soul and God that let us into the " secret place of the Most High," when we seem to " abide under the shadow of the Almighty." We go back again to the busy working world, feeling that this is not our rest ; and however hard we may toil for the bread that perisheth, there is a home in reserve for us, in which our nobler nature shall have free scope for enjoyments and relationships such as nothing on earth can afford.

Frequently have the words come, as it were instinctively, to my lips, as I have been gazing upon fair scenes such as I have adverted to, " all things are yours." Yes, if we have given up our rebellion, and have returned in penitence and love to our Father's heart and house, we may feel that we have a right and title to all that is around us in this fair and beautiful world. Of a Christian it may indeed be said—

> " He looks abroad into the varied field
> Of nature, and though poor perhaps, compared
> With those whose mansions glitter in his sight,
> Calls the delightful scenery all his own.
> His are the mountains, and the valleys his,
> And the resplendent rivers, his to enjoy

With a propriety that none can feel,
But who, with filial confidence inspired,
Can lift to Heaven an unpresumptuous eye,
And smiling say,—' My Father made them all !'
Are they not his by a peculiar right,
And by an emphasis of interest his,
Whose eye they fill with tears of holy joy,
Whose heart with praise, and whose exalted mind
With worthy thoughts of that unwearied love,
That plann'd and built, and still upholds, a world
So clothed with beauty for rebellious man !"

" Blessed are the meek, for they shall inherit the earth ;" and the richest worldling, though he may call himself " lord of the soil," and look around upon a thousand broad acres that he may rightly call his own, yet he has not the enjoyments of the man who, though he have not an inch of ground, has nevertheless the true enjoyment of all that is spread out before him. If I am a child of God by faith in Jesus Christ, the world and all that it contains are mine—

"For me kind Nature wakes her genial power,
Suckles each herb, and spreads out every flower ;
Annual for me the grape, the rose renew,
The juice nectareous, and the balmy dew ;
For me, the mine a thousand treasures brings :
For me, health gushes from a thousand springs :
Seas roll to waft me, suns to light me rise :
My footstool earth, my canopy the skies."

Shortly after my arrival at the quiet little village of East Rudham, a little incident occurred that caused a hearty laugh, not only among my relatives there, but also among my friends in London. I walked out through the straggling little village one evening, and was attracted to a plain red-brick building, standing back from the road, and which I afterwards found to be a Wesleyan Chapel. There were about half-a-dozen people standing at the entrance, and as I approached one of them made me a respectful bow, and remarked that I was rather late. I looked inquiringly for an explanation, when the person said that she thought I was the local preacher, who was expected from a neighbouring village, from the direction of which I had come. I told the friends that I was no preacher, but was a stranger in the neighbourhood in search of health and rest. They pressed me then to occupy the pulpit, as the preacher whom they expected-had not arrived. To this request I could not yield, as I had at that time never engaged in duties of that nature. They then proposed that a prayer-meeting should be held, and literally led me up to the chair to preside. I consented to this, more by quietly yielding, than by anything said; having learnt from them the order of the service, and arranged that they should call upon suitable people to pray, as I was an entire stranger. There were about thirty persons present, chiefly labourers and their wives, with one or two of a better class. I thought of my stammering tongue, and feared I might break down in giving out the hymn; but there was no time for hesitation, and having selected the hymn I read it out in solemn tones, and with great deliberation. This was followed by reading one of the Psalms; and as they were all strangers to me, I assumed a ministerial air, and did not stammer in the slightest degree. The reading being ended, I said, "Let us pray;" when, to my surprise, the soft voice of one of the females was heard. It was the first time that I had ever heard a woman pray in public, and I was a little afraid at what would follow; my fears were soon allayed, as the prayer was one suitable in all respects to the occasion. The language was simple, devout, and scriptural, and at the close of her prayer, a touching and delicate allusion was made as to the state of my health, and that I might be restored to my family benefited and in safety. This was followed by another hymn, and a second female prayed. This good sister was a great contrast to the last, and made up in fervour and warmth what she lacked in other ways. She was the wife of one of the labourers present, and her language, though scriptural and devout, was not the best specimen of the " Queen's English." To this succeeded a third prayer, offered by an

elderly man with venerable look and silvery hair. After
this I gave out another hymn, and at the close offered a
short prayer, and pronounced the benediction.

I was not a little glad to find the service over, as it was
the first time in my life that I had ever taken a public
part in devotional exercises. I did not tell the friends
this, and they appeared to be glad that I had taken the
presidency at the meeting, and thanked me for my services.

My relatives were not a little surprised when I told them
where I had been, and how I had been engaged. They
were Church people, and knew nothing of Dissenting practices, and therefore were at a loss to understand how I
could have consented to have been pressed into such a
service.

My London friends were not a little amused that I should
have been taken for a Dissenting parson, and I was joked
about it many times. However, I made a good impression
upon my Wesleyan friends there, and enjoyed the service
much; and I hear that, though twenty years have passed
since then, kind inquiries are even now made, by some
who were present at that meeting, about the pale-faced
gentleman who was staying there for the change of air.

After spending six or eight weeks in this delightful
neighbourhood, I returned to London, and resumed my
ordinary work. I was particularly cautioned by my doctor to avoid all violent exercises, such as running, jumping,
and lifting anything heavy.

Every possible indulgence was granted to me by the gentleman at the head of my department; and I am pleased
to record this as only one among many instances of his great
kindness and consideration to those under his command
who, from sickness, or other causes, needed his help and
sympathy. During a period of more than thirty years that I
have had the honour of serving under him, and in which I
have had more than ordinary opportunities of observing what
has taken place, I have known that, while he looks up
most keenly those who would attempt to abuse the privilege

accorded to invalids by the trustees of our National Library, I have never known a single instance of his refusing to obtain, for those who really needed it, the full benefit of absence from duty in cases of sickness and domestic affliction. In my own case I can truly say that, had he been my father, he could not have behaved to me with greater kindness and consideration.

During the next two years of my life, 1845-46, I do not recollect anything particularly to record beyond the fact that I had a terrible struggle to keep my expenditure below my income. The salaries of every one in the establishment to which I belonged were notoriously small, so much so, that the late Mr. Joseph Hume, who took much interest in the place, said that it was the worst paid of all our public institutions.

However, I was happy in having a wife who not only helped to improve our income by her own earnings in fancy-work and embroidery, but was also most careful in our expenditure; and I was often for my own part comforted by Sydney Smith's assurance, that, though " other rules vary, this is the only one you will find without exception,— that in this world, the salary or reward is always in the *inverse ratio* of the duties performed."

Privations, and difficulties, arising from slender means and sickness, are not pleasant things to bear; but they exert a salutary influence: and while one is compelled to go without many little luxuries which ample means can procure, yet there is a vast amount of enjoyment to be had from a wise and careful appropriation of even a small income. Some one has said that " more mean things have been done in this world under the shelter of wife and children, than under any other pretext that worldly-mindedness can resort to;" but it need not be so, if we cultivate a thankful acquiescence in whatever it may please the Great Father to appoint for us; and it is most true that—

" If in our daily course, our mind
 Be set to hallow all we find,

> New treasures still of costless price
> God will provide for sacrifice.
>
> The trivial round, the common task
> Would furnish all we ought to ask:
> Room to deny ourselves—a road
> To bring us daily nearer God."

One of the subjects of the greatest anxiety to us at this time, and all through the earlier part of our married life, was the difficulty in procuring suitable education for our children. Schools such as we should like to have sent them to were beyond our reach, and those that were within our means were not desirable on many accounts. The course of instruction was very meagre, and then the class of children sent to these cheaper schools was not such as we were desirous of our little ones making companions of.

It has been my lot all through life to have had friends and acquaintances whose means were far above my own; and although I cannot charge myself with being proud, yet I did feel anxious to maintain our social position, and in doing so we were obliged to cheerfully submit to many privations.

But what is there that a father will not forgo for his children; I never felt that any sacrifice was too great to make for them. Bless their little hearts, how have they gladdened my home when otherwise it would have been cheerless and dreary! No love is so pure, so disinterested, as that of a child. What indeed would the world be without children? They are the flowers of our homes and the delight of our hearts. What is more gladsome than their loud, happy, joyous ringing laugh? And Heaven seems nearer to us as we gaze into their innocent faces, and look into the soft depths of their loving eyes. I have often felt that the words of the poet have beautifully expressed my own thoughts as I have gazed admiringly at them:—

> "O little feet! that such long years
> Must wander on through hopes and fears,

Must ache and bleed beneath your load ;
I, nearer to the wayside inn
Where toil shall cease and hope begin,
    Am weary, thinking of your road !

O little hands ! that, weak or strong,
Have still to serve or rule so long,
    Have still so long to give or ask ;
I, who so much with book and pen
Have toil'd among my fellow-men,
    Am weary, thinking of your task.

O little hearts ! that throb and beat
With such impatient, feverish heat,
    Such limitless and strong desires ;
Mine that so long has glow'd and burn'd,
With passions into ashes turn'd,
    Now covers and conceals its fires."

Towards the close of 1846 my youngest, and now only surviving brother, returned from India with the remnant of his regiment. He had gone out a mere lad, and returned to us now in the prime of his manhood. He had gone through all the vicissitudes of a British soldier's life in a foreign land, under the burning suns of India. He had seen some actual service at the battles of Maharajpore, Buddiwal, Aliwal, and Sobraon, for which he had been rewarded by medals. He had left my eldest brother alone in his glory at Landour, sleeping in the dust, far away among the lofty Himalayas. He had closed the eyelids of another loved one, who had gone scatheless through some terrible battles, and was cut down like a flower, and buried by the side of the mighty Ganges, on his way home.

As might have been expected, our first meeting was a most affecting one. Some delay had occurred in his getting a furlough to visit us ; my father's health would not allow of his going to meet him at the ship, and my own doctor peremptorily forbade me to go, as any sudden emotion might produce a return of the hemorrhage from the lungs, and might be fatal to me.

We were assembled at my father's apartments in the vicinity of Russell-square, and I well remember the state of anxious suspense we endured as we awaited his arrival. Every cab that was heard in the streets made our hearts beat quicker; and when at length he arrived, and we heard his well-known voice at the door, we could hardly believe our ears. In another moment he stood in our midst, and was locked in his mother's embrace. It was a scene such as a painter would have delighted to have transferred to canvass. The tall and manly form of my brother, with the gay scarlet uniform of his regiment, with face bronzed by the scorching suns of India; my mother, almost always an invalid, clasping him about the neck as only a mother can; my father, bending in loving admiration over his long-expected, darling boy; my sisters and myself standing in speechless joy until our turn came to have the loving kiss and the hearty grip of the hand of him we loved so well.

Oh! it was a scene to be remembered, and one that gladdens this dark world of sin and woe. He told us of his voyage, of his troubles, of his battles and his hair-breadth escapes; but when he came to talk of those who had been left behind in that far-off land, there were sobs heard in that room,—Rachel weeping for her children because they were not,—as well as tears of joy and gratitude on account of him who had been so mercifully preserved in the day of battle, and safely returned to tell of the wondrous mercy of Him who had made him the object of His loving care.

All that long afternoon, and far into the hours of the night, did we sit and talk of all the things that had happened during his absence from us.

I was admiring the golden bars upon his arm, when he turned and whispered to me that the jacket he wore was that that had belonged to the poor fellow they left sleeping by the banks of the Ganges. It was a home-stroke that quite unmanned me, and I wept like a woman till I was fairly ashamed of my weakness.

My brother brought with him many little trinkets and curiosities from Lahore and other places for his mother and sisters; and he rewarded me with a silken sash, taken from some Sikh chieftain slain at Aliwal. A relic that I shall keep as long as I live.

In recalling the scene that I have attempted to describe, I am reminded of the Divine order and arrangements in the world around us and within us. We do not become all at once that which we have set our hearts upon; it must be the result of patient labour and untiring persistence :—

"'Tis first the true and then the beautiful,
    Not first the beautiful and then the true;
First the wild moor, with rock, and reed, and pool,
    Then the gay garden, rich in scent and hue.

'Tis first the good and then the beautiful,
    Not first the beautiful and then the good;
First the rough seed, sown in the rougher soil,
    Then the flower-blossom, or the branching wood.

Not first the glad, and then the sorrowful,
    But first the sorrowful and then the glad;
Tears for a day,—for earth of tears is full,—
    Then we forget that we were ever sad.

Not first the bright, and after that the dark,
    But first the dark, and after that the bright;
First the thick cloud, and then the rainbow's arc,
    First the dark grave, then resurrection-light.

'Tis first the night, stern night of storm and war,
    Long night of heavy clouds and veilèd skies,
Then the far-sparkle of the morning-star,
    That bids the saints awake and dawn arise.

'Tis first the fight and then the victory,
    Not first the victory and then the fight;
First the dark night, and then the dawning day
    Which ushers in the everlasting light."

Shortly after the arrival from India of my brother I lost my father. His death was very sudden, after a slight illness of only a few days. He was laid aside from duty for about a fortnight with an attack of influenza; but the immediate cause of death was the rupture of a blood-vessel in the neighbourhood of the heart. I had seen him on the evening of the night he died, and before I left assisted in lifting him into bed, as he had become very weak from the influenza. In bidding him good night, he held my hand within his for a long time, and appeared reluctant for me to leave. However, there was nothing to awaken our fears as to his recovery, and I left him about ten; but the lingering pressure of his hand within mine was what I have never forgotten. He was taken worse about two o'clock in the morning from the cause I have mentioned, and expired gently, as an infant would fall asleep, about four. My mother and brother were with him; but I did not know it till my arrival at my post the next morning, when it came upon me like a thunder-clap; and not only upon myself, but also all his colleagues; for no one imagined that from so slight an illness he would have died.

His loss was felt by many; but his own immediate family, and my dear mother, were well-nigh overwhelmed with sorrow. He was a man of singular amiability; quiet and undemonstrative in his manners, but full to overflowing of affection and love. Oh, that I could embalm his memory as he deserves! He was kindly, benevolent, and liberal, far beyond his means. He ever responded to affection's call, and was full of care for others: weary often with others' burdens, generous man, and yet his own loving heart was too little strong to bear it. Many mourned his loss; and he has left behind him a memory fragrant and beautiful. Oh, my father, how much do I owe thee? I can never pay the happy debt until I depart—

> " Then will I bless and love it all away
> In that bright world, my father, where thou art ! "

My father's affairs were left in a very unsettled state, and I was nearly ruined in my poor endeavours to adjust them. Had they been, however, still more complicated, no labour or sacrifice on my part would have been grudged for such a father. I had caused him much anxiety, and not a little grief, by my waywardness and wickedness in early life; but he never upbraided me for this in after days, and was not only a fond and loving father, but also a wise and faithful counsellor, ever ready to help me in all my difficulties.

The death of my father had a great effect upon my own health, and I began to find a decrease in the buoyancy and elasticity of mind that I had hitherto enjoyed. I know not what I should have done but for the consolation of religion. In the great truths of the Bible I found a never-failing source of comfort and help. I saw that these times of trouble came not by accident or chance; but were messengers from God to do me good—the chastisements not in anger, but in love, from One whose goodness and mercy had followed me all the days of my life. It is well in time of trouble to see God's fatherly hand, and—

> " Sorrow touch'd by *Thee* grows bright,
>   With more than rapture's ray;
> As darkness shows us worlds of light,
>   We never saw by day."

It is well to remember that *discipline* is the end of all God's dealings with his children. Good old Thomas à Kempis truly says that " the whole life of Christ was a cross and martyrdom: and dost thou seek rest and joy?" Some people, Christian people, seem to think that the end of life is to be as comfortable as possible, and to make the best of both worlds. I am not by any means unmindful about the good things of the present world—they were sent for our enjoyment, and are to be received with thanksgiving and prayer; but there are higher and nobler purposes to be accomplished in passing through this probationary state—we are to be educated for something beyond the present life.

For my own part I would not have been without my

N

troubles; they have done me good, and have, by God's blessing, produced within me the peaceable fruits of righteousness. In adverting to this subject I am reminded of some exquisite lines from the accomplished pen of the late Earl of Carlisle, which I am sure my readers will thank me for inserting here:—

" How little of ourselves we know,
    Before a grief the heart has felt !
The lessons that we learn of woe
    May brace the mind as well as melt.

The energies too stern for mirth,
    The reach of thought, the strength of will,
'Mid cloud and tempest have their birth,
    Through blight and blast their course fulfil !

And yet 'tis when it mourns and fears
    The loaded spirit feels forgiven ;
And through the mist of falling tears
    We catch the clearest glimpse of Heaven."

A few weeks before the death of my father we had born to us a little son. The birth of a child in a family is always a matter of no small joy, and this dear little fellow was welcomed most heartily. We hoped that he would grow up to be a companion and protector to his sisters, as well as " a son of consolation " to ourselves. I was so glad to have a boy that I might train him up so as to avoid the evils I had fallen into. He was a darling little fellow, and his mother was very proud of him ; but, alas ! all our hopes were blighted by his early death, and, as we thought, premature removal. He took the hooping-cough from his eldest sister, and in a few days sickened and died.

Everything that medical skill and tender nursing could do was called into requisition to save this little one ; but it was in vain. One who has gone through this trying ordeal has said, in words that will move every parent's heart who has watched by a sick-bed—

" We watch'd him breathing thro' the night,
   His breathing soft and low ;
As in his breast the wave of life
   Kept heaving to and fro.

So silently we seem'd to speak,
   So slowly moved about,
As we had lent him half our power
   To eke his living out.

Our very hopes belied our fears,
   Our fears our hopes belied ;
We thought him dying when he slept,
   And sleeping when he died.

For when the morn came dim and sad,
   And chill with early showers,
His quiet eyelids closed—he had
   Another morn than ours."

The death of our dear little boy, so soon after the removal of my father, was a great trial to us ; but, beyond the loss of the child, death brought with it no terrors. We could hardly bring ourselves to believe that the child was really dead, so beautiful did he look—the bloom was upon his little cheeks, and the pretty mouth looked more exquisite than ever. As we fondly gazed at him, the beautiful words of that great master of song came instinctively to my mind :—

" He who hath bent him o'er the dead,
   Ere the first day of death is fled;
   The first dark day of nothingness,
   The last of danger and distress,
   (Before Decay's effacing fingers
   Have swept the lines where beauty lingers),
   And mark'd the mild angelic air,
   The rapture of repose that's there,
   The fix'd, yet tender traits that streak
   The languor of the placid cheek;
   And, but for that sad shrouded eye,
   That fires not, wins not, weeps not now,
   And but for that chill, changeless brow,
   Where cold obstruction's apathy

> Appals the gazing mourner's heart,
> As if to him it could impart
> The doom he dreads, yet dwells upon.
> Yes, but for these, and these alone,
> Some moments, aye, one treacherous hour,
> We still might doubt the tyrant's power;
> So fair, so calm, so softly seal'd,
> The first, last look by death reveal'd."

His mother could not bear to leave him at night, and we carried his little coffin to our own bed-room, and placed him on the drawers by the bed-side. It was not until the day of the funeral that his eyes began to sink, and the bright coral of his baby lips to fade. To put such a treasure into the cold grave is no small trial of faith, and especially to her who bore him; but—

> " Oh! when a mother meets on high
>   The babe she lost in infancy,
> Hath she not then, for pains and fears,
>   The day of woe, the watchful night,
> For all her sorrow, all her tears,
>   An over payment of delight ? "

Among the many friends who condoled with us on the loss of our child was our pastor. He was a man preeminently fitted for pastoral visitation, as well as being so distinguished as a preacher. His presence in a sick chamber and the house of mourning was like the entrance of the light after a dark and stormy night. He moved so quietly, and his tones were so gentle, that the most excited felt soothed by his first few words of kindly greeting. He was a man of thoughtful brow, and meek full dark eye, with large projecting eyebrows. There was a tender and delicate sort of melancholy about him that the better qualified him to comfort and console the mourner or the invalid; and yet he was full of wit and quiet fun, and could say things on suitable occasions to make you hold your sides for laughter. The mind that has an equal mixture of melancholy and vivacity is sure to be attractive;

but to be lively without levity, and pensive without dejection, is a very rare quality. These qualities were found in a remarkable and unusual degree in our pastor; and his many visits made to me in sickness, and to our household in times of sorrow and bereavement, were among the most pleasant and profitable in my history.

He appeared ever to feel the great responsibility of his position, for—

> " 'Tis not a cause of small import
> The pastor's care demands;
> But what might fill an angel's heart,
> And fill'd a Saviour's hands."

It would be well if the members of our Churches would remember how valuable is the time of such a man, and how foolish it is to waste his precious moments in talk about a hundred things that are of no sort of importance. When prevented by sickness from attending the Sanctuary, our pastor would make frequent visits; he would tell me of what he had been preaching on the past Sabbath, and has often thus furnished me with profitable subjects for thought and meditation. His prayers on these occasions were the soft and tender breathings of a strong but loving nature; and when his visit was over, and he was gone, you felt that you had been holding intercourse with one of " Nature's noblemen," whose influence would last for many days.

Our children were very fond of him, and he was particularly partial to our eldest girl, who always ran to him with that intuitive knowledge that a child has of those who love them. He never, as a rule, visited his people while they were able to attend the services, as the congregation was so large that it would have been impossible; but if any of his flock were in trouble, or sick, he was always found among them, let their position in life be ever so humble. There were more than eight hundred registered members of the Church under his pastoral care at the time I am writing of, besides a great many occasional communicants; and it will be apparent that, with such a number, to visit in times of affliction was no small labour. His wife once told me, on my asking when he prepared his sermons, that they were generally written between the hours of twelve at night and three in the morning. He has himself informed me, when conversing on the subject of preaching, that he never let a train of thought escape him, let the hour of the night be what it may, he always got up and jotted it down. To meet the same congregation Sabbath after Sabbath with anything worth listening to, requires that a man should work hard, and my friend told me that wherever he was, or however he might be engaged, either at home or abroad, he was ever collecting materials for sermons. When a younger man he used to think that thoughts which came trooping unbidden, like a flock of birds, would come again when he wanted them, and had more leisure to entertain them, and put them to some good purpose; but he found they did not come again oftentimes, and therefore he formed the habit of securing them on paper whenever and wherever he might be.

To have to meet a London congregation from week to week, such as that which assembled in the house of prayer I attended, was no small drain on the intellectual and nervous powers of a man. It is not only the preaching that must be provided for, but there is to bring the many varied wants of such a multitude before God in prayer, and this in language that shall be edifying and profitable. Our reverend brother in the Establishment has no such drain upon him, inasmuch as a liturgy is provided, which, for comprehensiveness, as well as devotional feeling, cannot be excelled. And yet there is something in the exercise of free prayer, when conducted by a man of ability, and who himself cultivates the spirit and habit of devotion, that is very refreshing and helpful. I have heard Churchmen speak with contempt and ridicule of a Dissenting parson's prayers; but though this may be true of some, it is by no means applicable to many of the men who fill our metropolitan and provincial pulpits. I would for my own part far rather listen to the beautiful service of the Church of England, rich in devotional thought, and expressed in language simple and sublime, than the loud and noisy prayers, in hackneyed language and irreverent manner, that may be heard in some of our Dissenting Chapels.

I have often thought that Nonconformists might with much advantage use a liturgy occasionally; as well as that the reading of the Scriptures in our chapels should be more consecutive, as is the case in the lessons prescribed by the Church of England.

I have always been at a loss, however, to understand why in the public services of the Church of England the Book of Revelation has been entirely excluded, while the Apocryphal books form a part of the daily reading. I have been a little surprised sometimes to find that intelligent Churchmen had never noticed this strange anomaly.

I am a Nonconformist upon principle, and I glory in the freedom of our Churches, and would die the death of a martyr rather than relinquish one jot or tittle of the liberty and freedom obtained for us by our noble forefathers; yet, nevertheless, I am not so blind to some of the evils that obtain in our Churches, as not to desire that they should be removed. I know by making this confession I shall be charged by some of the old school of Dissenters with deserting their principles; but I care not for this, as I am not so wedded to Dissent as not to see that there are imperfections in our Church arrangements which we should do well to consider and remove.

The ability to remove any evils in our midst, either of doctrine or practice, is one of the distinguishing characteristics of Congregationalism; and there are to be found among us a noble body of men, both lay and clerical, equal to any in other denominations, who are well able to grapple with difficulties that may stand in the way of such improvements; and I would say to them with all humility, " I speak as unto wise men; judge ye what I say."

To return once more to my personal history. Trouble and bereavement had done their work upon me, and given me a more sober and serious view of life, but—

> " Was not earth's most auspicious hour
> One darksome, sad, and wild?
> When crucifixion was the birth,
> Redemption was the child."

I had a good many privations to undergo from slender means, and we rarely had the doctor out of the house for many weeks during the year: but I was enabled to breast the wave, and hold on; and I thought that—

> " If misfortune comes, she brings along
> The bravest virtues. And so many great
> Illustrious spirits have conversed with woe,
> Have in her school been taught, as are enough
> To consecrate distress, and make ambition
> E'en wish the frown beyond the smile of fortune."

In the next year or two of my life nothing occurs to me that is worth recording. Matters went on much as usual, excepting that in 1848 I gained promotion at my place of business that increased in a small degree my income, so that I was less anxious about the ways and means. Just about this time I joined a small society of friends for mutual improvement in reading aloud, and for the discussion of moral, political, and social questions. There were only about a dozen members, and the meetings were held at the houses of those who had the best accommodation for such purposes.

These meetings were very pleasant. In the reading meetings a certain number of the members would select pieces of prose or poetry, and these were read and criticised in the freest possible manner, both as to the compositions themselves, and the manner in which they had been read or delivered.

It is surprising how few really good readers are to be found either in private society or in our reading desks and pulpits. Reading is thought by some to be one of the easiest things in the world to do; but let any one go into our public courts, and churches and chapels, and it will soon be evident that to read well is by no means an easy accomplishment. Until lately very little attention had been given to the subject; but we have had many professional readings of late years, and the people generally appear to be more desirous of acquiring a correct and pleasurable mode of reading, instead of the careless, drawling habit that is for the most part seen and heard in our social circles, as well as public places.

No exercise is more conducive to health than good reading, providing certain rules are borne in mind. Those who are desirous of attaining a habit of good reading will do well to consult a small work lately published by a gentleman who has given more attention to the subject than almost any one that I know of. It is entitled, "The Right Management of the Voice, and on Delivery in Speaking and Reading. By the Rev. W. W. Cazalet, A.M."

The discussion meetings of the little society of which I was a member were always looked forward to with much pleasure. Almost all the topics of the day were brought under consideration, and it fell to my lot to prepare short essays on some subjects that could not but be interesting in discussing; and I am sure that the preparation required was a very healthful exercise in testing one's mental resources, and accustoming one's self to address a meeting without that fear and dread that is mostly the case when a man has never measured himself fairly with his fellows in intellectual combat. The subjects allotted to me were —" The Claims of our Roman Catholic Fellow-subjects to the Rights of Citizenship;" "Slavery; is it a thing sanctioned by God?" "In what Sense, and to what Extent, are the Scriptures Inspired?" "The Sovereignty of God and the Free-agency of Man," &c.

The discussion of these and kindred subjects was found to be exceedingly useful and interesting, and we were accustomed to express ourselves most freely and unreservedly

on the questions introduced. I recollect that the paper I
drew up on the Inspiration of the Scriptures caused a good
deal of discussion, and was useful to not a few of the members whose views upon that great subject had been very
loose or mistaken.

As the subject of the Inspiration of the Scriptures is one
that occupies a very prominent position just now, I may
be pardoned for adverting to the paper I drew up on that
important question.

I felt the solemnity of the subject, and at the same time
did not shrink from boldly and fearlessly speaking of some
of the theories which had been put forth by those who
have written on the Inspiration of the Scriptures; striving
earnestly, at the same time, not to forget the decorum which
becomes the discussion of solemn subjects.

I had seen sufficiently into the question to be most
thoroughly convinced that fully to grapple with the great
subject required an amount of scholarship and ability to
which I did not for a moment pretend. I was convinced
that that was a fitting task for a powerful and resolute
mind, which should bring to the subject not only profound
scholarship, but also an energy and earnestness commensu-
rate in some measure with an inquiry which had long been
felt by those who meditated on theology to be a most
pressing want of the Church.

I knew also that those who would be engaged in discussing the matter were men, like myself, desirous of
understanding the real merits of the question in a religious
aspect for our daily guidance in the perusal and meditation of the sacred volume.

That the book, or collection of books, which we call the
Bible was inspired in some sense, has been the current
belief of the Church in all ages, and this was most cordially
believed by those who were assembled with me to discuss
the subject. There was not in any one of us a perhaps,
or peradventure, as to whether the Bible was of God; we
all knew by an internal conviction, which no power of

argument or sophistry could in any way shake, that in receiving it as a Divine revelation we had not followed " cunningly devised fables ;" but were resting our faith upon " the oracles of God." And further, we knew, all of us, that the ultimate appeal in matters of faith and doctrine had ever been made to these venerable writings.

The Apostle Paul, in writing to the Corinthians, tells them that " the things of God knoweth no man, but the spirit of God," (1 Cor. ii. 11); but the writers of the Bible speak with as much familiarity of the " things of God," as they do of the things of man. They always speak as consciously authorized instructors : not only do they, as other historians, relate facts, and pass opinions fairly within the scope of their faculties, but they with equal confidence deliver judgments belonging to a far higher domain.

I did not in the paper referred to enter upon the question of the canon of Scripture, but accepted it as the Church has received it, and therefore confined my remarks to the inquiry, In what sense, and to what extent are the Scriptures inspired ?

In considering the subject I was bound to admit that a large and numerous body of Christians, from an early period, distinguished alike by piety, learning, and intellectual status, have affirmed, that the Bible is God's word in the same sense as if He had made use of no human agent, but had Himself spoken it as He did the Decalogue. These held that " every word, every syllable, every letter, is just what it would have been had God spoken from Heaven without any human intervention."

A writer of no small ability,* who sets forth this theory, says with much candour, " I am aware how large a claim this is to make for the Bible, and the very largeness of the claim has produced much painful doubt in many minds. But we must never argue from inconveniences. Truth

---

* Baylee, " On Verbal Inspiration of the Scriptures."

or falsehood is the only rational test by which to examine principles." He goes on to affirm that " this is indeed a large claim to make for the Bible, but it is not more than can be fully demonstrated. The Bible," he says, " is the word of God—it is appealed to as God's words, every natural image is found to be most wonderfully true, every scientific statement is infallibly accurate, its words and phrases have a grammatical and philological accuracy such as is possessed by no human composition ; it is not only God's word, but God's words : then it is indeed verbally inspired, every letter of it is stamped with the image of God, and with the superscription of His name as the unalloyed coin of His glorious kingdom."

Now I felt that this kind of dogmatism used by the advocates and defenders of a verbal theory of inspiration, while it is pleasing to a morbidly orthodox ear, and passes current with the disciples of a certain theological school, will never satisfy a calm and thoughtful inquirer, or a mind really anxious to " prove all things," as the proper preliminary to " holding fast that which is good."

I have no sympathy with those advocates of a theory of inspiration which ignores phenomena, and exalts *à priori* conclusions ; or, in other words, excludes the Baconian method of induction from the domain of theology.

If the sacred writers claimed this special inspiration, then indeed there would be nothing left us but to admit that a sound believer in Revelation must receive it, for inspired men best know the nature of the gift by which they are endowed. But they do not make any such claim, or give any such definition, as to exclude the inquiry as to what inspiration is, what are its characteristics, its extent, and its limits.

Now, while yielding to no man in my unwavering repose and unquestioning trust in the truth of God's word, yet it is in the truth of its great and saving statements, its revealed facts and doctrines that my faith rests : and not in the infallibility of its minute references to matters which in no way concern the competency of the writers to instruct us in Divine things.

Those who hold the verbal theory of inspiration represent the mind as the passive recipient of Divine truth ; and one illustration of this theory is, to quote their own language, " that the mental faculties of the Apostles and Prophets were like so many pipes of an organ into which the Divine Spirit breathed, and without any concurrence of their own, sent forth the music of Divine truth to ravish the ears of the world."

With reference to this theory, the idea is entertained by many, that a distinct commission to *write* was in every instance given to the sacred penmen by God ; that each book came forth with a specific impress of Deity upon it ; and that the whole of the canon of Scripture was gradually completed by so many distinct and decisive acts of Divine ordination. Now the evidence of this opinion must, I think, be regarded as totally defective, and its growth and progress in the Church can only be ascribed to the low and mechanical view of the whole question of inspiration itself. Let any one look carefully through the books composing the Old and New Testaments, and consider how many can lay claim to any *distinct commission ;* and consequently how their inspiration can be at all defended, if it be made to rest upon this condition, I am quite at a loss to determine. That Moses had a divine commission to institute the Jewish Theocracy, and to give both the moral and ceremonial law to the people, there can be no question ; but that does not prove any Divine commission to write the whole of the Pentateuch as we now have it. I would not have it thought by these remarks that I throw the slightest shade of doubt upon the *inspired source* of the Pentateuch, as perhaps no book of Scripture has greater internal arguments to vindicate its Divine origination. If we pass on to the books of Joshua, Judges, Ruth, Samuel, Kings, and Chronicles, where in any one of these books can we discover any specific Divine ordination that they should be written at all ? So far from finding this, the very authors are totally unknown ; and all that we can say is that they were universally received, both as veracious histories, and as containing correct religious sentiments, by the Jewish people.   In like manner the date and authorship of the book of Job are highly problematical, and the learned are quite at a loss to assign any other reason for its being received into the Jewish canon except the extraordinary religious value of its contents.

If we look again to the Psalms, respecting the authorship of many we are altogether ·in ignorance ; and those which are undoubtedly ascribed to David were evidently intended as sacred hymns and odes, some of them written for the Temple service, and others the natural outpourings of a mind at once devotional and poetic.   We cannot find in any case, as far as I can learn, that they were written by express commission, and all that we can say is that they embodied the religious consciousness, or, if the term be preferred, *the state of inspiration to which the mind of the writer was elevated.*

With regard to the prophetic writings, these certainly occupy a much higher position than the historical books, inasmuch as we learn that the authors actually received a prophetic commission to declare the counsels of God to the people.   This does not, however, necessarily involve any distinct and separate commission to *write* the books in question ; nor have we any reason, as far as I know, to regard their writings as inspired in any other sense than as containing the authentic announcements of their oral testimony.

Passing from the Old Testament to the New, the same entire absence of any distinct commission to the writers of the several books (with the exception perhaps of the Apocalypse) presents itself.   The Gospels, for example, were regarded in the second as in the nineteenth century, as authentic documents descending from the Apostolic age, and containing the substance of the Apostolic testimony.

I cannot but believe that upon the authenticity, or rather the apostolicity, of our Gospels rests their claim to inspiration. Containing the substance of the Apostles' testimony, they carry with them that special power of the Holy Spirit which rested on the Apostles in virtue of their office, and also on other teachers and preachers of the first age.

The subject is a very wide one, and second in importance to hardly any that can be raised ; but it seems to me, after a thoughtful consideration of the question, that the proper idea of inspiration, as applied to the Scriptures, does not include verbal dictation, or any distinct commission from God.

The inspiration of the sacred writers I believe to have consisted in the fulness of the influence of the Holy Spirit specially raising them to, and enabling them for, their work, in a manner which distinguishes them from all other writers in the world, and their writings from all other writings.

The *men* were full of the Holy Ghost, and "spake as they were moved" by His divine influence. The books of Scripture are the pouring out of that fulness through the men, the conservation of the treasure in "earthen vessels."

Some one has truly said that " the treasure is ours in all its richness, but it is ours, as it only can be ours, in the imperfections of human speech, in the limitations of human thought, in the variety incident first to individual character, and then to manifold transcription and the lapse of ages."

I would only add further my humble belief that the Scriptures contain all that is necessary to man's salvation. " It is not," to use the words of one who has written on the subject, " arithmetical truth, nor geographical truth, nor antiquarian truth, nor scientific truth, which we must go to the Scriptures to learn, but moral and religious truth. Errors may have crept in with the progress of time, and under the progress of transcription and translation; but, with all these errors and apparent discrepancies before us, they do not change a single fact, nor affect a single doctrine. The Bible is made up of facts and doctrines, not of the history of those facts and doctrines. The histories may vary, but the truths and the facts on which those truths are based are unchangeable."

What the Apostle John says, in concluding his gospel, is equally applicable to the entire Scriptures: — " These things are written that ye might believe that Jesus is the Christ, the Son of God, *and that believing ye might have life through His name.*"

There are those who would have us believe in the present day that a great part of the Old Testament is only valuable in an antiquarian point of view, and that much of its teaching has become obsolete. We are quite willing that the Bible should be put into the crucible, and subjected to the severest test that man can invent, as we have nothing to fear from true criticism. One who has devoted the labours of a life to the investigation of Biblical science,* has stated, that " the object of true criticism is not to alter Scripture dogmatically on the judgment of any individual, but it is to use the evidence which has been transmitted to us as to what the holy men of God, inspired by the Holy Ghost, actually wrote."

For my own part, I believe that one of the very greatest advantages an enlightened people can enjoy is the liberty of freely discussing every subject which can fall within the compass of the human mind. A great writer on moral and religious questions, lately removed from among us, says truly that, " however some may affect to dread controversy, it can never be of ultimate disadvantage to the interests of truth or the happiness of mankind. The colours with which wit or eloquence may have adorned a false system will gradually die away, sophistry be detected, and everything estimated at length according to its true value."

---

* Dr. Tregelles.

I have no fears as to the ultimate triumph of truth; and I firmly believe, in spite of all the open and avowed attacks made by infidels on the one hand, and by the more dangerous and insidious sophistries of those who hold high positions in the National Church on the other, that the Bible is the grandest, the noblest, the most sublime book anywhere to be found in the world.

About this period of my life my attention was called to the subject of Homœopathy; and, in order that I might know something as to the real merits of the question, I cast about for a book that would fairly present the matter for consideration. After looking at a good many works advocating its claims, written by members of the medical profession, I decided upon carefully reading a volume issued under the superintendence of the British Homœopathic Association, entitled, " Truths and their Reception, considered in relation to the Doctrine of Homœopathy," by Marmaduke Sampson.

I have never been deterred by ridicule from the examination of any subject; and it has always appeared to me to be a poor, miserable shift to smile or sneer at a thing you know nothing about, simply because a number of people have condemned it, and some great names have denounced it as a heresy not to be tolerated. Everything good in the world has been treated in this way, and I can recollect many things, that are now established and recognized facts, that for a man once to have confessed that he believed in, would have been a reason for his being counted a fanatic and a quack. Sometimes I have heard it sneeringly remarked, What can you expect from a man who believes in homœopathy? I can only say that, having examined as carefully as I could the evidence adduced for the correctness of the great truth, " Similia similibus curantur," I was thoroughly persuaded that reason and argument were in favour of homœopathy. Having ascertained that, I tried it first upon my own person with marked effect, and then upon my children with complete success. Since that period

o

I have had many serious attacks of illness, but have never doubted the soundness of Hahnemann's celebrated axiom; and I cannot but think that, had I been treated by what are called "the doctors of the old school," I should long ere this have "gone to the bourne from whence no traveller returns." More than fifteen years' experience of the correctness of the principle and practice, is not to be upset by a joke in "Punch," or a bitter paragraph from "The Lancet."

The Literature of Homœopathy now takes its place in the realms of thought, and among its practitioners are found some of the ablest physicians of the day.* There is a great advantage that the new system has over the old, namely, that Nature has a far better chance to right herself under Homœopathic treatment than by the large and ponderous doses of the old school; the longer I live the greater is my faith in the restorative powers of Nature. I do not forget the affirmation of Dr. Forbes, the late Editor of the "Medico-Chirurgical Review," than whom no one is more competent to judge, who says that the mortality, would not be so great if diseases were not treated medicinally.

I am not such a fool as to believe that Homœopathy is everything that could be desired, or that all that Hahnemann taught is to be believed; but I do believe that the world owes a large debt of gratitude to that great man for the discovery and application of a truth that must at no distant period be universally admitted and acted upon.

In 1850, I had another addition to my family—a little daughter. These arrivals were always looked forward to with very much pleasure, and never regarded as a misfortune, as I have sometimes heard friends, with what are

---

* For confirmation of this see the list of members of the British Homœopathic Association; and those who want further information upon the entire question will do well to consult a work entitled, "Homœopathy and its Principles explained," by John Epps, M.D.

called " slender means," remark. The birth of a child into a family ought ever to be regarded with joy. It was always so in my own case: I subscribe most heartily to what the author of " Proverbial Philosophy" says upon the subject :—

> "A babe in a house is a well-spring of pleasure, a messenger of
>   peace and love :
> A resting-place for innocence on earth; a link between angels
>   and men :
> Yet is it a talent of trust, a loan to be rendered back with
>   interest;
> A delight, but redolent of care; honey-sweet, but lacking not
>   the bitter."

Yes, these dear little ones always brought with them an increase of love : and that father is not to be envied, who, whatever else he may possess, has no love for his children, and does not feel it to be a happiness and privilege to toil for them. My children have been to me the occasion of my greatest joy, and some of the pleasantest hours of my life have been passed, not only in the enjoyment of their playful gambols, but also in working with hand and head for their welfare and happiness.

In 1851 we removed from St. John's-wood to the neighbourhood of Queen-square, that I might be nearer to my place of business, as my health began to awaken some apprehension on the part of my wife and family.

We were very loath to leave St. John's-wood for many reasons, but chiefly on account of our attachment to our dear pastor. However, I had learnt, among other things from him, that sacrifices must be made for duty, and that inclination must never stand in the way of a man's resolutely carrying out that which he sees to be right.

For seventeen years I had been a constant and careful attendant upon the ministry of this good man. I can never adequately express the deep sense of obligation I feel with reference to him. He was the means, under God, of first awakening within me a state of moral thoughtfulness, and of directing me to an Almighty Saviour. He gave me a taste for reading, and lent me from his own library books, the influence of which upon me will never cease. He instructed me in Divine things as "a workman that needeth not to be ashamed, rightly dividing the word of truth." He visited me in times of sickness and trouble, and comforted my heart when I have been well-nigh swallowed up of over-much sorrow. I feel, and I am right glad to record my obligation, that, whatever I am as a husband, a father, a friend, and a member of society, I owe it *mainly* to the preaching and influence of this great and good man upon me. He has recently retired from the ministry with a shattered nervous system and impaired health, and I trust that his declining years may be happy and peaceful, and that an abundant entrance may be ministered unto him, when he dies, into the everlasting kingdom of our Lord and Saviour Jesus Christ.

He has published only a few occasional sermons; but those who feel any interest in what he was as a preacher, can judge in some degree of his powers by a volume of sermons he has recently published, entitled, "Freedom and Happiness in the Truth and Ways of Christ."* The twenty sermons contained in this volume were selected as samples of his preaching, in the ordinary course of his ministry; and those who heard them with the living voice, and accompanied with the nervous power that he could put into them, will regret that such a man should no longer be heard in our metropolitan pulpits.

The apartments we occupied in Brunswick-row, Queen-square, were very commodious and healthy. It was one of the old-fashioned houses that abound in that neighbourhood. You might have driven a hackney-coach up the

---

* As this gentleman has now for many years retired altogether from public life, I may, without impropriety, give the title of his last published work: "A Retrospect of Forty Years in the Wilderness. A Sermon preached at Paddington Chapel, June 27th, 1858. By James Stratten. Ward and Co., 27, Paternoster Row."

staircase. Our front-rooms overlooked the garden of the Rev. Fred. Maurice, one of the most accomplished clergy-men of the Church of England, whose labours in con-nection with the Working-men's College will ever be remembered by a class that has, until lately, been sadly neglected. The back-windows overlooked the gardens in Queen-square, so that we had floral beauties and green trees both back and front.

There is, perhaps, no part of London more healthy than the neighbourhood of Russell-square. The soil is gravel, and the drainage for the most part good. The nearness to my official duties was a great convenience, as it enabled me to dine with my family instead of going to a tavern for that purpose. We missed, however, our walks in the Regent's-park, but, most of all, the ministry of our good pastor.

After hearing some of the Nonconformist ministers in the neighbourhood to which we had removed, we connected ourselves with a Church presided over by one of the most popular preachers of the day. Our new pastor was mainly distinguished by what I may call his hearty manner and devout demeanour in the pulpit, and which deservedly commends him to the sympathies of his large and highly respectable congregation.

The Church with which we were connected at Blooms-bury was what is denominated Baptist; but the constitution of its society was such that all Christians were admitted to its communion, and a large number of the communicants were Pædobaptists. Most of the Baptist Churches in Lon-don and the provinces are formed upon this Catholic basis, and the members of such Churches are found to work most harmoniously together. There is no compromise on the part of the Baptist, and his Pædobaptist brother is treated in all respects on an equality with himself, and has, more-over, the benefit, if he pleases, of seeing the ordinance of believers' baptism administered, and, consequently, of having the subject occasionally brought under his notice.

The services at this popular and crowded chapel were so conducted as to afford nourishment to the spiritual life, and the minister there is known to be a man eminently useful to a certain class of people. As a speaker from the platform, as well as a preacher, he is always listened to with attentive interest: and some of his lectures at Exeter Hall, before the Young Men's Christian Association, have produced a great and lasting effect.

This gentleman received me with his usual kindness and urbanity; and during the four years we attended his ministry he was everything that we could desire, both as a pastor and a friend.

For the next year or two of my life I cannot remember that anything occurred that would be interesting to my friends. I had still to work hard, not only at my ordinary duties, but also at other times whenever I could get any writing to do; and my vacations continued to be employed in earning money to meet the urgent necessities of our daily life, instead of being devoted to recreation and rest.

However, I had great reason to be thankful that my health was, for the most part, such as to enable me to devote my leisure hours in obtaining the means for making my home more comfortable, as well as procuring some suitable education for my children—a thing I have never been able to do from my ordinary salary.

In the spring of 1854 I obtained, quite unexpectedly, the office of Receiver of Publications delivered under the Copyright Act at the British Museum. I had some qualifications for this duty, having not only been connected with the bookselling trade from my earliest days, but I had already discharged the same duty for two of the privileged libraries from 1833 to 1842, so that I was fully acquainted with all the practical details of the work.

I had looked wistfully at the appointment ever since the death of my father in 1847; but as the duty of seeing that the Copyright Act was complied with, on the part of the Trustees of the British Museum, at that time rested with the secretary; the keeper of the printed books, strangely enough, had nothing whatever to do with the Act, but to receive the publications when they were transferred to the library from the secretary's office.

The Royal Commission* that was appointed to inquire into the constitution and management of the British Museum rectified many of the anomalies that existed up to that time; and among other things effected by that commission was, that the keeper of the printed books should henceforth have the entire management and control of the provisions of the Copyright Act, relating to the delivery of publications at the National Library.

As soon as a fitting opportunity presented itself, the gentleman at the head of the department I had served in, and without any application on my part, very kindly recommended me for the appointment as receiver.†

The work was most congenial to me, and the position it gave me in the establishment was in advance of that which I had previously occupied. The salary of the receiver of copyright publications, at the time I refer to, was but a few pounds a year more than I had received in

---

* An epitome of the voluminous evidence given before this Commission by Mr. Panizzi would, if published, be most interesting to those desirous of becoming acquainted with the rise and progress of the National Library. That evidence manifests a thorough knowledge and grasp of the subject; and with the new reading-room with its adjuncts, as a part of its practical development, will be a noble and an enduring monument to the fame of the eminent librarian to whom England and the literary world owe so much.

† This is only one of the many acts of unsolicited kindness that I have received from this gentleman. Since these pages were written, and while they are passing through the press, Mr. Panizzi has laid at Her Majesty's feet the high and responsible appointment she was pleased to confer upon him some years since. The Trustees of the British Museum, and the House of Commons, have alike acknowledged the eminent services of Mr. Panizzi, and I trust he may long enjoy, among his much-loved books and many friends, the rest and leisure so well earned, and so much needed, after a long and uninterrupted life of toil and anxiety.

my former position in the library; but the hours of attendance were lessened, and my vacation was increased.

I gave myself to the discharge of my new duties most unreservedly—so much so as to injure my already impaired health; but I was fond of the work, and I was also desirous of evincing my gratitude to the head of my department for having so kindly selected me for the office.

In the following year, 1855, my mother died very suddenly, after an illness of a single day. I was summoned to her bed-side immediately on hearing of her sickness; but it was believed that the medicines administered were of that powerful nature that she was perfectly stupified by them, and could not articulate a word, and was unconscious of anything that was passing around until she sunk gradually away.

There was no occasion for my mother to have made any expression of the state of her mind, as her previous life had sufficiently shown that she was a Christian of no mean attainments; and, after all, it is not so much how we die as how we have lived. She had been a woman of prayer from her early life; and her knowledge of the Scriptures, and delight in public worship were known to all her family circle. Towards the close of the day on which she died I whispered into her ear some passages of Scripture; she heard them, and tried to lift the heavy eyelids, but could not. There was a beautiful tranquil smile upon her countenance, and once I felt a slight pressure of her hand as I held it within mine. She slept away so softly, without a sigh or groan, that we could scarcely tell when she ceased to breathe. Her end was literally peace, and she fell asleep in Christ. As we knelt around her bed to pray, the feeling of every one present was, " Let me die the death of the righteous, and let my last end be like hers."

I had now lost both parents, and when that is the case there seems to be only a step between ourselves and death. How true are the words—

" 'Tis strange that those we lean on most,
   Those in whose laps our limbs are nursed,
Fall into shadow, soonest lost:
   Those we love first are taken first.

God gives us love. Something to love
   He lends us; but, when love is grown
To ripeness, that on which it throve
   Falls off, and love is left alone."

On the death of my mother we removed from Queen-square to what was then known as the New-road, near Albany-street. At this time the building long known as the " Diorama " was undergoing a transformation, and was just about being opened as a place of worship. It was one of the many commodious and elegant chapels erected in London and its suburbs by a worthy baronet, who is an enlightened and influential member of the legislature, and a man of truly noble and catholic spirit. His praise is in all the Churches, and his liberal purse is ever ready to help any movement that will benefit his fellow-countrymen. There are not a few such men among the ranks of Nonconformists; would that their number were increased a hundredfold !

I attended the opening services of this new chapel, and was much interested in all its proceedings. We had been induced to remove to the neighbourhood mainly that we might attend the ministry of the gentleman who had been prevailed upon by the generous baronet, who had erected this noble chapel, to leave a large and influential Church and congregation in one of our chief provincial towns, and enter upon this new and important sphere of labour.

I had heard some occasional sermons and lectures by this young minister on his visits to the metropolis, and believed him to be a man of rare and singular ability. We accordingly provided ourselves with sittings at this new chapel. Many of those who enter the Regent's-park by Park-square East, from Portland-place and the Euston-road, would not imagine, from the plain exterior of the building, long known as the "Diorama," that there is behind that unadorned entrance one of the most beautiful chapels in London. The style of architecture of this chapel is Byzantine. The pulpit is very elegant, from a design by Thomas, the late eminent architect; it is constructed of Caen stone, with panels of alabaster in each of the sides. The chapel contains sittings for more than twelve hundred; and there are also, in addition to these, two hundred free seats for strangers and the poor, with about a hundred and sixty sittings for the Sunday-school children connected with the chapel. It is said that the converting the " Diorama " into a chapel cost the wealthy baronet upwards of £20,000.

It has sometimes been sneeringly and contemptuously asked, What has Congregationalism and Voluntaryism done in connection with Dissenters? We might, in answer to this inquiry, point to the thousands of chapels that have been erected throughout the length and breadth of our Fatherland, where freedom to worship God according to the dictates of our consciences is the birthright of every Englishman; and also to the many schools that have been founded by Nonconformists, where not only the children of the poor receive a good plain education, that shall fit them to be intelligent members of the community, but where what are termed the middle classes may obtain a first-class commercial and classical education for their sons, and suitable instruction for their daughters, without subjecting them to the test of the Church Catechism, or requiring their assent and consent to any creed of man's devising. To quote from one who has paid some attention to this particular subject,* in an interesting paper, entitled, " The Position of Nonconformists:"—" We would remind our friends of other denominations that a Baptist minister was the founder of the Bible Society, and also of the Religious Tract Society; an Independent minister was the founder of the Deaf and

---

* Rev. R. Ainslie.

Dumb Asylum. Dissenters founded the Orphan Asylum at Clapton, since taken from them by Churchmen. An Independent minister founded the Infant Orphan Asylum, also taken from them by the wicked test of the Church Catechism; and then he founded the Infant Orphan Establishment, where there is no test, and where there is given to the child of the Churchman, in a Christian spirit, what the Churchman denies to the child of a Dissenter in a sectarian spirit. Dissenters founded the Orphan Working School, now on Haverstock-hill; a Dissenter founded the London City Mission; a Dissenter was the origin of the British and Foreign School Society; Dissenters have, with Churchmen, aided in building and supporting British schools over the whole kingdom. The Voluntary principle sent a Baptist missionary to India before a Church missionary, or a bishop, had planted foot on that soil, and when, to the disgrace of England and English law, he was obliged to take refuge in a Dutch settlement; and a Congregationalist was the first Protestant missionary to China: he translated the Scriptures into the Chinese language, compiled a lexicon, and both of these men—Carey and Morrison—rose to the highest distinction in India and China. The South Seas, Africa, Greenland, and every part of the world, have been visited and blessed by men of God, sent forth and sustained by the Voluntary principle. They have reduced spoken to written languages, translated the Scriptures, founded schools and colleges, made large contributions to literature and science, and have conferred on Britain immortal honour. The Church of England, as an establishment, has done nothing in other lands but what she has done on the same principle."

Lest I should be deemed partial and biased in what I have said and quoted upon this subject, let me transfer to these humble pages the testimony of the secretary of the Committee of the Council of Education,* who, in his work

---

* Sir J. P. Kay Shuttleworth.

on education, says : "The Congregational Dissenters havo ever been friends of freedom, defenders of the rights of the minority, and missionaries to the benighted villages of England, to the wild valleys of the Welch mountains, or the turbulent colonists of its mines, and to the regions of darkness and death, where typhus and cholera find their victims in our towns. They comprise a large and influential portion of the middle classes ; they claim to be descendants of the Puritans, who, whatever were their own errors, were stern and successful champions of the English Reformation, and have left a deep trace, not only in the history, but in the institutions, the manners, observances and character of the nation. They have just cause to point to their own independence of the State, as the first conspicuous triumph in this country of religion, unaided by traditional authority, by the power of a foreign hierarchy, or the protection of domestic princes. They embody principles of self-government, of which our race and country have in civil affairs exhibited the most successful examples, and they are at least sincere and earnest in their endeavours after a primitive and apostolic simplicity in their discipline and ceremonial. Communions having these high claims to respect, comprising not less than 4,000 congregations, and of 1,500,000 of members, representing 2,250,000 of the population, must wield no small influence on opinion."

Surely such a testimony as that I have just quoted, from a man occupying a distinguished position in the forefront of the advocates for the National Church, should have its due weight in silencing some of the small-fry of the Church of England, who are ever affecting to sneer at Dissent and Dissenters, as people beneath their contempt.

It would be an easy and pleasant task to quote from writers that are termed authorities in ecclesiastical questions, to justify our position as Nonconformists, and this from men who are notable members of the Church of

England, and in no way likely to favour Dissent. Congregationalists concur with Bishop Gibson, that "the
Christians in particular cities and countries are everywhere in the New Testament styled Churches, which
properly denotes an assembly of persons called together
in one body." We accept the 'statement of Dr. Isaac
Barrow, that "each Church did separately order its own
affairs, without recourse to others;" and that the apostolic
writings assume individual churches to be " able to exercise spiritual power for establishing decency, removing
disorders, correcting offences, deciding cases," &c. We
endorse the testimony of Gibbon, the historian, that "the
societies which were instituted in the cities of the Roman
empire were united only by the ties of faith and charity.
Independence and equality formed the basis of their internal constitution. Each formed within itself a separate
and independent republic." We believe with Mosheim,
the ecclesiastical historian of the Church, that "the churches,
in those early times were entirely independent, every one
governed by its own rulers, and its own laws;" that it is
" out of all doubt that every one of them enjoyed the same
rights, and was considered as being on a footing of a most
perfect equality with the rest."

Hence Congregationalists demand, in the words of Bishop
Stillingfleet,—" What ground can there be why Christians
should not stand on the same terms now as they did in the
time of Christ and His apostles? What charter has Christ
given the Church to bind men up to more than He hath
done?" Archbishop Whately tells us that in the constitution of the Primitive Churches each was " a distinct,
independent community on earth, united by the common
principles on which they were founded, and by their mutual
agreement, affection, and respect; but not having any
recognized head on earth; . . . and as for, so called,
general councils, we find not even any mention of them,
or allusion to any such expedient;" and that " each bishop
originally presided over one entire Church."

We believe, with Dr. Merle D'Aubigné, that "the Church, in the first three centuries, in the period of her simplicity, her charity, and her martyrs, was independent of the State. This was of immense advantage to her; for she could develope herself freely, conformably to her nature, while no foreign power interfered in her affairs, corrupting her purity."

Milton tells us, in the avowal of his belief, that "forced consecrations, out of another man's estate, are no better than forced vows, hateful to God, 'who loves a cheerful giver.'" And the learned Archbishop before quoted says, that, in proportion as any man has a right understanding of the Gospel, "will he perceive that the employment of secular coercion in the cause of the Gospel is at variance with the true spirit of the Gospel. . . . Parliament should have none other than civil functions. The Church of Christ should be legislated for by none but its own members."

John Locke affirmed that "the Church itself is a thing absolutely separate and distinct from the Commonwealth. He jumbles heaven and earth together, the things most remote and opposite, who mixes these two societies which are in their original, end, business, and in everything, perfectly distinct and infinitely different from each other."

"Christianity," says Archdeacon Paley, "is not a code of civil law. It can only reach public institutions through private character. . . . A religious establishment is no part of Christianity." Bishop Shipley said in the House of Lords, "The Dissenting clergy, I am told, declaim against all human authority in matters of religion. They hold that no Church has a right to impose an article of faith on any other Christian community. I believe from my heart they are right; at least, if they be not, he that can refute them is a much abler man than myself."

For my own part I repudiate the name "Dissenter," except in accommodation to a conventional usage of language. We are no Nonconformists to the "faith once delivered to the saints." Ours is not the sin of innovation. Ours is not the guilt of schism. We are as intimately allied with a National Church and a political religion as ever were Tertullian, or Polycarp, or Ignatius; as ever were Peter, or Paul, or John. In the words of one of the noblest Nonconformist ministers of our own day,* we may say :— "*We* have never dissented from the Church of the New Testament. It is not *we* who have forsaken the apostles' doctrine and fellowship. We abide by the primitive rule. We repudiate altogether the notion that our origin is to be sought for in the troubled reigns of the Tudors and the Stuarts. Brown was not our founder. The ejected Nonconformists were not the first Congregationalists. The persecuted Puritans did not originate our order. Geneva was not our cradle. To Calvin and Luther we owe not our birth. We trace beyond the Reformation. We are older than the Waldenses. The ancient fathers are to us but modern names. We have a higher antiquity than Rome. We are successors of the Apostles; our Church government is as old as the New Testament, and our founder is Christ Himself."

I return once more from this renewed digression upon Nonconformity to my own personal history.

It was a most inspiring sight to see that large and beautiful sanctuary which I now attended, crowded on the Lord's-day with intelligent and attentive worshippers; and still more gratifying to hear, from its manly and earnest minister, the glad tidings of salvation through a crucified and exalted Saviour.

In common with most other successful men, the minister of this chapel has had his detractors; he has been ignorantly and recklessly accused of not preaching the Gospel. Every strong and thoughtful man has his own way of treating particular subjects, and there is something more to do than declare from time to time from the pulpit that

---

* Rev. Newman Hall.

" God is in Christ reconciling the world unto Himself, and not imputing unto men their trespasses." This is only a part of the "glorious Gospel of the blessed God ;" but upon this great central truth the minister referred to was, and is, wont to dwell most clearly and fully. If men and women are to be taught "that the grace of God that bringeth salvation," is to be proved in its reception by "teaching us that denying ungodliness and worldly lusts, we should live soberly, righteously, and godly, in this present world," (Titus i. 11, 12), then these great moral lessons must be enforced. This is the grand end of all God's dealings with the world ; and in my humble opinion he is the defective and false teacher who dwells only upon the promises of pardon and forgiveness, justification by faith, and admission to the favour and love of God, without re- ference to worthiness of any kind, and who in doing so neglects to enforce the Divine requirements as to the moral duties of the Gospel. However, the published sermons of the man against whom this charge has been made, by those who have never regularly attended his ministry, will suffi- ciently answer this groundless calumny. It will be found by those who are interested in the matter that the sermons of this eminent preacher are, as one observes, " not only distinguished by a careful and a cultured style, but they abound in just evangelical thought. In varied and reite- rated forms the great doctrines of the incarnation and sacrificial atonement of Christ are fully and earnestly stated, and all this free from the mawkish and unctuous senti- mentalism which is so common in many of our pulpits, and which chiefly affects the most sacred themes. The ser- mons of this good man are at once manly and tender, full of just thought and reverential feeling."

Some of the truest and most lasting friendships I have made in life have been those that I have formed from the frank and spontaneous expression of my sentiments. This was the case with the gentleman that I have been advert- ing to. After hearing him for several successive Sundays,

and attending the week-night lecture, I introduced myself
to him at the close of one of the services as an admirer
of his preaching, and one that was willing to render him
any help that lay in my power. He received me in the
most kind and cordial manner, thanked me for my sympathy, and invited me to help him in the work of forming
a Church, and organizing a Sunday-school. To these
duties I set myself in right earnest; and when a provi-
sional committee was appointed for carrying out these and
other desirable objects, I had the honour of being selected
as honorary secretary, both for the chapel and also for the
schools.

Not long after this I was elected to the office of an elder
in this Church. I shall never forget the strange sensation
that came over me when I received the first intimation that
it was the intention of the members of the Church to elect
me to that office. I should as soon have thought of being
made Archbishop of Canterbury as that I should be selected as one to fill so sacred an office as that which I have
referred to.

For the information of such of my readers as may be
desirous of being informed on the subject, I may mention
that, in the apostolic churches, elders were an order of laymen who assisted those to whom was committed the stated
work of the Christian ministry. Dr. Macknight, an undoubted authority in all matters relating to the constitution
and discipline of the Church of the New Testament, thinks
that, in the apostolic age, the term elder was applied to
"all who exercised any sacred office in the Christian
Church," (Acts xx. 17-28).

Elders, in the Presbyterian discipline, are officers who,
in conjunction with the minister and deacons, compose
what is called the Kirk Sessions, to take cognizance, not
only of all grosser immoralities, but on some occasions to
carry their jurisdiction into the bosom of families, to dis-
arm private resentments, and arbitrate in cases of domestic
variance. In the Christian society to which I refer, the

elders discharged the office which originally belonged to the deacons—of attending to the interests of the poor. They were chosen from among the people, who had the power to dismiss them from the office at any properly constituted meeting of the Church.

The appointment of deacons in the first Christian Church is distinctly recorded, (Acts vi. 1-16). Their qualifications are stated by the Apostle Paul, (1 Tim. iii. 8-12). These weighty and solemn words were *again*, and *again*, and *again*, read and pondered by me. The standard of the New Testament is very high as to all who hold offices in the Churches of Christ; and I found it profitable to keep it in view, though I never could attain perfectly to its sacred requirements.

In 1856 I had the first of a succession of serious attacks of nervous exhaustion and mental depression. Hard work, and scarcely a day's vacation that I could afford to take as a holiday, began to tell upon me, and I felt it very much. I had hitherto been equal to any reasonable requirement made upon my energies, and I fear that I had drawn too much upon my resources. The work that I was officially engaged upon was of a highly responsible and harassing nature; and although the hours of attendance were not such as to press heavily, yet, unfortunately, my temperament was of that character as to lead me to tax my powers to the full extent while engaged in business; and not only so, but I carried all my anxieties about with me, and could not divest myself of them at home. I was compelled, in the spring of this year, to spend six weeks in the country; and though the rest and change were very grateful, after the many years of almost uninterrupted labour, yet I was so depressed that, though I had always been a lover of the country, and in former years had enjoyed the most exquisite pleasure in rambling about over hill and dale, finding " sermons in stones and good in everything," I could now find little or no enjoyment. Jaded and worn out, I felt most keenly and painfully that—

"The pleasant heights of breezy life,
The pleasant heights are past;
The sunny slopes of buoyant life,
The sunny slopes are past."

Surrounded by beautiful scenery, and in the midst of kind and loving friends, but I could derive no pleasure from the one, and would have shunned the other. In former years I had been as joyous and glad as were the birds that sang among the woods and the hedgerows; but now I wandered about silent and sad in the midst of all that was calculated to produce happiness and joy. I had many a time in earlier years roamed abroad in the same meadows, and along the same green lanes, feeling as light-hearted and gladsome as a child; but now a gloom and sadness had settled down upon me that made life a burden, and society of almost every kind an intolerable nuisance. I could derive no comfort from the consideration of the great verities of God's revelation to man, and thought myself shut out from all hope. I have taken a favourite book in my pocket, and have sought some quiet nook, or sat upon a stile, and have tried to read it, but could not. I have taken out my Bible, and turned to the most consolatory passages; but they all seemed to be intended for anybody but me. Everything within me was dry, barren, and lifeless, and I almost envied the sheep as they snipped off the short grass around me, and would have exchanged willingly my existence with one of the cows that grazed so complacently about my path.

This period of gloom and depression lasted for about three or four months, and it was not till the autumn came that I was better. I shall have occasion to speak of other returns of this fearfully trying disease, and will therefore now leave the unwelcome subject.

About this time I was introduced to a gentleman who had spent many years on the study of the human voice, and whose attention had led him necessarily to the investigation of the causes of what is called stammering.

I had made up my mind, sometime previous to this, not to try any more pseudo-curers of impediments of speech, as I had not only given considerable attention to the subject myself, and had read everything within my reach that had been written upon stammering, but I had also had the benefit of the treatment of no less than five of the most distinguished advertised curers of that distressing malady, without having derived any real and permanent benefit from any one of them.

As stammerers form a somewhat large class of the community it may not be uninteresting, to many of my readers, if I enter into a few particulars relating to this distressing calamity. I scarcely think that it is possible to speak in too strong language of the intense mortification endured by a sensitive mind suffering from this vitiated habit of speaking. I can subscribe, without any mental reservation, to what has been said of it by one who has suffered more or less from stammering all through a long life that

" It is as lack of breath or bread, *life hath no grief more galling.*"

What I have to say is not that which I have obtained from a careful and extensive perusal of the literature of the subject, but what I have myself endured, and from a close observation of its terrible effects upon sufferers with whom I have come in contact.

It is the uniform practice of pseudo-curers of stammering —and their name is legion—when they are unsuccessful, to throw the entire blame upon their poor mortified and dispirited patient. It has been my misfortune to bear this cruel and cowardly treatment, in addition to the bitter mortification of feeling that you must carry your infirmity still about with you ; and it has raised my righteous indignation against the men who have done this after procuring you as a patient by the most undoubted promises of " a certain and permanent cure."

There are happily exceptions to this rule, and it was

my good fortune to fall into the hands of a man who was at once a scholar and a gentleman, and whose knowledge of the difficulties which a stammerer had to encounter made him patient and persevering in his intelligent and gentle treatment.

I owe so much of my present freedom from stammering to the skilful instructions of this gentleman that I am glad of making this public acknowledgment of my great obligations to him; for, although the impediment of speech that I have laboured under from my boyhood is not entirely removed, I am enabled freely to enjoy the delightful interchange of thought in friendly and social converse, as well as occasionally to take part in public services, which would try a man who had never been afflicted with a stammering tongue.

The gentleman referred to is the Rev. W. W. Cazalet, A.M., who, in addition to his little work on " Stammering, the Cause and Cure," has written also a very able treatise " On the right Management of the Voice in speaking and reading," which has passed through several editions, and will be found to contain some truly valuable hints to those who are called upon to make public speaking and reading aloud a part of their daily business.

I have already stated in a former part of this work that I became a stammerer from being placed with a relative who had a bad impediment in his speech. The habit, like most other habits, was the result of imitation in the first instance, and it was not until I was sent to a boys' school that I began fully to feel the annoyances of stammering. It subjected me to a good deal of ridicule, as well as made it difficult at times for me to take part in the classes. The constant mortification, arising not only from the impediment of speech, but also from the ridicule of my school-fellows, produced in me an irritability of temper that has been a great source of sorrow to me all through life. If I was strong enough to thrash a boy who scornfully mocked me, I did; and if he were a great big bully

of a fellow, which was frequently the case, I looked upon
him with a silent angry contempt, and was obliged to bear
his unkind and cowardly treatment as best I could.

On leaving school I found that it was a serious objection
to my entering upon many avocations where talking was
required.   It was this that led my father to place me in
a conveyancer's office, where my pen, and not my tongue,
was chiefly called into requisition.

My stammering tongue did not, however, keep me from
making love to the pretty conveyancer's daughter, who
taught me to exercise my vocal powers in song, where the
words would warble on flowingly enough.   On leaving my
native place for the army it was a serious difficulty, and
turned my career into a widely different channel.   I found
it a great annoyance in business, and was glad enough
when I obtained employment in the National Library,
where my duties were chiefly confined to the pen.   There,
however, I have sometimes felt most keenly that—

> " 'Tis to be mortified in every point,
> Baffled at every turn of life, for want
> Of that most common privilege of man,
> The merest drug of gorged society,
> Words—windy words."

I have been often asked how I managed to get on in
courting, and have replied, that there are a thousand ways
of winning a woman's heart besides talking twaddle and
trash to her.   There is the language of the eye, and the
manly thought struggling, it may be, for utterance, but
still it is there ; and then there is the pen, by which a
man may put the woman he loves in possession of what he
feels in burning words, which his tongue would never let
him freely utter.

It is in society, and in public, that I have found my
infirmity the most annoying.   Though friends sometimes
" wound deeper by their compassion," yet they know us,
and will estimate us, not from what we say, but from what
we are : yet this is not the case with strangers.   I have

many a time been looked upon with pity by those to whom
I have been trying to make myself understood, and have
been obliged to mutilate and mangle a sentence which
would have been intelligible enough had I been able to
have given it uninterrupted utterance.

The most trying of all hearers to a stammerer is the
cold and unresponsive listener—one who will, perhaps, in
kindness, avert his face from yours, instead of looking at
you and expecting the answer. I have seen sometimes in
the quick, restless, anxious eye of a stammerer the terrible
struggle that was going on within, and have taken his
trembling hand, hot and feverish, that he might feel that
one understood his feeling of mortification, and sympathized in his sufferings.

It is not so much in reading that stammerers have the
greatest difficulty. I could always read aloud the grand
majestic lines of "Paradise Lost," or Gray's "Elegy,"
with little or no hesitation, as they flow on so musically,
that when you have once started it is almost impossible to
stammer. It is very different in dialogue, where quickness is required in taking up the various parts of a conversation; and the different characters must be borne in
mind, so that the voice, as well as the manner, may be
adapted to each in succession.

In my early days I read a great deal of poetry, and
committed large portions to memory, which I have found
in after-life most valuable, not only for the purposes of
practising the voice, but also from the pleasure to be
derived from the oral utterance of great and beautiful
truths in choice and elegant words.

In my solitary rambles oftentimes passages from "the
bards sublime" have been my never-wearying companions,
and have helped me to understand fully the beautiful words
of the author of the "Christian Year," when he says:—

> " There are in this loud stunning tide
> Of human care and crime,
> With whom the melodies abide
> Of th' everlasting chime;

Who carry music in their heart
Through dusky lane and wrangling mart,
Plying their daily task with busier feet,
Because their secret souls a holy strain repeat.

A stammerer will find the greatest difficulty in reading aloud, even when no one is present, some of the dialogue scenes in Shakespeare. Let him try, for example, the fourth scene in the first part of " Henry IV ; " and by the time he has endeavoured to personify the characters there introduced, he will find it no small relief to close the favourite author, for the more flowing lines of Milton, or the pensive musings of Gray.

Reading aloud is one of the most healthful, as well as agreeable exercises, when care is taken not to strain the voice or make any undue effort to give effect to what we are reading. We have high medical authority for affirming that reading aloud, even where there is a tendency to pulmonary disorder, is, when proper care is taken, salutary in promoting the healthy development of the organs of respiration.

Sir Henry Holland, in his " Medical Notes," chap. xx. p. 422, makes some most valuable remarks on this subject, and speaks of one or two remarkable cases known to him where a constitutional tendency to asthma showing itself in early life has been subdued to a great extent by exercising the chest on certain regulated efforts, of which recitation formed a part.

It must be borne in mind, however, that it is not mere recitation or reading aloud that will produce these salutary effects. The great matter is to acquire the right method of using the organs of the voice ; and for this purpose I can refer my readers with all confidence to the work of Mr. Cazalet, " On the right Management of the Voice," already referred to.

The subject of correct reading and speaking is treated in that work by a man who has thoroughly studied and mastered the whole philosophy of the question, and with an entire absence of that ignorant dogmatism and disgusting quackery which characterize many similar productions of men whose advertisements meet the eye in our public journals.

The literature of stammering is very interesting to those who are desirous of becoming conversant with the subject; and if the statistics of stammering could be correctly ascertained it would, I fear, present a sad picture of the wide-spread misery produced by this distressing· malady. Two well-known and distinguished literary men of the present day are not only the subjects of this painful habit, but have also written their experiences. I allude to the deservedly popular author of " Proverbial Philosophy," and to a distinguished clergyman and novelist, who has recently reprinted an article on the subject that originally appeared in " Fraser's Magazine."

An anonymous work purporting to be the experiences of a stammerer was published a few years since, under the title of " The Unspeakable." It is an amusing book for a wet day, or a country ramble; but it is, however, painful to read the experiences of those who have suffered from this " tyrannical Argus."

Many ludicrous stories have been told of stammerers, and I could add a few to the number, but that I question the propriety of repeating stories relating to others who have suffered from this mortifying and painful habit. I recollect some years ago calling at the house of a friend, where, from being well known to the servants, I was always allowed to pass in at once : a new servant answered the door one day I called, and of course waited for me to state my name and business. I made several ineffectual attempts, first of all, to ask if my friend was at home, and then, not having a card with me, to tell her my name. The girl stood very patiently holding the door in her hand for some minutes, when finding that all my efforts were unavailing, she left me in the passage to call her mistress. The lady, who was in an adjoining apartment, hearing that some one was a long time at the door, came forward, and I heard the girl say, " Oh ma'am ! here's a foreigner at the door wants something—but I can't understand a word he says." I was much amused, and called out to the lady, who immediately recognized my voice, and we enjoyed a hearty laugh at the adventure.

It has been remarked that stammerers can always sing and swear, without any interruption from their malady. I can in my own case attest the truthfulness of this statement. In my early life I used to chant what I was desirous of saying, when I had much to communicate, and I could always do this without the slightest difficulty, as the continuous flow of sound was uninterrupted. I regret to say that I also acquired a bad habit of interlarding my conversation with oaths, where I could do this without giving offence, and it helped me very much in my utterance by giving emphasis and force to what I had to say. I had great difficulty in after-life to break myself of this profane and vulgar habit, and I remember one instance in particular where the force of habit was rather singularly developed, when I thought I had gained the complete mastery of it. One day at the Museum the gentleman at the head of my department came to me in haste, asking for "Facciolati's Italian Lexicon:" it was out of its place, and I made several abortive attempts to tell him who had taken it. Finding that I was baffled at every point, I so far forgot myself as to recur to my old habit, and with a most emphatic oath told him at once who had taken the book. Of course I immediately apologized for this unwarrantable rudeness, and was forgiven as quickly.

This habit of swearing had become as inveterate as my stammering, and even in more advanced life, I have had to lay considerable restraint upon my " unruly member " whenever I have been stirred with strong feelings, lest I should inadvertently forget myself and recur to my old habit. Swearing is like swimming, when once acquired it can never be forgotten.

I always felt the annoyance of my stammering most of all in conversation, and it has denied me the privilege of that free and unrestrained interchange of thought which is the chief charm of friendship.

Hundreds of times have I gone away from the society of men and women of cultivated minds, who would have freely responded to any demands made upon them, but the thoughts that came to my lips rarely or ever found expression ; and I have sought, when I have left·their company, to relieve my labouring chest and wounded feelings by holding an imaginary conversation with myself, just by way of letting off the steam.

The poor timid man, that may sometimes be seen in company,—

> "who stands aloof, nor mingles with
> The wise and good in rational argument,
> The young in brilliant quickness of reply,
> Friendship's ingenuous interchange of mind,
> Affection's open-hearted sympathies,—
> That feels himself an isolated being,
> A very wilderness of widow'd thought !"—

demands our tenderest sympathy, for he loves sweet social converse, but he is forced to sit silent, because—

> "Nervous dread and sensitive shame
> Freeze the current of his speech."

Those only can fully sympathize with these sufferers who have themselves gone through the agonizing ordeal.

I recollect some years since meeting with a man, of distinguished ability as a civil engineer, who stammered so fearfully that he could scarcely articulate two words in succession without the most painful and distressing contortions of countenance. The anxious and beseeching look of this sufferer, when attempting to speak, was most painful, and I have sometimes grasped his hand and begged him to desist, as the efforts he made were so violent that I dreaded the consequences to himself.

It is fortunate that the habit of stammering is rarely
seen to afflict females, although the instance named by
me in the early part of my history was a notable exception.   To see the countenance of a woman distorted by
this terrible malady would be a sad drawback upon the
pleasure we derive from the uninterrupted flow of their
eloquent tongues.   If Lord Byron disliked to see women
eat, it is questionable if he would have enjoyed the society
of his fair friends, the Countesses of Guicciolo and Bles-
sington, had they been stammerers.

After all my experiences of pseudo-curers of stammering,
it is a consolation to me to know that the disease, or habit,
bad as it is, will really give way under skilful and persevering treatment.   In my own case I have had the double
misfortune of not only suffering the mortification incident
to the malady itself, but also the bitter feeling of having
fallen into the hands of those who promised me " a perfect
cure," and when that failed, cast the entire blame of their
failure upon myself.   It is no small pleasure to be able to
refer to one among the many who offer their professional
services to those who suffer from this affliction, who, I
know, possesses all the means at his disposal of relieving
the most deeply-seated impediment of speech ; and with
this concluding remark I will dismiss the subject.   I may
add, however, that the gentleman I have referred to is
not aware, until these pages meet his eye, that I should so
pointedly allude to himself in this matter of stammering.

In the spring of the following year I had a return of
the mental depression that I had previously suffered, which
lasted for several months, during which period I found that
it was with very great difficulty I continued to discharge
my ordinary daily duties.

These attacks of depression were the more trying from
the fact of there being little or nothing in my outward appearance to indicate ill-health ; and as sufferers from these
complaints are generally supposed to be persons too ready
to yield to despondency, I had abundance of advice from

my friends not to let anything worry me, and to try and take matters quietly and easily.

It is in vain to recount to any but a medical man the long catalogue of melancholy symptoms incident to this form of disease; and it has been a great relief to me to pour out my complaints to one both skilful and kind. The medical profession are justly famed for their tender and delicate treatment of some of the more trying maladies that " flesh is heir to," and but for this intelligent and sympathizing treatment in my own case, I think my sufferings would have ended in black despair.

Everything was done for me that medical skill could suggest, but my doctor insisted upon my appropriating my vacation to obtaining rest and recreation, instead of using it, as had been the case for many years, to purposes of business with the view of increasing my finances. I saw and felt the necessity of this advice, and acted accordingly.

As these vacation rambles are amongst the most pleasant reminiscences of my life, I shall endeavour to recall a few particulars relating to them.

IV.

BRIEF RECOLLECTIONS OF SOME VACATION RAMBLES, WITH THOUGHTS AND GLEANINGS BY THE WAY.

> " When thou haply seest
> Some rare note-worthy object in thy travels,
> Make me partaker of thy happiness."

> " As odours, press'd in summer hours
> From summer's bloom, remain
> To soothe and comfort, till the flowers
> Of Spring revive again,

> So memory's magic wand restores
> Gladness too bright to last,
> And in a flood of music pours
> Sweet echoes of the past."

IN recording these wanderings, of course, I do not write for the information of those who have gone over the ground themselves, nor for those who contemplate such rambles, as the world-known " Handbooks " of John Murray, and Adam and Charles Black; the " Practical Guides," and the " special edition " of " Bradshaw's Continental Guide," will afford correct and ample information upon all points connected with such peregrinations.

I simply record my own impressions of places that I have visited, and people that I have seen, for the amusement of my friends and the entertainment of those who, from various causes, have never had the opportunity of seeing much beyond their own immediate homes.

In the autumn of one year I accepted the invitation of a friend, who had known me for a long period, to accompany him in a short trip to the Continent. Up to this time I had never gone out of sight of the white cliffs of my native land, and the thought of seeing something of foreign lands charmed me much.

Our route was Paris, *viâ* Southampton and Hâvre. On arriving at Hâvre we visited the museum and other places of note there. I was much struck with the different manners and customs of the people, so entirely unlike our own; and everything was new and interesting, so that it was with difficulty one could believe that so great a change could be found in a people living so near our own shores. To hear every one speaking a strange language, and at every point to be wanting some information which you could only obtain by asking, taxed our little stock of French very amusingly, and convinced us how truly valuable is a thorough knowledge of a language spoken by a great people so near our own shores.

The ride by rail from Hâvre to Paris is very picturesque; and I began to be convinced that Frenchmen may be justly proud of " La Belle France." I should have liked to have had a day to have looked over the fine old town of Rouen; but our time was limited, and we were booked through to Paris direct.

Paris more than came up to all that I had expected.

The day we arrived there was fine, and the atmosphere clear and beautiful. We engaged apartments in a pleasant street in the suburbs, near the Barrière de Clichy; and having deposited our luggage and refreshed ourselves, we sallied forth to see the great city. The cheerfulness and activity of the people, as well as the handsome and tastefully fitted-up shops of the principal streets, were objects of admiration. Our first dinner in Paris was a very unsatisfactory affair, though we appeared to have partaken of many dishes. We got on much better at breakfast: the nice fancy bread and beautiful butter, with the incomparable coffee, made us praise our neighbours very much. The substantial meat-breakfasts of our own land are needed by the difference of climate; but such a meal in Paris would never be thought of.

The atmosphere, though so clear and light, I found very enervating; there seemed to be nothing for the lungs to bite at. The streets, though well watered, were not cool, and there was a disagreeable, faint, vegetable odour about them which was sickly and unpleasant. Frenchmen may, however, well be proud of such streets as the Rue Richelieu, St. Honoré, and Vivienne. We wandered along, almost unconscious of the distances we were traversing, being so much taken up with admiration at the Place Royale, the Place Vendôme, the Place de la Concorde, the Place des Victoires, the Place de la Bastile, the Place Richelieu, and others, too numerous to be noted down, but which are familiar enough to all our country cousins who have visited Paris. Our apartments overlooked pretty gardens, and the backs of some large houses in an adjoining street. I was not a little amused to see the windows thrown open, and men come out upon the balconies to shake the bed-clothes, and then help the women to make the beds. I can hardly imagine some of my friends in England doing this. A fellow that we saw every morning engaged in these domestic duties with his wife, went about his work very cheerfully, and enlivened us by whistling some lively tunes. One of these he gave us so frequently that I find myself even now often whistling it.

On the next day we visited the Palace of the Tuileries and the Louvre, where we spent some delightful hours in gazing upon the statuary and pictures, and were much interested in the fine collection of models of marine architecture. We returned again and again to the Louvre, and every time with renewed admiration. It is a truly magnificent collection, and is displayed with the most exquisite taste. The contrast with our own national collection, in point of arrangement, tells most unmistakeably in favour of our neighbours over the way.

We missed seeing the Imperial Library, in consequence of its being closed for some purpose, during the week we remained in Paris, and could only look up at the fine building in the Rue Richelieu, containing perhaps the largest, if not the choicest, collection of books in Europe. Our own National Library is rapidly coming up to it in point of numbers; and from all accounts there is no comparison as to the superior facilities afforded to readers who use our own magnificent reading-room, and those who seek to make themselves acquainted with the Imperial Library of France.

A stroll round the colonnade of the Palais Royale, to look at the shop windows, was a never-ending source of amusement to us. Frenchmen certainly possess the happy knack of displaying their wares to the best advantage. We may be " a nation of shopkeepers," but we have yet to learn the art of setting out a window in a way properly to display the articles for sale, and at the same time please the eye and not offend the taste.

The bridges are numerous, and some of them highly picturesque. The elegant suspension bridge De la Cité, with its ornamental Gothic gates at either end, is very beautiful; and so is the Pont Neuf, the largest and most frequented in Paris: but I do not recollect any that will bear a comparison in all respects with our London, Waterloo, and Westminster bridges.

We visited most of the principal churches, and I suppose the palm must be yielded to the Cathedral of Notre Dame, though I confess I was far more pleased with the exterior than the interior of that most noble building. The interior of most of the continental cathedrals that I have seen very much disappointed me, with the exception of Strasbourg and Cologne; there is, for the most part, so much bright ornament and colouring that meet the eye on every side, and such a close and vitiated atmosphere

Q

from the constant daily services, that I always felt glad to get outside and breathe the fresh air.

The Madeleine is a splendid temple; but it hardly looks like a place dedicated to religious services. We were much pleased, however, with the choral and instrumental service there, and heard a very earnest sermon from no mean preacher. We saw the sacrament of the Eucharist administered, and were not a little amused to see afterwards the collecting-bag handed round by a tall footman with a cocked hat.

We visited the far-famed Pantheon, or, as it is now called, the Church of Saint Geneviève. It is unquestionably a fine building, but nothing about it to inspire the mind of the beholder with lofty aspirations and noble resolves. The fact that the remains of two of the greatest minds that France has produced repose there,—Voltaire and Rousseau, —excite a melancholy train of thought, to think that such commanding talents should have been devoted to blot out the name, if that were possible, of that benign and beautiful religion introduced by Jesus Christ, and which blesses and ennobles any nation that will listen to its sacred teaching, and yield a willing obedience to its heavenly laws. What would France be if it were thoroughly imbued with a real and life-giving Christianity!

Our visit to the Jardin des Plantes was a most pleasant and agreeable one. It shows the desirableness of combining in one place, where it can be accomplished, not only the living animals and birds, but also a complete collection of prepared specimens, in order that the natural history student may have the two-fold advantage of studying the objects, both living and dead. Such an arrangement in our own National Museum would not only be a boon to the student of that particular branch of science, but would also afford room for the more ample development of other departments which it is desirable should not be separated.

The fine collection in the Museum of the Luxembourg, of paintings by modern artists, afforded us a rich treat.

The magnificent line of road terminated by the Arc de Triomphe was traversed by us repeatedly. We have nothing at all comparable with this elegant and gorgeous work of art in London. Our own " Marble Arch," at the top of Oxford-street, must not be named in the same day with this beautiful Parisian structure.

Every day of our week in Paris was so fully taken up that we omitted to visit the cemetery of Père la Chaise, and some other of the lions. We returned every evening to our apartments so thoroughly knocked up, that we had no desire to venture out to see Paris by night; so that that phase of Parisian life must be reserved for some future visit.

We did not leave Paris without going to see Versailles. If Paris is France, no one would have a very intelligent idea of Paris who had not seen Versailles. It is indeed a palace; and a long day spent in wandering through its almost endless galleries and saloons gives one a better idea of the history of France than any work that I know of. You are reminded almost at every point by some gorgeous article of furniture, or some splendid picture by Vernet or Delaroche, of the great national events that have taken place in the history of the country; and there is an air of princely magnificence in everything you see around, both within and without, of that truly regal place.

The extensive gardens and pleasure-grounds are in keeping with the Palace, and it is altogether a place of which any nation may be justly proud. The only Palace in England that at all approaches it is that of Hampton Court; but the comparison is greatly in favour of Versailles, both in extent and in the variety and beauty of its contents.

My impressions of the French people from what I saw of them are that they are a highly intelligent, active, quick, and responsive race. A glance at them will convince any one that they are a people that will continue to exert a great influence in the world. I was much struck with the frank and cheerful appearance of most of the men; but there was a care-worn, anxious look about the women that indicated their need of what we understand in England by home influences. During the short time spent in Paris and its environs I only saw one really pretty woman. The ladies in France know far better than our own fair countrywomen how to blend the colours in their costume so as to make a plain woman elegant and attractive; but they are wanting in that womanliness that gives such a charm to an English face.

Let any one take a stroll through the fashionable boulevards and parks of Paris who has been accustomed to Kensington-gardens and Rotten-row, or Brighton during the season, and if he has an eye for the beautiful, the palm will be yielded to our countrywomen.

Whatever may have been said in praise of French beauties, I am prepared to say of the women of England—

> "I deem the daughters of thy soil
> Have greater share of beauty's spoil.
> The clear blue eye, the ruddy lips,
> The cheek where rose in lily dips.
> The auburn locks that lightly throw
> A shade upon the temple's snow.
> The silver tones that sweetly tell
> The love that in your bosoms dwell."

Frenchmen are perhaps more gallant than ourselves in their treatment of the opposite sex; but women look more for strength and stability in men than for mere politeness, which after all may be only a covering for selfishness. I have seen a Frenchman almost overwhelm a lady near him with his attentions at dinner, but take care at the same time to keep the best parts of a cold fowl for himself.

The military have a very smart and soldier-like appearance, and for light service would, I have no doubt, fully bear out all that we have heard of their daring and dashing services in the field; but they contrast strangely with the firm and measured tread of our Coldstream Guards: and one can easily imagine that though our neighbours over the way are not wanting in courage, they have neither the power of endurance, nor the immoveable firmness of our fellow-countrymen.

After spending a very pleasant week or ten days at Paris, and seeing St. Cloud, we left the gay city by an early train one morning for Strasbourg, *en route* to the Rhine. The Strasbourg Railway is one of the longest lines in France, the distance being about four hundred miles. We left the handsome terminus by the 7 A.M. train, and had a most delightful ride through some of the fairest provinces of France, where the scenery, produce, manners and character of the people differ considerably. To have looked at the lofty towers of Notre Dame in the morning, and find oneself gazing up at the magnificent spire of Strasbourg Cathedral in the evening of the same day is a luxury that kings could not have purchased a quarter of a century ago; but railways and locomotives have so altered distances that now it is an every day occurrence to see the sun rise on the banks of the Seine in the morning, and before its last beams are seen in the west you may find yourself quietly reposing on the banks of the lovely Rhine.

After resting for the night at Strasbourg, we spent the greater part of the next day in exploring the cathedral, with its wondrous clock and its complete astronomical almanack. The tower of the cathedral is nearly five hundred feet above the pavement, and is indeed a master-piece of architecture. As my companion, as well as myself, was interested in "the black art," we did not forget that Strasbourg claims the honour of using the first printing press by Gutenburg.

We made our way from Strasbourg to Frankfort, where we spent a day in seeing the principal objects of interest in this lively city. The Goethe monument is a worthy memorial of the greatest writer that Germany has produced; and one could not but look upon the house in which the great child-like Goethe was born with something of the same interest that we attach to that in which our own great Shakespeare first saw the light. He was unquestionably one of the great lights of the world ; but a " lesser light " than the bard of Avon. The walks and promenades about Frankfort are very picturesque and beautiful.

The next morning found us on our way to Mannheim, where we embarked on one of the Rhine boats, to see that far-famed river. As we went down the stream the voyage to Cologne was a very rapid one, and in the evening it seemed more like a fair vision than a reality, that we had beheld in one short day the unequalled scenery of that majestic river, and its never-to-be-forgotten surroundings. As point after point came into view, we could only look up in silent admiration at the castellated ruins and vine-terraced hills as they succeeded each other in picturesque confusion, and longed for the quiet leisure and ample means to explore the inland glories of the Rhine.

We were landed in the evening at Cologne ; and the next day being Sunday, we visited the cathedral and most of the other churches. The views about Cologne are not famed for their beauty ; but in the evening we strolled up the Rhine for some miles, and obtained a fine view of the Seven Mountains bathed in the last rays of the setting sun, and lit up with those beautiful violet tints that must be seen to be fully understood.

We left the next day by rail for Calais, and found ourselves in the evening taking a mutton chop with our tea at the "Gun Inn," Dover. So ended my first Continental trip ; and I promise myself, on some future day, should my finances allow of such a luxury, the pleasure of a pedestrian tour through the Tyrol and Switzerland, and a run through Northern Italy. I should much like to see Rome.

EDINBURGH AND THE HIGHLANDS

INCE reading the "Waverley Novels," the poems of Burns and Scott, the "Noctes Ambrosianæ," and the "Recreations" of Christopher North, to which I must add the sermons of Dr. Chalmers and those of Edward Irving, together with the writings of Thomas Carlyle, the most profound and original thinker of our day, I had a strong desire to see the land that gave birth to these illustrious men—the famous

> " Land of brown heath and shaggy wood,
> Land of the mountain and the flood."

In 1858, and again in 1861, I spent two vacations in Scotland. My first visit was chiefly confined to Edinburgh and the adjacent neighbourhood, supplemented by a very pleasant week's run through some of the Highlands, with one of Scotia's sons, who had left his father's farm when a young man, and, like most of his persevering and persistent countrymen, had been successful on this side of the Tweed.

It is scarcely possible to speak too highly of the metropolis of Scotland. Edinburgh probably stands unrivalled as a city—its situation is magnificent; and there are few, if any, of my readers who have not read the glowing accounts from the gifted pens of Dr. Johnson, Sir Walter Scott, Christopher North, Hugh Miller, and Professor Aytoun.

Poets have sung its praises, and historians and novelists have dwelt upon its many beauties. In reading the glowing accounts of their fatherland I had sometimes thought them extravagant in their praises; but I must candidly confess that all the descriptions I have ever met with, even including those of Lord Macaulay, fell far short of the reality. Scotland exceeds in beauty and picturesqueness all that her many bards have sung concerning her; and even the accomplished and eloquent pen of the late Professor Wilson has failed fully to make her beauties known.

I do not wonder that Byron should have been charmed as he roamed about "through its open glades, dark glens, and secret dells," and that he could say of it—

> "England! thy beauties are tame and domestic
> To one who has roved on the mountains afar;
> Oh! for the crags that are wild and majestic,
> The steep, frowning glories of dark Lochnagar."

On my first visit to Scotland I spent some weeks in Edinburgh and its immediate neighbourhood. The city itself teems with interest, not only on account of its unequalled natural scenery, but also for its rich and varied historical associations.

If "that man is little to be envied whose patriotism would not gain force upon the plain of Marathon, or whose piety would not grow warmer among the ruins of Iona," as our great moralist observes, surely he must have a very small soul who could ramble about the old town of Edinburgh, and not feel his heart beat quicker as he is reminded almost at every turn of men who walked with kingly step to the scaffold, or who suffered in Christian firmness and meekness at the stake.

The Castle, with its many traditions, real and legendary, and the magnificent views to be seen from its ramparts, was a never-failing attraction to me. I visited it at early morn, and saw the sun rise with orient beams upon its black and frowning walls; and at even-tide have I lovingly lingered about its fortifications and look-outs, musing over the startling and interesting events connected with its chequered history and renowned story.

"Mons Meg" contrasts strangely with the more destructive "Armstrongs" of the present day, and the view from the

Bomb Battery is magnificent. Among other objects of interest in the castle are the small Norman Chapel, built by the queen of Malcolm Canmore, the Scottish Regalia, and the window from which the young prince was let down in a basket. Perhaps the best view of the castle is that which may be seen from the Grassmarket—the Smithfield, in more senses than one, of Edinburgh; but there are also some fine views of the fortress from the Castle Gardens in the valley below.

Heriot's Hospital, Parliament Square, the University, John Knox's House, Tolbooth, the Lawn-market, St. Giles's, Calton Hill, the Canongate, and Holyrood Palace were visited many times. I was particularly interested in the churches where the great Chalmers, and his no less illustrious colleague, Edward Irving, spent their best days. The Queen's Park, with its beautiful undulations, and its breezy healthful heather hills, was a place of daily resort with me; while Salisbury Crags, crowned by Arthur's Seat, were classic grounds. I have sat for hours together on the summit of Arthur's Seat, in the favourite niche of the great Sir Walter, reading from the Heart of Midlothian, and other of his works, faithful and graphic representations of the surrounding scenery; drinking in the invigorating breezes that may always be enjoyed there, let the day be never so hot and close in the streets of the city.

There are several Cemeteries in the vicinity of Edinburgh, some of them very beautifully laid out as gardens, and made as attractive as possible. They contain the precious dust of many of Scotland's noblest sons. I visited the "Grange Cemetery" frequently, and was glad to linger about the last resting-place of such men as Chalmers, M'Cheyne, Mackintosh, the "Earnest Student," and the lamented Hugh Miller, who fell a victim to an overwrought brain, and from whose writings I gratefully and lovingly acknowledge to have derived much pleasure.

"Dean Cemetery" contains the ashes of Lords Jeffrey, Cockburn, and Rutherford; and some of the aristocracy of Edinburgh; while not a few names of note are to be seen on the monuments, erected in the very pretty garden-like burying-place called the "Rose Cemetery." There is an interesting monument here, erected by her Majesty the Queen, to the memory of one of her faithful servants, to whom she was much attached. The environs of Edinburgh are very picturesque and beautiful, and I paid frequent visits to Granton, Trinity, New-Haven, Leith, Portobello, Musselburgh, Melville Castle, Dalkeith Palace, Roslin, and Hawthornden.

Hawthornden and Roslin are to the dwellers and visitors at Edinburgh very much what our Hampstead and Highgate are to us Londoners; although in point of beauty we must yield the preference to these Scottish places of resort.

One day at Hawthornden I met a party of three young ladies at the entrance of the grounds, who were annoyed by the attentions of some young fellows, who seemed disposed to make too free with them. Seeing the embarrassment of these young ladies, and being a man in advanced life, I offered my services to escort them through the grounds. My offer was courteously accepted, and it added very much to the day's enjoyment to ramble about this charming place in company with those who could not only appreciate its many beauties, but who could chat pleasantly upon the various subjects brought to recollection in connection with Roslin Chapel and Castle, as well as talk about the people who had visited William Drummond, one of the most distinguished of Scotland's earlier poets, and the friend of our Shakespeare and Ben Jonson.

We occasionally came across the gay gallant young fellows who were making too free with my fair companions, and they appeared to be a little vexed that I had supplanted them. They followed us on to Dalkeith Palace, and we found them again at Edinburgh in the evening.

I will not attempt any description of Roslin and Hawthornden; they are places which every visitor will be sure

to see : and those who are not so fortunate as to get so far
north will be better pleased to read some account of these
lovely places from those who have written specially about
them.

Dalkeith Palace, the property of the Duke of Buccleugh,
is about two miles from Lasswade, and is well worthy of
a visit. The Duke allows parties to see the palace and
grounds on Wednesdays and Saturdays ; while Hawthornden and Roslin can only be seen by visitors on 'Wednesdays. These attractive places can be reached from Edinburgh either by coach or rail. If you go by coach you
should be put down at Lasswade, and walk up the glen to
Roslin. The distance is only three miles, and the scenery
so beautiful that you will be well repaid for undertaking
the walk.

Lasswade, it will be remembered, is a little village, said
to have derived its name from a sturdy *lass*, who, in days
of yore, was wont to carry travellers over the Esk on her
back. It is interesting also as containing a cottage in
which Sir Walter Scott spent some of his happiest years.

I had arranged to spend my last week in Scotland with
a reverend friend from London. We met at Glasgow,
and set out from thence for a run through the Highlands.
Taking the steamer on the Clyde, we steamed down to
Dumbarton, and from thence by rail to Balloch, and soon
found ourselves on one of the fine steamers on Loch
Lomond. The day was showery and misty, so that we did
not see to perfection the enchanting scenery of this king
of Scottish lakes. The glimpses that we obtained at
several points were very beautiful, and the mist acted
like a thin veil, through which we gained occasional views
of the graceful slopes and monarch crown of Ben Lomond.
Had the day been fine we should have landed at Rowerdennan, and climbed the mountain, but it would have been
labour in vain to have done so.

My fellow tourist was a Scotchman, familiar with the
scenery, and he pointed out to me, as we steamed along

over its placid waters, many beautiful views. Loch Lomond is so extensive that different views may be obtained of its beautiful scenery at every turn of the vessel.

We landed at Inversnaid, and walked across the moor to Stronachlacher, a distance of about six miles, to Loch Katrine. The rain now came down peltingly, as rain does in Scotland, and we were glad to find both shelter and refreshment at the little inn that stands at the head of the loch. The rain continued to pour down in torrents; but finding that there was no probability of its holding up, we took our places on the smart little steamer that plies up and down this queen of Scottish lakes. All the passengers but ourselves took refuge in the cabin, but as we were furnished with waterproofs, we continued on deck, as the steamer moved silently and leisurely through the dark and deep waters. In spite of the rain we enjoyed the ten miles sail down this beautiful lake; and as we were both pretty well up in Scott's poems, we recited to each other some of the well-known passages of the great Sir Walter, so faithfully descriptive of the scenery through which we were passing. The views of "Ellen's Isle" and the surrounding scenery at the bottom of the lake can hardly be surpassed for quiet beauty. The grey mist hid the giant form of Benvenue, with its wild crags, from our gaze; and as the pitiless rain continued to fall, we could not linger to look at the views at the lower end of the lake, and were compelled to hurry through the far-famed Trossachs, to find shelter at the castellated hotel, about half a mile from the lake.

It is curious to observe, while passing through this classic district, how tradition may spring from pure fiction. Events which were the creation of the fertile brain of the great "Wizard of the North," half a century ago, are now gradually coming to be believed as veritable history by the people around, and the guides will point out to you the exact spot where Fitz-James's horse fell, as if it were a well authenticated historical fact.

The Trossachs' Hotel demands more than a mere passing mention. It is really a magnificent turreted edifice, which owes its present proud condition to the constant stream of tourists through these romantic scenes during the summer and autumn. We ascertained that this excellent, and well-conducted hotel was, not very many years since, a little cottage, owned by a farmer of the neighbourhood; but that soon after the "Lady of the Lake" was published, the cottage was so crowded by visitors to Loch Katrine, that further accommodation was required. The present building owes its erection to Lord Willoughby d'Eresby, and is quite a princely-looking place. The fare is all that could be desired, and the sleeping apartments most comfortable, the crowning glory is, that the charges are very moderate, and the attentions of the officials most courteous and intelligent. After resting for the night in these very comfortable quarters, we awoke early in the morning, and climbed to the summit of Ben An, which lies immediately behind the hotel. The rain had ceased, and the morning was clear and bright, so that we obtained a splendid view of Loch Katrine, Benvenue, Ben Ledi, and the renowned scenery of that classic spot through which we had passed on the preceding day.

Our walk gave us a keen appetite for a good breakfast; after which we shouldered our knapsacks to pursue our wanderings in search of the beautiful. We soon found ourselves by the side of Loch Vennacher, a pretty lake of five miles long, and about a mile and a half broad. Two small islands rest upon its bosom, and the scenery around is soft and verdant. Scott says of it—

> "Here Vennacher in silver flows,
> Here, ridge on ridge, Benledi rose;
> Even the hollow path twined on
> Beneath steep bank and thundering stone;
> The rugged mountains' scanty cloak
> Was dwarfish shrubs of birch and oak,
> With shingles bare, and cliffs between,
> And patches bright of bracken green,—

> But where the lake swept deep and still,
> Dark osiers fringed the swampy hill;
> And oft both path and hill were torn
> Where wintry torrent down had borne,
> And heaped upon the cumber'd land
> Its wreck of gravel, rocks, and sand."

Leaving Callender on our right we marched on through the rugged pass of Leny to Loch Lubnaig, obtaining some fine views of Ben Ledi, which from its position has been called " the advance guard of the Highland hills." As we had a long day's walking in prospect we did not ascend Ben Ledi ; but we were informed that the view from the top is very fine, embracing the entire breadth of Scotland, from the Pass of Jura on the west, to the Bass Rock on the east ; while the prospect northward extends to Inverness, and southward to the English border. The scenery in the vicinity of Loch Lubnaig gives you a general impression of grandeur, but on the immediate margin of the lake the banks are soft and verdant, contrasting pleasantly with the rugged steeps of Ben Ledi. We strolled on leisurely by the side of the lake through Ardchulleric to King's House, where we arrived in time to see the sun go down behind Ben Voirlich, as we took a ramble after an early tea.

We started early the next morning, and walked to Lochearn Head to breakfast; after which, leaving the lonely and desolate scenery of Loch Voil and the Braes of Balquhidder on our left, we pursued our way to Glen Ogle, a wild and picturesque walk to Killin. This latter place is very beautiful, and to an artist would afford some fine sketches ; but as neither of us possessed this accomplishment, we lingered at Killin, and took into our mind's eye all the beauties of the place. Having taken some bitter beer and biscuit at the inn, we reached Loch Tay, and took the left-hand road by the side of the lake, with Ben Lawers towering just above us all the way to Kenmore. On arriving at Kenmore we took a hasty early dinner, and set out to see the far-famed Taymouth Castle.

Both the castle and the grounds in which it is embosomed are thrown open to the tourist; on applying at the entrance lodge, we were furnished with a fine young intelligent fellow, in full Highland costume, to conduct us through the park, and point out the more beautiful views to be obtained from this matchless domain, where Nature has lavished her bounties so profusely, and where wealth has called in the aid of art, and the most exquisite taste, to make Taymouth Castle and its surroundings a kingly place. The interior of this baronial castle is very spacious, and furnished fit for a monarch. The proprietor of this noble domain, the Marquis of Breadalbane, is married, but there is no offspring. His grounds are so extensive that he can ride a hundred miles, to the broad Atlantic, through lands he calls his own; but no child is there to run to him on his return, and to call him father. Who that has a child to love him would exchange with the noble owner of Taymouth Castle? A man may not have an inch of ground to call his own, but may nevertheless be an inheritor of the earth, and possess all things. It reminded us of the poet's lines—

> "Cleon hath a million acres,
>   Ne'er a one have I;
> Cleon dwelleth in a palace,
>   In a cottage I;
> Cleon hath a dozen fortunes,
>   Not a penny I;
> Yet the poorer of the twain is
>   Cleon, and not I.
>
> Cleon, true, possesseth acres,
>   But the landscape I;
> Half the charms to me it yieldeth
>   Money cannot buy;
> Cleon harbours sloth and dulness,
>   Freshening vigour I;
> He in velvet, I in fustain—
>   Richer man am I.
>
> *   *   *   *   *
>
> Cleon sees no charm in nature,

> In a daisy I;
> Cleon hears no anthems singing
>   In the sea and sky;
> Nature sings to me for ever,
>   Earnest listener I;
> State for state, with all attendants,
>   Who would change? NOT I."

We left Taymouth Castle with the persuasion that very few of the ancestral halls renowned in ancient story can equal this Highland home of the Marquis of Breadalbane; and we wondered not that our good Queen, when on a visit to the noble owner with her late lamented consort, should have remarked to their host that " she lived in a house— he in a palace."

On the following morning we left Kenmore, and walked about three miles through the grounds of the noble marquis, to Cusheville Inn, where we breakfasted. By the way, I may just mention that these morning walks gave us always a good appetite for breakfast, and that it would have been a saving to the innkeepers if we had adopted the more usual custom of taking this important repast before setting out for our daily peregrinations.

We left the coach-road and crossed the moors to Blair Athole. Though we were occasionally rather at a loss to pick out our way, and missed the comforts of an inn, yet by the aid of a good tourist's map, and a little inquiry of the shepherds we met with in these lonely plains, we got on pretty well, and were rewarded for all our pains by seeing a good deal of fine scenery not mentioned in any of the guide-books.

On reaching the high ground a few miles from Cusheville, we sighted Schichallion—a mountain between three and four thousand feet high, and having a peculiar summit resembling a half-crescent. In crossing the moor to the river Tummel we had this fine mountain in view under various aspects the greater part of the day. We wandered along upon the beautiful heather in the direction, as nearly as we could guess, of Blair Athole, and about noon found ourselves at a little straggling village called Foss.

The long walk and the bracing air had reminded us that "the inner man" needed attention, and we cast about to find an inn. Upon inquiry we regretted to learn that there was nothing of the kind within two or three miles. "Tummel Inn" was the nearest, and to go there would lead us some miles out of our projected route to Blair Athole. Tired and hungry, we looked round the little hamlet to see if there was any house that we might venture to ask for a bason of milk and a little oatcake. The mánse was the best house to be seen, and I suggested to my reverend friend that he should make himself known to the minister as " a brother chip," and ask for " a cup of cold water." After some little hesitation my proposition was agreed upon.

As we approached the neat little house we saw a tall, reverend-looking man pacing up and down the lawn by the side of the manse, apparently meditating upon some abstruse question, or thinking out a sermon for the next Sabbath. He was a man of middle-age, with a thoughtful, benevolent countenance; and as we approached the low wall that separated the garden from the road, he came forward to meet us. We inquired of him if there was any inn in the place, and found our village friends were right in the information they gave us. On learning this my companion, who was the chief speaker upon all occasions, rather hesitatingly told him that he was a brother minister, that I was an elder in his kirk, and that we needed a little refreshment. He immediately came to the gate and invited us into his pretty little house. In a few minutes we found ourselves quite at home with our good brother, and there was placed before us a plentiful supply of bread and cheese, butter, oatcake, honey, and a large jug of milk. We found our good Samaritan was a bachelor, and a very intelligent fellow. The welcome was so cordial, and the fare so good, that we did justice to our friend's luncheon,

B

and chatted away for an hour or more upon all sorts of
subjects. Our host would not let us leave without taking
"a wee drop of whiskey." Having regaled ourselves and
being rested, our kind brother walked with us down to the
ferry at the Tummel. We parted with many mutual good
wishes, and on our part with most grateful expressions for
the kind and generous treatment we had found at this
Highland manse. We left our cards with the minister,
and hope some day to see him in London, that we may
reciprocate his timely and brotherly hospitality. There
are thousands of kindly hearts behind a somewhat cold
exterior, if we would but put them to the test; and I verily
believe that, in the present instance, it was "more blessed
to give than to receive." If a cup of cold water, given in
the name of a disciple, will not go unrewarded, this kindly
hospitality of the minister at Foss shall not be forgotten.

Having crossed the Tummel, we pursued our journey,
and reached Blair Athole by way of Glen Rannoch, and
so concluded a very pleasant day. We had a great desire
to see Glen Tilt; but the Duke of Athole had shut up
that picturesque and romantic spot to tourists, and consequently we could not gain admission. On my next visit
to the Highlands I was more fortunate, and enjoyed a
day's ramble through its wild and beautiful scenery by
way of Castleton of Braemar.

The next morning we mounted our knapsacks and
strolled leisurely on to the celebrated Pass of Killiecrankie,
the well-known scene of "the bloody Clavers," one of
Scotland's most hated foes. The Pass stretches away for
a mile or more by the side of the river Garry. The hills
rise from the bed of the river perpendicularly, forming a
solid wall of rock. On either side the banks are clothed
to the height of several hundred feet with waving birch-
trees, while Ben Vracky looks frowningly down upon the
Pass. The terraced slopes approaching this beautiful
valley are adorned by several picturesque villa residences.
I did not enjoy our ramble so much on this occasion, as I

walked with a large blister under my great toe, produced by the rather hard walking of the previous days.

We made Pitlochrie our resting-place for the night, and the next day found us at the pretty little city of Dunkeld. The entrance to this beautiful place is most imposing and magnificent, as the hills on the opposite valley approach each other, clothed with dark pine-forests and interspersed with immense masses of naked rock. The Tay runs through the town towards the sea, and the plain upon which the city stands is embosomed among wooded hills and mountains.

We took the rail from Dunkeld to Perth, but could not stay there; but continued our way to Edinburgh by Dysart, Kirkaldy, Kinghorn, Burnt Island, and Granton.

So finished my first tour in the Highlands. I had seen in a week more than enough to make me desirous of visiting other famous places of

> " The land of the mountain and flood,
> Where the pines of the forest for ages have stood;
> Where the eagle comes forth on the wings of the storm,
> And her young ones are rocked on the high Cairngorm."

SECOND VISIT TO THE HIGHLANDS.

MY next visit to Scotland was in 1861. I had for my fellow-tourists two old and valued friends, in addition to my Caledonian companion on the last occasion. I cannot resist the desire to let my readers know that the addition to our party was a very happy one. One was an Australian merchant on a visit to England for two or three years, and who, since his return to the land of his adoption, has been elected an M.P. for one of the most important constituencies in South Australia. He was a man of middle

age, with irresistible energy and quickness of perception.
During our month's tour he was ever ready to do any, or
all of us, a service—as genuine and kind-hearted a fellow
as ever stood in shoe-leather, never thinking anything a
trouble, singularly free from selfishness, full of fun and
frolic, and as genial as a May morning.   Our other
companion was a warm-hearted, active fellow, who by his
rare mechanical skill has a hundred times supplemented
the accomplished knife of Liston and his cutting colleagues.   He has made for himself a name famous among
surgeons for inventing and manufacturing anything needed
by the profession, from a cork-leg fit for a duchess, to a nose
that would adorn the face of a duke.   Mechanical skill of
this delicate character is rather rare in the world, and we
could but congratulate ourselves upon having such a man
with us, in case of any mishap in our own wanderings.

With such men as companions, a month's pedestrian
tour in the Highlands, or indeed anywhere else, could not
but prove a treat.   Whether we were walking by the
way, fondly gazing upon the beautiful scenes around us,
or sitting in an inn enjoying our " creature comforts," we
were as " jolly as sand-boys "—however jolly those happy
fellows may be.   It added no little to our enjoyment,
that, being all of one mind as Christian brethren, we could
present together our united and grateful adorations to the
great loving God who had spread out before us so many
scenes of beauty and grandeur, and who watched over our
wanderings with more than a Father's tenderness.

Having parted with our wives at King's Cross Station,
we started by the mail-train, and found ourselves next
morning at Edinburgh, where, after getting a wash and a
substantial breakfast, we left at once by rail for Stirling,
through Linlithgow and the memorable field of Bannock-
burn.

As we came upon these stirring spots our reverend
brother warmed up, and began to praise his native land,
for—

"Dear to him was Scotland,
In her sons and in her daughters,
In her Highlands, Lowlands, islands,
Regal woods and rushing waters;
In the glory of her story,
When the tartans fired the field,
Scotland! oft betray'd—beleaguer'd—
Scotland! never known to yield."

Stirling and its Castle are very interesting in an historical point of view. It was not, however, on account of the many sieges it had sustained; nor that it was the birthplace of kings; nor that it was the favourite residence of the Stuarts that we came to it—not that the place was less interesting to us on these accounts, but we were pilgrims in search of the picturesque and the beautiful, and there are few spots, even in Scotland, that can equal Stirling in this respect. The views from the castle and the adjacent churchyard are perhaps unequalled by any to be seen in the Highlands, as they combine, with great extent and extreme fertility, a magnificent range of mountains stretching away through the valley. Any description of such a scene from my humble pen would be an impertinence; it must be gazed upon to be appreciated; and without being extravagant in my praises, for my own part I should have been fully repaid for the long journey if Stirling alone had been the object of our visit. Two of our party had seen Stirling before, but it was all new to our Australian friend and myself. In addition to the information supplied by Adam and Charles Black, in their excellent "Scottish Tourist," we had the benefit of our bishop, who was full to overflowing in everything relating to the land of his nativity. We were also joined by Mr. Culross, the Baptist minister there—a man of refined taste and elegant mind, and a poet of no mean order. This gentleman gave us the benefit of his genial society, and kindly pointed out to us all the points of peculiar interest in the glorious panorama stretched out around us on every side for many miles.

The churchyard on the opposite hill to that on which stands the castle has been tastefully laid out, chiefly at the cost of the well-known Peter Drummond, who has also erected statues to the memory of James Guthrie, the Stirling martyr, John Knox, Andrew Melville, Ebenezer Erskine, and other illustrious Scottish worthies. There is an exquisite group in white marble, to commemorate " Margaret Wilson of Glenervoch, the Virgin Martyr of the Ocean Wave, and her like-minded sister Agnes."

Here also, in this beautiful spot, you may slake your thirst at a fountain from which flows a stream of the coolest and most delicious water. There is a crag to the south of the valley called " The Ladies' Look-out," from having been used by the fair maidens, during the courtly days of Stirling, as a natural gallery from which might be seen the tournaments, and other sports which were then displayed in the valley beneath.

After lingering upon the ramparts of the castle, and resting ourselves in the pleasure-grounds adjoining, we reluctantly descended into the town, where we hired a conveyance to the Trossachs. The scenery from Stirling, through the Bridge of Allan and Callender, is very picturesque. The first view of the Trossachs from the banks of Loch Achray is possibly the finest—certainly it is the most striking. The great Sir Walter has depicted this scene with his usual faithfulness and power, though even his description falls immensely short of the reality.

We took a stroll after tea to Loch Katrine, and wandered by the margin of the lake by moonlight for a couple of hours. Ben An, Ben Ledi, and Ben Lomond, were at times distinctly visible, though their bald heads were occasionally half veiled by mists, which only made them look, if possible, more beautiful, as does the fair face of a bride seen through her veil. The scene all around was beautiful; everything so still and quiet that we hardly liked to break the silence by our own voices. After taking our fill of this enchanting lake, we returned through the Trossachs, and by the side of the little fairy-looking Loch Achray, the waters of which wash the road. The moonbeams were resting upon its peaceful and quiet bosom, and we went happily to our comfortable beds at the hotel, sleeping soundly enough after our previous night's journey from London.

Breakfast over on the following morning, we walked up to the foot of the lake, where, finding that we had an hour or more to wait for the steamer, we hired a boat and rowed up to "Ellen's Isle," the spot immortalized in "The Lady of the Lake." Having landed, we ascended by a natural staircase to the centre of the island, where such a scene of quiet beauty surrounded us on every side, that for a while we gazed upon it in silent admiration. One of the party proposed that we should sing the beautiful lines beginning with—

"Triumphant Lord ! Thy goodness shines."

The words were so expressive of our joy and gladness that we sang them out right manfully; and if our voices were not the most musical, our hearts fully responded to this well-known sacred lyric.

We did not like leaving this lovely spot; but as our time was limited, we rowed back to our starting-point, and took our places on board the pretty little steamer, "Rob Roy," to sail up the lake. The morning was bright, with occasional showers ; and as we steamed up the loch we amused each other by repeating portions of "The Lady of the Lake " as the scenery around suggested passages from that beautiful poem. No one should pass through this classic scenery who has not read Scott's poems and the Waverley Novels. Every point of interest has been noticed and faithfully delineated by the great novelist and poet, and it is quite a relief to find your own exhausted vocabulary of epithets of admiration supplemented by the magic pen of the great "Wizard of the North."

Some one has said :—

> " The world is full of poetry; the air
> Is living with its spirit; and the waves
> Dance to the music of its melodies,
> And sparkle in its brightness."

Poetry is never so beautiful as when that which gave rise to it is around you : it is then you feel it to be a relief to the pent-up feelings to repeat stanzas of immortal verse, such as the circumstances demand, and as only a master-mind could have penned.

Having gained the head of the lake, some of us tried to repeat the unpronounceable name of the inn there : we could only do it satisfactorily after repeated lessons from our reverend friend, who always put us right in all matters relating to his country. We set out to walk across the moor to Loch Lomond, instead of coaching it, and in about an hour and a-half found ourselves at Inversnaid. The graceful and classic scenery of Loch Katrine should always be seen first, as it prepares the way for the grander beauties of Loch Lomond.

From Inversnaid we steamed up the loch to Rowerdennan, the best point for ascending Ben Lomond, which rises immediately from the small inn that lies at its base. Having refreshed ourselves with beer and biscuits and ordered dinner, we started for the mountain ; but on climbing about two miles my respiratory organs reminded me that I was not quite so young a man as I imagined ; and as I had been an invalid for some months before taking this Highland tour, I though it wise to give up the thought of climbing to the summit. My disappointment was very great, as may be imagined ; but I sat down on a mossy bank and philosophised upon my condition as well as I could, and contented myself with the scenery around. I could not, however, forget that Dr. Chalmers had said, on seeing the view from the summit of this grand old mountain, that he " scarcely thought anything even in heaven could be more beautiful."

As I sat pensively musing I took out my Bible, and

thought of the analogy between Nature and that sacred record. In both we may trace the hand of God. His creation is broken at every point: here a sheltered valley, there a profound abyss on one side of a mountain whose summit is in the clouds, whilst on the other there is a leaping, noisy cataract. Here we may have spread out before us soft and verdant pastoral scenery, with

> " Quiet breadths of evening sky,"

and off in the distance the great and wide sea, where the waves lift up their voice. In the heavens above the stars move in separate paths, and shine with varied degrees of glory. And when we look into the Bible there is the same sublime diversity: on one page there are, as it were, pastures clothed with flocks, and valleys covered over with the yellow corn; on the next page we look up to heights, and down into depths, where there are such hidings of God's purposes that the loftiest faculties of man are baffled and abased. We may follow our blessed Lord to the quiet home of the Marys and Lazarus, his "own familiar friend," where kind and loving words drop from His divine lips; or we may go up with Him to the mountain of transfiguration, where the brightness of Heaven glows and glistens from His face; and then, again, walk with Him mournfully to dark Gethsemane, and gaze in silent admiring wonder at the wondrous scene at Calvary. The blending of the divine and human in the person of Christ is, to my mind, one of the most convincing of all proofs that " certainly this was the Son of God; " and there is an irresistible charm about it. While we know and love Him as a brother, He has also a fulness of glory about Him too dazzling for mortal eyes. He is so human that we may lean on His bosom, and kiss His blessed feet; and yet when His glory bursts out upon us, we fall at His feet as dead, and can only cry, " My Lord, and my God."

These pensive musings were interrupted by the return of my companions, who had been four hours in making the ascent and descent, but were amply rewarded for their labours by the splendid view they obtained from the top. Though their appetites had been sharpened by their exertions and the keen mountain air, they could hardly get on with their dinner, so desirous were they to give expression to the admiration of the scene they had been rewarded with from the summit of Bèn Lomond.

Such a scene of majestic beauty as that which Loch Lomond presents, either at early morn or dewy eve, when the sun descends beneath its distant waters, I think, is hardly to be met with this side of Heaven.

We stayed at the quiet little inn at Rowerdennan for the night, and walked out the next morning, as soon as it was light, by the margin of the lake. The mountain top was hid by a grey mist, that seemed, as it slowly curled away, like incense rising from an altar. We took a boat and rowed out for a mile upon the lake, and returned to breakfast with a good appetite. We got on the first steamer and crossed to Tarbet, where we mounted our knapsacks and walked leisurely on to Arrochar, for Glencroe. To avoid a couple of miles needless walking we hired a boat at Loch Long, and crossed to the Glencroe road. The boat leaked so in the stern that it was as much as our surgical friend and myself could do to ladle out the water with a small bucket. It would have been rather a serious matter if the boat had gone down, as only two of the party could swim, and there were no other boats in sight.

Having put us ashore opposite the bend of the road leading to Glencroe, we trudged on, with one of the mountains at the head of Loch Long on our right, called "The Cobbler," so designated from its remarkably bold and fantastic outline. This glen resembles in some respects Glencoe; the lower slopes are broken and jagged by protruding masses of rock, while the hills above are split into separate summits of all imaginable shapes. Some parts of the valley present a pleasing aspect of grey rock, purpling heath, and verdant pasture. It is at the head of this glen that the stone is found bearing the inscription, "Rest, and be thankful;" words inscribed on it by the soldiers who made the fine road, with the date, "1748," and an addition by a succeeding party, "Repaired by the 23rd Regiment, 1768." One who has lately visited the spot says, "This seat was erected by General Wade, while engaged in his great work of Highland road-making; and so long as it exists the general will be remembered—and Earl Russell too." We took out our whiskey-flasks, and drank to the memory of the general and the noble fellows who made the road. This stone has been rendered more memorable since by Earl Russell making the inscription his motto for a time with reference to political measures.

I am not the man to underrate the services of that eminently patriotic statesman, and would say that I believe Earl Russell to be one of the few public men of our time who would make almost any sacrifice for his country's welfare. His private character will always command the respect of all who can admire the stirling virtues which constitute the real glory of an English noble-man. Never has a whisper of scandal been heard of this Christian statesman, who is both loved and looked up to, by a large circle of distinguished relatives and friends, as well as the numerous and increasing moderate Reform party in the country.

Earl Russell * has contributed somewhat largely to our political and historical literature, and all his writings evince a thorough knowledge of the subject in hand, combined with a healthy moral tone. His "Life of Tom

---

* While these pages are passing through the press, his lordship has, through the sudden and lamented death of Lord Palmerston, been again called to the helm of the State. May he be enabled to develope his first Reform Bill, as the extension of the franchise is the cause of right, of justice, of expediency, of safety, and, I think, of the highest political wisdom.

Moore " is a most charming book ; and every man interested in the political welfare of his country should read
his work " On the English Government and Constitution,
from the Reign of Henry VII. to the present time."*   I
remember, when a boy, that " Lord John " was to my
mind the *beau ideal* of a reformer, and my admiration of
this Christian statesman has increased with years.

A mile or two from the " Rest-and-be-thankful " stone
we found a farm-house, where we obtained some milk and
oatcake.   Leaving Cairndow on our right, we made for
St. Catherines through Kinglass.   We reached the ferry
at the head of Loch Fyne after a toilsome and wearisome
walk, which had completely knocked up our surgical
friend, who, though a man of indomitable pluck, was fairly
taken off his legs.   He had, unfortunately, set out
upon this tour wearing a pair of smart Wellington boots,
which would have done well enough in Regent-street,
but were very poor articles to carry a man through a
pedestrian tour in the Highlands.   They got so twisted
and out of shape by the rain, and the roughness of the
roads, that we were obliged two or three times in the
course of the day to draw them off his tender and blistered
feet, to try and straighten them.   Our good Australian
brother was of much service in offices of this nature, as he,
had had in early life considerable experience in traversing
the rough, half-formed roads of his adopted country.

The sail across Loch Fyne to Inverary is about three
miles, and we did not forget that this fine salt-water lake
is famous for its herrings.   We were told that sometimes
as many as 800 boats may be seen in pursuit of these
breakfast luxuries, sold in London and elsewhere as " real
Yarmouth bloaters."

After resting and refreshing ourselves at the " Argyle
Head Inn," we set out to find, if possible, a more suitable
pair of boots for our poor crippled friend.   We sought in

---

* 3rd Ed. Published by Longman and Co. Crown 8vo. 1865.

vain among the shops at Inverary, a somewhat large town, for a pair of boots that would fit our friend, as he had so small a foot. He was obliged at length to put up with a pair of women's highlows; and I believe he preserves both these and the Wellingtons as interesting relics of his first tour in the Highlands, as well as occasionally exhibits them when the tale is told to a few select friends around his hospitable fireside.

We spent our first Sunday in the Highlands at Invèrary, and the rest and refreshment of the sacred day were most grateful to us after the wanderings of the preceding week. After inquiring as to the places of worship in the town, we decided upon going to the U. P. kirk, where I witnessed for the first time the mode of administering the ordinance of Baptism among the Presbyterians. This Christian rite, as administered by our Scotch Pædobaptist brethren, differs very little from the mode that obtains in the Church of England, only that the parent takes upon himself the responsibilities of bringing up the child religiously as a son or daughter of the Church. This appears to me to be a much more sensible and scriptural idea of the matter than that of the Church of England, where sponsors, under the name of godfathers and godmothers, are made to take upon themselves vows which they never for a moment intend to fulfil, and which, if they did, a parent would of course resist as an infringement upon the parental authority, which, be it ever remembered, steps in before all Church authority. The minister was a good man, but very dull and prosy. Oh! when shall we see men in earnest in the pulpit? If we walk into any of our Courts of Law we shall find the advocate, who is feed simply to defend or prosecute either side, as the case may be, doing his work right earnestly and skilfully, carrying the jurymen with him, and obtaining a verdict for his client. A doctor who goes in and out among his patients without being thoroughly in earnest, would not be likely to extend his practice. The man of science, who never was sure of anything, but always doubtingly putting his half-digested theories forward, would never be a foremost man among his fellows. The statesman who hesitatingly addresses a listening senate, will not be likely to "bring down the house" upon him, except he speaks from a firm conviction that he can move the minds of his audience, and influence their judgment. Then why should our preachers, for the most part, be such a dull, passionless, wearisome set of men? Theirs is the highest vocation that can be entrusted to man. To be an "Ambassador of Christ" is to fill an office that an angel might covet. To rescue a sinner from the error of his ways is a God-like work, and to bind up the broken-hearted a man must be tenderly in earnest. If you were in a position of imminent peril, you would not think much of the man who coolly told you that you had better get out of it, but gave you no warm hand to grasp your sinking and exhausted form. When you are crushed sometimes under the pressure of some great domestic trial or heart conflict, you would not care very much for the poor lifeless twaddle that we hear oftentimes from the pulpit. We want *sympathy* in our preachers: we want them to be like the impassioned and tender-hearted Paul, who not only thundered out the divine threatenings against sin in high places, so that "Felix trembled" and King Agrippa quaked with cowardly fear, but who could also, in accents soft and loving as a mother's words, whisper peace to the troubled soul. I know that this will cost a man something to do, and that he cannot benefit others to any profit except by self-sacrifice. But it is a noble work, and there will be the recompense of the reward. I like to see our soldiers, brown and tawny from an Indian sun, wearing their well-earned medals on their breast, which tell of hard-fought fields and dangers in the deadly strife. I love to talk with the bluff old heroes at Chelsea and at Greenwich, who, with maimed limbs and crooked forms, garrulously tell of the glorious deeds of their early days. And why should we not have in our churches and pulpits men whose love for souls should be, like their Master's,—a love " stronger than death."

But to return from this digression, which has been occasioned by the pastor of the U. P. Church at Inverary. After kirk was over we sought the banks of Loch Fyne, and as the day was hot and scorching, we sat upon the rocks and bathed our feet in its refreshing waters. The scenery of Loch Fyne is rather tame, and devoid of any striking or remarkable feature ; the shores are well wooded, and the surrounding hills completely covered with trees.

The town of Inverary is built on an elongated indentation of Loch Fyne, and on a level space in front of Glen Aray, a little elevated above the lake, stands the castle. The Duke of Argyll, unlike his compeer of Athole, takes no fees from tourists for admission to his castle and beautiful grounds, and it added no little to our enjoyment to feel that here—

> " Nature's charms, the hills and woods,
> The sweeping vales, and foaming floods,
> Are free alike to all."

Inverary Castle is not remarkable for its architectural beauty, but the park in which it stands is very picturesque. There are some magnificent trees, some of very curious growth ; and from Duniquoich, which shoots up its conical head above the contiguous range seven hundred feet, you gain a splendid view of the surrounding country.

We spent a pleasant Sabbath evening in wandering about the grounds of this distinguished Scottish nobleman. Oh ! it is a marvellous proof of God's love to put such rebellious creatures as we are into a world so filled with beauty ;—and it is a greater marvel still if we have been brought back to filial obedience, and can look up and say with tearful eye, " Our Father made all these mountains, and lakes, and woodland heights, and running streams, and peaceful valleys for our enjoyment ! "

We laid ourselves down on the mossy summit of Duni-

quoich, that Sabbath evening, and read the 67th and the
104th Psalms, and sang in unison the hymn beginning—

> "O God of Bethel, by whose hand
> 　Thy people still are fed;
> Who through this weary pilgrimage
> 　Hast all our fathers lead."

The evening was soft and balmy, and we lingered about
this lovely spot till the shades of night warned us that " this
is not our rest." One of the party recited some beautiful
lines ascribed to Tom Moore ;. but as they are not found
in his acknowledged writings, I am sure the reader will
be pleased to have them :—

> " There is a world we have not seen,
> 　That time shall never dare destroy ;
> Where mortal footstep hath not been,
> 　Nor ear has caught its sounds of joy.
>
> There is a region, lovelier far
> 　Than sages tell, or poets sing ;
> Brighter than summer's beauties are,
> 　And softer than the tints of spring.
>
> There is a world, and oh! how blest !
> 　Fairer than prophets ever told ;
> And never did an angel-guest
> 　One half its blessedness unfold.
>
> It is all holy and serene,
> 　The land of glory and repose ;
> And there, to dim the radiant scene,
> 　The tear of sorrow never flows.
>
> It is not fann'd by summer gale,
> 　'Tis not refresh'd by vernal showers,
> It never needs the moon-beam pale,
> 　For there are known no evening hours.
>
> No; for that world is ever bright,
> 　With a pure radiance all its own ;
> And streams of uncreated light
> 　Flow round it from the eternal throne.
>
> There, forms that mortals may not see,
> 　Too glorious for the eye to trace,
> And clad in peerless majesty,
> 　Move with unutterable grace.

In vain the philosophic eye
  May seek to view the fair abode,
  Or find it in the curtain'd sky,—
    It is the dwelling-place of God."

As we returned to our inn we took a glimpse by moon-light of the little obelisk, erected in a garden beside the church, to commemorate the execution there, in 1685, of several patriotic gentlemen by the name of Campbell, who were among the last individuals that suffered for their unflinching and faithful opposition to Popery.

The next morning, as soon as it was light, we shouldered our knapsacks, and set out for Dalmally, leaving our foot-sore surgical friend to come on to us by coach, as the Wellington boots had made our brother not very nimble on his legs, and we were afraid of his knocking up alto-gether. The rain was falling heavily when we left In-verary, and after walking about three miles through the grounds of the Duke of Argyll, we called at a peasant's cottage by the road-side, and obtained not only shelter from the rain, but some milk and oatcake. The rain hav-ing a little subsided, we marched on merrily enough through some fine scenery, half obscured by the mists occasioned by the heavy showers, until we reached Cladich, a cele-brated village for anglers. There we dried our feet, and got a good substantial breakfast; and as neither of us happened to be disciples of Izaac Walton, we pushed on to Dalmally.

Just before entering Cladich we obtained a splendid view of the far-spreading sides, and towering broadly-peaked summit of the gigantic Ben Cruachan, with its innumerable lines of silver, caused by the rains running down its rugged sides. It is a magnificent mountain, and we had it as a companion almost the whole of the following day, as we walked slowly by the margin of Loch Awe.

On arriving at Dalmally, we found our crippled friend all the better for the ride and the rest. He had ordered dinner and beds for the night. He remarked that he

s

found it a dull place without us ; but this would not have been the case had he been a Waltonian, as there is some fine fishing there.

We left our quarters at break of day next morning, and soon found ourselves by the side of Loch Awe. It is a lake about twenty-four miles in length, varying from half a mile to three miles in width. There are several little islands scattered over its surface, some of them beautifully crowned with dark nodding pines ; indeed the eastern end of the lake possesses innumerable beauties. We saw Kilchurn Castle from the same point that Turner did when the great painter made that silent and deserted ruin the subject of one of his celebrated pictures. On another of these beautiful islands are the ruins of a small nunnery of the Cistercian order ; and on a third, called Fraoch Elan, those of a castle, which we were told was granted, in 1267, to Gilbert Macnaughten by Alexander III. Tradition informs us that this latter island was named from Fraoch, an adventurous lover, who, attempting to gratify the wishes of his fair lady for the delicious fruit of the isle, encountered and destroyed the serpent by which it was guarded, but fell himself a victim to his gallant temerity.

Ben Cruachan rises in solemn grandeur from the margin of the lake, and is twenty miles in circumference at its base. The sheep that were feeding quietly on its green slopes looked like little white specks ; and as we laid down to rest ourselves at its feet the scene appeared altogether so strangely beautiful that we could almost have imagined ourselves gazing upon some fair vision in a dream.

On approaching the eastern end of the lake the scenery increased in beauty and grandeur. As we neared the Pass of Bradner, where on one side Ben Cruachan rises abruptly, while on the other, the rock ascends from the brink of the water almost perpendicularly, the dark waters of the lake stealing slowly and silently into a deep narrow gorge, the scene is magnificent. We stood in silent admiration for some time, for all our epithets of the beautiful were exhausted; and sometimes, when we are surrounded with scenery of this character, speech is almost an impertinence, and you would gag the man who would profane such sacred moments by his noisy and meaningless twaddle. This celebrated Pass was one of the grandest and wildest scenes we had as yet met with in the Highlands, and we lingered about it until we had got the whole scene photographed in our mind's eye.

We were compelled at length to leave this piece of magnificent scenery, and strolled on by the side of the River Awe, which rolls on majestically over a rocky bed, about four miles, to Bunaw. Our walk terminated at the "Inn of Taynuilt," where we found very comfortable quarters for the night. In the evening we had a ramble by the side of Loch Etive, a salt-water lake of about twenty miles long and a mile broad. Bathing in these salt-water lochs is a great luxury, and after a day's hard walking it is most refreshing. I found that I could always sleep well during my tour in the Highlands,—a thing I had not done for many months before; and that I awoke about four in the morning, fresh and invigorated, as in days of yore.

The next morning, instead of going on from Taynuilt to Oban, the usual route for tourists, we hired a boat and two stout young fellows to row us up the inland arm of Loch Etive in the direction of Glencoe. We were well repaid for this *détour*, as the scenery both of the lake and the glen is wild and picturesque. The distance from Taynuilt to the head of the loch is about twelve miles, and we enjoyed the row exceedingly. Glen Etive is one of the most secluded and out-of-the-way places you can imagine. We walked on for some miles without any sign of human habitation, save here and there a shepherd's hut. These cabins are of the most primitive construction, and are of the rudest description. The entrance to them is so low that you must stoop to get in at the door, and there is nothing within to ensure comfort in any way. The light admitted is so small that it takes some time before you can see anything at all distinctly. We found here, as in all the dwellings of the peasantry of Scotland, something to feed the mind as well as the body. We remarked in one of these huts a well-worn Gaelic New Testament, a small Halifax edition of the "Pilgrim's Progress," and some other religious books. Very nearly all the Scottish peasantry can read and write, and in this respect they strangely contrast with the labouring classes in our own agricultural districts.

After walking ten or twelve miles up this glen, we turned into one of these cabins to seek for some refreshment, and as the shepherds were driving in the sheep preparatory to deer-stalking, they had fortunately laid in a larger stock of food than usual. We had set before us, by a tidy lassie, some basons of milk and oatcake, which we much enjoyed. As we were tired with our morning's walk, we stayed an hour or more reciting poetry and singing snatches of well-known songs. One of the party was called upon to sing "Nora Creina." Little did Tom Moore ever dream that that beautiful Irish melody would ever be sung in a Scotch glen. Our visit and uproarious voices had induced the wives and children from some of the adjacent huts to gather round the door, so that we had quite a large audience. The shepherds came in to their dinner before we started, and we left a few shillings with them to be distributed among the children. We wound up our concert by giving them the National Anthem, and left with many hearty good wishes that we might have a pleasant journey.

Those who love romantic scenery should go to Glen Etive. The guide-books say nothing about it; but any one in search of the beautiful will find this unfrequented glen abounding in scenery of the choicest and most exquisite character. We sat ourselves down many times to look leisurely round upon the scene, and as we had had our fun at the shepherd's hut, we gave way to quiet thoughts, produced by the objects before us. It must

have been in some such scene of beauty as this that the
poet sang—

"Far opening down some woodland deep,
In their own quiet glade should sleep
The relics dear to thought;
And wild-flower wreaths from side to side
Their waving tracery hang, to hide
What ruthless time has wrought."

The walk up this glen was by a rough and unused road,
but the scenery on either side and before us was very fine.
The conical bold head of Buchael Etive on our left, the
Royal Deer Forest on our right, with the high ridge of
black rocks known as the Devil's Staircase in front. We
were glad, however, to find we were not far from Kings
House, for we had walked about fourteen miles through a
bad road, though there was everything around us to make
us forget our poor blistered feet. How sweet it is, after
such a day's toil,—for toil it must be, if you get anything
worth your labour,—to take off your boots and "stretch
your tired limbs" on a comfortable bed! Verily "the rest
of the labouring man is sweet."

After refreshing ourselves at this welcome lonely inn,
standing in the midst of a bleak moor, we set off for Glencoe, the grandest and most romantic scene in the Highlands. Our expectations were raised to the highest pitch,
and we were not at all disappointed. Glencoe is about six
miles in length, and the upper part of it is wild and terrific beyond the power of description. It would need a
Ruskin, a Macaulay, or a Kinglake, to do anything like
justice to such a scene of unmingled wildness and terrific
grandeur. On the one side immense black ranges of rock
rise in a continuous series of high, naked, sharp-edged
precipices. The mountains on the southern side are lofty
and bold, and appear to have been crowded together by a
mighty hand, and then split up the centre by some subter-
ranean and irresistible force that carried everything before
it. The mountains on the north side of the glen are so

sharp and pointed as to resemble the roof of a house. Numerous torrents pour down their waters from these inaccessible fastnesses, and the streams are so rapid, carrying so much stony matter along with them, that they make the road through the glen dangerous, and at times almost impassable. The gloomy grandeur of this wild and tragic glen is such as to impress the most unreflecting mind with awe and solemnity. We paused, and turned again, and yet again, to gaze silently upon the strange and imposing scene around us, so different to the soft and peaceful scenery through which we had wandered for some days past. Evening was coming on, and the sun was already below the black crags, and lighting up the naked summit of Buchael Etive with those beauteous violet tints that only Turner's pencil can place on canvass, and which must be seen to be appreciated. The lower part of Glencoe, next Loch Leven, is covered with rich verdure, and the course of the river that runs through it is fringed by alder and birch trees. It has been truly said that " Glencoe is to the other glens what Tennyson is to contemporary poets. If Glencoe did not exist, Glencroe would be famous."

As we left Glencoe behind us, the mountains of Morven came into view, bathed in the glowing colours of a Highland sunset. On arriving at the charming little village of Ballahulish, on the banks of Loch Leven, we were literally filled to overflowing with the scenes through which we had passed. However, good scenery, like good sermons and every other earthly good, must, after all, end in " creature comforts." We were wearied with sight-seeing, and were both tired and hungry, and consequently did ample justice to the mutton chops and salmon steaks provided by the very civil landlord of the little inn that stands on the very margin of the lake.

After making a substantial tea, we took a stroll by the side of Loch Leven by moonlight, and enjoyed a bathe in its transparent and refreshing waters before going to roost for the night.

We awoke refreshed the next morning, mounted our knapsacks, and crossed the ferry for Fort William and Bannavie, by way of Onich and Corran Ferry. We walked on, talking of the beauties of yesterday, by the side of Linnhe Loch, fourteen miles, to Fort William, where we dined and engaged beds for the night. I would say, for the information of tourists, that the accommodation at the "Caledonian Hotel" at Fort William is far inferior to that which can be obtained at the "Lochiel Arms" at Bannavie, which is only three miles farther on the road. Not only is the commissariat department bad at Fort William, but we found that the charges were considerably higher than at any other inn that we stayed at during a month's tour in the Highlands.

At Bannavie the hotel stands in a fine situation, the accommodation good, and the charges moderate, and where Ben Nevis can be seen to the greatest advantage, who

"Looks from his throne of clouds o'er half the land."

A little incident occurred at the hotel at Fort William that caused some amusement at the time. On going to our bed-rooms at night, one of our party, who was famous for imitating all sorts of noises, employed his powers at cat-a-wauling along the passages. So true to nature was the imitation that some of the tourists, who had retired for the night, opened their doors and came out to drive such unwelcome visitors away. When we were assembled at breakfast next morning in the coffee-room, we were rather amused to hear one of the party remark to the waiter how they had been annoyed during the night by cats. The waiter expressed his surprise, and replied that the gentleman must have been mistaken, as they had not a cat in the house. One of the party remarked that probably the gentleman had been dreaming, while the real delinquent sat quietly eating his breakfast.

On inquiry of one of the guides at Fort William, we found that to climb Ben Nevis was both difficult and tedious. The ascent usually occupies nearly four hours from the base of the mountain, and the descent rather more than half that time. The weather was doubtful, and we decided upon not making the ascent, as there would have been the risk of being disappointed when we had gained the summit.

Ben Nevis rises majestically above the surrounding hills, and looks over a vast and wide sweep of mountain and moor, glen and lake, far away to the Highlands that lie amid the western sea; its base is almost washed by the sea, and none of its vast proportions are lost to the eye. The summit is not peaked but tabular, and admirably harmonises with its general massiveness and grandeur: its circumference at the base is said to exceed twenty-four miles. We wandered up the glen from which Ben Nevis rises, for some miles, that we might look up upon this mighty mass of creative power in various aspects. Impressive and almost overwhelming as it is to look down from the bald summit of some of these everlasting hills upon the glorious view unfolded, and the lesser undulations around, it is to me far more impressive and inspiring to look up from some green and quiet glen to one of these grand old mountains, whose summit is either bathed in the sunlight, or veiled by the mists of heaven. I love to lie down and silently let the eye wander from point to point, and as you do so, you gradually take in the vast and magnificent proportions of such a mountain as Ben Nevis. Musing silently upon the scene, the mind instinctively turns to the Almighty power that lifted these enormous masses from the plain below. Man feels at once his littleness and his greatness:— " crushed before the moth," but at the same time having within him something that will live when " the mountains shall depart, and the hills be removed."

Glen Nevis is one of the most beautiful valleys in Scotland, and as we wandered leisurely along by the side of the stream that runs through it, we gained ever and anon varied views of the great monarch of Scottish mountains, that lifted its towering head above us. The grass was so green, and the heather in full bloom, that we laid ourselves down for some hours. Everything around was quiet and serene, and the silence only broken by our own voices, and the mournfully plaintive note of the plover : but for those birds of the mountain this beautiful wilderness would have been silent as the grave. We felt ourselves so completely shut out from the world, and the scene around and above us so surpassingly beautiful, that it would not have required much effort to have imagined ourselves fondly gazing upon a second Eden. So beautiful was the scene altogether, that we should not have wondered very much to have seen a flock of angels settle down upon some of the fair projecting peaks of this wondrous mass of creative power and beauty. An object worthy of the great Architect, who had placed it there for so many ages, for the admiration of His rebellious children. Oh! what a luxury is wealth ; that one may, without crippling matters at home, go abroad in God's great world, and see the many manifestations of His creative power ; and gratefully adore the hand and the heart that has so lavishly filled man's probationary resting-place with objects to please his eye, and gratify his taste.

Having lingered long and lovingly in this charming valley, we retraced our steps to the head of the glen, and called at a farm-house to refresh the inner man. The good farmer's wife gave us each a tumbler full of new milk, and chatted very friendly to us. She called our attention to photographs of her son and daughter,—for where is the mother that is not proud of her children ? The son was a fine strapping fellow, in the Volunteer uniform, and the daughter a pretty fair-haired innocent looking lassie of nineteen.

An hour's walk brought us to the "Lochiel Arms," Bannavie, one of the finest and best-managed hotels in the Highlands. There is an excellent *table d'hôte* every day at five : we sat down in a splendid dining-room with about sixty tourists and visitors, among whom we found some very agreeable people, especially three or four from America. There is a magnificent view of Ben Nevis from this hotel. We spent a pleasant evening in strolling about the neighbourhood, and making inquiries as to time of starting of the steamer that sails through the Caledonian Canal, from Bannavie to Inverness, twice a week.

The Caledonian Canal, through a valley of sixty miles, called " The Great Glen of Scotland," deserves more than a passing notice, as it is one of the grandest pieces of workmanship ever executed by the hand of man. This great and wonderful national work was projected and carried out, at an expenditure of little short of a million pounds sterling, by the genius and energy of the late Thomas Telford, a man of whom Scotland may be justly proud. There were, of course, many obstacles to be surmounted in such a gigantic undertaking ; but they were all overcome by the skill and persistency of the great engineer who had been selected for the work. In 1803 the work was commenced, and the canal finally opened in the autumn of 1822, with all due ceremony. The dimensions of the canal originally resolved on were as follows, viz. " The bottom width, 50 feet, with slopes of 18 inches to a foot, so that a depth of cutting of 15 feet earth will be obtained, to make the banks contain 20 feet of water, which will be 110 feet in width at its surface." As the summit level of the canal between Lochs Oich and Lochy is more than ninety feet above high-water mark, at Fort William and Inverness, the two extreme points, vessels navigating this silent highway are raised and lowered by locks. These locks are twenty-eight in number, and are none of them less than 170 feet long, and forty feet wide ; and each affording an average rise of eight feet, capable of admitting a 32-gun frigate. At Bannavie there are eight magnificent locks, within about a mile of the sea, called Neptune's Staircase. The original intention of making the depth twenty feet was abandoned on

account of the immense expense that it would have
occasioned. The present depth is only fifteen feet, which
limits the navigation to vessels of that draught of water.
It is said that an additional expenditure of £50,000
would be required to carry out the full depth contem-
plated. However, it presents, as it is, an enduring monument, not only of the genius and talents of Telford, but
also of the national enterprise that could carry out so
grand an undertaking.

The following beautiful and graceful tribute to the
great man who originated and completed this wonderful
work, is from the pen of Southey, and was written by
him during a temporary sojourn at Bannavie in 1819,
while on a tour through the Highlands :—

> " Where these capacious basins, by the laws
>   Of the subjacent element, receive
>   The ship, descending or upraised, eight times
>   From stage to stage with unfelt agency
>   Translated, fitliest may the marble here
>   Record the architect's immortal fame.
> *Telford* it was by whose presiding mind
>   The whole great work was plann'd and perfected;
> *Telford*, who o'er the vale of Cambrian Dee,
>   Aloft in air at giddy height upborne,
>   Carried his navigable road, and hung
>   High o'er Menai's Strait the bending bridge—
>   Structures of more ambitious enterprise
>   Than minstrels, in the age of old romance,
>   To their own Merlin's magic lore ascribed.
>   Nor hath he for his native land perform'd
>   Less in this proud design; and where his piers
>   Around her coast from many a fisher's creek,
>   Unshelter'd else, and many an ample port,
>   Repel the assailing storm; and where his roads
>   In beautiful and sinuous line far seen,
>   Wind with the vale and win the long ascent;
>   Now o'er the deep morass sustain'd, and now
>   Across ravine, or glen, or estuary,
>   Opening a passage through the wilds subdued."

It must be remembered that the construction of a canal

on so large a scale, to connect the German and Atlantic Oceans, was to be regarded as an experiment to ascertain the probable advantages, of which there was no previous test of a similar description that could be applied. The Isthmus of Suez Canal, that is now almost completed, is but the development on a larger scale of that constructed by Telford. I must return, however, again to our tour, with the hope that I have not wearied my readers by this short digression from the immediate subject in hand.

We took our places in one of the splendid steamers that sail through this "silent highway" from Bannavie, and were very much delighted with our trip. The tour by the Caledonian Canal has become a favourite one, and the steamer was crowded by tourists, all of whom seemed thoroughly to enjoy the varied and continuous extent of beautiful, romantic, and picturesque scenery through which we passed, which probably is not to be met with, within the same distance, in any other part of the British Isles.

The steamer stopped at Port Augusta, to enable passengers to see Gordon Cumming's exhibition; but as we all voted him a humbug, we preferred a stroll by the side of the canal to patronising such a pretentious fellow. The exhibition was displayed in a large tent close to the spot where the steamer pulled up, and the gentleman himself, in full Highland costume, stood at the door to entice visitors within. Such an illustration of Barnumism, in the midst of so much that was beautiful and attractive in nature around, made us the more disgusted with this attempt to minister to the love of the marvellous that is found in most of our countrymen.

On leaving Port Augusta, the route is continued through Loch Ness, a lake about twenty-four miles in length, and varying in breadth from three quarters of a mile to a mile and a quarter. The mountain ranges on either side are about of equal elevation, averaging between twelve and fifteen hundred feet in height. Mealfourvonie, about midway on the north side, rears his dome-like head far above the neighbouring hills, to a height of upwards of three thousand feet.

The steamer stopped again at a landing-place on Loch Ness to allow passengers to see the Falls of Fowers. These celebrated Falls, which have been the subject of many a poet's lay, and Burns among the number, are situated about a mile from the lake. The tourist will be well repaid for making this *détour*, as it is the finest thing of the kind in Scotland. The principal fall dashes through a narrow gap, over a height of about ninety feet, and is very imposing. At the point we viewed it from, the spray wetted us through, but we saw it to the best advantage. Two rainbows spanned the bottom of the Falls, which added not a little to the beauty of the scene. As there had been a good deal of rain just before our visit, the volume of water was considerably increased, so as to make the ground tremble around us from the shock of the tumbling waters, and our ears were stunned with its ceaseless roar. From the rocks surrounding the Falls, you obtain a fine view of Loch Ness, backed by the steep and ample sides of Mealfourvonic, while the foreground descending to the margin of the lake is beautifully covered by woods of the weeping birch.

On regaining the boat, we steamed along the lake, admiring the noble scenery on either side. We longed to wander up Glen Urquhart, one of the richest and most beautiful of the Highland valleys, but our time would not permit us to do so, and we reached Inverness about five in the afternoon. Having secured comfortable quarters at a quiet inn, we took a walk about this famous Highland city.

Inverness is the largest town in the Highlands, having a population of nearly 20,000. Some have gone as far as to compare it with Edinburgh as to its situation and surroundings. However this may be, the scenery round Inverness is very picturesque and beautiful. Everything has been done that can be effected by wood and cultiva-

tion, and the character of the country around combines not
only the rich open lowland views, but also the wildest
mountain scenery, and to this must be added the Moray
Frith, a maritime landscape not often equalled. From
the Castle Hill the views are very fine: the mountains
about Loch Ness terminating in the dome-shaped summit
of Mealfourvonie. Towards the west the hills rise in
clusters, and, we were told, present in winter a fine sight,
with their many snow-clad peaks, while to the north rises
the huge, shapeless mountain called Ben Weavis, towering above the surrounding hills to the height of 3,700
feet. Towards the east the waters of the Moray Frith
are seen stretching out into the German Ocean, and conducting the eye to the dim distant mountain-ranges of
Sutherland, Caithness, and Banffshire.

The gaol is a fine building, lately erected in place of
the old prison, which we were told consisted of a single
chamber in one of the arches of the bridge that spans the
River Ness. It is said that this dungeon was only abandoned after a poor madman confined there had been
devoured by rats. There are some good churches, in the
steeple of one of which is a sweet clear-toned bell, placed
there by Oliver Cromwell, who brought it from the Cathedral of Fortrose. The great so-called usurper has left
other marks of his presence here in the destruction of the
Monastery of Black Friars. A citadel and fort were also
constructed by him on the north side of the town, near the
mouth of the river. This fort was, however, demolished
at the Restoration to please some of the Highland chiefs,
whose loyalty was no longer doubtful. A considerable
part of the ramparts remain to remind the good people at
Inverness of England's greatest monarch.

We saw the spot where Macbeth's Castle once stood;
and although there are some doubts among antiquarians
as to whether Duncan's foul murder was perpetrated there,
we could not but look with interest at a place rendered so
memorable by our " Divine Shakespeare." Within about

a mile of the town the river is divided into two branches by a series of islands luxuriantly wooded. These islands are connected by light and elegant suspension bridges, and have been laid out into walks for the recreation of the inhabitants.

We spent a Sabbath at Inverness, and in no place that we visited in Scotland had we seen the outward reverence for the sacred day so rigidly observed. The streets during the hours of divine service were as silent as those of Pompeii; not a carriage of any description, hired or private, was to be seen. We went in the morning to hear a gentleman who was considered the best preacher in the place; the church was well filled, and the preacher rather a good-looking fellow, but a little conceited and theatrical in his manners. When will those who fill the sacred office learn to be natural and unaffected, instead of assuming an artificial style and mannerism in the pulpit, which is disgusting to a cultivated audience, and an insult to the God of Heaven? The great charm about Mr. Spurgeon is his perfect naturalness; there is no straining after effect. He stands simple and reverent as a man ought to do before God and his fellow men, and you forget the man in the services in which you are engaged. Every one with any pretensions to correct taste in these matters will concur with the bard of Olney when he says,—

> " In man or woman, but far most in man,
> And most of all, in man that ministers
> And serves the altar, in my soul I loath
> All affectation. 'Tis my perfect scorn;
> Object of my implacable disgust.
> What! will a man play tricks, will he indulge
> A silly, fond conceit of his fair form,
> And just proportion, fashionable mien,
> And pretty face, *in presence of his God?*
> Or, will he seek to dazzle me with tropes,
> As with the diamond on his lily hand,
> And play his brilliant parts before my eyes,
> When I am hungry for the bread of life?
> He mocks his Maker, prostitutes and shames

His noble office, and, instead of truth,
Displaying his own beauty, starves his flock!
Therefore, avaunt all attitude, and stare,
And start theatric, practised at the glass!
I seek divine simplicity in him
Who handles things divine; and all besides,
Though learn'd with labour, and though much admired
By curious eyes, and judgments ill inform'd,
To me is odious."

The sermon of this rather conceited fashionable Scotch preacher was a very ordinary affair, and we could not help remarking that he appeared to think far more of himself than of his subject. In the afternoon we went to another of the Free Churches, for our sympathies were chiefly with our brethren who had emancipated themselves from State control. The church was crowded, and the atmosphere so intolerably hot and close that it was anything but inviting. The minister, a man advanced in years, was well enough; but he was dull and drowsy, and the place so unwholesomely oppressive, that when the devotional exercises were over two of our party, who were sitting by themselves near the door, quietly withdrew, leaving our brethren to benefit by the good man's sermon.

In leaving the church at this hour we could not but be impressed with the silence and solitude of the streets. An hour before every thoroughfare was literally crowded with people on their way to the different churches, but now not a single person was to be seen in many of the streets. I was much struck, during my two visits to Scotland, at the way in which the outward observance of the Sabbath is characterized. It is a beautiful and cheering sight on the Sabbath morning to see such a " multitude " going up to " the House of the Lord;" and in this respect Scotland contrasts very favourably, as far as the outward observance of the day is concerned, with our own land.

The Sabbath question is undoubtedly one of the very first importance to any country and community; but to legislate on the subject is confessedly a difficult and delicate matter. It should always be remembered by Christian statesmen, and indeed by every man possessing the elective franchise, that the generous and confiding spirit of Christianity has not imposed a single restriction upon us with reference to the observance of the Sabbath. While I heartily believe that those who from conscience and principle turn their thoughts most entirely out of the current of worldly cares on that day fulfil, unconsciously, a great law of health; and that, whether their moral nature be thereby advanced or not, their brain will work more healthfully and actively for it, even in physical and worldly matters. "I have often thought," remarks one, "that it must strike every thoughtful observer that it is because the Sabbath thus harmonizes the physical and moral laws of our being, that the injunction concerning it is placed among the ten great commandments, from the lips of God Himself, each of which represents some one of the immutable needs of humanity." Now, although this is most true, yet I believe that the observance of the Sabbath must ever be treated as a question of *religious authority.* I recollect reading a work, many years since, by the late Winter Hamilton, of Leeds, a man of much original thought, and "mighty in the Scriptures," that exercised a considerable influence upon me. I had been educated a Churchman, and had a most superstitious reverence in my mind as to the outward observance of the Sabbath, but the work referred to had the effect of deepening my reverence, as a Christian man, for the religious observance of the sacred day; but at the same time it set me right as to what should be done by the nation in its legislative capacity, as to the outward observance of the day. I hold that in the keeping of the Sabbath, as of any other religious observance, to our own Master we stand or fall. I protest most emphatically against the principle that recognizes human magistracy in the province of conscience. The law may defend, and it is one of its plainest duties, the worship of religion; for as this is the first right of man, civil go-

T

vernments are bound to protect its subjects in it: but having done this, the civil power must not, however, enjoin or enforce it. The writer above referred to says, in his own vigorous language, " Civil governments may not dictate the form; it may not arrogate the power of personal responsibility. It may not distribute lure or disfranchisement. Rulers, in matters of religion, are on a perfect level with their subjects; they are seldom so well informed or so well disposed. They owe, whatever may be the accident of their rank, in common with the meanest, the same individual accountableness. And it becomes every Christian man not only to forbear to seek, but to solemnly abjure, every political enforcement of the Sabbath. Because it is a state of things established and convenient, let them do nothing to reprove it. Let their protest resound, but let them never call in the avengement of human law for any such case. Trade and pleasure on the Lord's-day may annoy, and if these strictly interrupt Divine worship, we may demand protection from it, but nothing else. Let it never be ours to wage a petty crusade on religious grounds against the shop or the stall. Let it never be ours, on every such pretext, to close the rivers, the railways, and the parks, whither city populations vent themselves. To do this would only debar, not convince. It would only be an outforce, and not an inward homage. As Christians and advocates of free trade in everything, we must accord to all worship the same safeguard as we challenge for our own. We must leave all men alone in religious matters, as we plead to be left alone."

These just and equitable sentiments from so great a writer will, I am sure, have their weight and influence with all my readers, whether they agree with him or not; and in Scotland our Christian brethren very much need a word of exhortation on this subject. They are very zealous on the Sabbath question, but I think it is " a zeal not according to knowledge," and it would be well to ask them " by what authority doest thou these things, and who gave you this authority ?" To stop the railways and shut up the rivers, and, if they could, to close the parks, may be in perfect accordance with both the letter and spirit of the law of Scotland ; but he must be a bold and reckless man who shall attempt to defend such a state of things from the New Testament—the statute-book of Christians. It is well known that our Lord, and also His apostles, both by precept and example, taught their disciples, in those.early and purer days of Christianity, that recreation was a necessary and essential part of our life, in such a world of toil and weariness as this.

Our Scotch Sabbatarians, who call public meetings in its chief provincial cities to maintain this state of things, and advocate their principles from the press and the pulpit, profess to be marvellously careful of the railway and steamboat officials. This is a very commendable thing to do ; but any one can see that, by a wise and equitable adjustment of these practical matters, it would not fall more heavily upon this class than it does upon those who are obliged every Sabbath to be in attendance almost the entire day in our churches and chapels. To do any good to a large number, must always be a tax upon self-sacrifice. The greatest happiness to the greatest number ought to be our maxim in all legislative enactments.

The Sabbatarians affirm that to run a limited number of trains on Sunday, and to man a few steam-boats, is an infringement upon the law of heaven, and that it keeps men employed without intermission. This assertion will be found upon examination to be without foundation. We readily admit that no class of men could toil all the year round without rest and relief, but surely they have the right to decide for themselves whether they shall make the attempt. I would not for a moment advocate the principle that man should be *obliged* to work on the Sabbath: that is the farthest from my thoughts, and I would resist such a thing with all my might and main ; but if the few choose to labour on that day, that the many may more completely enjoy and be grateful for their day's rest and recreation, that is the choice of the few; and all honour to the noble fellows, it is always found that they will gladly and willingly make the sacrifice. To work on this day is what our Sunday School Teachers do almost every Sabbath throughout the year; and they are for the most part composed of those who through the week are engaged in warehouses and shops, and would be glad enough to get out into the country for a day's rest and change. The claims, however, of Him whom their souls love, and their yearning tenderness to the children of their less favoured brethren, constrain them to make the sacrifice: in my humble opinion no class of workers in the vineyard of Christ are so deserving of the sympathy of their fellow-Christians as are these self-forgetting and self-sacrificing Sabbath-workers. From my own personal knowledge and observation of this noble class for more than thirty years, I can bear testimony to the fact that they forgo on the Sabbath the pleasures of the family circle, the pleasant walk in one of the parks, or the comfortable afternoon nap indulged in by many of their Christian brethren. If any class will be more entitled to the reward of grace than others, I think it will be those who persistingly and prayerfully pursue their unpaid and unpurchasable labours in the heated and buzzing atmosphere of a Sunday School. They will have the recompense of the reward from the Master's lips in the " well done, good and faithful servant, enter thou into the joy of thy Lord "—as well as meeting many in Heaven who never would have been there, but for their loving ministrations on the Sunday. Think also of the large staff of church and chapel keepers and pew-openers, who on that day work harder than any other in the week, while others sit comfortably in their well-cushioned seats; to say nothing of the men who use their mental powers, and expend their physical energies in the ten thousand pulpits of our own and other lands.

After considering the matter carefully in all its bear-

ings for many years, I am led to the conclusion that it is
far better that our crowded millions should get abroad
in the country and visit absent relatives, and soul-born
friends, and walk through the yellow corn-fields, as some
One else did, who declared, with an authority that none will
dare to question, " *The Sabbath was made for man, and
not man for the Sabbath*"—than to sit in some dark un-
wholesome room, drinking whisky and smoking tobacco,
as may be seen in almost innumerable instances in Edinburgh, Glasgow, and other large towns in Scotland. Our
Scotch Sabbatarians would have their fellow-subjects attend
punctually at kirk in the morning and afternoon, though
they might spend their evenings either in getting drunk
upon whisky-toddy or indulging in licentiousness.

For my own part, I cannot see sufficient reasons for
shutting out the large majority of our fellow-countrymen
from such places as the British Museum, the National
Gallery, the South Kensington Museum, and the Crystal
Palace, on the only day of leisure when they can visit them
without deduction from their hard-earned wages. I fear
I may have shocked the religious feelings of some of my
friends by this frank avowal of my mind on the Sabbath
question. It is, however, a subject that occupies at the
present time a large share of public attention, and as
public opinion is the result of individual judgment, I must
be allowed to speak out my sentiments, and leave them
to the consideration of my readers.

It does not follow that because we would obtain, if
we could, as much rest and recreation for our hard-worked
countrymen on the Sunday as possible, that we desire to
see the reckless profanation of the sacred day as it unhappily obtains on the Continent and other places, where
the people have not been subjected to Christianity divested
of the additions and mummeries of Popery.

I am almost ashamed at having trespassed so largely on
the time and patience of my readers about this vexed question ; but those who have gone north of the Tweed will

bear me out in my assertions as to the outward reverence of the Sabbath there, and some of them may have had opportunities at the same time of ascertaining what is going on behind the scenes.

To return, however, from this digression to my narrative. We took the rail from Inverness to Aberdeen, by way of Fories, Elgin, and Keith, and from thence to Aboyne. Aberdeen is an interesting quaint old city, and the grey granite buildings in the principal streets have a very fine effect. Our stay there was short, as we were anxious to get into the open country again. Having arrived at Aboyne, of late years so interesting as the point where her Majesty leaves the railway for Balmoral, we again shouldered our knapsacks, and walked on leisurely to Ballater, where we rested for the night. The next morning we started for Balmoral, passing Abergeldie Castle, and Crathie, two places now endeared to us in connection with the Queen and her illustrious mother, and known almost as well as the Bank of England and the General Post Office.

Leaving the little village of Crathie, we soon found ourselves in the grounds of Balmoral. We called at the palace, and sent our cards to the housekeeper for permission to see the interior of the castle and the grounds. This lady received us most courteously, and regretted that as they were making arrangements for the arrival of the Queen, who was expected in a few days, no visitors were allowed within the palace. She gave us permission to see the gardens and plantations, and also to range about the extensive grounds surrounding this Highland home of our beloved Sovereign, rendered, however, desolate by the absence of one who taxed his good taste to the uttermost in making this beautiful retired spot as attractive as possible to his illustrious wife, and their royal children.

The palace, though a chaste and beautiful structure, does not strike the beholder as being very regal. Taymouth Castle and Dalkeith Palace have both a much more palatial appearance, and the grounds surrounding them are more extensive and attractive than are those at Balmoral; yet there is something about the severely classic pile at Balmoral that reminds you at once of the exquisite taste and refined mind of her Majesty and the illustrious Prince, under whose immediate superintendence the new palace was reared. The locality is far away from the fashionable and frequented parts of the Highlands, and is, indeed, in all respects just such a spot as might have been expected would have been selected by its lamented owner and his Royal lady, as a quiet resting-place after the wearisome round of courtly duties in the south.

The gardens and plantations in the immediate vicinity of the palace are laid out, as may be imagined, in the best taste; but trees must have time to grow, and the alterations that were made under the direction of the Prince Consort will be seen to greater advantage as years roll on.

Having rambled for a couple of hours or more about this Highland home of our beloved Queen, we bade farewell to Balmoral, and took the private road through the Pine Forest to Castletown of Braemar. It came on to rain, as it does in these northerly regions, without any previous indication, and we were glad to have the shelter afforded by the dark and sombre pines as we walked on for some miles through the forest. The pelting rain, however, did not prevent us from turning out of our way, for some distance, to see the Falls of Garrawalt, a favourite resort of her Majesty and her royal children. We looked at them from several points of view; and not with the less interest from the fact that the Queen has made several sketches of the more beautiful scenes with her own pencil.

We called at one of the gamekeeper's lodges not far from the falls, and were shown by the good woman of the house the chair where her Majesty had sat very often to rest herself after a long walk. We were directed also to portraits of the Queen and the late Prince Consort on the walls of the little cottage, that were presented by the royal widow. This gamekeeper's wife told us several very inte-

resting anecdotes of her Majesty; but as they were mentioned incidentally as we conversed with her, I do not feel
at liberty to repeat them. I may say, however, that they
were such as to reflect the highest honour upon the great
personage in question, and convinced us more than ever
that, exalted as are the virtues of our Queen in her public
and regal capacity, she shines still more in her womanliness. There was not one of us there who did not lift up
our hearts to the Fountain of all Goodness, that He would
continue to manifest His care to her; and that He would
bind up her sorrowing heart, and wipe the tears from her
sad countenance. How true it is that " one touch of
nature makes the whole world kin."

The day cleared up as we neared Braemar, and we
obtained some fine views of " dark Lochnagarr," towering
proudly pre-eminent in these northern Highlands. We
did not forget that Lord Byron considered it " one of the
most sublime and picturesque amongst our Caledonian
Alps." It was near here that poor Byron spent some of
his early happy years; and in after-life, when in a foreign
land, the recollections of his youthful days came back upon
him, and while he mused his pen recorded some of the
thoughts that filled his heaving bosom:—

" Away, ye gay landscapes, ye gardens of roses!
    In you let the minions of luxury rove;
Restore me the rocks, where the snow flake reposes,
    Though still they are sacred to freedom and love.
Yet, Caledonia, beloved are thy mountains,
    Round their white summits though elements war,
Though cataracts foam 'stead of smooth flowing fountains,
    I sigh for the valley of dark Loch na Garr.

Ah! there my young footsteps in infancy wander'd;
    My cap was the bonnet, my cloak was the plaid;
On chieftains long perish'd my memory ponder'd,
    As daily I strode through the pine-cover'd glade.
I sought not my home till the day's dying glory
    Gave place to the rays of the bright polar star;
For fancy was cheer'd by traditional story,
    Disclosed by the natives of dark Loch na Garr.

*   *   *   *   *

Years have roll'd on, Loch na Garr, since I left you,
Years must elapse ere I tread you again :
Nature of verdure and flowers has bereft you,
· Yet still are you dearer than Albion's plain.
England ! thy beauties are tame and domestic
To one who has roved o'er the mountains afar:
Oh ! for the crags that are wild and majestic !
The steep frowning glories of dark Loch na Garr !"

We turned again, and yet again, to get this fine mountain fully impressed upon our mind's eye ; but as the day wore on we were compelled to leave its sombre beauties, and pursue our course to Braemar.

Castletown of Braemar is, as most of my readers will recollect, the highest land in Scotland, as well as being one of the healthiest places in the United Kingdom. It formerly consisted of only a few cottages clustering round Braemar Castle, but of late years it has been the resort of many who are in search of health, and has already grown to be a place of some importance. Its nearness to Balmoral will always make it attractive ; but one would hope that those who visit it will never intrude too much upon the royal domain, the chief charm of which is, that it is far removed from sight-seers. There are now two commodious inns at Castletown, where every comfort may be obtained ; and the surrounding scenery, though not so fine as some parts of the Highlands, is still highly picturesque and beautiful. The annual gathering of the clans at Braemar, sometimes honoured by the presence of royal personages, is a sight I imagine that would be exceedingly interesting. The view from the bridge of Dee, both up and down the river, is very imposing. Forests of fir clothe both sides of the valley, which is cultivated in many parts. The corn-fields and green pastures contrast well with the woods which occupy the gentle slopes on either hand, while these are crowned by amphitheatres of bare and lofty Alps, that rise in frowning majesty in the background.

We obtained the best accommodation at Fisher's Hotel, and learnt from its intelligent and obliging proprietor some valuable information as to reaching Blair Athole through the far-famed Glen Tilt. Information such as " mine host " kindly furnished us with is of late years very necessary to the tourist, as the Duke of Athole has not only demolished the huts and houses that once stood in the glen, and that were built by his ancestors, but he has also removed the bridge over the Tarff that divides the glen, in order, if possible, to prevent tourists from passing through this wild and beautiful valley.

Glen Tilt, it will be remembered, is a celebrated sporting rendezvous and deer-stalking region. Its ducal owner boasts that he possesses the best stocked and most extensive deer forest in all the country. It is said that no less than a hundred thousand acres of the surrounding ground are appropriated for the use of these noble animals. It is somewhat singular that we wended our way through this sequestered glen without catching a glimpse of one of them. We were informed, however, that they are frequently to be seen leisurely and majestically pacing along the edge of the impending cliffs.

Having provided ourselves with a good supply of sandwiches and whisky for our perambulations through the glen, as there was no chance of getting even a bason of milk by the way, we set off for Blair Athole, distant from Braemar about thirty miles. Our Australian brother had made a sketch of the route from instructions obtained from Mr. Fisher, of Braemar, and but for this precaution, I question if we should ever have found our way through some parts of this roadless and pathless region.

We engaged a waggonet to convey us as far as any vehicle can travel, which put us down at the hunting-box of the Earl of Fife, about twelve miles from Braemar. On our way there we alighted to see Carrymulzee Linn, Mar Lodge, and the beautiful Linn of Dee. The last-mentioned is a spot where the river has worn a long narrow passage, between thirty and forty feet deep, through rocks that have opposed its progress, and forms four small falls. Below the falls the water has scooped out a series of basons, where it sleeps deep, dark, and motionless. We were informed that when the water is low, some of the connecting channels are not more than a yard wide, but that it is subject to floods, which sometimes fill the chasm to the brim. Our coachman told us that the daring feat of leaping across the Linn has been occasionally performed.

On leaving our conveyance, we took our way over a bleak and barren moor, through a heavy rain, for about two hours, before reaching the head of the glen. Three hours' walk further brought us to the point of the Tarff, where the bridge formerly stood, and where we had been instructed to cross, as the water was not deep there. The rains had, however, considerably increased the volume of water in the river; but there was nothing to do but to ford the stream since the ducal owner had removed the bridge. This we at once proceeded to do by removing the lower parts of our dress; and having packed them up, and placed them on our heads, we slowly commenced the passage in single file. The river was about sixty feet wide at the point we crossed, and we found, before proceeding far, that the water nearly reached the middle of the tallest of us. We had some fears about our surgical friend, as he was some inches shorter than either of us; but he was a sturdy little fellow, and not at all wanting in pluck. The stream was so rapid that it was as much as any of us could do to keep our feet. We had not only to be careful to keep our standing, but as we had to hold the bundle of clothes and boots on our heads some of the party let slip their coat-tails into the water. The scene was most ludicrous and amusing, and we laughed heartily at the fun, though we did not forget to bless his grace of Athole for removing the bridge and thus risking the valuable life of our surgical friend, who more than once stumbled; and had he been carried away by the flood the consequences would have been very serious, as just below where we crossed the river narrowed and deepened into a black pool of unknown depth. We were glad, however, to find ourselves safe on the other side, and discover that the only damage done was that the sandwiches had got a wetting. As we put ourselves into marching order, we made the valley ring with roars of laughter at our little adventure. Fording the Tarff would have afforded a good sketch for George Cruikshank, especially if he could have depicted the grave and frightened look of our short brother as he reeled and stumbled in the dark and rapid waters.

Having demolished the sandwiches and taken a little whisky, we rambled on through a very wildly beautiful scene for some miles. A black deep river below us, and high wooded banks some hundred feet above our heads. The scenery of Glen Tilt, a few miles before reaching Blair Athole, is very beautiful.

The comforts of a good hotel are never so appreciated as when you have had a long wearisome walk of eighteen or twenty miles: tired, hungry, and footsore, the rest and refreshment to be had in these Highland hotels, after such a pleasurable day, must be enjoyed to be understood.

The next morning we visited the Falls of Bruar, and loitered about the woods in its vicinity for some hours. Here one of our party, who could sing a good song and spout poetry to almost any extent, finished up by dancing a hornpipe on the road, amid roars of laughter that were echoed again and again from the surrounding hills.

We returned to Blair Athole to dinner, and then set off leisurely through the Pass of Killiekrankie, and saw the Falls of Tummel—scenery which none of us will ever forget, for " a thing of beauty is a joy for ever." We found ourselves at Pitlochrie by tea-time, slept there, and next day marched on to Dunkeld.

The entrance to this Scottish city is most imposing. It stands on the banks of the Tay, on a broad plain embosomed among wooded hills and sloping mountains.

Rather a fine bridge spans the river, above which stand the ruins of the venerable cathedral: the choir has been restored by a former Duke of Athole, and is now used as a place of worship.

A little incident occurred here that I may mention. One of our brethren, feeling a little fatigued with the sight-seeing and journeyings of the last few days, retired to bed rather early, but not, alas! to sleep. A frolicsome brother stole softly into the room, and piled upon the bed, where his friend was resting, the wash-stand and its accompaniments, a chest of drawers, and almost all the furniture in the room. Having done this he called his brother tourists in to see the wearied friend who had laid him down to rest. A sketch was taken of the scene that our dear ones at home might have the benefit of the fun. The laughing that followed, I fear, sadly disturbed some of our more staid and serious neighbours, who must have been shocked at this breach of decorum at such an unseasonable hour of the night.

The next day being very wet, we did not explore the Duke of Athole's grounds at Dunkeld, the "policies" of which, we were informed, are upwards of fifty miles, independent of a carriage-drive of thirty. The duke makes a regular charge to visitors desirous of seeing his wide domains; and as we thought this to be not quite worthy of "a peer of the realm," &c. &c, we turned away from his broad acres to lands where we could wander at "our own sweet will." It would not surprise us to hear that this noble duke had put up a turnstile in Glen Tilt, to take toll of tourists as they do at Waterloo Bridge. I can understand a man being selfish enough to keep his hereditary palace and lands to himself; but for a duke to take half-a-crown as a fee for admission to his estates does not raise him very high in the estimation of his more plebeian brethren. He seems to be a stranger to the feeling that " good communicated becomes greater good."

How frequently during my wanderings through the

Highlands, and also when passing through some of the ancestral halls of our English nobility, have the beautiful words of Cowper come to my lips as the natural utterances of a Christian heart:—

> " He looks abroad into the varied field
>   Of nature, and though poor, perhaps, compared
>   With those whose mansions glitter in his sight,
>   Calls the delightful scenery all his own.
>   His are the mountains, and the valleys his,
>   And the resplendent rivers: his to enjoy
>   With a propriety that none can feel,
>   But who, with filial confidence inspired,
>   Can lift to heaven an unpresumptuous eye,
>   And smile and say—'My Father made them all!'
>   Are they not his by a peculiar right,
>   And by an emphasis of interest his,
>   Whose eye they fill with tears of holy joy,
>   Whose heart with praise, and whose exalted mind
>   With worthy thoughts of that unwearied love
>   That plann'd, and built, and still upholds, a world
>   So clothed with beauty for rebellious man?"

This is the crowning joy to all earth's beauties—it is our Father's world.

> " There's not a strain to memory dear,
>   Nor flower in classic grove,
>   There's not a sweet note warbled here
>   But minds us of Thy love.
>   O Lord, our Lord, and spoiler of our foes,
>   There is no light but Thine; with Thee all beauty glows."

Our ramblings were drawing now to a close, and as some of the party were desirous of seeing Edinburgh before our return to London, we held a consultation at Dunkeld as to where we should spend the next Sabbath. We looked each other up and down, and came to the conclusion that we were hardly presentable at Edinburgh on the Sunday. As we carried our wardrobe with us, and looking rather seedy after our hard walking, we determined upon spending the Sunday at Perth.

Accordingly we took the train from Dunkeld, and found

ourselves in " the fair city of Perth " on Saturday afternoon. As our clerical brother was well-known to many
of the good people here, he was hailed with a right hearty
welcome, and at once solicited to preach on the following
day. It was in vain that he pleaded to be excused, both
on account of his being holiday-making, and that he had
nothing but the grey suit he stood in; and to appear in
such a costume in the pulpit would never be forgiven by
his carefully correct countrymen and countrywomen. The
difficulty as to costume was surmounted by a proposition
that he should preach in the Town Hall, which would hold
a far greater number than could be assembled in any of
the churches or chapels of the city. In less than a couple
of hours the streets of Perth were placarded that our
reverend friend would preach on the following evening at
the Town Hall.

The arrangements for this special service having been
completed, and " the inner man " refreshed, we set out for
a walk through this pretty Highland city. Perth is, in
every way, what may be called a handsome and beautifully
situated city. Its historical reminiscences render it interesting to the antiquary as the scene of the Gowrie con-
spiracy; but to us it was the more interesting as having
been the scene of some of the earlier labours of the great
Reformer—John Knox.

We concluded our day's ramblings by ascending Kinnoul
Hill, and were delighted with one of the richest and most
extensive views in Scotland. The view from this point is
equal to, if it does not surpass, that from Stirling Castle;
and after giving expression to our feelings in one general
burst of admiration, we spent a couple of hours in quietly
taking in all the parts of this magnificent and almost
boundless panorama. We remained fondly gazing upon
this beautiful scene till the sun had gone down, and the
shades of evening reminded us that " nought on earth
abideth."

The evening was spent at the hospitable mansion of

one of the baillics of the city—a man of wealth and influence—where we met a select circle of friends, to whom we
recounted some of our wanderings through their noble
land.

Our appearance may be judged of from the fact that
when we called at the "Railway Hotel," to engage beds
for the night, the chambermaid conducted us to some
attics at the top of the house, as suitable apartments for
such a company of pilgrims. It was only when we mentioned the name of the gentleman at whose house we had
spent the evening that we were shown more comfortable
rooms. The proprietor of this hotel also came forward
with an apology for the very natural mistake of his
domestic.

This rather amusing incident was followed by one,
which, though somewhat ludicrous, was likely to have
ended in a more tragical story. Some hours after we
had retired to our respective rooms for the night, I was
awoke by a gentle tap at my door. I found, on opening
it, one of our brethren in what appeared to me the last
stage of cholera. He had partaken rather freely of the
viands at the party of the preceding evening, regardless
of the advice of "Thomas Ingoldsby, Esquire," of my
native county, who tells of one who—

> " Was seized
> With a tiresome complaint, which, in some seasons,
> People are apt to be seized
> With, who're not on their guard against plum-seasons."

On getting a light I found that my poor friend was in
a most woeful plight. The cold perspiration stood on his
face and forehead in large drops, and he was literally
brought to " death's door." Being alarmed at his pitiable
appearance, I found the room of our Australian brother,
and got him up to assist in attending to our prostrate
patient. By this time his pulse was so feeble, and the
exhaustion so great, that we awoke our clerical brother and

held a council as to what should be done. There was evidently no time to lose, as our sick friend lay across the bed, partly dressed, writhing in agony and looking most ghastly. He pointed to his " Daily Journal of Proceedings " that was open on the chimney-piece, in which he had carefully recorded his symptoms from hour to hour, and that in a tone that evidently implied that our little merry friend thought it not at all unlikely that he might " turn up his toes to the daisies." Unfortunately our whisky flask was empty ; but after some delay we roused the house and procured some brandy, that never-failing and invaluable remedy for this " horrid complaint." Having administered a pretty good dose of this domestic remedy to our prostrate friend, and wrapping him well up in the blankets, he began to revive, and before the morning he was so much better that we congratulated both him and ourselves that a doctor was not called in. If medical aid had been summoned, it is most probable that our little friend would have been laid up for some days. On getting him down stairs to breakfast we recommended him for the future, by way of " moral " to this serio-comic exhibition,—

> " Of stone-fruits in general be shy,
>   And reflect, it's a fact beyond question,
> That grapes, when spelt with an *i*,
>   Promote anything else but digestion."

We spent a quiet Sunday in Perth, and enjoyed the rest and refreshment of the day with its hallowed services. The meeting in the evening at the Town Hall was a crowded one, and I never heard a more useful sermon than that preached on the occasion by our reverend brother. The platform was filled with the ministers of the various churches and chapels of the city, there being no evening service at Perth. The sun-burnt face of the preacher, in his light tweed suit and blue cravat, contrasted strangely enough with the grave countenances and the ministerial costume of the reverend brethren by whom he was surrounded.

U

I hope it will be seen elsewhere one day that this "special service" was made useful to not a few.

We left Perth for Edinburgh, *en route* for home, by the first train in the morning, and spent the remainder of the day in seeing the principal "lions" of that famous "city set on a hill." A young fellow who resided at Edinburgh, and was known to our clerical brother, took us up Arthur's Seat by what he called a short cut. He led the way and we followed, and instead of going round by St. Catherine's well, and gradually making the ascent by that ordinary and safe route, he took us up the face of the rock, a part of which is nearly perpendicular. What we saved in distance was more than made up in risk : in fact it was the only really venturesome thing that we did during our ramblings.

We concluded our very happy Highland tour by having ourselves photographed in a group by one of the best artists in Edinburgh, as a memento of our holiday, and took the train in the evening from the Caledonian Station for King's Cross, where we arrived safely the next morning.

One who has lately spent "a summer in Skye," and has visited the Highlands,* gives the following good advice, which I transcribe with much pleasure for the information of those of my readers who may be thinking of seeing Scotland for themselves :—" The Highlands can be enjoyed in the utmost simplicity ; and the best preparations are, money to a moderate extent in one's pocket, a knapsack containing a spare shirt and a tooth-brush, and a courage that does not fear to breast the steep of the hill, and to encounter the pelting of a Highland shower. No man knows a country till he has walked through it ; he then tastes the sweets and the bitters of it ; he beholds its grand and important points, and all the subtler and concealed beauties that lie out of the beaten track. Then, oh Reader ! in the most glorious of the months, the very

---

* Alexander Smith.

crown and summit of the fruitful year, hanging in equal poise between summer and autumn, leave London or Edinburgh, or whatever city your lot may happen to be cast in, and accompany me in my wanderings. Our course will lead us by ancient battle-fields, by castles standing in hearing of the surge; by the bases of mighty mountains, and along the wanderings of hollow glens." I can give my hearty amen to this invitation of the eloquent author of " A Summer in Skye," etc. and would say to all who have the time and the means at their disposal, go and see this glorious land for yourselves.

I feel that what has been imperfectly said of Scotland, and the scenery of the Highlands, will not come up to what a Scotchman may think of his native country; but they are the grateful utterances of a son of the south who laments his inability to do more ample justice to such scenes of beauty, grandeur, and magnificence.

UPSTREET AND CHISLETT.

AMONG the places visited by me not unfrequently of late years, during my vacations, is a small village in the parish of Chislett, known by the name of Upstreet. That rural and salubrious little place is interesting to me on many accounts.

For more than half a century an uncle of mine rented a farm under Sir John Bridges, which lies to the right and left of the road leading from Canterbury to the Isle of Thanet. It is situated just below the road leading to Grove-Ferry, which in my early days, before railways were introduced, was one of the most lovely and retired spots in the fair county of Kent. Often, as a boy, have I sat on the stile, at the top of the bank that overlooks the river Stour, gazing in silent rapture on the beautiful scene spread out before the eye from that spot. From there may be seen a great part of the Isle of Thanet, and on a clear day the cliffs at Ramsgate. Nearer home the villages of Minster, Sarre, Stourmouth, Preston, Ash, Stodmarsh, Ickham, Wickham, Wingham, and Littlebourne are seen with the embattled towers and angel-finger spires of the churches, always the crowning features of an English landscape, and, but for a projecting bank, Canterbury Cathedral would add to the interest of the scene. The towers of this noble cathedral may, however, be seen to great advantage by those who will take the footpath by the side of the river, into a park-like meadow at the top, where they will be rewarded by as fine a view of the kind as may be seen in all the county.

Grove-Ferry is now one of the well-known stations on the South-Eastern Railway, and many are the parties from Margate and Ramsgate, during the summer, who frequent the pretty and attractive " Tea-Gardens " on the other side of the river.

How a railway alters a scene, and puts to flight much of the poetry of a place! Of late years I have sat on the stile which I was wont to linger about as a boy, and have watched the thin white line of smoke as the train has made its way from Minster through the Sarre marshes to Grove-Ferry; and while one cannot but rejoice that the iron road has opened up a way for the tired and used-up Londoners to reach the healthful watering-places of the Isle of Thanet, where they may recruit their wasted powers without a sea voyage, yet the lover of quiet and repose at Grove-Ferry will look upon it as an innovation.

What a contrast is presented by the hissing and rattling express-train as it rushes thundering past the station, to " the silent highway " of the river Stour, whose tranquil waters glide softly by its side! The one is noisy and ostentatious, as are all the works of man; the other is silent and unobtrusive, as are the works of God, and the tired and wearied mind lingers with loving fondness by its side.

Every visitor to Canterbury and the Isle of Thanet who loves English scenery, should not omit to spend an afternoon at Grove-Ferry. It can be reached either by rail or coach, as the visitor may desire. The accommodation and civility of the worthy host and hostess at the Ferry "Tea-Gardens," will, I am sure, be appreciated by those who are as fond of good cheer as of beautiful scenery.

On visiting this pretty place, not long since, I could not help repeating to myself, as I looked lingeringly once more at the winding river,—

> " Men may come, and men may go ;
> But Stour flows on for ever."

When quite a child, I remember to have been sent to stay with my aunt at Upstreet, for months together, so that almost every tree and blade of grass on my uncle's farm was familiar to me ; and in after years, when I could leave London, and afford the time to take a holiday, no place had so many charms for me.

The old farm-house and its surroundings are very picturesque, and no one who loves English homesteads could pass down the road without admiring it. The house is of red-brick, and literally covered with grape-vine, jessamine, honeysuckle, and ivy. In front was a lawn, soft and yielding as Genoa velvet, and kept during my uncle's time in the most perfect order; to the left was a large orchard, where once grew some of the choicest apples that my native county could produce. The principal entrance to the house was through a Gothic porch, where roses, honeysuckle, and jessamine were blended with the best taste. A little to the left of the house was the dairy, a semi-detached building, so much resembling an ecclesiastical structure that we always called it "the Priory." This building is so embosomed in ivy that not a single brick is to be seen.

Such was the house where I spent many happy months

of my childhood; and as a boy I loved to ramble with my uncle through the green pastures and the waving corn-fields, and to assist him at even-tide to take an account of the sheep and cattle.

I was particularly fond of fetching up the cows in the afternoon for milking, and used to sit and watch the dairy-maid as she drew from them their rich and yielding trea-sures. The way from the marshes where the cows were pastured lay through a small wood, called Walmer's-hill. The pathway was at the bottom of a sandy slope, clothed with hawthorn bushes, the wild rose, and honeysuckle, and with a rich profusion of primroses in the Spring. The rabbits ran about as thick as blackberries, and one evening when I had driven the cows down from milking and was returning home alone, a full-grown fox came out into the pathway within a few yards of me, and stared me in the face. I was a little startled at Reynard's boldness, and we both gazed steadfastly at each other for some moments, when the little fellow looked so fierce and resolute that I put a cow's-horn that was slung at my back to my lips, and blew as loud a blast as I could. This was more than master Reynard expected, and he cantered off leisurely up the slope to his quarters. My uncle was much amused at this incident, and would have liked to have had the chance of putting a little shot into the gentleman, who had often made too free with my aunt's poultry.

My uncle was devotedly attached to farming; but while he was well up in Sir John Sinclair, and freely availed himself of all the practical knowledge of that eminent agriculturist, his library contained not a few choice volumes in general literature. He was " a fine old English gen-tleman, one of the olden time;" and though by no means wealthy, was known to all the neighbours round as a con-tributor to everything that would add to the comfort and happiness of those who tilled his farm and reaped his harvests.

My aunt was a very loveable woman, and always treated

me as one of her own children. I have stood by her side and watched her many a time moulding the butter into pyramidal pounds and pretty little tempting pats, as she, with upturned sleeve, displayed an arm of finest shape, and a rounded dimpled elbow that would have gratified Peter Paul Rubens, and which charmed me even as a boy. She was married before she was eighteen, and must, when young, have been a lovely "maid of Kent."

There were seven cousins in that farm-house, and as most of them were about my own age, many were the pranks and gambols we indulged in.

I visited this old familiar place not very long since, and how changed is the scene! My uncle has been for some years gathered to his fathers, and has exchanged a life of toil and labour for a land where "the weary are at rest." My dear old aunt has long since left the farm, and resides at Canterbury, with a daughter who was some years since disappointed in love, and will, in all probability, "remain unmarried till her death."

The farm-house, once so snug and comfortable, is now little better than a ruin; the garden, once so carefully tended, has become almost a wilderness; and the farm-yard, once so trim and neat, is now little cared for. There has come over the whole scene a melancholy change, and as I have gone round and round the old familiar place, endeared to me by a thousand hallowed recollections of early happy days, I have felt the cheek moistened, and the words swell up from my heart—

"It is not now as it hath been of yore;
  Turn wheresoe'er I may,
    By night or day,
The things which I have seen, I now can see no more."

Although my uncle is gone, and a stranger now owns the house that once received me as one of its own, I occasionally visit this well-remembered spot. A septuagenarian cousin, who is a retired purser in the Royal Navy, resides not far from where my uncle lived, and many happy hours have I spent of late in his jovial society. He is as full of health and vigour as a man of forty, and is a most genial companion, teeming with ready wit and quiet fun. An old schoolfellow lives within a mile of the place, around whose hospitable board I have met with many old and valued friends.

The walks about Upstreet are very picturesque. I well remember a ramble across the marshes to the little village of Reculver, by the sea, to look at the interesting ruins of the old church there. It is a favourite resort of the archæologist ; but as my study has been man, rather than his surroundings, I leave the antiquities of the place to wiser heads, who find "sermons in stones, and good in everything." On the day referred to, I had a fair cousin for my companion ; and after wandering about among the broken fragments of the old church, and looking out upon the deep blue sea, we sat down, musing upon the past, thinking of those who once worshipped within its sacred walls, and whose dust was beneath our feet. I recollect full well, though many years have passed since then, sending a boy for a flagon of Cobbs' Margate ale, from the "King Ethelbert," and while feasting upon meat patties, my fair cousin read to me some "lines from the bards sublime," which never seemed so sublime before, as the ale and patties were most grateful after the long and pleasant walk. The day was fine, and we were within hearing

"Of the grand majestic symphonies of ocean."

A pleasing melancholy pervaded our kindred minds, so that the couple of hours spent at Reculver will ever be a red-letter-day in my vacation rambles.

TUNBRIDGE WELLS AND ITS SURROUNDINGS.

UNBRIDGE WELLS was a place where I spent a part of several vacations, not only on account of its attractive scenery, its pure and bracing air, and its health-restoring waters, but that it also afforded me an opportunity of spending a few weeks with an old and valued friend whose society I much enjoyed.

Perhaps there are few places so near London where the scenery is so diversified and picturesque as at Tunbridge Wells. If you are fond of walking, you may ramble over open downs and through green lanes, where, at almost every turn of the road, you get glimpses of the beautiful country around; and if the reader is there in the autumn, and is fond of blackberries and nuts, he may be satisfied to his heart's content. "The common" at Tunbridge Wells is a fine open ground, almost always dry, as it is a sandy soil, and where have been placed many rustic seats, from any of which may be obtained a view of the surrounding country. Rusthall Common, and "the Happy Valley," will always have its admirers while English scenery has a charm for visitors; and those who want to see a pretty village must go to Southborough, only three miles from the town, where a man, weary of London and its endless work, may here surround himself with rural beauty such as can rarely be surpassed.

Bishop's Down, and Hurst Wood, are within an easy walk of the town. Bishop's Down overlooks a wide and fertile landscape, which, when you have enjoyed, you may turn your footsteps to a lane overshadowed with lofty trees to a beautifully secluded retreat called Hurst Wood, where one can be reminded of the poet's words :—

> " Reader, if thou hast learnt a truth which needs
> No school of long experience, that the world

Is full of guilt and misery, and hast seen
Enough of all its sorrows, crimes, and cares,
To tire thee of it—enter the wild wood
And view the haunts of Nature. The calm shade
Shall bring a kindred calm, and the sweet breeze
That makes the green leaves dance, shall waft a balm
To thy sick heart."

The owner of this wood has kindly placed seats in the most attractive parts of this sylvan retreat, where you may enjoy Tennyson, or Keble, or any other favourite author you happen to have in your pocket, or, what is perhaps better, a chat with some loving sympathetic " friend, with whom to whisper, solitude is sweet."

The pretty village of Frant, about two miles from the " wells," was a favourite resort with me; and from the tower of its church can be seen, in a clear day, a panorama of great beauty, including the Sussex Downs, the hills of Surrey, and the heights of Kent, and even extending to Dungeness and Beachy Head. The rector of this little church is one of the most aristocratic looking parsons I ever saw. He is, I believe, brother-in-law of Lord Abergavenny, the owner of Eridge Castle, in the immediate neighbourhood. I once saw this kingly-looking clergyman bury a pauper, and was not a little pleased with the devout and reverent manner in which he read the beautiful service of the Church of England over the remains of one who had no mourning friends to gather around his grave, but only the workhouse officials to bear him to his last long home. If he had been one of the greatest in the land, the officiating clergyman could not have behaved with greater seriousness and decorum. The rector of Frant will always be embalmed in my memory as one of nature's noblemen for this act, which contrasted so happily with the cold and flippant way which I had sometimes seen a London clergyman of " the poor man's church " perform this last office for a pauper. He is a baronet; and I found, from inquiries made in the village, that he is a kind-hearted man, ever ready to help and sympathize with, the wants and necessities of his needy parishioners.

The invalid at Tunbridge Wells can suit himself with a carriage of any description, from a donkey-chaise to the stylish well-horsed open barouche ; and the many beautiful drives in the neighbourhood are probably nowhere to be surpassed in any of the fair counties of our merrie England. If you are a horseman, and have no nag of your own, you can be well mounted at riding-master Cramps, who owns a large stud of well-trained horses ; and should you be an early riser you can enter into the joy of one who pencilled the following lines on the crown of his hat :—

" At five on a dewy morning,
   Before the blazing day,
To be up and off on a high-mettled horse,
   Over the hills away.
To drink the sweet breath of the gorse,
   And bathe in the breeze of the Downs.
Ha ! man, if you can, match bliss like this
   In all the joys of towns !

With glad and grateful tongue to join
   The lark at his matin hymn ;
And hence on faith's own wing to spring
   And sing with Cherubim !
To pray from a deep and tender heart,
   With all things praying anew,
The birds and the bees, and the whispering trees,
   And heather bedropt with dew,
To be one with those early worshippers,
   And pour the pæan too !

Then off again with a slacken'd rein,
   And a bounding heart within ;
To dash at a gallop over the plain,
   Health's golden cup to win !
This, this is the race for gain and grace,
   Richer than vases and crowns ;
And you that boast your pleasures the most,
   Amid the steam of towns,
Come, taste true bliss, in a morning like this,
   Galloping over the Downs ! "

If you make your first attempt at horsemanship, let it be early in the morning, and not in the middle of the day, as was the case with me. My friend with whom I was staying was accustomed to take a couple of hours' ride for the benefit of his health at mid-day, and he prevailed upon me to accompany him, and provided me with a fine, tall, sleek animal, such as would not have disgraced "Rotten Row." I had not crossed a horse for more than twenty years, and felt a little nervous at first. However, we started through the town at a walking pace, and I began to feel my feet pretty comfortably; but on getting on the sandy ground of Broadwater Forest, my friend started for a gallop, and my nag followed as a matter of course. I stuck my knees well into the saddle, and held on all right; but I soon lost my "wide-awake:" and before we pulled up my trousers had worked up over my boots and above my knees, very much to the amusement of my friend, who thoroughly enjoyed this, my first lesson, in riding. Some equestrians were mightily pleased at the figure I cut; but I congratulated myself at keeping my seat in the saddle, and was quite careless as to the appearance I presented. However, with a little instruction from my friend, and a pair of straps to my trousers, I managed to take my daily ride after this with great comfort, and occasionally was in the saddle soon after break of day.

Most of the places of interest in the neighbourhood of Tunbridge Wells are within reach of an easy walk, or a short ride. Bayham Abbey, with its beautiful ruins, lies about six miles south-east of the "wells," and is well deserving a visit. Mayfield Place, once a palace of the Archbishop of Canterbury, and at a later date the favourite residence of Sir Thomas Gresham, founder of the Royal Exchange, and where Queen Elizabeth became his guest, is now in ruins. Here it is tradition affirms that St. Dunstan manifested his miraculous power; and there are still to be seen, by those who are of an antiquarian turn of mind, the sword, hammer, anvil, and tongs with which that hot-headed and redoubtable prelate, according to monastic fables, flattened the nose of a distinguished personage when he intruded on his meditations.

> " For of course you have read,
>   That St. Dunstan was bred!
>   A goldsmith, and never quite gave up the trade !
>   The company—richest in London, 'tis said—
>   Acknowledge him still as their patron and head."

Near the entrance to the ruins of Mayfield Place is the famous St. Dunstan's Well, said to be more than three hundred feet deep. Crowburgh Beacon, the highest hill in Sussex, is not far distant, where on a fine day can be seen a magnificent prospect, extending many miles on every side.

The ride, on the top of the coach that runs from Uckfield to Tunbridge Wells, is one of the prettiest pieces of scenery to be met with in Kent or Surrey. There is also Brambletye, which will ever be interesting to all who have read Horace Smith's clever story of " Brambletye House," where you may recal the incidents upon which the novelist founded that charming tale of history and fiction. Lamberhurst, about two miles south-east of Bayham Abbey, quite comes up to what Cobbett calls it, " one of the most beautiful villages that man ever set his eyes on."

Knole House, with its invaluable collection of paintings, entitling it to the distinction of the " Picture Gallery of Kent," and the " Louvre of England," will always be an object of great attraction. It is a beautiful drive of about fourteen miles, and near Sevenoaks, one of the healthiest and most picturesque villages in my native county. The noble park at Knole contains some of the finest oaks, elms, and beeches in the kingdom.

Penshurst, however, to me presented the greatest charms. The walk there, by way of Southborough, and through Bidborough Park, will never be forgotten. My companion was one who knew all the localities well, and pointed out to me the numerous places of interest to be seen on the road. The village of Penshurst is charmingly situated on the banks of the Medway; and the place, as everybody knows, has been associated for centuries with genius, worth, chivalry, and patriotism. Penshurst, the birthplace and home of the Sidneys, with its noble mansion, its gardens, and extensive park, is classic ground. Here you may see, in its fine old hall, the sword of Sir Philip Sidney, and a right stalwart hero he must have been to have handled such a weapon. On the walls of the hall are suspended weapons of war and armour that have seen good service on many a hard-fought field, where laurels were gained by the chivalrous and patriotic Sidneys. As I looked round this fine old hall the famous lines of Campbell came to my lips—

" Men of England! who inherit
   Rights that cost your sires their blood!
Men whose undegenerate spirit
   Has been proved on land and flood!

By the foes ye've fought uncounted,
   By the glorious deeds ye've done,
Trophies captured, breaches mounted,
   Navies conquer'd, kingdoms won!

Yet remember! England gathers
   Hence but fruitless wreaths of fame,
If the virtues of your fathers
   Glow not in your hearts the same.

    *   *   *   *

Yours are Hampden's, Russell's glory,
   Sidney's matchless shade is yours,
Martyrs in heroic story!
   Worth a thousand Agincourts!

We're the sons of sires that baffled
   Crown'd and mitred tyranny!
They defied the field and scaffold,
   For their birthrights; *so will we!*"

In the ball-room here, tradition relates that the maiden queen opened the ball with Sir Philip Sidney; "her Philip," as she used to call him, in contrast to Philip of Spain. All the apartments abound with interesting relics of Elizabeth and her age, a description of which would fill a volume, and also demand an abler pen than mine. In every room almost may be seen gems of the old masters, including Titian, Vandyck, Guido, Poussin, Teniers, Caracci, and a host of others. The tapestry-room well deserves its name, for it contains some matchless specimens of art. Never did loom more faithfully delineate figures and landscapes, or weave more brilliant colours—colours which time has been unable to fade.

Of course I visited the beauties of Eridge Park, the princely seat of the Earl of Abergavenny. Eridge Castle is a magnificent pile, in the castellated style, occupying a bold eminence in a well wooded and watered park of more than two thousand acres. The visitor should enter the park from the Frant road, and he may spend a day very pleasantly in rambling about among its many beauties.

To go to Tunbridge Wells, and not see the "High Rocks," would be almost impossible. They are highly interesting, and to my humble judgment perfectly inexplicable, after all that the learned have theorized about them. There they stand in all their awful grandeur, placed there by One "who weigheth the mountains in scales, and the hills in a balance." Thousands of centuries have rolled on since their formation, and how they came to be placed where they are no one seems to know.

One place especially retains very much its original appearance, and carries us back a century since. It is the quaint old Parade, the *boulevard* of Tunbridge Wells. It is still a fashionable promenade, and at certain hours during the summer months a private band performs all the popular music of the day in the orchestra, which bears the appearance of having been erected when the town was the resort of illustrious worthies long since passed away. The old Parade and its accompaniments vividly recal the celebrated personages who once thronged its promenade.

Among them may be mentioned Dr. Johnson, Colley Cibber, the frail and beautiful Miss Chudleigh, afterwards Duchess of Kingston, Garrick, the Earl of Chatham, Mrs. Thrale, and a host of others of inferior name in the annals of that age.

I fear that I have tired the patience of my readers in lingering so long at Tunbridge Wells; but it is a place very interesting to me, inasmuch as I have spent many happy weeks there in the society of a valued friend, who has been my companion in many a ramble, and who was cut down in a day, and withered like a flower, save that his memory is cherished by a large circle of friends, who could not but love a man in whom was found so many excellences, and whose Christian character commanded the respect and admiration of all who knew him. Some one has truly said, that—

> " To live in hearts we leave behind
> Is not to die."

And this is eminently true of him whose mortal remains are laid in a secluded spot of the little cemetery near the town, where he spent the last few years of his short, but happy and useful life, and within a few yards of the last resting-place of the late distinguished physician, Dr. Golding Bird, who was also removed in the meridian of life—another martyr to an overworked brain—and one who will not soon be forgotten by the many patients that have profited by his great professional skill. The plain simple slab, that bears the name of " Edward Millard,"* covers the remains of a friend that will ever be embalmed in the memory of the writer of these pages.

---

* See a useful and elegant funeral Sermon preached by the Rev. W. Landels, on the occasion of the sudden death of this good man, entitled, " In Memoriam. A Tribute to the Memory of Edward Millard. London, 1863. 12mo. Published by Simpkin and Co." Young men would do well to read and ponder this Sermon.

DORKING AND BOX HILL.

T was late in the autumn of the year that I took the train from London Bridge to Dorking, to pay my first visit to some newly-married friends. Having spent their honeymoon at Rome, where they remained for three months, they returned to England, and had settled down into domestic life in a very pretty villa residence at Dorking. A boy nearly twelve months old, the first fond pledge of their married life, a sweet little fat, chubby fellow, such as Caracci or Raphael would have delighted to have painted, gladdened their home with his infantile crowing and crying. The husband was a man in the prime and vigour of life, who, with ample means, had spent a good deal of time on the Continent, and knew as much of Paris, Rome, Florence, and Naples as of London.

I found that he had adorned his home with choice pictures from " the grand old masters," as well as good copies by Roman and Florentine artists of one or two of the great pictures of Raphael, Caracci, and Domenichino. Three exquisite water-colour views of the Bay of Naples, by a Neapolitan hand, shone upon his drawing-room walls, and a few genuine bronzes were seen in the dining-room, amongst which were the Fawn, the Apollo Belvidere, and the Medici Venus. Photographs of the Transfiguration, Gibson's Venus, and other art favourites, met your eye on every side, and everything in the house manifested most unmistakably that no expense had been spared to make their home a little paragon of comfort and good taste.

His wife was a fair young creature in her twenty-first year, whom I had known as a school girl. She was pretty and fascinating as a girl of fifteen, but now she had fairly blossomed into womanhood. Rather below the average

x

height, she had a form that any sculptor would have been glad to have moulded as a model. Her face was an oval, and with a bloom upon it resembling a peach. Mouth small, and lips as thin as they well could be. Her nose was perhaps what an artist would have deemed rather too small, and the lower part of the face a little too full to be classical. Her hair was light and wavy, and arranged in the simplest manner. She had the tiniest foot for a woman that I ever beheld, and a hand such as a duke would have delighted to kiss. Her conversational powers were brilliant, and when speaking her face was full of dimples, and such as to fix your gaze admiringly. Her soft blue eyes looked out lovingly upon you like that of an angel, as full of purity as of love. She was an accomplished pianist, and possessed a voice of silvery sweetness.

I could but congratulate my friend upon having such an " angel in the house ;" and as the first few days of my visit were wet, cold, and uninviting as to out-door exercises, I had ample opportunities of enjoying the society of this charming woman. I fear that some of my more staid and unromantic readers will smile at the description I have vainly attempted to make of this fair young wife. If so, they can turn over the page and leave it for more congenial readers. For my own part, I have always been a most enthusiastic admirer of fair women ; and in such a prosaic world surely a man who numbers fifty summers may be pardoned for indulging in so innocent a weakness as that which I have been attempting.

I set out one fine clear morning with this lady for my guide, her husband being unavoidably detained at home, to see some of the beauties in the neighbourhood of Dorking. I gave myself up most unreservedly to her own sweet will, as it was the first time I had visited this picturesque and surpassingly beautiful locality. We passed through the principal street of the town,—of which the author of " Proverbial Philosophy " says, " Name a third country-town for beauty and cleanliness, and all that makes a place pleasant, worthy to be numbered with Dorking and Guildford,"—to Betchley Park, and soon found ourselves under the stately beeches there, treading upon the brown broad leaves which lay around us " thick as those in Vallambrosa." Having strolled through this noble park, we passed through a gate and crossed the road into the opposite meadow, to see the famed " Betchley Avenue," justly celebrated as the finest natural cathedral to be seen in all England ; a triple avenue of lime trees resembling the nave of a cathedral, but greatly surpassing in grandeur and beauty any " temple made with hands." If there were nothing else at Dorking but this wondrously beautiful avenue, it would be worth taking a day from London to see it. I am not going to attempt any further description of this grand sight, as it is so well known ; and, moreover, it would require the pen of a Ruskin, and the pencil of a Creswick or Birket Foster, to reproduce such a scene with any credit.

Returning from this avenue, we took the road to the right of the bridge, from the centre of which a pretty view presents itself. The heavy rains of the preceding days had so swollen the river Mole as to produce quite a flood ; and so wide was it in the vicinity of the bridge, as to resemble a small lake. You get a fine view of the grounds and mansion at Denbies* from this spot. We passed along, keeping to the right, till we came to two gates, one on either side of the road ; here we paused and rested awhile. The scene was rural and delightful ; a newly-ploughed field was between us and the river, whose swollen waters we could hear murmuring at our feet, though hidden by trees. At a gap to the right we caught a glimpse of the river, with Betchley Park for a background, with its patches of verdure and its thousand golden trees. The

* The estate of Denbies is now in the possession of George Cubitt, Esq. M.P., who, we are informed, has effected considerable alterations in the grounds, as well as having erected a spacious and handsome mansion in place of the small house that once stood there.

spire of Dorking church, just pointing above the trees, in
the distance, while further to the right was Denbies, with
its park and princely mansion, and the pretty steeple of
Ranmore church standing like an angel by its side. We
lingered here to let the eye wander slowly along the crown
of the hill, which is broken to the extreme right by the
valley between that and Box Hill, the back of which you
see, and terminating with a dark pine plantation, contrasting finely with the golden crowns of the surrounding woodland. Proceeding on the road to Reigate, we continued
our walk till we came to two pretty red-brick cottages with
rose trees growing up the walls ; passing these we turned
up a narrow lane to the left, and crossing the wooden bridge
over the railway, we took the road by the chalk pit, and
began to ascend the steep and precipitous hill. My young
guide tripped along gaily enough ; but it sadly taxed my
respiratory organs, and we were obliged to sit down more
than once that I might " get my wind." It reminded me,
however, that nothing worth having is to be obtained without labour, and when you have toiled hard and manfully
for something, how great is the enjoyment of fruition.

Having at length gained the summit of this hill we were
rewarded by a magnificent view of the surrounding country,
rich and fertile as an English landscape always is. Immediately at our feet was a ploughed field, with the
husbandman casting in the seed-corn from his basket ;
further on the river Mole wandered between its green
banks, and in the distance soft undulating hills and slopes,
crowned with woodland, stretched out for many a mile as
far as the eye could reach. The railway is just below you
in the valley ; but as a train passed which in some measure
destroyed for a moment the poetry of the scene, it was at
such a distance as to make the interruption rather pleasant
than otherwise. Passing through a field we gained the
road, and, turning to the right, walked on for about half a
mile with a plantation on either side ; a little further on
there is an opening in the road to the left, so that you can

walk out upon the open Downs. Here we had a glorious view of the country, and as we strolled leisurely along the crown of Box Hill the scene was far more beautiful than any words of mine can describe. The broken bottles, corks, and fragments of paper strewn about, suggested gipsy parties, and young loving couples, who always, for some reasons known only to themselves, wander away from the rest of the party to tell to each other, as they walk hand-in-hand, " truths that perish never." The owner of this beautiful domain has not only thrown it open for all the world to range in, but has also placed seats where the best views can be obtained, so that you may sit down and at your leisure take in the scene before you. In one charming nook is a comfortable seat to hold a dozen, with a round table that would have pleased good King Arthur himself.

After resting awhile we continued our way along the crown of the hill, and turning into the plantation walked through its darkened pathway till we came to an opening where a view bursts at once upon you that is certainly unequalled by anything of the kind I have ever beheld. Immediately below were clusters of beech, chestnut, and oak trees, crowned with glory; a little to the left the park and mansion at Denbies. Looking through the valley, hill upon hill in long and varied succession meets the eye, and as you gaze language fails to express the beauty and loveliness of the scene. As I had no guide-book, many of the places in the distance were unknown to me, and also to my fair .conductress; but I believe St. Paul's and Westminster Abbey can be seen by the naked eye on a clear day, as well as the hills beyond London.

My fair friend pointed out to me the pretty little Burford Bridge Hotel, at the foot of the hill; a place not only associated with great names in the literary world, but also a favourite resort for young newly-married couples. I can hardly conceive a more fitting place for beginning wedded life. It is well to surround oneself on such occasions with all that is beautiful, so that in after-life, when trials and sorrows come, we may look back to such green spots with pleasure and delight.

After remaining on the hill till we had taken our fill of the lovely scene, and had exhausted all our stock of descriptive epithets—helped not a little by quotations from many a son of song—we descended the steep path leading to the road.   Coming down hill, to a man of my years, is even more trying than the going up, as it tries the knees, which are terribly inclined to " bow themselves."   The keen air and breezy heights had quickened my appetite, so that I could not resist going into the Burford Bridge Hotel for a glass of stout and a biscuit.   It is a most comfortable little hotel—a place where young fellows may take their sweethearts, and old fellows their wives.

Leaving the hotel, we took the road to Dorking, over the bridge, till we came to a turning on the road leading to Mr. Cubitt's.   A handsome lodge fronts the road, and a good carriage-way, through a pretty plantation, winds its way to the residence of this wealthy commoner.   About half a mile from the entrance you approach the open ground, and before you is a picturesque view of Dorking, with its pretty church, and its many villa residences jotted about in every direction.   We pursued our way to within a few yards of the house, when we turned off to the right, by a pathway, to Ranmore church and common.   The view from the lodge leading from the park to Ranmore Common is very extensive and beautiful.   The church, a modern structure in the Gothic style, is all that an ecclesiologist could desire ; and we were informed that the interior presents an appearance that would satisfy the most careful admirer of church adornments.   The church, with its accompaniments, are all the product of Mr. Cubitt's munificence.   Nonconformist as I am, I cannot but admire the beautiful structures raised at the present day by private individuals, whom God has prospered in this world's good, and who, I think, make a grateful and graceful acknowledgment of the same by erecting a temple to His praise.

Leaving this very pretty little church, with its commodious schools, we made our way for a footpath through a small plantation by the side of the road, where again is spread out before you such a view as an artist would be enamoured of, but which no pencil of mine can adequately pourtray. There are the stumps of some trees cut down to make seats large enough for two—by sitting rather close,—at short intervals, so that you may sit down on these "quiet resting-places," and at your leisure enjoy the fine scene before you.

The best things must, however, come to a close, and the dinner hour warned us that we must wend our way homewards. Half-an-hour's walk brought us to our friend's house, and a good dinner was doubly good after four hours' walking through such scenery, and in such society, as I have vainly attempted to describe.

Dorking abounds in varied and beautiful walks, and my only regret was that my brief sojourn there would only allow of my visiting some of the more notable places.

I hope one day to walk from Reigate to Dorking along the top of the hills; and from what I saw of the country a great treat is in store for me. How pleasant and healthful it is to make a right use of one's legs. When I have heard sentimentalists quote the words, "Oh, that I had the wings of a dove, that I might fly away and be at peace!" I have been devoutly thankful that I have the legs of a man, and am contented to wait for the wings till we shall be made "like unto the angels."

"God made the country and man made the town,"

were the familiar words of one who drank at the fountain of nature, and the sentiments conveyed in these words I have often most heartily endorsed, and have felt that—

> "In the wonders all around,
> Ever is Thy spirit found;
> And of each good thing we see,
> All the good is born of Thee.

Thine the beauteous skill that lurks
Everywhere in Nature's works;
Thine is art, with all its worth,
Thine each master-piece on earth!

Yea, and foremost in the van,
Springs from Thee the mind of man;
On its light, for this is Thine,
Shed abroad the love divine."

Very frequently, when I have been brought low in body
and in mind, have I in wakeful hours of the night derived
comfort in my sadness from the grateful recollection of
hours and days spent in communion and fellowship with
the fair and beautiful scenes of Nature, when my heart
sang as gladsomely as the birds in the hawthorn hedgerows, and my mind was as free and happy as a child's.

I do not forget that Dorking and its neighbourhood is
rich in literary associations, as well as being famous for
its lime and fowls.   The river Mole has been rendered
poetically famous by Spenser, Drayton, Milton, Pope, and
Thomson, who, in his " Summer," tells of the

" Soft windings of the silent Mole."

I am not unmindful that Daniel Defoe lived some
time at Dorking, as well as other distinguished Nonconformists, such as the Rev. John Mason, the author of
" Self Knowledge," who was succeeded in the pastorate
by Dr. Kippis, a man of considerable note, and the com-
piler of the " Biographia Britannica."   Abraham Tucker,
author of the " Light of Nature pursued," a favourite
book with Robert Hall, the great Baptist preacher, lived
here also.

I was reminded by my accomplished Cicerone that the
Burford Bridge Hotel is a spot illustrious as the occasional
resort of many of the literary men of our own time.   There
Keats wrote the latter part of his " Endymion."   There
we are informed that the hero of Trafalgar and the Nile,
spent some days with that frail and beautiful woman Lady

Hamilton, before leaving England for his last great fight. There also, sitting under the apple-trees, Hazlitt read with delight the " Astronomical Discourses " of Dr. Chalmers ; and it is a spot, too, where many young hearts have retired in the first golden days of matrimony, when the opening promise of the future came to them—

> " In whispers, like the whispers of the leaves
> That tremble round a nightingale."

One who knows the neighbourhood well says that " Denbies is perhaps the best spot to get a good view of Dorking. The town itself lies clearly before you, with the Glory* in the background, and the Deepdene† a little to the left, beyond which he will see the avenues of Betchworth Park, nearly a thousand feet in length, and the pretty village church of Brookham, whose white spire with—

> ' Silent finger points to heaven.'

Then the long and straight line of railroad running beneath him, Markland's old house beyond it,—easily distinguishable by the adjacent pond,—the hamlet of Westcott on his right, with its picturesque church,—to which Birket Foster alone could do justice,—the wide expanse of country looming in the distance, and the somewhat faint outline of the Evelyn woods, which have become classic by association,—will give the visitor no vague notion of his ' where-

---

* A name given *par excellence* to a clump of Scotch firs, standing on a rather lofty ascent, and commanding some noble views through the open spaces which have been cut for that purpose in the wood.

† This beautiful place was in bygone days the favourite residence of Thomas Hope, where he wrote his famous works on the "Costumes of the Ancients and Moderns," and where he gathered around him a collection of sculpture, paintings, books, and Etruscan vases, such as cannot be surpassed by any similar collection in the kingdom. Here also, we understand, Mr. Disraeli wrote his "Coningsby."

abouts,' and of the pleasant rambles which are in store
for him. The Mole pursues a meandering course around
the base of Box Hill, whence it proceeds in a sinuous
direction through the picturesque vale of Mickleham to
Leatherhead on to Guildford."

One thing must ever be borne in mind by those who want
to enjoy such scenery as this, that—

> " We receive but what we give,
> And in our life alone does Nature live."

Seek to bring with you to such scenes a love of the
beautiful, and a heart at peace with God, and I know not
a more pure and serene joy than is to be found in such
rambles as these—

> " To one who has been long in city pent,
> 'Tis very sweet to look into the fair
> And open face of heaven,—to breathe a prayer
> Full in the smile of the blue firmament."

The neighbourhood of Dorking, like that of Tunbridge
Wells, abounds in green lanes ; and who can wander along
an English lane, whose banks are bright with primroses
and wild hyacinths, and not feel the gladness which these
" flowers of the field " produce? The love of flowers, like
all other love, deepens as we advance in years. They have
often with me exercised a soothing influence, and they
recal the memory of early and happy days, and keep the
heart fresh when other influences are calculated to harden
and corrode it. Our Lord knew what was in man when
He said, " Consider the lilies of the field, how they grow."

Often, when among " the flowers of the field," have the
beautiful lines of Campbell come to my lips—

> " Ye field flowers! the gardens eclipse you, 'tis true,
> Yet wildings of Nature, I doat upon you,
> For ye waft me to summers of old,
> When the earth teem'd around me with fairy delight,
> And when daisies and buttercups gladden'd my sight,
> Like treasures of silver and gold."

I look forward at some future day, if life be spared, to visit Dorking and its surroundings again. There are many places there yet in store well worth seeing, such as Norbury Park, Brockham, the Deepdene, Bury Hill, Wotton, Holmswood, and Ockley. I quite long to stand on Leith Hill, and look through the vale at its foot of thirty miles in breadth and sixty miles in length, when—

"Autumn lays his fiery finger on the leaves."

Pardon me, gentle reader, in detaining you so long at Dorking and its environs—and also for attempting to describe scenes that have taxed the eloquent and facile pens of writers from John Evelyn down to the author of "Proverbial Philosophy."

HEREFORD AND ITS NEIGHBOURHOOD.

 VISITED the old and interesting city of Hereford many times, not only in my vacations, but also when ill-health obliged me to seek change of air and scene. Hereford stands in the midst of orchards, corn-fields, and pastoral scenes, such as can scarcely be surpassed for rural beauty. The river Wye, in its wandering course, washes the old walls of the city; which, indeed, for its rich scenery of rock, of wood, and of water, has been generally allowed to be equal, if not superior, to any stream in the kingdom. From its fountain-head to its junction with the Severn, the banks of this classic river present a continuance of views picturesque and magnificent, or, as Gray the poet remarks exultingly, "a succession of endless beauties."

The principal building in this old city is the cathedral, erected in the time of William the Conqueror. It is one of the finest specimens of the Norman-Saxon and Early-English style to be seen in England.

The cathedral of Hereford, as representing an Episcopal see, is so ancient as to induce antiquarians to suppose it to have existed before the arrival of St. Augustine. This cathedral, like some others in the land, has suffered, not only from the hand of time, but more, perhaps, from so-called restoration. Wyatt the architect, between the years 1788 and 1797, expended, we are informed, £20,000 on this cathedral. He did much to destroy the original character of the sacred building, and introduced in its place a good deal of his own. It was afterwards taken in hand by Professor Willis, an authority in all matters of this nature, and " restorations " were effected between 1841 and 1852 at a cost of nearly £30,000. The architect then employed was Mr. Cottingham, who carried out his work under the personal superintendence of Dean Merewether, whose zeal for the good work will ever entitle him to the greatest respect. A memorial window of great beauty has been placed in " the house of the Lord " as a fitting expression of gratitude and respect to this good man.

Since 1858 the final restoration of the cathedral has been placed in the hands of Mr. G. G. Scott, whose plans have been most ably and efficiently carried out by the resident architect of the dean and chapter, Mr. William Chick, a gentleman who was an articled pupil of Mr. Scott.

Some of the monuments are as old as the eleventh century, but they have been sadly mutilated. The Parliamentary soldiery in 1645 have the credit of removing the fine sepulchral brasses which were once so numerous, as well as having defaced several of the monuments.

Hereford cathedral is interesting to a " Man of Kent " as the last resting-place of good King Ethelbert, though the magnificent and costly tomb erected to his memory by Offa, king of Mercia, perished by fire at the invasion of the city by one Griffith, a prince of Wales, who, according to chronologists, visited the city in 1055.

The Cathedral Library contains, we are informed, a goodly number of books and MSS. There are in all about

2000 volumes, many of great rarity and interest. Among the most remarkable printed books may be named a collection of Bibles ranging from 1480 to 1690; Higden's " Polychronicon," by Caxton, 1495; Caxton's " Legenda Aurea," 1483; and Lyndewoode's " Super Constitutiones Provinciales," 1475. Of the MSS. may be named an ancient " Antiphonarium," containing the old " Hereford Use." A fine map of the world on vellum is exhibited on the walls of the cathedral, which· is interesting, not only from its great age, but also as having Jerusalem placed in the *centre* of the world. It is one of the most valuable relics of mediæval geography, and is the work of the latter part of the thirteenth century.

The magnificent screen of wrought-iron work, executed by Messrs. Skidmore of Coventry, from the designs of Mr. G. G. Scott, is an object of great attraction to every lover of high art, not only for its beauty, but as showing how metal work can be used for the purpose to which it is here applied. As a whole, it may with safety be affirmed that this screen is one of the finest and most complete works of its class that has been produced in modern times; nor would it be easy to mention any piece of ancient metalwork which will bear comparison with it.

This sacred and highly interesting building is well deserving a visit, not only from the antiquarian, but also from everybody who loves old places, and " temples made with hands." The building itself is altogether of a different character to that of my native city; but I have spent many pleasant and profitable hours under its sacred roof, both in attending the services, as well as looking around at its monuments. The dean and chapter have made an excellent arrangement in throwing open the doors of the cathedral to the public at a charge of sixpence. This small fee is one that every visitor would gladly pay; and the proceeds are appropriated to " the building and restoration fund." This fixed charge for admission, when Divine service is not performed, is a much better practice than

that of leaving the attendants to get as much out of visitors as they can.   How much better it would be if our
cathedrals should be thrown open as " a dwelling-place for
all generations," where the devout and thoughtful might
leave the busy street, and the outside world, and be reminded that there is a " Father's house " awaiting those
who love the " outer sanctuary."   Cathedral corporations
are rich enough in all conscience without taking toll of
visitors ; and surely that which boasts itself as the " Church
of the people " should be made as popular as possible.
There are always pensioners connected with our cathedrals,
and they might be well employed as attendants to see that
no injury is done to the sacred buildings, as well as to
preserve a proper order and decorum.

There are three other old churches in the city, All
Saints, St. Margaret's, and St. Peter's.   The rector of the
latter is the Rev. John Venn, whose evangelical and apostolic labours have endeared him to the largest and most
influential congregation in the ancient city.   This excellent clergyman is one of the well-known and highly-
esteemed secretaries of the Church Missionary Society,
and is as distinguished by the quiet, unobtrusive virtues of
his private life as he is for his pulpit labours.   He is a
bachelor, and gives himself wholly to his spiritual work,
and has at the head of his home an accomplished sister,
like-minded with himself, whose gentle ministries among
the sick and the needy, have made her a welcome visitor in
every humble home, as well as an honoured guest in the
higher circles of the neighbourhood.

The other public buildings of note in the city are the
Shire Hall, the Bishop's Palace, beautifully situated on
the banks of the Wye, the College, and the County
Gaol.   The theatre seems entirely to have disappeared :
it was for many years under the direction of the Kemble
family.   There are the ruins of a monastery of Black-
friars, the pulpit of which, an interesting relic of ancient
architecture, has recently been restored by Lord Saye and

Sele. To this nobleman Hereford is also indebted for the restoration of "the White Cross," about a mile west of the city, erected by Bishop Charlton at a time when the people of the surrounding places were afraid to approach the city on account of the plague that raged there. It is recorded that there were large reservoirs of vinegar on the east side of the cross, in which were dipped whatever article was deemed infectious brought from the city. This fearful scourge committed great ravages in 1347.

The County Gaol is a prominent building, and occupies, we were informed, the site of an old priory, which was dedicated to Saint Guthlac. The present building was completed in 1797, on Howard's plan of solitary confinement, under the superintendence, and from the designs of John Nash, the architect. It is enclosed within a high, red-brick wall, having a handsome rusticated entrance, with Tuscan pillars, over which is the place of execution. The governor's residence was formerly in the centre of the prison; but a spacious and comfortable house adjoining the prison has recently been erected. It is almost too much to expect that a man possessing the qualifications for such a post should consent to live always in a prison, surrounded by criminals, and with nothing to look out upon but bare walls. The deteriorated health of the present governor, as well as that of his family, induced the magistrates of the county to erect a suitable house for his residence, so communicating with the prison as to be near at any moment that his presence might be required. The prison itself is spacious, having workshops, inspection rooms, infirmary, chapel, and large exercise-yards for the prisoners. Most of the cells are fitted up in accordance with all the modern "regulation" improvements; and every possible care is taken, not only for the safe custody of the inmates, but also of their health and well-being.

Having been rather a frequent inmate of this prison, as a visitor of the governor, I may be allowed to make a few remarks on the treatment of our criminals, which my observation and thinkings have forced upon me.

Prison discipline is confessedly a very difficult question, and has been for many years discussed with the earnestness and ability that the subject demands. Penal service appears to me to consist in the withdrawal from criminals those privileges which can safely be allowed only to the peaceable and honest members of society, and to cure them, if possible, of their bad habits; both these objects being subordinate to the more general one of the prevention of crime.

Our prisons are, with all the improvements that have of late years been introduced, far from attaining these desirable objects in any high degree; but it is consolatory to know that they have at any rate been much improved, especially since the establishment of a responsible system of Government inspection.

It seems to me that the first essential requisite of a good system of imprisonment is, that the condition of the prisoner should be inferior to that of the honest and industrious labourer. If our criminals are simply to be well fed and housed, and comfortably clothed, they will care little or nothing about being in prison. Whatever care may be taken of the health and habitudes of our criminals, a prison should never be divested of its *penal character*. The tendency, I fear, has of late years been rather to make prison discipline such as to act rather as a premium to crime than as a terror to evil-doers.

I cannot help believing that prisons should be made, as much as possible, self-supporting, and that not only in order that the cost of supporting these necessary institutions should be made less burdensome to the state and the ratepayers; but that the criminals should be taught habits of industry, I would make it a rule everywhere, if I could, that "except a man worked neither should he eat."

The "hard labour" of the crank, or the tread-wheel, which obtains in almost all our prisons, may have its beneficial effect upon some who perhaps could not be made to work in any other way; but it is a cumbersome and profitless part of the machinery of a prison.

Productive labour is, I think, the thing to be encouraged on all accounts. I was glad to see this to be the case in Hereford County Gaol, and to know that the visiting justices did all in their power to further the very praiseworthy efforts made by the present governor to carry out this principle. The practice has been tried now for some years with the best possible results, not only in diminishing the cost of the maintenance of prisoners, but also in exerting a most salutary influence upon the criminals themselves. Many a man has, to my knowledge, left that gaol able honestly to earn his living, who, before becoming an inmate of the prison, was not able to work at any trade whatever, except that of picking pockets and similar nefarious practices.

I cannot see why this productive labour should be confined to the walls of the prison. As respects agricultural and out-door labour the objections are obvious—the difficulty of guarding against escape. This objection might be overcome if the governor were allowed to select such prisoners for employment in out-door work as he might consider safe to be so employed. If land could be attached to our prisons it would be possible to grow all the potatoes and other vegetables needed for consumption in a gaol.

It is a great mistake to suppose that most of the prisoners are watching for opportunities to escape. They know well enough that to do so would only be to subject themselves to perpetual banishment from their homes. Generally speaking, it is only wandering offenders, and what are called "tramps," under serious charges, who make any attempt to escape.

Why should there not be inaugurated a "criminal corps" of convicts, under sentence for penal servitude, who could be employed, under proper *surveillance*, upon great national undertakings, such as the Thames' embankment, railways, &c. We have in our Home Secretary a man of vigour and energy, and I think the thing could be accomplished.

Of transportation, in the ordinary sense of the term, few can have a lower opinion than myself; in fact, I believe the system has generated some of the most monstrous and terrible evils. The colonists themselves are now fully alive to its baneful effects, and are not only resolutely opposed to a system inconsistent with a high tone of morality, but one that is also dangerous to life and property, and even to the personal honour of the female part of the population. The evils of transportation are not confined to the penal colonies alone, for the convicts soon find their way into other colonies. It appears that most of the crimes in South Australia are committed by released convicts; and we know full well what "ticket-of-leave men" can do at home.

The custom of teaching criminals a trade, and making their labour productive, is one that I am sure will be found to work well. The great difficulty is to know what to do with those who will not work, and who by their influence and example upon other prisoners make them most dangerous. As these form a very small proportion of our criminals, they might be dealt with as exceptional cases; I would send such worthless and refractory members of the community to Sierra Leone, Bermuda, Cape Castle, and other suitable places, where the climate is such as to exert a salutary check upon their more gross and criminal propensities, and where they might be employed and punished as such refuse require. This may appear to be rather a barbarous way of disposing of such characters; but if the well-being of the community is to be considered, there must be a "Norfolk Island" somewhere; and if reformatory and remedial treatment fail, punishment and severity must inevitably follow.

I am conscious that it is a subject difficult to grapple with; but as we owe much to the great loving-hearted

Howard, and the gentle Christ-like Caroline Fry, for their never-to-be-forgotten labours in our prisons, so we may look to such men as Sir Walter Croker, and the late estimable Colonel Jebb, for effecting reforms in the treatment of our criminals that shall be crowned with success. Having made these few remarks upon an unpleasant topic, I leave the subject for my readers to think about, and to suggest such remedies for these great evils as their wisdom may dictate.

The walks about Hereford are very beautiful and picturesque; there is the fashionable promenade, the Castle Green, so named from being on the site of the old castle that once stood here. Very little remains of this once celebrated stronghold but a few broken fragments of the original walls, a part of which has been appropriated to a "Museum;" a poor miserable affair, with a public reading-room on the basement floor. The river Wye glides by one side of Castle Green, and the views of the surrounding country from the grounds are very fine. There are some splendid trees on Castle Green, of large girth and magnificently spreading foliage, such as would gratify Creswick and Birket Foster.

There are also some fine walks by the side of the winding river, round the Bartonsham meadows, though the stiles and bridges are in too dilapidated and dangerous a state for ladies to make the attempt to walk there. Surely some of the enterprising citizens of Hereford should take such a matter in hand, and see that this very beautiful walk by this classic stream should be passable. The river Wye has been described by Gilpin, Ireland, and many others of inferior name. At this point it may be said of it, in the words of the poet of "Grongar Hill,"—

> "And see the waters how they run
> Thro' woods and meads, in shade and sun,
> Sometimes swift, sometimes slow,
> Wave succeeding wave, they go
> A hasty journey to the deep,
> Like human life to endless sleep!

Thus in Nature's verdure wrought,
To instruct our wand'ring thought,
Thus she dresses green and gay
To disperse our cares away.
Ever charming, ever new,
When will the landscape tire the view?"

One of the prettiest walks about Hereford is that to Dynedor Hill, once a Roman encampment, and about two miles from the city. The views from the summit are very extensive and beautiful. To the N.E. the Malvern Hills in Worcestershire, and the Clee Hills in Shropshire, terminate the view. Towards the N.W. the vale stretches out for many miles, presenting at one view Credenhill Camp, Tillington and Foxley Woods, Lady-Lift, Bishopstone Hill, Moccas Park, and Merbidge Hill, bounded by the mountains of Radnorshire. To the S.W. the Black Mountains appear as a grand natural boundary to England and Wales. The celebrated St. Michael's Mount, with the Blorinch and Pen-y-Vale Mountains, near Abergavenny, in Monmouthshire, are the distant objects, and are very beautiful when seen under the favourable effect of an evening sunset. The view to the S.E., though not so extensive, has much to recommend it to the admirers of picturesque scenery. The Wye is here seen nearer than from the opposite side, and makes a graceful sweep through a tract of fine meadow lands, inclosed on one side of the river by the woodlands of Fownhope and Capler Camp, rising above the bed of the river with much grandeur; over all you see May Hill in Gloucestershire. On the opposite side, the park of Holm Lacy, with the mansion half-hidden by the trees, adds to the beauty of the scene.

Dynedor Hill is the property of Mr. Bodenham, of Rotherwas, to whom the public are indebted for the privilege of beholding the charming views to be seen from its summit. This gentleman has not only thrown open these beautiful grounds, but he has placed comfortable seats at all the best points, where you may " rest-and-be-thankful."

I should never think of going to Hereford without visiting Dynedor Hill.

There are other fine walks and pleasant drives in the vicinity of Hereford, such as Foxley, Credenhill, Sufton, Mordiford, Broomy Hill, and Wareham Wood. Stoke Edith is within an easy walk of a few miles. It is so called because it was to St. Edith that the parish church was dedicated. The church is a very ancient building, dating from the time of Canute. The princely mansion that stands upon this estate was built by Paul Foley in the reign of Charles II. The park is well wooded, and contains some fine scenery.

There is also Holm Lacy, Aconbury Hill, and Belmont, with its fine cathedral, all within reach of an easy walk of a few miles.

I fear that I am lingering too long in attempting to describe some of the fine scenery of Hereford; but I have passed many weeks in the neighbourhood, and dearly love rural scenes. I must, however, leave the banks of this beautiful river; and though I have some knowledge of the "silvery Thames," the "silent Mole," the "meandering Stour," and the dark pools and rapid shallows of Scottish rivers, yet I am compelled to say, with a dash perhaps of romantic rapture—

"No stream boasts such banks as the banks of the Wye."

Many eminent men have adorned the bishop's office in this diocese. Dr. Hampden, the present bishop, is distinguished for his learning and solid attainments. He is no orator; and it will be remembered that his orthodoxy was called in question on his promotion to the high office.

Among the literary celebrities of Hereford may be mentioned Bishop Breton, preferred to the see in 1268, who wrote a work on the "Laws of England," which is yet extant; Adam de Orlton, also a bishop, and promoted to the see, on account of his literary attainments, in 1316; Roger of Hereford, who lived in the reign of Henry II, was the author of two well-known works, the one on "Judicial Astrology," the other on "Mines and Minerals." Miles Smith, D.D. who is said to have been one of the most celebrated scholars of his time, was a canon residentiary of Hereford for many years, and was promoted to the see of Gloucester in 1612. This eminent man was selected by James I. as one of the translators of the Bible—to him and Bilson, Bishop of Winchester, was committed the revisal of the whole translation at its completion. To him we are indebted for the preface to what is called the original edition of the authorized version of the sacred volume, published in 1611.

Garrick, the player, and the beautiful Nell Gwynne, were both natives of Hereford, and both famous in their own way. The inimitable actor was born at the Angel Inn, in Widemarsh-street, in 1717. His father was a French refugee, and held a lieutenant's commission in a regiment of horse then quartered in the city. Poor Nelly was unhappily born beautiful, and became the mistress of a monarch, who, with all his weaknesses, was not a bad fellow in many respects. Greenwich Hospital is a noble monument to the memory of this beautiful woman; and among those who have swayed the regal sceptre in England, have been men far more deserving of execration than "the merry monarch."

John Philips, the author of "Cyder," etc. calls Hereford his native soil, though not born in the county. John Gwillim, the celebrated author of "Heraldry Displayed," was born at, or near, Hereford, and died in 1621. Here also was born Humphrey Ely, a Romish exile of eminence, who afterwards became professor of canon and civil law at Lorraine, about 1604. John Davies and Richard Gerthinge, natives of Hereford, were so proficient in penmanship, as to be noticed by Fuller in his "British Worthies." Davies was writing-master to Henry Prince of Wales, son of James I.

William Brome, afterwards famed for his learning, was

born at Ewithington, near Hereford. He formed the plan of compiling the history of his native county; and, according to all accounts, he was a man eminently qualified to do this laborious work, not only on account of his general learning, but also as being a good naturalist and antiquary. Having made considerable progress in this praiseworthy work, he gave up his project, and unhappily destroyed the materials he had collected.

At Hereford was born also the brave and fearless Captain Cornwall, who fell in the action before Toulon, in 1744. He was commander of the "Marlborough," of 90 guns, and at the commencement of the engagement had both his legs carried away by a chain-shot. Nothing daunted by this terrible casualty, he remained on deck, and continued his directions for the fight. Soon after his own accident, his nephew, who was First Lieutenant of the ship, lost his arm, and being desired to go below by the surgeon, he refused to do so, alleging that his uncle, who was much more dangerously wounded, still kept on deck. The Captain, hearing the reply of his noble nephew, said to him, "Fred, go down, and be dressed; you may live and be an honour to the Navy; as for me, I cannot exist for many hours, but while I live, must, and will, *do my duty.*" The words had scarcely escaped from his lips, when he received a fatal shot through his breast, which killed him instantly. With such men in our Navies, and happily they are not extinct, what has England to fear?

Whatever Hereford may have been in past time, it is not by any means famous for its love of books now. There is not, as far as my observation goes, a single second-hand book-stall in the city; and there is a sad dearth of intellectual society.

Attempts have been made, on the part of some, to rouse the people to a sense of intellectual life, but without much success. An occasional concert, and a visit from Mr. and Mrs. Howard Paul, call the people together; but in this age of progress and intellectual activity Hereford should not be left too much to past fame. I speak of the intellectual status of the city as a whole, as of course there are many happy exceptions to this general charge of want of mental culture.

I would only say, in conclusion, that I have spent many pleasant hours at Hereford, not only in admiring its many beauties, but also have enjoyed the society of not a few of its hospitable citizens.*

I have already lingered so long over these vacation rambles that I am afraid of having taxed the patience of my readers. I should like to have included some other places I have visited in my holidays, such as the Isle of Wight; Rochester, Chatham, and Stroud; Maidstone; Brighton and its splendid downs, &c; but I have said already too much, and will therefore resume the thread of my little history.

* I am indebted to John Price's "Historical Account of the City of Hereford," published in 1796, for some interesting particulars relating to the city; and to Mr. J. R. King's very able account of the Cathedral in "Murray's Handbook to the Cathedrals of England."

REMOVAL TO HAMPSTEAD.

N 1859 my health had assumed so serious an aspect as to induce my doctor to recommend my immediate removal from London, and also to require me to give up everything in the shape of work that I could, so as to reserve what little energy was left for my everyday duties at my place of business.

I had sometimes gone without sleep for nearly a fortnight; and as we then lived in a great thoroughfare (in a house built by Braithwaite, the engineer), now known as Euston-road, there was a continuous stream of cabs and carriages passing and repassing all through the weary night. Sometimes, when there was a lull for a few minutes, the silence was the more trying, as I began to listen for the noise again, so as to prevent entirely my getting any sleep. The house stood at the corner of a street which was the principal thoroughfare for Pickford's heavy vans from their Camden Town depôt. The passing of these vans would shake the house to its foundations; and that alone, to one of shattered nervous system, was of itself no small trial.

It was no easy matter for a man of my slender income to find a house a few miles out of London at a rent such as I could afford, and, at the same time, either within a reasonable walking distance from my office, or where a cheap omnibus would help me in case of bad weather, or increasingly failing health.

I have always found a difficulty in obtaining a house such as one was obliged to live in to keep one's standing in society, at a rent that I could afford. There are plenty of "villa residences," and good substantial houses, in the suburbs for those who have four or five times my income. There are houses also in abundance for mechanics and the labouring classes ; but a man holding the official position of a gentleman could not, if he would, avail himself of them. I am glad to find that a Christian lady of high rank, and possessed of ample means, has, near Highgate, erected some charmingly built villas for those who have worked hard as clerks in her employ, and who would prefer paying a rent from their income for a residence, than be voted into an almshouse. Those who are interested in these matters will probably have seen the houses referred to, in Swane's Lane, Highgate, erected at the expense of Miss Burdett Coutts, a lady who has done so much to benefit her less favoured countrymen and country-women.

After making many careful inquiries in the neighbourhood of Hampstead, Hornsey, Highgate, Colney Hatch, Finchley, Muswell-hill, and Pinner, I met with a little house at Holly-hill, Hampstead.

We removed there in the autumn of 1859, and I soon found the change most beneficial. The bracing air, a ramble over the heath, and the quiet nights, made a marked and visible improvement in my health, aided, doubtless, very much by deep and refreshful sleep, though it rarely or ever lasted beyond the usual hour of four in the morning.

At the time referred to I was honorary secretary to the church with which I was connected in London, as well as holding the office of an elder in the same church. The responsible duties connected with these offices pressed rather heavily upon my waning powers, and I was very reluctantly compelled to give them up. I was thoroughly persuaded not only by the doctor, but also by my own consciousness of failing health, and powers of endurance, that such a step was my bounden duty ; and having once seen it to be so, I had no hesitation in at once carrying it out.

Though most thoroughly enjoying the rest and healthful invigorating change at Hampstead, we all missed the services of the sanctuary on the Sabbath, and the earnest manly sermons of our reverend friend in London.

One of the first things I did at my new home was to make myself acquainted with the religious aliment to be found at the churches and chapels of the neighbourhood : for this purpose I visited in succession all the places of worship there. As there was no Independent chapel in the place, it was not unnatural that I should seek out the places occupied by the Baptist denomination. We all, as a rule, go to "our own place," as certainly as Judas Iscariot did to his, though up to this period I was not a Baptist in principle. I enjoyed an occasional visit to my old Episcopalian friends ; but felt far more at home among my Congregational brethren. I found upon inquiry that there were two Baptist churches in the parish, one immediately under the shadow of the beautiful spire of Christ Church, and the other only a few doors from my own house, and known as Holly-bush Chapel, though the founder had called it "Ebenezer." The society meeting at "Bethel," near the church, was what are termed "Particular Baptists" of the hyper-Calvinistic school, with close communion. For the information of my Episcopalian, and other uninitiated readers, I may say that "close communion" means that none but baptized believers are admitted as members of the church. These good people would not do for me at all, as I had never as yet seen it to be right and Scriptural to conform to their requirements. The other was a small society of Christian people, that met in a queer little building erected by the late Mr. Castleden, who used it for a residence, as well as for the more sacred purposes of divine worship. This gentleman, I was informed, was a very remarkable man, and so respected and beloved in the parish that many of the highest Episcopal families of the neighbourhood invited him to their houses, and some of them regularly attended the week-night service at his chapel. I regret that I cannot furnish any particulars relating to this good man ; but I found that he had left behind him a name beloved and honoured among the people that he laboured for in holy things.

The pulpit of this chapel was supplied at the time of my removal to Hampstead by a worthy man who had formerly been a schoolmaster, but who had relinquished that calling, and had passed through a course of preparatory training for the ministry at Regent's Park College. He was a jolly-looking, genial man, of middle age, a bachelor, and intelligent and companionable. With an entire absence of what is called " ministerial dignity," there was found in him very much to respect and venerate, and as he was a thorough hater of cant, we soon became great friends, and he was a frequent visitor at our fireside. I have mentioned that, although I had been attending what are called Baptist Churches since removing from Paddington, I was not a Baptist in principle, and had there been a church of the Independent order at Hampstead, with a minister that we could have heard with pleasure and profit, we should in all probability have connected ourselves with such a church.

The worthy minister of Holly-bush Chapel did not remain at Hampstead more than about twelve months after my removal there, as the church over which he presided was too poor to maintain a stated minister. I have mentioned that he was a bachelor ; but this was not from choice, but necessity, as he had been courting a lady for seventeen years, who would not marry while her mother lived. Our good friend was waiting in patient hope and joyful anticipation for " a consummation most devoutly to be wished," and has now for some years been rewarded for his long probation with a loving, if not a very youthful wife. Happily for him, as well as the lady of his choice, that he had not such a temperament as mine. I have often wondered how Jacob could have served seven years for his lovely Rachel, " though they seemed unto him but a few days, for the love he had to her," for I question if I could have done so, even for an angel from heaven. Long and protracted courtships are, as a rule, I think, to be deprecated. When two young fond hearts are " initiate in love," and circumstances are at all favourable, the sooner the consummation comes the better. Delays are always dangerous ; and a courtship extending over many years loses much of its poetry and romance.

Since the time I am writing of, Holly-bush Chapel has been converted into some secular hall, and an elegant and commodious chapel has been erected in Heath-street, principally through the generous and efficient help rendered by Mr. James Harvey, a gentleman well known and very highly esteemed at Hampstead. This Church, though professedly Baptist in principle, is composed of persons of all denominations, giving credible evidence of their being Christians, and is presided over by the son of one of our most popular Baptist ministers of the metropolis. This able young minister has much to contend with from his episcopalian neighbours ; but he is labouring with quiet and persistent efforts, and happily not without success. Heath-street Chapel is one of the most comfortable places of worship in the neighbourhood of London, and my heart's desire and prayer for its minister is, that he may be as wise to win souls as his worthy father, who has laboured so long and successfully at " Bloomsbury Chapel."

It was quite a new thing to feel in attending the Sanctuary that I had nothing to think of, and to do, but to enjoy the rest and refreshment of the service. For many years previous to my removal to Hampstead, Sunday had been my most fatiguing day. My duties as secretary and elder of the church to which I had belonged were such as to tax my energies sometimes to the utmost. How little do those who sit quietly and comfortably in their pews imagine how a hundred things may be passing in the minds of those whose heads and hands are thinking and planning for their comfort and edification. Five years' connection with one of the largest Baptist churches in London qualifies me in some measure to speak of the arduous and responsible duties devolving upon a class of men whose chief and only reward is the approbation of their Master, and the consciousness of doing something to promote the accomplishment of His mission to our lost world. I do not know what are the duties of a church-warden, but I can hardly imagine that our Episcopalian laymen work as do the deacons in our Nonconformist churches. Where the ordinary income of a chapel is derived exclusively from the pew rents, and the expenditure is large, the duties and anxieties of those who attend to the adjuncts of Divine worship are both heavy and manifold. It should be remembered that all the secular arrangements of a chapel, such as providing the stipend of the minister, the repairs of the building, coals, gas, taxes, etc. etc. rest entirely with the deacons. The men who mostly are selected to fill this office, are those who have businesses or professional duties, taxing their utmost energies, and absorbing their time during the day; and these are the men who, to serve their brethren and their Master, forsake their quiet, cheerful fireside and family circle many evenings a week to make arrangements, not only for matters connected with the public worship of Almighty God, but a variety of other things constantly turning up in a large congregation.

As my failing health has obliged me to retire from all official connection with churches, I am glad of the present opportunity of reminding my lay brethren of their obligation to a class of men who render valuable service in our churches without any remuneration whatever.

The other religious places at Hampstead, at the time

referred to, were the Parish Church, with, to a Londoner, its well-known steeple, and its ivy-covered walls, the vicar of which was a man of sound learning, but very "High Church" in his ideas and practices. We not unfrequently attended the services at Christ Church, and much enjoyed the useful and fervent evangelical sermons of the amiable and hard-working clergyman there. This good man has laboured most successfully for many years, both from the pulpit and the press, to correct the High Church tendencies of his neighbour the vicar. He is most indefatigable in his pastoral visitations, and ever to be found at the bed-side of the sick, and among the bereaved. This excellent clergyman would have delighted good old George Herbert, as he is a poet as well as a preacher and pastor, and always to be found among his people, stirring them up to every good word and work.

Among other things instituted by this good man, to whom Hampstead owes so much, is what is termed a "Union Prayer-meeting," at which all the religious people in the neighbourhood were invited, irrespective of sectarian differences. These meetings for prayer and praise were at first held in the large schoolroom adjoining the Church; but as Dissenters as well as Churchmen, both lay and clerical, were called upon to lead the devotions in common with their Episcopal brethren, it was considered rather *outré* for Nonconformists to pray on consecrated ground; and to avoid this the good man, who had originated the movement, erected a large lecture-room in his own garden, which was subsequently used for the purpose. These meetings were remarkably well attended; and I should mention that they were presided over by clergymen and laymen in alternation, including the Baptist and Free Church ministers in the parish. The only matter of regret in connection with these services was, that our Episcopal brethren in the ministry could never be persuaded to attend meetings of a similar kind held alternately at Heath-street Chapel and Trinity Free Church. Evangelical Churchmen are ready enough to receive into their community Dissenting brethren, but they are not so ready to reciprocate these Christian advances of Nonconformists.

In attending the various places of worship at Hampstead, we did not omit that in Well-walk—certainly one of the most melancholy and miserable buildings ever used for purposes of Divine service. It was originally, I believe, the "Pump-room," in the palmy days of Hampstead, when fashionable and courtly people went there to drink its mineral waters. After that it was converted into a "Chapel of Ease;" and when given up by our Episcopal friends for the beautiful church that now stands out so conspicuously in the landscape, on the borders of the heath, was taken by the Free Church. The pews were tall and ugly, and resembled a condemned cell; and the place altogether presented such a sombre and gloomy appearance that my children begged as a great favour that we might never go again.

I saw at a glance, however, that the minister of this place was no ordinary man; and as he has been since cut down in the flower and ripeness of his manhood, and gone to his reward, I shall be pardoned if I record some of the impressions produced upon my mind on first seeing and hearing this highly-gifted man.

In personal appearance he was tall and slender, with a countenance singularly thoughtful and meditative; a finely-shaped angular nose, dark brilliant eyes, and a mouth that indicated both playfulness and power; dark brown hair, with a good deal of whisker, but carefully shaven, so as to exhibit the mouth and chin. His voice was deep and musical, but gave evidence that his respiratory organs were not healthy. His reading was good, and his manner of conducting Divine worship most impressive. The long prayer he offered struck me as one of the most solemn and child-like utterances I had ever listened to and united with. The sermon was far beyond the average quality, and struck me as being calculated to produce great effect upon a select and educated congregation.

The many empty pews told most unmistakeably that such preaching is not calculated to be popular in the best sense, as it would fail to reach those who would not, from any cause, give the requisite attention.

In spite of the dingy place and high pews, so distasteful to the young, I was a frequent attendant on the ministry of this gentleman; and soon after my residence at Hampstead, I had the privilege of making his acquaintance. I owe this pleasure to the united prayer-meetings, held at the lecture-room there; and this is not the only friendship resulting from those hallowed meetings.

As he was a man of nervous temperament, and had, like most of us that are so constituted, suffered a good deal from depression of spirits, there were many points that brought us into more intimate relationship, and frequent were the quiet walks, when we had long talks upon all sorts of subjects. I had the mournful pleasure of spending an hour with him alone, the evening before he left Hampstead for Mentone, never again to return alive.

All that could die of this good and gifted man lies buried in the cemetery on the neighbouring hill, where the sacred ashes of so many of God's saints repose, watched over by the Eye that never sleeps, and whence the Almighty Voice will one day call them forth to be clothed upon with immortality.

I was a privileged and delighted listener to the beautiful tribute to his memory by his illustrious countryman, Dr. James Hamilton, of the Scotch Church, Regent-square, a man in every respect able to do justice to the high Christian character and great attainments of the late lamented James Drummond Burns.

The poems of Mr. Burns, re-published in a collective form, with a biographical notice of the poet, from the accomplished pen of Dr. Hamilton, as a memorial volume, would be highly valued by the personal friends of the poet, and would moreover extend his fame among all lovers of good poetry.

z

What Mr. Burns was as a poet and preacher was known to many beyond his own denomination; but only those who knew him in the private walks of life could estimate him as he deserved. His conversational powers were of a high order; but he was so modest and retiring that he was always more ready to listen than to speak. His removal from his much-loved work, just as an elegant sanctuary had been erected for him by a wealthy and attached congregation, was felt to be a great loss; he has, however, been succeeded by a gentleman well qualified to carry out the work so ably begun by one who will ever be gratefully remembered at Hampstead. Mr. Burns has left a young widow and some dear little ones to mourn his loss, as only those do who have been bereft of such a husband and father.

As I was desirous of seeing and judging for myself of the various places of worship in the neighbourhood, I went once or twice to the Unitarian Chapel. The minister of this chapel was a man of superior mental attainments, and one highly respected in the parish. There was, however, a coldness and chilliness about the service that was anything but attractive, and which it seems to me is the necessary consequence of excluding from their belief the heart-stirring, and deeply felt want, not only of the sympathy and help to be found in the human nature of Christ, but also that which our inner and deeper nature yearns for, His vicarious sacrifice and death. This want has been felt and acknowledged by some of their best writers. A denomination that can number among their ranks such men as Priestley, Channing, Theodore Parker, Martineau, Thom, and Sadler, will ever command the respect and admiration of their Christian brethren. To all of these writers I gratefully acknowledge my own obligations for many profitable hours spent in perusing their writings.

I visited our Wesleyan brethren, who met in what was once the Independent Chapel. The congregation was small and uninfluential, and the preaching very ordinary. I have often wondered that the shrewd and active men who compose the " Conference" should neglect such a place as Hampstead. My attachment to the Wesleyans is great. I have heard sermons from Robert Newton and Morley Punshon that I shall never forget, and my obligation to John Wesley and Richard Watson, for the pleasure and profit derived from their writings, is greater than I can express. The sermons of Richard Watson, I think, are equal to any that I have ever read ; in times of sickness and sorrow, I have found them a source of never-failing comfort and help. I regret that I never had the opportunity of hearing the living voice of this great preacher. The memoir of his life and writings, by Thomas Jackson, is one of the most interesting and instructive biographies I have ever read.

About this time, in my ordinary course of reading, I met with " The Life of Adoniram Judson," the American Missionary, by the late Professor Wayland, President of Brown University, U.S. ; a book in every respect worthy of perusal, as containing a highly interesting and able account of the life and labours of one of the grandest men and most heroic missionaries of modern times.

Among many other things, in the life of that extraordinary man, that made a deep impression on me was the account there given of the alteration that took place in his views on baptism.

When Dr. Judson and his wife left the American shores for the scene of their missionary labours they were Pædo-Baptists, and were sent out as missionaries to India under the auspices of the American Board for Foreign Missions. At the commencement of the voyage to India it occurred to Dr. Judson and his wife that, as they were going to make known the Gospel of Christ to the heathen, they might reasonably expect to make converts from heathenism to Christianity, and the question naturally arose in their minds as to how they should treat the servants and children of these converts. Was he authorized to baptize the children and servants of converts that might be made to Christianity ?

And if so, what would be their relation to the Christian Church afterwards?

In addition to this, Dr. Judson knew that he was going, in the first instance, to Serampore, to reside for a time with the Baptist missionaries there. He felt, therefore, the necessity for re-examining the subject of baptism, as he thought he might be called upon to defend his position as a Pædo-Baptist. In this latter respect, however, he found himself singularly disappointed; the Baptist missionaries at Serampore, as might have been expected when such men as Carey, Marshman, and Ward were among that noble band, made it a matter of principle never to introduce the subject of their peculiar belief to any of their brethren of other denominations who happened to be their guests.

Under these circumstances, Dr. Judson and his devoted wife set themselves, during the voyage, to examine, *from the Scriptures alone*, the question of baptism—its subjects and mode. The result of this investigation, extending through several weeks, landed them in the full belief that in apostolic times none but believers were baptized, and that the mode of administering the ordinance was by immersion.

The change thus brought about in the minds of these devoted servants of Christ and His Church, placed them in a most painful position. They had been sent out to India as the Agents of the American Board for Foreign Missions, who were Pædo-Baptists; and having so entirely changed their views on the important subject of Baptism, they felt that they must at once avow the alteration that had taken place with reference to this point of faith and practice, whatever the consequences might be.

Dr. Judson and his wife were baptized at Calcutta shortly after their arrival there, and they wrote home to their family connections, as well as to the association under whose auspices they had left their native shores, informing them of their altered views on baptism.

As may be supposed, Dr. Judson's friends in America,

as well as the Board of Missions, were not a little sur-
prised at the alteration that had taken place in their views.
Arrangements were at once made that Dr. and Mrs.
Judson should be transferred from the American Board for
Foreign Missions to the American Baptist Missionary
Society, with whom they continued to work most honour-
ably and successfully to the end of their lives.

The account given in the " Life of Dr. Judson " referred
to is highly interesting ; and I was very much struck, not
only with the conduct of these devoted and self-denying
servants of Christ, but also with the arguments brought
forward by Dr. Judson as those which had wrought the
change in his views relating to baptism as we find it in the
New Testament.

I pondered the matter a good deal in my own mind,
and was induced, without the knowledge of any one, to
renew my inquiry into the Scriptures as to the correctness
of my own views on this important subject.   After a careful and thoughtful examination I was led to the conclusion
that infant baptism *is nowhere to be found in the New
Testament*, and that only those who believed the Gospel, and made a profession of their faith in Christ, were
baptized in apostolic times.

My wife and more intimate friends were astounded at the
change that had taken place in my mind, as I had been
known to hold very positive views on the opposite side.

I may here mention the fact that, though the Church of
which I was a member was composed of Christians of
almost every denomination, I do not remember a single
instance where this diversity of sentiment was the means,
in any way, of interrupting the Christian intercourse
of its members, or of impeding the various associations
for Christian work that distinguished that church and
congregation.   The ordinance of believers' baptism is
administered there as often as occasion requires, and the
minister is a determined Baptist ; yet all the members of
that Christian society, whether Pædo-Baptist or Baptist,

meet upon a perfect equality in all matters as church members, and work most harmoniously together.

As I had removed from London on account of my health, I might have been baptized at a church of that order in the neighbourhood where I resided ; but I thought it better, on many accounts, that I should avow the change in my opinions and practice by submitting to the ordinance in the church of which I was an office-bearer, and among the people who had known me as a Pædo-Baptist.

Now, although I have no doubt whatever as to the fact that baptism was only administered in the days of the apostles to those who heard and accepted the Gospel, I am not so certain that those who were so baptized were immersed. The *only* instance recorded in the New Testament in which parties are said to have gone to the water is that of Philip and the eunuch, (Acts viii. 36-39). In *all* the other instances the water may have been brought to them for aught that appears to the contrary. Neither Christ nor the apostles, as far as we know, ever gave any directions whatever as to *how* the ordinance of baptism should be administered. At all events, the absence of any definite direction on the mode of baptism proves, I think, that neither our Lord nor his apostles attached much importance to the *modus operandi;* and it follows that this very silence as to the mode leads me to infer that there must have been a previously-existing custom prevailing, and which, without any direction being given to the contrary, they naturally adopted.

After thinking a good deal upon the subject, and keeping the point in mind when I have been reading the New Testament, the conclusion I have arrived at is, that immersion is probably a human invention, originating in a feeling like that which the impetuous Peter was impressed with when he said, " Not my feet only, but also my hands and my head." He very naturally thought that if a little water was good, that more would be better ; but I cannot help thinking that he was mistaken, and so are the immersionists.

In hazarding this expression of an opinion, contrary to the views of a large and learned body of Christian brethren, I know that I expose myself to the most rigid criticism; but as my only object is to arrive at the truth, I shall be satisfied if this contrary opinion of mine lead any one more gifted than myself to re-examine the subject.   I am not so old, or so bigoted to any opinions that I entertain, as not to be open to conviction; and I have learned to give up the most cherished practices when my judgment has been convinced that they are unscriptural.   However this may be, I think the mode of administering the ordinance in modern times has much about it very un-apostolic, (if I may use such a word); and I cannot but think that our churches are open to some improvement in their mode of administering this solemn and significant ordinance of our Lord.

It is the practice in most of the churches of the Baptist denomination to give a prominence to the administration of the ordinance that I think quite unnecessary and uncalled for; and also, that in so doing they make an ordinance that is simple in itself a cumbersome and unsightly thing; and further, I think there is no precedent in the Scripture for its being made so.

A baptism in most of our churches—though, I am glad to say, there are exceptions to this rule—is made a separate and distinct service on one evening of the week; and this is made known by announcement from the pulpit, generally on the preceding Sabbath.   This announcement to a large congregation is pretty sure to bring a considerable number of persons together on the evening in question; not only of the members of the Church, who naturally feel an interest in seeing any come forward to make a profession of their faith in the risen Saviour, but it also attracts a class of persons to be found in all our congregations who have a love for anything *outré*, or unusual, and who would attend the baptism of a believer as they would the execution of a criminal, simply for the gratification of sight-seeing.

Now, with all due deference to the practice of the Churches, and the opinions of my fathers in the Faith—men many of whom I have the greatest possible respect for,—yet, nevertheless, I cannot find precedents for these public exhibitions, either in the New Testament or in the practice of the early churches, as recorded by ecclesiastical historians. Where is the necessity for our baptistries being placed in front of the pulpit, or that they should be in our chapels or churches at all? Would it not be much better that they should be provided for in some convenient apartment adjoining the place of preaching, and so arranged that the ordinance could be administered at the close of the proclamation of the Gospel, *as was the case with the Apostles and Evangelists in the primitive times?*

The office-bearers of the churches might administer the ordinance (for it is by no means necessary that the preacher should perform this ceremony), in the presence of any friends more immediately interested. Surely this would be far more in accordance with apostolic precedents than the custom in modern times of making this simple and unobtrusive Institute of Christ a " special service," and sounding a trumpet for the purpose of calling together a number of idle people who love excitement; and whose presence, moreover, upon these sacred occasions goes very far to mar the pleasure, and prevent the profit that would otherwise result from witnessing the baptism of those who have been induced not only to accept the offer of salvation through a crucified Saviour, but who also comply at once with His requirements, that " He that believeth and is baptized shall be saved."

I feel that I am treading upon very delicate ground by advancing these opinions; but, as I think that I have Scriptural authority for so doing, I am not over careful as to whether what I have stated be in accordance with the opinions and practices of men whose learning I admire and honour, and whose Christian character I revere and love.

A few examples from the New Testament will, I am

sure, bear me out in what I have said in relation to this matter; and I trust that the importance of the subject will be a sufficient apology to any Christian reader who will bear with me in calling his attention to the passages I adduce in support of what I have stated.

Our Lord, as the Source and Fountain of authority, in His last great commission to His Apostles before His ascension, leads them clearly to understand that baptism should follow immediately on believing:—"Go ye, therefore, and teach all nations, baptizing them in the name of the Father, and of the Son, and of the Holy Ghost: teaching them to observe all things whatsoever I have commanded you," (Matt. xxviii. 19, 20). It is plain, from this passage, not only that all who are made disciples, or that believe in the Divine mission of Christ, are to be baptized; but that it is the solemn initiatory rite of admission into the visible Church, and is designed as a public profession of faith in the character of Christ, and the word of God, as revealed in the Scriptures.

After Peter's address to the multitude on the Day of Pentecost, it is added, "Then they that gladly received his word were baptized: *and the same day* there were added to them about three thousand souls," (Acts ii. 41). When Philip, one of the colleagues of Stephen the protomartyr, and a deacon, had preached in Samaria "the things concerning the kingdom of God, and the name of Jesus Christ, they were baptized, both men and women," (Acts viii. 12); and again when preaching to the devout Ethiopian, the baptism of that distinguished convert followed immediately on his conversion, (Acts viii. 36-38).

When Ananias, "a certain disciple," was sent to Saul to remove his blindness, that he might "be filled with the Holy Ghost . . . he received sight forthwith, and arose, and was baptized," (Acts ix. 18).

Peter, after preaching to Cornelius and those who were assembled with him, said, when many of them had received the message, "Can any man forbid water, that these should not be baptized, which have received the Holy Ghost as well as we ? And he commanded them to be baptized in the name of the Lord," (Acts ix. 47, 48).

Lydia, " whose heart the Lord opened, that she attended unto the things which were spoken of Paul," was " baptized, and her household," as soon as they were converted, (Acts xvi. 15).

When the Philippian jailor and his household were converted, the sacred historian tells us that they were " baptized, he and all his, *straightway*," (Acts xvi. 33).

When Paul preached at Corinth to the Gentiles, we are told that " Crispus, the chief ruler of the synagogue, believed on the Lord with all his house : and many of the Corinthians hearing believed, and were baptized," (Acts xviii. 8).

Paul, when preaching at Ephesus to " certain disciples," who had been but imperfectly instructed, revealed the faith unto them more perfectly ; and " *when* they heard this, they were baptized in the name of the Lord Jesus," (Acts xix. 5).

I think any candid reader will, after reading these instances which I have adduced, admit that the Apostles and first preachers of the Gospel never delayed baptism after a person believed in the divine mission of Christ. From these instances, and others that might be mentioned, I am led to believe that any disciple of Christ, lay or clerical, may preach or make known the Gospel to those who are in ignorance, from any cause, of the great salvation ; and further, that he has the authority of Christ to baptize all such as believe in His name without any reference whatever to what are termed Church authorities upon the subject.

There is a superstitious and unscriptural reverence in all our churches for what is denominated an " ordained ministry."

For my own part I have no great reverence for the sacred office in itself, except when the men who fill it are deserving of our esteem, and command our respect by their Christian character. I do not find in the New Testament anything at all like the ordination of ministers as practised either in our Congregational Churches, or among those which are known as Episcopalian or Presbyterian. And even if it could be shown from the New Testament that a distinct order of men are to be specially set apart as evangelists and pastors, yet we have the highest authority for refusing to accord to them any submission in matters of faith and conscience.

The Jewish teachers—and there are men among all our Christian churches who have the same feeling—were fond of being publicly and loudly hailed by their followers with cries of "Rabbi! Rabbi!" but our Lord rebuked them, and said, "Be ye not called Rabbi: for one is your Master, even Christ; *and all ye are brethren,*" (Matt. xxiii. 8-10). Our Lord here condemns not only vanity, but also all that assumption of superior authority in religious matters which the terms "Teacher," "Father," "Master," or "Reverend" are held to imply; as being derogatory to the claims of our Heavenly Father, and of our Lord and Saviour, and inconsistent with the fraternal relations of Christians as brethren.

I cannot see, from what I know of the New Testament, that an "ordained minister" is essential to the valid celebration either of Baptism or the Lord's Supper. While believing that, in ordinary circumstances, the recognized office-bearers are the natural and proper agents in their celebration, I can see nothing in Scripture restricting either that, or the preaching of the Gospel, to ordained ministers by any absolute necessity.

Ananias, "a certain disciple," baptized the Apostle Paul, (Acts ix. 10-18). Philip, the Deacon, baptized the Samaritans, and the eunuch, (Acts viii. 12; 36-38). It was not Peter, but the brethren who came with him, that baptized Cornelius and his friends, (Acts x. 23; 44-48). To assume that an ordained minister is essential to the administration of either of the New Testament ordinances makes virtually a priesthood of the ministry, standing between the body of believers and the Saviour's ordinances.

With reference to all these and similar matters, I verily believe that living attachment to Christ is the only legitimate bond of Church fellowship ; and that gifts from Christ are the only legitimate qualification for ministry of any kind, within the body of which He is the head.

I may here take occasion to observe that though I am a Baptist, that is to say, a believer in Christian Baptism, as administered to those who have made a confession of their faith in Christ and His Gospel, I by no means adopt all the views held by those who are commonly known as Baptists.

My brethren of that persuasion will, I trust, bear with me while I mention a few things in which I differ from them. I know their deep and profound reverence for Scripture ; and everything that is really excellent will not only bear examination, but it will even invite it ; and the more narrowly it is surveyed, to the more advantage it will appear.

In the larger proportion of our Baptist Churches none are admitted to the ordinance of baptism whose spiritual state has not first been made known to the members of the particular church they desire to become connected with, and their fitness for baptism been approved by those members. Now where our brethren find apostolic precedent for such a procedure I am quite at a loss to determine ; certainly they do not find it in the early Christian Churches of which we are informed in the Acts of the Apostles. But this is not the only thing done in churches of the Baptist order that is not in accordance with apostolic precedent. This will be seen by glancing at a few particulars.

John the Baptist and the Apostles, baptized " unto repentance ;" that cannot be done by those who require repentance unto life as a necessary preliminary. Paul and the three thousand on the day of Pentecost were baptized " for the remission of sins ;" our Baptist brethren generally contend for justifying faith as a qualification. The Apostles exhorted people to be baptized, that they might "receive the gift of the Holy Ghost; our brethren look for proofs of the reception of the Spirit before they administer the ordinance. The Apostles and first Evangelists administered the right before they taught the peculiarities of the Christian religion ; our brethren require a knowledge of these peculiarities as a qualification for it. The primitive Christians " were baptized into Christ ;" our brethren insist upon our being in Christ preparatory to the ordinance. The Apostles placed baptism *before* the putting on of Christ, (Gal. iii. 27); our brethren the contrary. Baptism, in the Scriptures, stands before sanctification, (1 Cor. vi. 11), and is the appointed means of producing it, (Eph. v. 26); our brethren reverse this order. Peter tells us that . . . " Baptism doth save us," (1 Pet. iii. 21); and Paul, to the same purpose, says, " He saved us by the washing of regeneration, and the renewing of the Holy Ghost," (Titus iii. 5); our brethren require us to be in a state of salvation prior to baptism : and therefore, according to them, there is no sense in which they can be said to be saved by baptism.

In commending these few hints to the consideration of my Baptist brethren, I am sure they will receive them in the spirit in which they are offered. I have found, from my own experience, that it has been a wholesome thing to be contradicted sometimes, as it has set me to examine a question again ; and this cannot be done in a Christian spirit without advantage. Custom and habit cling to all of us, and we hold most tenaciously opinions that we have received from our ancestors, whose wisdom we do well occasionally to call in question.

I return from this rather long digression upon a knotty point to my personal history. I have mentioned the removal from Hampstead of the minister who officiated at Holly-bush Chapel. As the people were neither numerous nor wealthy, it was found impossible to invite a stated minister to take the oversight of the church. Under these circumstances those who had the management of matters at the chapel made the best arrangement they could in securing the services of students from the Baptist College, and others, to supply the pulpit. Just about this time a gentleman of wealth and influence, from the North of England, came to reside at Hampstead for the benefit of his health. This gentleman had been wont for many years " to teach and preach Jesus Christ," not only from house to house, but wherever he could find opportunity. Hearing of the destitute state of Holly-bush Chapel, he very kindly engaged to take the morning service, and gave them the benefit of his Christian services. The congregation, from having no regular pastor, had become very small ; but this good man's preaching put new life into the people, and soon the place was filled with attentive and devout worshippers, who could but profit under a ministry fraught with the life and soul of the Gospel. This Christian " brother of high degree" continued his kind services for several months, when the chapel passed out of the hands of the deacons, for the purpose of being appropriated to some other than a sacred use.

Under these circumstances the gentleman who had so kindly given the people there the benefit of his gratuitous services offered them the use of a large room in " his own hired house," for the purpose of holding their meetings for Divine worship. This offer was most gladly accepted, and by far the larger proportion of the congregation continued for some years to meet in a comfortable room at Montague Grove, where a Christian Church was formed, and where the ordinances of Christ were administered, with the exception of believers' baptism, which, as often as occasion required, and that was not unfrequent, was carried out in some of the Baptist churches in the vicinity.

There, in Montague Grove, under the hospitable roof of a Christian gentleman, was a " Church in the house," as nearly resembling as possible those that were assembled in the first days of Christianity, when "they who feared the Lord spake often one to another," (Mal. iii. 16-18).

As this Christian gentleman's work was of that public character as to be thoroughly known and felt at Hampstead, and as he has recently gone to his reward, I may be allowed to mention his name in this humble narrative.

The late Mr. Richard Burdon-Sanderson, of West Jesmond, Northumberland, and lately of Montague Grove, Hampstead, was born 31st March, 1791; and married, in 1815, Elizabeth, only daughter of the late Sir James Sanderson, Bart. He was son of the late Sir Thomas Burdon, whose wife was sister of Lords Eldon and Stowell. Mr. Sanderson was intended for the Church, and for this purpose was entered as a student at Oriel College, Oxford, where he was the colleague of the late Archbishop Whately, Mr. Baden Powell, Dean Milman, Professor Keble, and Dr. Pusey. In this galaxy of eminent men Mr. Sanderson was a star of no mean magnitude. He was the author of "Parthenon," the prize poem for 1811; and also "A Comparative Estimate of the English Literature of the seventeenth and eighteenth centuries," the prize essay of 1814. I possess copies of these interesting compositions of his early life, with his autograph attached, and preserve them among my choicest literary treasures. Mr. Sanderson was the author of several works, many of which were published anonymously. One little volume, entitled "The Dew of Hermon, by a Son of Consolation," containing a short exposition of a text of Scripture for every day in the year, has had a very wide circulation, and has comforted the hearts of many sorrowful ones, as well as increased the gladness of others.

On leaving college, Mr. Sanderson was invited by his uncle, Lord Eldon, at that time Lord High Chancellor of England, to act as his private secretary, and undertake the management of the Church patronage attached to that high office. The duties connected with these ecclesiastical

matters brought of necessity some phases of the Church of
England under his notice, and so astounded was he at the
anomalous condition in which he found the system of
Church promotion, that he determined to examine for himself the whole system; the result of this investigation
led him to resign the appointment conferred upon him by
his illustrious uncle, and to renounce, once and for ever,
his connection with a Church, in his opinion so opposed to
that of the New Testament. His retirement was a source
of much sorrow to his uncle; but his attachment to his
Nonconformist nephew continued to the day of his death.

Mr. Sanderson, on leaving the Church of England,
identified himself with the Independents, and afterwards
became a Baptist. As a memoir of this distinguished
gentleman is preparing, and will shortly be published, there
is no occasion to enter more fully into the particulars of
his remarkable and eventful life, as that will be done by
those who, in every respect, are far better able to perform
such a work than the writer of these pages.

For more than four years this truly apostolic man provided all the accommodation necessary for the purposes of
Christian worship, and did himself preach, not only on the
morning of the Sabbath, but also on an evening in the week.
The Sunday-evening service at the " Church in the
House" was taken by Christian brethren in the neighbourhood, or by one of the deacons, who occasionally officiated when no other helpers were forthcoming.

I was privileged, with my family, to attend these services
throughout the entire period that they were held, which
was up to within a few months of his lamented death; and
I gladly bear testimony to the effects produced both upon
myself, and many that were stated attendants upon the
ministry of the Word there.

The whole range of Christian doctrine and practice was
brought repeatedly and authoritatively before us with an
affectionate earnestness that was irresistible. Our venerable friend—for he was a man nearly seventy—came to

the sacred work under a deep sense of the responsibility of speaking to his fellow-men on subjects of the most tremendous importance. He felt that preaching the Gospel was, as the great Apostle states, (Rom. xvi. 26), " According to the commandment of the everlasting God, to be made known to all nations, for the obedience of faith." I have many times listened to these invitations with the intensest interest, and have seen the effects produced upon others, as well as having experienced them in my own case. No man could go away from such services without feeling that he had had presented to him, and pressed upon him, the offer of salvation, free and immediate, through a crucified and risen Saviour; and men and women were brought to decide for Christ who had lived for many years borderers, with reference to the claims of the Saviour. These instances of conversion were fervently and perseveringly prayed for; and when the good work was accomplished, and an open profession of the change that had been wrought by Divine power was made by baptism, the joy of the aged pastor was such as to light up his beaming countenance with a heavenly radiance.

His preaching was eminently calculated to build up the faith of the believer, and " to comfort those that mourn in Zion; " and many were the instances in which he was made very helpful to desponding Christians. His prayers were the most fervent I ever heard : they were short, simple, and importunate. His reading of the Scriptures was peculiarly impressive, and brought out " the mind of the Spirit" in a way that I have seldom seen equalled. The Bible was literally " the man of his counsel : " he spent large portions of every day in its perusal, and, as a consequence of this, he was " mighty in the Scriptures."

About a year after the services were established at the " Church in the House," one of the deacons died, and the writer of this narrative was elected in his stead. I well remember the address that was delivered by the pastor on

A A

the evening appointed for the election of a new deacon. He selected for his motto, " Show whether of these two thou hast chosen," (Acts i. 24). It was the most lucid statement of the Divine sovereignty in harmony with human agency that I ever heard.

I endeavoured to excuse myself the duty of acting as a deacon in this little Christian society, on the score of ill-health, but was persuaded by my venerable friend to accept the office, as by so doing I should be able to help him in matters connected with the church, and particularly in the arrangements for the Sunday evening services. I felt it to be no small privilege to be associated with such a man, and entered heartily into the good work.

My official position as a deacon, and a friendship that had preceded my election to that office, gave me frequent opportunities of enjoying the society of this eminent Christian. I have conversed with him upon all the great subjects in theological science, and was always glad to be a silent listener when he could be prevailed upon to talk upon any theme.

It was hardly possible to hold frank and friendly inter-course with such a man without benefit: all his learning and attainments were consecrated to the study of the sacred volume, the results of which were apparent in his public expositions, as well as in private and social inter-course. Sometimes he would write to me on subjects that had come under our notice. I have one such letter before me now in reference to an address that I delivered at the service where I had him for one of my hearers. The letter is as follows, and contains some good hints on preaching to those who are desirous of speaking so as to be useful :—

" Montague Grove, December 10th, 1862.

" My Dear Friend,—There are some persons to whom I can say anything that it is right to be said, because I know they will not take it amiss ; and there are others to whom one can say nothing for fear of giving offence. I class you among the first of these characters, of which you have given proof in your construction of my remarks on Sunday last. The fact is, that your address was too much of a finished composition for the purpose of edification. I know of no better rule in this matter than the Apostle's, ' And I, brethren, when I came to you, came not with *excellence of speech,* or of wisdom, declaring unto you the testimony of God.' No, we want nothing but a plain unvarnished tale of Jesus Christ and Him crucified, in demonstration of the Spirit and of power, if we would have the faith of the hearers to stand, not in the wisdom of men, but in the power of God.

" My plan is to *meditate* closely on a chapter, or two chapters (one in the Old and the other in the New Testament), and endeavour to elicit from them one or more propositions to illustrate by the chapters themselves, leaving the language to look after itself, or rather trusting to the promise in this particular.

" Yours very truly and affectionately,

" R. B. SANDERSON."

Such a letter, from such a man, could not but be valuable, and I endeavoured in my future attempts to carry out in my public addresses these excellent rules. The late Mr. Sanderson was by far the best lay preacher I ever heard ; and to have such a man as a hearer was enough to intimidate a man who, like myself, had only been accustomed to give an occasional address to a village congregation, or at a meeting of the Young Men's Christian Association. I have always found, however, that the most charitable hearers of sermons are those who preach themselves ; and I derived many valuable hints from this aged and eloquent man.

It is hardly possible to speak of Mr. Sanderson without also coupling him with his devoted wife. She was " a

helpmate" indeed, and was indefatigable in her unobtrusive efforts to second the Christ-like labours of her devoted
husband. The affection subsisting between them was
most romantic and beautiful to behold. I believe that
for nearly half a century of married life they had never
once been separated a single day; and the attachment, as
is always the case when it is genuine, increased with
years.

The sudden and unexpected death of this excellent
Christian lady occasioned such a shock to her husband
that he never recovered it; and in a few months he suc-
cumbed, and followed her to the final rest. As "they
were lovely in their lives," so "in death they were not
divided."

I should not omit to mention, though the best record is
on high, that the help afforded to the aged and infirm
poor connected with the "Church in the House," at Hampstead and elsewhere, was such as ample means and large
and loving hearts would minister.

They made many a widow's heart to sing for joy, as well
as gladdened the desolate orphan, and cheered the sick-
bed of those who, but for such help, would have been left
to die in poverty and want. Oh! what a luxury is wealth
when it is used not to embellish a home, or entertain
select circles of intelligent friends *only*, but where, in addition to this, care is taken to search out cases where a
little timely and kindly help comes like a message from
Heaven!

Occasional social gatherings of the Church and congregation were held under the roof of this hospitable man,
when the venerable pastor might be seen, surrounded by
his family and the people of his charge, looking quite
patriarchal. I have known him, more than once, at the
close of a week-night service, invite the congregation
to his dining-room to take a glass of wine, and partake of
some of the choice fruits from his garden. At these social

gatherings he would express the pleasure it afforded him to see so many around his table.

As there were no " pew rents," collections were made for various Christian and benevolent objects, such as the Baptist Missionary Society, the Hartley Colliery catastrophe, and always for the poorer members of the Church. It was most gratifying to see, in actual working, a Christian society, held together by the bonds of the Gospel, having the ordinances of Christ administered, and discipline exercised, without much of the machinery that encumbers many of our Christian churches.

The last illness and death of this good man cast a sad gloom over the little company that were wont to worship at the " Church in the House." It was a mournful day at Hampstead when the remains of this eminent saint were removed from his hospitable mansion to the cemetery at Highgate, followed, not only by his children and relatives, but also by the deacons, and most of those who had so often listened to his earnest and affectionate preaching. As we gathered around the open grave, and took a last, long, lingering look at the coffin that contained all that could perish of this Christian gentleman, we united in singing the well-known hymn—

" For ever with the Lord."

" We buried him in peace, but his name liveth for evermore."

I must again return to my personal history. During my residence at Hampstead I was frequently invited, as an office-bearer in the church, to visit the sick and bereaved. As I had had a good deal of ill health, and had drunk deeply of the cup of sorrow myself, I found my visits always acceptable. These visitations to the house of mourning and the bed of sickness were quite as profitable to me as they were helpful to others. I could record many instances of good done in this way. It is a time when the mind and heart are both open to Christian influences, and a few kindly words at such a season are sometimes never forgotten. I will mention one instance of this nature, as an illustration of others that might be named.

In the winter of 1862 I was sent for suddenly to see a person I had known intimately in my early life, who was seriously ill, and had expressed a strong desire to see me. The address given me was to a street on the Surrey side of the Thames. On finding the house I saw that I had been expected, and was immediately ushered into an apartment on the first floor. On entering the room the first object that attracted my notice was a woman between forty and fifty, reclining on a bed, supported by a young man whom I knew to be her son. A young woman sat by the bed-side looking on, whom I ascertained to be his wife. I recognized the poor invalid at a glance as one whom I had known thirty years ago, and took her thin, hot, feverish hand in mine, and seated myself by the side of the bed. I could see plain enough, by the great difficulty she had in breathing, and also by her wild and restless eye, that she was near the last great crisis.

She made several ineffectual attempts to tell me how ill she had been, and what agony of mind she had endured at the thought of dying. She trembled so at this recital that the bed shook under her. I spoke to her at once of Christ —of his sacrificial death and his dying love. A Bible lay open upon the bed, and I read to her the 51st Psalm—that penitential prayer of millions now in heaven. I could see, by her eagerness to listen, how exactly suited was this inspired prayer of a royal penitent to her agonized mind. After waiting for a few minutes, I read to her the 53rd chapter of Isaiah; and without any word of explanation on my part, she appeared to see at once the great and comforting doctrine therein contained, of substitution and sacrifice.

She then asked me to pray with her. We knelt around

her bed, and brief, and earnest, and importunate, were the prayers we offered. Those feeble utterances of the heart reached the throne of the Eternal, and entered the listening ear of the Lord of Hosts.

I said a few brief words to her of the willingness of the Father to receive back an erring but penitent child, of the all-sufficiency of the sacrifice of Christ to atone for the sins of the whole world, and of the readiness of the Holy Spirit to bring these precious truths home to her heart and conscience.

The great work was done; the mental eye was opened, and a flood of sacred light flowed in upon her soul, and she could lay hold of the promise of salvation, free and immediate. As the afternoon sun streamed in at the window, the countenance of this dying woman shone with a radiance like that of an angel. Turning to her son, and looking upon him as only a mother can, she said, in accents soft and sweet, "Edward, I have now no fear of death ; I know that I am forgiven. My only anxiety is for you and Lizzie," pointing to his wife. She added, in words that I shall never forget,—"Oh, mind that you both meet me in heaven !"

After a short silence she asked me again to read from the Scriptures, and I selected the 23rd Psalm. She said that it was what she herself felt, and that she now could depart in peace. I knelt once again by her side, and commended her to God: bade her farewell, and returned to my home.

She died on the following day, and a note from her son informed me that her departure was peaceful and happy.

Here was one among many instances that I could recount where the Gospel of Christ has been found equal to any case. This brief interview was to me most memorable, inasmuch as this woman was the person referred to in my early history, the intimacy with whom was the immediate occasion of my leaving Canterbury. How true it is that—

"God moves in a mysterious way,
  His wonders to perform."

A death-bed repentance, and a late conversion, are to
be deprecated, as far as their practical influence upon the
world is concerned, as time is needed to establish the
reality of the change : be this as it may, " the Lord knoweth them that are His," and " delighteth in mercy ;" and
" He is able to save unto the uttermost "—the uttermost
point of time, as well as of guilt—" all that come unto Him."

About this time I had another return of physical exhaustion and mental depression, and many were the remedies that were proposed by my friends for its alleviation
and removal. I thought at one time of entering into some
particulars of this distressing depression to which I have been
so frequently subjected for the last five or six years ; but it
is a dark passage in my life, and perhaps, after all, to recount my sufferings would only be interesting to the
physiologist. Those who are interested in such matters
may find a most vivid account given in the " Autobiography
of the Rev. William Walford," published in 1851, Letters
xviii-xxi, in which the diagnosis of the disease is described
with terrible correctness, and the cure effected is most
marvellously related.

Among the many remedies proposed in my case were
perfect rest, generous diet, cold water, gymnastics, the
Turkish bath, and tobacco. I yielded to the advice of my
friends, and tried in succession all these remedies ; rest and
good-living were both very grateful, although I am not
likely to have occasion to " do Banting." Cold water, applied outwardly, I most thoroughly believe in, and, with
few interruptions, I take a cold bath every morning, winter
and summer, immediately on getting out of bed. Like
some other good habits, it is somewhat difficult to begin ;
but having once mastered that difficulty it is easy enough,
and is, moreover, most refreshing and invigorating. It
promotes cheerfulness and a healthy action of the brain
that is very delightful. I tried among the remedial measures

a course of gymnastics, for three months, at Professor Georgii's establishment in Wimpole-street, Cavendish-square. The Professor is, both physically and intellectually, a little Hercules; and he is a gentleman by birth and education. The system carried out by the Professor is that of the late Swedish poet and gymnasiarch, Peter Henry Ling.

Before commencing the exercises the patient is subjected to a rigid and careful medical investigation, so that the mode of treatment to be adopted may accord with the *physique* of the applicant. I invited the Professor to tell me candidly what he thought of my case, informing him that I should not be alarmed at anything he might say. He told me at the close of the investigation that I had a sound and healthy body, but that it was *vitality* that I needed.

I went through a course of the exercises for three months with very much enjoyment, but without deriving any very great benefit from them, as before I had concluded the course I had a return of the depression.

Professor Georgii's establishment is conducted most efficiently, under his own personal superintendence. While taking the exercises I met persons of all ages, from the youth at school to the man at seventy; among the patients were not a few military men returned from India, who need something of this kind to brace and invigorate the system after a residence in that enervating climate.

At certain hours of the day the Professor gives his attention to ladies; in this he is aided by an efficient staff of female assistants, so that there is nothing to offend the most fastidious.

If men need gymnastic exercises to develope fully the physical part of their being, it is as much needed by women. I am persuaded that if the physical education of woman was more intelligently attended to, it would tend very much to lighten the sad curse pronounced upon our first mother. Will my fair young readers permit me, as a

brother and a father, to recommend them to learn the full
and free use of their limbs in walking and gymnastic exercises? The latter process, under proper advice, will bring
about the happiest results. Gymnastic exercises should, I
think, form an important part of the course of discipline in
all our schools, both for girls and boys.

The Turkish bath was recommended to me among other
things, and I well remember my first experience of this
process. For the information of my country friends I will
endeavour to describe, as briefly as I can, my first adventure
in the matter of a Turkish bath.

The particular establishment that had been indicated to
me is one well known in the north-west of London, and
has been converted from a private dwelling-house to the
purpose for which it is now used. Having found my way
there one evening, I was introduced into a room with ten
or a dozen compartments of about four feet square, separated
the one from the other by a red curtain, in one of which I
was instructed to divest myself of my clothes. The attendant handed me an apron, consisting of a piece of striped
calico with strings to tie round my waist. I had pointed
out to me a stair-case down which I was to proceed when
I had undressed. As nothing was told me to the contrary,
I simply tied the apron on, and thought of Uncle Tiff, who
wore one behind, as well as in front, to hide his ragged
trousers. At the bottom of the stairs I found a door leading into an apartment, with two wooden benches on either
side of the room, and the gas burning brightly; the temperature of which was about 120 degrees. Here I found
the officiating attendant, a man about thirty years of age,
naked as myself, save a towel bound about his loins; he
informed me that I must remain in this apartment until I
perspired pretty profusely, and then proceed to an inner
room where the temperature was at about 150 degrees.
The attendant having retired, I was left alone, and began
to want something to do; the floor was so hot as to be disagreeable to stand on, and the wooden benches so intolerably

heated that to have sat long upon them would have baked
me.

I had been in this first sweating-room about a quarter
of an hour, when there entered a jolly-looking man of
about sixty, short and stout, little hair on his head, and a
good deal of beard and whisker. It was this gentleman's
first visit to the bath, and he, like myself, had simply tied
his apron on in the usual way ; but as he was one, of whom
Shakespeare tells us, with

"Fair, round belly, with good capon lin'd,

he presented such an odd appearance that I could not
refrain from laughing outright. He looked at me, now
profusely bathed with perspiration, and was probably
as much amused with the figure I cut as I was with him.
If our first parents, when "they made themselves aprons,"
looked half as ludicrous as we did, it must have required
no small effort on their part to have preserved a serious
countenance. I found afterwards that the apron, though
tied in front, should have been passed between the legs,
and fastened behind, so as to have presented very much
the appearance of the tights worn by an acrobat.

As there were no others in the room we chatted away
pleasantly enough, when by this time the attendant returned to conduct me into the second chamber, with a
temperature of 150 degrees.

I could not stand this so well as the first ; but it is necessary, and I thought it better quietly to submit to the
process. Pieces of cork were laid down upon the floor to
walk upon ; but these were so intolerably hot that I was
compelled to move from one to the other as quickly as I
could. Ten minutes in such a temperature was quite
enough, and I entered a third apartment to undergo the
shampooing process. I found the shampooer very intelligent ; he had originally been educated for the medical
profession, and understood his business thoroughly. After
a good deal of rubbing, punching, slapping, cracking the

joints, &c, there comes out a pretty considerable coating of dirt. I could not help thinking that a good shampooing would be a cure for self-righteousness. If a man think himself to be clean, the process I have been attempting to describe would demonstrate to him the fact that we cannot make ourselves clean. The lavatory follows upon the shampooing, where you are well washed with warm water, and subjected to the gentle friction of a hair glove.

The cold plunge, or *douche*, is the culminating process, and this is the crowning luxury. The bath being over, you are furnished with a couple of hot towels, your head is bound up in the eastern style, and you recline upon a couch until you feel disposed to resume your apparel.

Such, in brief, were my first experiences of a Turkish bath; and in returning to the street, I could not help feeling that I was a cleaner and a wiser, if not a better man.

The application of caloric, or dry heat, to the human system, by means of the hot-air bath, is beginning to be understood and appreciated in England; it is a luxury of no small magnitude.

We are indebted to Mr. Urquhart, not only for the introduction of the Turkish bath into England, but also for "the finest Turkish bath in the world," according to the testimony of an Arab sheikh, who was conversant with the baths at Cairo, Jerusalem, Constantinople, and Damascus. This son of the East, on being asked at Stamboul one day, at a dinner-table, by a Frenchman, to tell him where he could find the best Turkish bath, replied, "God is great, and effendis are wise; but if you ask your servant, he must say the best bath of all is to be found near Piccadilly, in London."

Some time after I had taken the bath which I have attempted to describe, I ventured one evening to test the accuracy of the eastern testimony, and accordingly paid a visit to "the Hummums" (Turkish bath) in Jermyn-street.

· Having paid the fee and put off your shoes, you enter an

elegant and spacious hall, beautifully cool and clean, and where there is every convenience for making the necessary preparations for what is to follow. There is a large marble tank of cold water in the centre of the hall, and on either side are oriental couches on which you may recline, and divest yourself of your apparel at your leisure. A boy in Turkish costume waits upon you, with a couple of coloured wrappers, one of which he attaches to your waist, and the other is thrown loosely over the shoulders. Thus habited, you proceed to what is called the *tepidarium*, where the light is dim, the couches voluptuous, and the heat such as speedily to make you freely perspire. From this apartment you proceed, after staying about twenty minutes or half an hour, to what is termed the *sudatorium*, where the temperature is considerably higher, and where you have an out-and-out sweating. When you have remained here as long as you can stand it, you return to the *tepidarium*, and lie down on a marble slab for the shampooer to commence his operations upon you. This was, in my case, performed by a swarthy son of the Desert, who did his work in the most delicate and efficient manner. Every part of the body in turn came in for its share of rubbing and kneading, and you rise from the operation with no inconsiderable coating of animal matter removable.

The lavatory follows upon this, with an abundant supply of Castile soap, and a free use of the hair glove; and in a few minutes you are "clean every whit." This being over, you descend to another chamber, where an icy *douche* awaits you; and the bath ends by your taking a dive under the plate-glass window that separates between the *tepidarium* and the great hall. On stepping out of this deliciously cold-plunge-bath, you are enveloped in hot linen, and look as much like a genuine Mussulman as John Bull can be made to appear.

Such, my country friends, is the sum of the matter; and when you are in London and can afford the time and will pay the fee, small in comparison for the princely accommodation afforded, I would advise you by all means to indulge in a luxury which when once enjoyed will never be forgotten. If Mr. Urquhart can carry out his truly philanthropic project of establishing such baths throughout London and the provinces, as those which are to be had in Jermyn-street, to be used for the fee of a shilling, it would be a national boon, and he would deserve a monument in Westminster Abbey, or St. Paul's.

The last remedy recommended for my ailments that I shall speak of, is tobacco. In my early Canterbury days I was a great smoker, but broke myself of the habit soon after coming to London, and for thirty years was " a total abstainer" from the much-abused weed. However, long attacks of nervous depression, lasting sometimes four or five months, and sleepless nights, made me willing to try almost anything to obtain relief. I have always resolutely avoided the quack remedies, for this and other similar maladies, that meet the eye in all our public prints ; and finding that the medical profession could do little or nothing to alleviate my wearisome symptoms, I tried tobacco.

Let not my readers be startled at the sound of the soothing plant, for my habit is never to take more than a single pipe of " golden shag," or one " mild Havannah" before going to bed. I have found the happiest results follow upon this simple remedy. My sleep has been sweet and refreshful, and I wake at my usual hour with a desire to get up. I have tried what is known as " a nightcap,"—a tumbler of grog—the last thing on going to roost, but not with the " desired effect," as my sleep has been disturbed, and a headache invariably followed it in the morning. My pipe has the contrary effect upon me, and I regret that I did not avail myself of its soothing qualities before. I believe that to a man of active brain the moderate use of tobacco is almost indispensable. In seasons of mental activity it will exert a gently-soothing and quieting influence ; and in times of depression, a man may sit and enjoy his pipe in silence, when he is unfitted to take part in conversation. To sit

and *do nothing*, and feel that you are of no use to anybody, is a terrible feeling ; but a man *looks* comfortable, if
he is not so, with a good old-fashioned " yard of clay" in
his mouth.

It should be remembered that some of the profoundest
thinkers have been men addicted to tobacco ; and we know
not how much we owe to the influence of this much-abused
plant. Some of the mightiest intellectual efforts of the late
Robert Hall followed upon a pipe, which was almost as familiar to him as the Bible, and his favourite Cicero. It is said
that his celebrated sermon on " Modern Infidelity" was
prepared and delivered after he had been rolling in agony,
on the floor of his vestry, from an internal disease which
gave him the most intense agony, and from which his pipe
was his best relief.

The author of " Alton Locke" and " Yeast" is a great
smoker ; and I know several eminent preachers who indulge
a little in this innocent weakness. Some of the best sermons have been meditated in the easy-chair by the fireside, under the soothing influence of a pipe. Sermonic
reveries, if they take no more tangible embodiment, will
pass away as poetic imaginings do : the better way is to
hold them fast until these bright creations are clothed in
suitable presentments for the pulpit.

I would not have my readers imagine that I recommend
the wholesale use of tobacco ; or that I have the smallest
sympathy with the half-fledged boys who crowd our streets,
with short vulgar pipes stuck in their mouths. All that I
go in for is this, that in my own case it has produced the
very happiest effects ; and the true enjoyment of tobacco,
like all other good things, is to be found in its moderate
and temperate use. The only interdict that I know of is to
be found in the Apostolic injunction, " Do thyself no harm."

I should like to say a few words on the part I have
taken in politics through my humble career. I have never
been afraid of being denominated " a Political Dissenter :"
I rather glory in the fact of being so. It is my thought-

ful belief that nothing is more consistent than for a Christian man to assert his citizenship, not only in the open and manly support of what is right; but also, if need be, in resisting to the uttermost, by constitutional measures, anything and everything that would retard the progress of the freest inquiry, and the most perfect equality in matters religious, let a man's creed be what it may. As a Christian man and a citizen, I am ready to " render unto Cæsar the things that are Cæsar's;" but at the same time I do not forget my obligation to "render unto God the things that are His."

I have no sympathy with so-called religious men who think that a Christian should not meddle with politics. It has sometimes been my misfortune to come in contact with small-souled, narrow-minded, and bigoted men, calling themselves Christians, that any sect or party in the world would be ashamed of.

I am old enough to recollect the repeal of the Test and Corporation Acts, and also the removal of the disabilities that oppressed and degraded the Roman Catholics.

The political state of the country ought always to be a subject of interest to every Christian man. A man who is a Christian should never lose sight of the fact that he is a citizen, and in the best and truest sense of the term, " a man of the world."

The passing of the Reform Bill I well remember; and though too young to see fully the great benefits conferred by that wise measure, yet I was old enough to take no small interest in the subject, and was present at the festival held at Canterbury to commemorate the passing of that Bill.

I hope to live to see that great measure developed and enlarged by a generous admission to the elective franchise of a great part of the five millions of my fellow-countrymen still unrepresented in Parliament.

With such a man as Earl Russell at the head of the Government, backed by Messrs. Gladstone, Bright,

Baines, and a host of minor names to support him,
surely a bill might be introduced and carried that shall be
another instalment of what will one day come to every
man, not convicted of crime, in England. Education and
social training are fast preparing the way for this great
boon.

I have great sympathy with the hard-worked unenfranchised millions of my fellow-countrymen. I know
something of their struggles, their narrow scanty means,
their sorrows, and the brave and silent way they bear them.

My humble efforts, while life is spared, and health will
permit, shall, as opportunity offers, be given to help on
the desirable object of obtaining for them the political
position that is their due. It is not the " Lord Dun-
drearys " that have made England what she is. Oh no!—

> " The noblest men I know on earth
>   Are men whose hands are brown with toil;
> Who, back'd by no ancestral birth,
>   Hew down the woods, and till the soil;
> And thereby win a prouder fame
> Than crowns a king's or warrior's name.
>
> The working men, whate'er their task,
>   To carve the stone, or bear the hod,
> They wear upon their honest brows
>   The royal stamp and seal of God!
> And brighter are their drops of sweat
> Than diamonds in a coronet.
>
> God bless the noble working men,
>   Who rear the cities of the plain,
> Who dig the mines and build the ships,
>   Who drive the commerce of the main!
> God bless them! for their swarthy hands
> Have wrought the glory of all lands."

The working men of England have in William Ewart
Gladstone and John Bright two eloquent and true-hearted
advocates ; but it is still true, in its best sense, that—

> " Who would be free,
> Themselves must strike the blow."

No one can help those, to any purpose, who will not help themselves. Working men should, in public meetings and every constitutional manner, show that they are in earnest; and that being the case, public opinion will become so educated and enlightened upon the subject that their demands must be complied with. In this way all the great national measures for the benefit of the masses have been conceded. Lord Brougham once eloquently remarked, that "the anger of the Deity is sometimes heard in the murmurs of the people." When will the Parliament of England learn that "the voice of the people is the voice of God?"

In spite, however, of all that may be said of the House of Commons as it is at present constituted, we look around Europe, and to our colonies, and across the Atlantic, and that legislative assembly will honourably compare with any representative parliament in the world, not only for ability, but also for high moral worth, and all that makes a nation great.

There are no evils that exist among us as a nation that cannot be removed by the people themselves, and therefore I look with hope and confidence to the final settlement of such vexed questions as the Abolition of Church Rates, the Dissolution of the unrighteous Union subsisting between what is called the National Church and the State; the fair and just appropriation of national property now absorbed by the Church of England; the equitable adjustment of the Income Tax; and the extension of the Elective Franchise to all who may with safety be brought within the pale of the constitution.

I know the opposition that has been made, and will be continued on the part of some, to oppose these reforms in the body corporate, but courage and persistent effort will attain anything that is really right in itself, and therefore ultimate success is certain.

I was present at most of the meetings held in London during the agitation and conflict that took place before the Corn Laws were repealed. I recollect the telling speeches that were made by the late revered Richard Cobden, John Bright, and William Johnson Fox. Two of these champions have fought the good fight, saw the victory, and are gone to their reward. One, as able, and more eloquent than either, remains; and to John Bright the people look as to a standard-bearer, around whom they will rally. I may yet live to see the fondest hopes and intensest yearnings of that great and good man fulfilled, and those who most abuse him now, admit him to be not only one of our best orators, but also a statesman of whom the country may be justly proud.

Of John Bright it may be said, in the glowing words of one who has passed from among us, " Distinguished merit will ever rise superior to slander, and will draw lustre from reproach. The vapours which gather round the rising sun, and follow it in its course, seldom fail, at the close of it, to form a magnificent theatre for its reception, and to invest with variegated tints, and with a softened effulgence, the luminary which they cannot hide."

As preaching and preachers is a subject of interest at the present day, and has been made the theme of discussion in some of the leading organs of public opinion lately, I make no apology for presenting a few thoughts for the consideration of my readers, relating to this interesting and important topic.

I have been a reader and hearer of sermons for the greater part of my life, and what I have to say is just a few remarks upon a subject that has occupied my mind frequently, and is also the result of some lengthened observation.

Preaching, in its legitimate sense, is, I presume, discoursing publicly on any religious subject. It is as old as the antediluvian era, as we learn that " Enoch prophesied,"

(Jude, 14, 15). Noah "was a preacher of righteousness," (1 Peter iii. 19, 20). Moses, "the servant of God," was an eminent preacher, as well as "the prophet of the Lord." Aaron was perhaps the more naturally eloquent of the two, but that they both were preachers we learn from several parts of the sacred writings. Joshua, Solomon, and Amos, "the herdsman of Tekoa," were preachers. They were dark days in the Jewish Church when they were left without "a teaching priest." Ezra was a famous preacher. John the Baptist was the most celebrated preacher that arose before the "Great Teacher," who preached "as never man spake." The preaching of the Son of God was such that "the common people heard Him gladly." His style was simple, solemn, and majestic, sometimes terribly severe and vehement; His imagery natural and beautiful, His deportment graceful and becoming, and, above all, His life was consistent with His teaching.

The Apostles copied their Divine Master, and Paul and Peter stand out, in bold relief, as men not only "mighty in the Scriptures," but also as grand living illustrations of what preachers ought to be.

The first centuries of the Christian Church produced some grand preachers: Basil, Bishop of Cæsarea, John Chrysostom, preacher at Antioch, and afterwards Patriarch of Constantinople, with Gregory Nazianzen, were distinguished preachers in the Greek Church, while Jerome and the great Augustine were foremost preachers in the Latin Church.

Sermons in those early days were, we are told, always in the "vulgar tongue," and they were short or long, as the audience or the occasion required. Preaching and preachers appear to have degenerated during the "dark ages," but revived again at the Reformation, when the great body of the people gladly thronged together to hear the Scriptures read and expounded.

The Church of Rome has produced some great preachers, such as Savonarola, Massillon, Bossuet, and Bourdaloue.

The Church of England can point with just and honest pride to such men as Bishops Latimer and Ridley, Archbishop Usher, the protesting Chillingworth, the poetic and imaginative Jeremy Taylor, Isaac Barrow, Tillotson, Sherlock, South, Baxter, Hoadley, Lowth, and Butler, whose sermons are as deserving of study as is his celebrated "Analogy;" Donne, the Dean of St. Paul's, Bishop Hall, and the good Bishop Jewel, should not be omitted from the muster-roll of preachers, which the National Church can number among her pulpit orators.

There are the great preachers of the Reformation, of whom Luther and Knox are the most prominent. The Puritan preachers also stand out as demanding our attentive study, as, for example, Dr. Owen, John Howe, Gurnall, and others.

We come down then to the days of Whitefield, Wesley, Romaine, and John Newton; as well as Robert Hall, the prince of modern preachers, Andrew Fuller, John Foster, Kinghorn, the great Chalmers, with his overwhelming torrent of eloquence, and his no less distinguished colleague the trumpet-tongued Edward Irving.

All who want to know anything of preaching and preachers should make themselves acquainted with the sermons of these famous men, and learn how they put the great subjects of the Christian Ministry before their hearers. I should not omit to mention among the list of great preachers James Foster, originally an Independent, but afterwards a Baptist, and one of the most effective preachers of his time.

Having just glanced at some of the more prominent preachers of ancient and modern times, I trust my readers will bear with me while I say something as to what I humbly consider preaching should be.

I may say at once that the pulpit is a solemn place, and should never be entered without thoughtfulness and prayer, because preaching has to do with the Eternal God, and with man's everlasting welfare. I look upon the office of the Christian Ministry as one of peculiar responsibility, and of unspeakable importance, as a man's own soul is not only at stake, but also those of many others. An unfaithful minister cannot sink alone to the world of woe, but in his fall he will drag others down with him.

While I do not think that secular professions and trades are inconsistent with the Christian Ministry, it should be looked on as a life-long lesson and service. If an artist, or a surgeon, or an architect need to apply himself *wholly* to his profession, surely a preacher should, if possible, devote himself exclusively to his sacred work. If freedom from the cares and anxieties of business be desirable for those who are set apart to the work of the Christian Ministry, then a Church is bound to make a liberal and suitable provision for the man who thus serves them; and if he be a man of the right stamp he will abundantly earn his stipend.

Prayer is the first duty of a Christian minister, and is essential to spiritual life and growth in grace. Love to God and to the Saviour, benevolence and love to man, elevated piety and self-consecration are undoubted necessaries in a preacher. An apostolic portrait of what a preacher ought to be is given in 2 Cor. vi. 3-10.

A cold-hearted preacher will do no good. A preacher without experience and knowledge will not be influential. You must be a *heart-preacher*, and feel yourself the truths you preach, if you expect your hearers to feel them: you must illustrate their influence in your own life if you would have that influence displayed in the life and deportment of your hearers. A holy and consistent life preaches to the consciences of men as nothing else does, and gives weight and influence to every word the preacher speaks: but if his moral conduct be not exemplary, he may preach with the eloquence of men and of angels, but it will be disregarded. The worst men and women among your hearers, and—

> "Oh, what may man within him hide,
> While angel on the outward side!"

And men, bad as they sometimes are,—

> "At most differ as heaven and earth;
> But women, worst and best, as heaven and hell."

Yet they all feel the force of a consistent and holy life. They may hate the preacher because he reproves their sins, but in their inmost souls they fear and respect him; and are, moreover, more persuaded of the reality of true religion by one such example than by a thousand arguments. Nothing upon earth is so lovely as a holy life. Some men never preach a standard of morality beyond which they have themselves attained to; but this should never be done. Let the standard be *the life of Christ.*

A preacher, in delivering his message, acts as an ambassador, who entreats men "in Christ's stead to be reconciled to God," so that nothing should be substituted in its place. "Preach the Word;" let nothing else occupy the sacred hour devoted to religious instruction. Amuse not dying men with the refinements of literature or the discoveries of science. "Preach the Gospel to every creature" is the great commission, and "woe to that man if he preach not the Gospel!" Let every one who hears you know that "he that believeth and is baptized shall be saved, but he that believeth not shall be damned," (Mark xvi. 16).

He who preaches should do so with deep compassion, of weeping, melting, beseeching pity; and let your soul burn with that holy ardour for the salvation of the hearers which becomes alike their situation and your own. I recollect having it said to me on one occasion by "an old disciple" of a certain school of theology, when I had been endeavouring to illustrate this that I am recommending in my own case, "My good brother, you speak as if you could do the work of conversion yourself; God will do His own work without your earnestness." My reply was, "Hear Paul at Athens and Corinth, or Peter on the day of Pentecost, or Whitefield in Moorfields, or Spurgeon at the

Tabernacle, and if they took God's work out of His hands, so do I." My reply was greeted by a quiet smile from the good old man. Now I know full well that as God alone can create a soul, so He alone can convert one ; but as human instrumentality is called into requisition in the one case, so the other is also brought about by what may be called " the foolishness of preaching," and " the feebleness of prayer."

Preaching, to be effectual, must be the work of the heart. Mere intellectual preaching will never move the people to do anything to rectify what is wrong in themselves. I have not unfrequently gone away from hearing sermons of this description, full of admiration both of the preacher and also of his subject-matter ; but it has not set me to work more manfully and determinately to bring my daily life into greater and more perfect conformity and harmony with God's requirements. Heart-preaching is hard work in every way, and it tells as much upon the preacher as the hearer, but it is effectual. We all yield an internal homage to that which is true, and we respect the man who has the courage and the heart to tell out to us the demands that God makes upon us as subjects of His moral government.

Extempore preaching is by far the most generally acceptable, and one of the strongest arguments in its favour is that the speaker is more likely to feel the truth which he utters than when he sits down to write in his study. Extempore preaching, however, sometimes falls into a round of common-place ideas, or mere generalities, by which the speaker is not affected himself, and as a consequence of this, the interest of the hearer flags. There are people who are so attached to extempore preaching that they will not tolerate a written sermon ; and such is their vitiated taste that a man may talk any twaddle he pleases, as long as he does not read it from a manuscript.

The practice of reading written sermons extensively prevails, and I cannot see the objection to it that some affirm. Of course it will very much depend, let the composition be what it may, upon the mode of delivery. A good reader will make a written composition tell in every word and in every syllable. If a man who knows how to do it will but throw his whole soul into the work, he will move his hearers, be they plebeian or patrician. A preacher, to be in any way effective, must be in earnest, for however he may exert his voice and assume the appearance of earnestness, if he feels it not he can never affect the intelligent hearer.

Though, for my own part, I cannot see any sufficient reasons why sermons should not occasionally be read, I think there can be no question that extempore preaching is by far the most effective. By extempore preaching I do not mean the unpremeditated effusions of a man too idle to study; but the delivery of an unwritten discourse, the subject of which the preacher has studied till he has it in his mind, and the spirit of which he has imbibed till he feels its impression on his own heart. Who that makes himself familiar with the great subjects about which he would speak, and that deeply feels their influence himself, can long be at a loss to find words expressive of the emotions of his heart, and the truths that he has been meditating?

If a man habitually lives under the lively impression of the truths he preaches—of the love of Christ, the preciousness of time, the vanity of all earthly good, the glories of heaven, the nearness of eternity and its tremendously solemn realities—let these truths deeply affect his own soul, and they will be manifestly felt and seen in his preaching. Under such feelings a man will never trifle in the presence of God; he will select no merely amusing and interesting, but comparatively unimportant subjects; he will not fill up sermons with dry, hard discussions, or cold, metaphysical speculations: but will solemnly and affectionately utter truths of eternal importance, and as an ambassador of Christ, will deliver his weighty message, " whether men will hear, or whether they will forbear."

The glory of Christ, and the eternal welfare of his hearers should be the ruling passion in the mind of a preacher, and never let him seek to please the refined and wealthy few while the poor and illiterate are uninstructed.

Dr. Owen remarked, that it would be worth preaching to a whole nation, for many years, to secure the salvation of one soul; and Robert Hall, the prince of modern preachers, has said, " that to a mind that rightly estimates the weight of eternal things, it will appear a greater honour to have been instrumental in converting one sinner from the error of his ways than to have wielded the thunder of a Demosthenes, or to have lighted up the fire of a Cicero."

Having said thus much of preaching and the preachers of the past, let me, for the information of those who, with myself, are fond of good sermons, indicate a few of the published discourses of some of the preachers of our own day that I have read and studied with advantage. I am well aware that as a general rule a volume of sermons is about as good a sedative as anything that can be taken. Sydney Smith recommends it as an invaluable soporific, though in my case it has often proved unavailing. The thousands of volumes of printed sermons, most of them "published by particular request," that repose quietly on the shelves of the National Library, uncut and undisturbed, save for the purposes of airing and dusting, sufficiently attest the interest generally felt for this class of literature. Still there are, happily, some noble exceptions to this rule, and among the volumes most in demand, both at the reading-room of the National Library as well as at "Mudie's," are good sermons.

One of the truest tests of the readable merits of a book is its appearance at a public library; and I have had from Mudie's volumes of sermons that had been so read as to be in anything but a presentable condition as to the binding and general appearance.

Among the best published sermons by clergymen of the Church of England of the present day may be mentioned

those by the late Mr. Robertson of Brighton, though some
of them are terribly heretical; but they are thoughtful,
bold, and suggestive; Melvill's Sermons, even those that
are taken in short-hand, and published in the "Pulpit" as
the "Golden Lectures," are a great treat; would that this
distinguished preacher could be persuaded to prepare a se-
lection of his sermons for the press, as a legacy to the
Church and his many admirers. Dean Alford's "Quebec
Sermons" are full of interest and intelligent criticism. A
series of "Lenten Sermons," published under the auspices
of the Bishop of Oxford, are many of them of great power
and eloquence. Those by the late Archbishop Whately, and
his worthy successor Dr. Trench, are also deserving of attentive perusal. Then there are volumes by Archdeacon Hare,
Dean Stanley, Dr. Pusey, Christopher Wordsworth, Dr.
Vaughan of Doncaster, and Charles Kingsley, that will repay
a careful study. As orators, these men are by no means
conspicuous, except Robertson and Melvill, who will ever
take high rank. Dr. M'Neile, the late Hugh Stowell, and
Sanderson Robins; Capel Molyneux, and the Bishop of
Oxford, would bear away the palm in the pulpit, though
these men are not so distinguished in their published
writings.

Among the Independents there have been some noble
preachers, in such men as the late Stephen M'All of Manchester, Winter Hamilton of Leeds, Dr. Raffles of Liverpool, Dr. Wardlaw of Glasgow, William Jay of Bath,
Angell James of Birmingham, and Dr. Leifchild of Craven
Chapel. These eminent preachers have gone to their reward; but there still remains in that denomination some
worthy successors in such men as Parsons of Leeds,
Thomas Binney, Samuel Martin, Dr. Raleigh, Thomas
Jones, and Newman Hall.

The Baptists have had some great preachers among
them, as Robert Hall and Andrew Fuller; and they have
now a goodly band of living pulpit orators, with the inimitable and incomparable Spurgeon at their head, who, I

rejoice to say, has falsified all his defamers, and is as fresh and as popular as ever. Let any one, fond of sermons, take the ten volumes of this justly celebrated preacher, and read them as productions taken down weekly from his lips, without a note to help him, and they will be astounded at the noble series of volumes even as a literary production, as well as for the amount of sound theology they contain.

Our Free-Church brethren can point to Dr. Guthrie as a host in himself, though, from ill-health, obliged to relinquish his pulpit labours, and is now only heard of through the press; his "Gospel in Ezekiel," and "Speaking to the Heart," contain sermons that cannot fail to be useful, and may be read over and over again as an intellectual treat. Drs. Candlish of Edinburgh, and James Hamilton of London, still hold foremost places, in their denomination, as first-class preachers; while Dr. Cumming and Norman Macleod may be said to stand at the head of their brethren in the "Establishment."

The Wesleyans have had among them, as eloquent preachers, Richard Watson, Robert Newton, and Dr. Beaumont. The published sermons of the late Richard Watson are among the best I have ever read; and, according to the testimony of James Montgomery the poet, and others, he was a most commanding preacher. Mr. Morley Punshon is perhaps the foremost living orator among the Wesleyans of the present day; I have listened with the greatest delight to some of his famous lectures, and occasional sermons, and have no hesitation in pronouncing him to be an orator of a high order.

I fear that I may have wearied my readers with this somewhat lengthy digression upon preaching and preachers, and I can only plead in excuse that I have always had a great liking for good sermons and earnest eloquent preaching; and this must be my apology for saying so much upon the subject. I would rather be a good preacher than the owner of a thousand acres, as to move men and women to attend to eternal realities, and to be the means of bringing them to the knowledge of Christ and His salvation, is, I think, the noblest and the most glorious office that a man can fill:—" They that be wise (to win souls) shall shine as the light; and they that turn many to righteousness as the stars for ever and ever."

The Bard of Olney has told us what a Preacher should be; and with his graphic description I close :—

" Would I describe a Preacher, such as Paul,
    Were he on earth, would hear, approve, and own,—
    Paul should himself direct me. I would trace
    His master-strokes, and draw from his design.
    I would express him simple, grave, sincere;
    In doctrine uncorrupt; in language plain,
    And plain in manner; decent, solemn, chaste,
    And natural in gesture; much impress'd
    Himself, as conscious of his awful charge,
    And anxious mainly, that the flock he feeds,
    May feel it too; affectionate in look,
    And tender in address, as well becomes
    A messenger of grace to guilty man.

         *   *   *   *

    In man, or woman, but far most in man,
    And most of all in man that ministers,
    And serves the altar, in my soul I loath
    All affectation. 'Tis my perfect scorn;
    Object of my implacable disgust.

         *   *   *   *

    Therefore, avaunt all attitude, and stare,
    And start theatric, practised at the glass !
    I seek divine simplicity in him,
    Who handles things divine; and all besides,
    Though learn'd with labour, and though much admired
    By curious eyes, and judgments ill inform'd,
    To me is odious."

CONCLUSION.

"Beyond the grave there doubtless is a sphere,
Where all will be right which so puzzles us here;
Where the false glare, the glitter, and tinsel of time
Fade and die, in the light of that region sublime;
Where the soul, disenchanted of flesh and of sense,
Undeceived by its happiness, its show, and pretence,
Will be clothed for the life and the service above,
With purity, truth, faith, meekness, and love!"

"I would not live always,
    I would not if I could;
But, I need not fret about it,
    'Cause I couldn't if I would."

HERE is something very solemn and affecting in leaving the work and the places which you have been accustomed to frequent for many years. The house of business, the well-known office, the desk at which you have worked for many a weary hour, the people you have been daily in the habit of meeting, all your surroundings become, after many years, a part of yourself.

And yet it must be so, whether you are a strong robust man of iron frame and full of nervous power and energy; or one with a more fragile and delicately-adjusted organization, upon whose mental and physical system contact with the world has done its sure work, the time must come when you must relinquish it all. Under these fixed and unalterable circumstances he is wise who, with calmness and composure, addresses himself to the duty of not only leaving that which has occupied and filled his hands and his head, it may be for a long series of years, but who also thinks soberly and thoughtfully of the great work of preparing to die.

I can understand, in some measure, the feelings of one in advanced life, and full of years and honours, contemplating his departure with serenity and even satisfaction; but to be compelled, through ill health and declining powers, to give up, at a time of life which may be regarded as the palmy state of man, and when, from the greater maturity of the judgment and his more accumulated experience, he is fitted for greater usefulness and more tranquil enjoyment, this is indeed no small trial. It is only when we regard sickness and health, and life and death, as being at the disposal of an infinitely wise and good Being that we can cheerfully acquiesce in such a procedure.

Except in cases of sudden death, the day must inevitably come to the most busy when he must formally resign and give up all public business. It is an interesting study to witness a thoughtful man endeavouring to make this retirement from public life a prelude and preparation for the still more important and momentous fact that he must shortly enter upon all the awful realities of death and eternity.

Every Christian man should make the necessary arrangement as to his affairs and his family, so that no needless hurry and unbecoming bustle should be allowed to interfere with the calmness and composure that should be the attendants of his last hours.

My declining health and impaired mental powers have continually reminded me that the day cannot be very far distant when the work which I have engaged in must be given up, and the subjects I have thought of and mused over for many years will no longer be seen " as through a glass darkly," but they will break in upon my mental

vision as a great and tremendous reality. Repeated attacks
of mental depression and nervous exhaustion have much
impaired any intellectual strength and vigour I may have
once possessed. I have known, not unfrequently, the terrible languor and complete prostration of a wearied and
exhausted mind, and the weaknesses incident to a feeble
and sickly body, and sometimes the feelings arising from
this state of things have been so strong as almost to overcome the natural desire to live. Frequently this has so
pressed upon my spirit as to prompt me to give expression
to thoughts and longings that have thrown sadness and
gloom over those around me, whose tenderest sympathies
I possessed.

To borrow the eloquent words of one who has truthfully
and beautifully spoken of this state of things—" The strong
men bow themselves: the years *will* draw nigh" when
the firmest fibre slackens, and the fullest well-spring of
human energy sinks below the brim. The process of declining health is humbling to sense though not to faith.
Weak points are felt in the frame which were never felt
before. The active mind discovers with surprise that the
body cannot answer all its wonted demands, and it is apt
to chide and urge its worn servant. When the truth can
no longer be concealed, a certain gravity shades the beaming countenance, and withdraws a few shades of light from
the full-orbed eye. Yet that conscious weakness gives maturity to wisdom. Humility throws its graceful mantle
over goodness. By how much man's stout-heartedness is
subdued, by so much are the lines of his character mellowed. Laden with fruit, and clothed with rich autumnal
tints, he is most admired as he enters on the last stage of
life; but as his sap recedes towards the root, and leaf
falls after leaf, he naturally seeks retirement from the
public eye. Not willing to relinquish his loved activity and
usefulness, he gradually withdraws from being the actor,
and becomes the counsellor. Happy the man who can
walk calmly down into the vale of years, lay aside his

labours and honours with modest dignity, and humbly await his rest." *

This touching passage, from one of the most interesting biographies of modern times, is appropriately descriptive of that which precedes the departure of a man who had been for many years extensively useful in his generation ; but it does seem hard for one just arriving at the meridian of life to feel in himself unmistakeable indications that he must no longer engage in many things that once were pleasurable and exhilarating. The mind, once capable of revelling in questions and subjects that taxed its utmost powers, is now weary, and is, at best, as " a wild bird hopelessly straining its broken wing ;" the step that was once elastic and firm is slow and measured ; and though the process of decay be with silent and stealthy approaches, so that one may say with the poet, that

> "Time has laid his hand
> Upon my heart, gently, not smiting it,
> But as a harper lays his open palm
> Upon his harp to deaden its vibrations,"

yet I cannot but feel that with me " the day is far spent, and the night is at hand ;" and though we naturally cling the closer to those we love when the shades of eternity are falling upon us, " until the day break and the shadows flee away," the prominent and uppermost feeling of my mind is that which a great and profound thinker of our own day has given expression to in writing to a bereaved and sorrowing friend.† He says, " I congratulate you and myself that life is passing away. What a superlatively grand and consoling idea is that of death ! Without this radiant idea, this delightful morning-star, indicating that the luminary of eternity is going to rise, life would, to

---

* Life of Edward Baines, by his son, E. Baines, Esq. M.P. 8vo. London, 1851.

† John Foster.

c c

my view, darken into midnight melancholy. Oh! the expectation of living *here*, and living *thus*, always, would be indeed a prospect of overwhelming despair! But thanks to that fatal decree that dooms us to die, thanks to that Gospel which opens the vision of an endless life, and thanks, above all, to that Saviour Friend who has promised to conduct all the faithful through the sacred trance of death into scenes of paradise and everlasting delight! Shall not this divine prospect console you for all you have lost and suffered, and animate you to triumph over every desolate feeling by which you are environed? If you are fatigued in life's journey, if the scenes and the persons through which you pass are inhospitable—see yonder, the palace divine, the angel-friends, and the ever-blooming flowers are nigh. It is not far to go; be patient, go on, and live for ever!"

In bringing these brief memorials to a close, I feel that some apology is due from me to my readers for having had so much of their time and attention in these rough-and-ready sketches of my life and history. It has been, however, with me a labour of love, and has pleasantly occupied my morning hours through many years, and intervals of leisure when more pressing duties have not engaged my hands and head, in jotting down for my many friends some few particulars of a somewhat chequered and eventful career.

The composition of this " story of my life " has been a good deal interrupted by ill health, and at other times by hard work. This will, I trust, in some way account for the occasional broken and disconnected character of the book; and also for other defects, for which the kind forbearance of the reader is requested. The writer disclaims every other pretension to merit but that of drawing his materials either from personal observation or from the most reliable sources. How far he has succeeded he must leave to the judgment of his friends and readers. He can only say that—

> " Whoever thinks a faultless piece to see,
> Thinks what ne'er was, nor is, nor e'er shall be.
> In every work regard the writer's end,
> Since none can compass more than they intend."

I fear that I have sometimes inadvertently made use of that which others have written, inasmuch as I have been accustomed in my reading to make extracts of particular passages that have pleased me, with comments of my own, without in many cases stating the source from whence they were obtained. These extracts have been accumulating for more than a quarter of a century, and often in stumbling over some of them I have been not a little puzzled to distinguish my own compositions from those of others, as, when they were written, I had not the most remote intention of giving them publicity. Should this be the case, I ask to be forgiven, as I am fully and gratefully conscious that I owe very much to books. I have no claim to originality, and am glad of the opportunity thus afforded me of publicly acknowledging my obligations, not only to the great and illustrious dead, but also to many living authors for having enriched my mind with treasures that are priceless.

I can never fully express the delight and gratification that I have derived from reading. My stammering tongue drove me into solitude as a youth, from a feeling of nervous sensitive shame, and I found in books the friends and companionship that I could not hope for in society. At the time referred to I could truly say—

> " That I can never with unmingled joy
> Meet a long-loved, and long-expected friend,
> Because I feel, but cannot vent my feelings,—
> Because I know I ought,—but must not speak,
> Because I mark his quick, impatient eye
> Striving in kindness to anticipate
> The word of welcome, strangled in its birth !
> Is it not sorrow, while I truly love
> Sweet social converse, to be forced to shun
> The happy circle, from a nervous sense,
> An agonizing, poignant consciousness

That I must stand aloof, nor mingle with
The wise and good, in rational argument,
The young in brilliant quickness of reply,
Friendship's ingenuous interchange of mind,
Affection's open-hearted sympathies,
But feel myself an isolated being,
A very wilderness of widow'd thought!"

I have made acquaintances with men in books that I
shall hope to meet elsewhere, there to tell them how much
I loved them here, and tried hard to tread in their foot-
prints. What a world of worthies is thrown open to the
man or woman that will read. And among books, there is
first and foremost the grand old volume of sacred story—
the wonderful book that we learnt to reverence at our
mother's knee; and let me say, that no man or woman,
learned or unlearned, be they of noble birth and lofty
lineage, can boast to be well-informed if they have never
read and studied the Scriptures. I can hardly imagine
that these pages will meet the eye of one who has not
made himself acquainted with the Bible; but if there
should be even one among my readers of whom this is
true, let me entreat him to read at once this hitherto neglected volume, which, even as a literary production, is
intensely interesting, and which, by God's grace, may
make him " wise unto salvation."

For my own part, I can say, with the great Scotch
divine,* " I do think that, without disparagement to human
authorship—which in many instances is in the highest
degree helpful to the inquirer—still, the main road to
light and comfort, and a solid establishment in the way
that leadeth to life everlasting, is the reading the Scriptures with prayer."

What should we have known of our first great pro-
genitor and his beauteous helpmeet, fresh and fair from
the hand of their Maker, but for the Bible? How often
have I gazed upon them in their primal glory, when all

---

* Dr. Chalmers.

around was bathed in beauty, and have joined them in their orisons, as—

> " Lowly they bow'd adoring."

And when they had partaken of—

> " The fruit
> Of that forbidden tree, whose mortal taste
> Brought death into the world, and all our woe,"

my sympathies have been so stirred that I would almost have left even the garden of the Lord to have gone with them, as—

> "They hand in hand, with wandering steps and slow,
> Through Eden took their solitary way."

What should we have known of Noah, " faithful among the faithless," when " all flesh had corrupted his way upon the earth," and when he stood unmoved at the sneers and derision of a ribald and godless multitude, if the sacred historian had not informed us ?

To the same sacred source are we indebted for what we know of Abraham, the father of a great multitude. His personal history, as therein recorded, is intensely interesting, as also are the typical circumstances connected with it. The Divine command to offer up Isaac as " a burnt offering," is to my mind the most staggering fact recorded in the Bible. It has been to me the greatest moral difficulty in the whole range of revelation, and I have turned to commentators in vain for any satisfactory exposition. The immolation of human victims, particularly of that which was the most precious, the first-born child, appears to have been a common usage among many early nations, and more especially by the tribes by which Abraham was surrounded. But it must be remembered that the Mosaic religion held human sacrifices in abhorrence, and the God of the Patriarchs had hitherto imposed no duties which were repugnant to the better feelings of our nature. For these reasons the trial was the more severe to

Abraham's faith. He must, therefore, have not only been fully assured of the Divine command, but he must have, at the same time, believed in the Divine rectitude. The only conclusion that I can arrive at is that his was a simple and sublime act of unhesitating obedience to the command of God. To see the real and terrible difficulties of the good old man is to place yourself in his stead, and as the conflicting feelings of the father on the one hand, and the desire to obey God on the other, are struggling in his heaving bosom, we shall see the last proof of perfect reliance on the Divine rectitude, and the certain accomplishment of the Divine promises. The father of the faithful believed that Isaac, so miraculously bestowed, could be as miraculously restored.

Who can think of Isaac but with admiration, as he stands before his father, in the prime and strength of his manhood, the willing victim to parental requirements, when, from his age, he might have resisted his aged father? How strikingly calculated this remarkable history to direct our thoughts to a more exalted personage whom Isaac prefigured, and to a more astounding transaction represented by that on Mount Moriah!

Who among us that is familiar with sacred story has not gone out with the thoughtful and meditative Isaac at even-tide as he mused in his mind relating to the wife to be selected for him by his father's faithful servant, although there are few among us in these days that would render such a proof of their filial attachment?

But for the Bible, what should we have known of the interesting and chequered life of Jacob?

To the same old book are we indebted for the full-length portraiture of the illustrious legislator of the Israelites, Moses, a prince among the nobles of the earth, and second only to Him of whom he wrote. There also we read of his successor, Joshua, the son of Nun; and who can follow him in his wanderings with the ancient Israelites and not admire the piety, courage, and disinterested integrity which are so conspicuous throughout the whole history of that great general?

Then there is Elijah the Tishbite, one of the most eminent of the Jewish prophets, who set himself like a wall of brass in opposition to the idolatry of the times; and afterwards his disciple and successor in the prophetic office, Elisha, a worthy follower of one of the heroes of sacred story.

We come on to David, the shepherd king, who, in addition to his regal qualities, was the " sweet singer of Israel," a singularly valiant man, of a comely person, and one favoured of the Lord. Who can listen to his sacred harp without getting some of its melodies into his own heart? Who can go out with him, when he was but a mere stripling, to fight with the gigantic champion who defied the armies of Israel, and hear him saying with the confidence of a child, " The Lord that delivered me out of the paw of the lion, and out of the paw of the bear, He will deliver me out of the hand of this Philistine?" And yet, with all this trust in God, we see David's wisdom in selecting the best means to bring about the giant's destruction. Where is the Christian who has not had his inner life fed and cherished by the hymns of David, which excel no less in sublimity and tenderness of expression, than in loftiness and purity of religious sentiment? In comparison with these inspired productions the sacred poetry of all time sinks into mediocrity. The songs which cheered the solitude of the desert caves of Engedi, or resounded from the united voices of the Hebrew people as they wandered through the glens, and climbed the hill-sides of Judæa, have been repeated for ages in almost every part of the habitable world; in the remotest islands of the ocean; among the primeval forests of America, and the scorching sands of Africa. How many human hearts have these inspired songs softened, purified, and exalted! Of how many wretched beings have they been the sacred consolation.

Who can read of Solomon, at once the wisest and the weakest of men, the builder of the first temple made with hands, where dwelt the miraculous cloud of the Divine presence, so that the priests could no longer stand to perform the functions of their ministry, without seeing in him the type of one who was greater than Solomon and the temple also? It is from the Bible that we learn that he exceeded in riches and wisdom all the kings of the earth, and from the same impartial source we see how, with all his wisdom and wealth, that he was weak as water, when, in his declining years, his wives and concubines perverted his heart, so that he worshipped Ashtoreth, Molech, and Chemosh, for whom he built temples in Jerusalem, and thus openly insulted the Majesty he had once adored.

In the Bible we learn how the princely Daniel was faithful to the God of Heaven, in the midst of the idolatries and wickednesses of the courts of Babylon and Persia.

Passing over many others that might be named, who may be denominated " the lesser lights " of sacred story, we come into the New Testament, and are confronted at once with Incarnate Wisdom and Almighty Love, and are introduced to all the great and illustrious names recorded for our imitation in those sacred writings.

And what shall I more say? for the time would fail me to tell of the muster-roll of worthies, "who through faith subdued kingdoms, wrought righteousness, obtained promises, stopped the mouths of lions, quenched the violence of fire, escaped the edge of the sword, out of weakness were made strong, waxed valiant in fight, turned to flight the armies of the aliens. Women received their dead raised to life again; and others were tortured, not accepting deliverance; and others had trial of cruel mockings and scourgings, yea, moreover, of bonds and imprisonment; they were stoned, they were sawn asunder, were tempted, were slain with the sword; they wandered about in sheepskins and goatskins; being destitute, afflicted, tormented;

(of whom the world was not worthy); they wandered in deserts, and in mountains, and in dens and caves of the earth."

And now my work is done. These pages that have for many years been the companions of my solitude, that have wooed me to record my thoughts and feelings, whether they have been joyous or sad, will be placed in other hands, and looked at and read not only by kind and loving friends, for whose entertainment they were at first written, but to be scrutinized and conned by the critic whose office it is to pronounce judgment upon those who, for any reason, claim the right of authorship.

Be it so, "what I have written I have written." I know there are many blunders, both of style and composition, that I would fain have corrected, but which must now stand as they are. My book is, like myself, a strange mixture of good and evil; of mirth and sadness, of some follies that are hardly becoming in a man who has long since passed the meridian of his days, and whose thoughts do now take a more sober colouring as the shadows of life darken and deepen. But judge not harshly of my early follies, gentle reader,—

> " The cold in heart are cold in blood,
>   Their love can scarce deserve the name ;
> But mine was like a lava flood
>   That boils in Ætna's breast of flame.
>
> *   *   *   *
>
> 'Tis true, I could not whine, nor sigh,
> I knew but to obtain or die."

I fear that some of my Kentish friends will think that I have not said very much of my native county. I left it for the " Great Metropolis" when I was a youth, and since then my time has been so occupied that, until lately, I have only been able to spend parts of my vacation amid its beauties.

I go back to Kent always as to my first love ; and if I have said little of the county where I first saw the light, I am glad to find that our great Shakespeare has worthily embalmed it in his wondrous pages, as,—

> " Kent, in the Commentaries Cæsar writ,
> Is term'd the civil'st place of all this Isle;
> Sweet is the country, because full of riches;
> The people liberal, valiant, active, wealthy."

I am writing these concluding pages where I spent some years of my early life; and as I look round with never-wearying eye upon the brown and golden autumnal woods, and see on every hand the ripened and mellowed fruits carefully gathered, I am reminded not only that we "fade as the leaf," but that we also fall as they do ; and that as the fruits of the earth are gathered into garners, so we also must wait patiently till the Great Husbandman shall beckon us away. And although such scenes and reflections awaken within us a chastened and pensive feeling as the truth comes home to each heart that " it is appointed unto men once to die," yet wherefore should we fear? The many assurances from the Book of the Lord that He who made this beautiful world for man's enjoyment here, and has surrounded him with all the loving ministries that sweeten life, has provided another place, " our Father's house," where there are joys that " eye hath not seen, ear hath not heard, neither has the heart of man conceived."

And not only so, but when man had fallen hopelessly from his ancestral glory, " God so loved the world, that He gave His only-begotten Son, that whosoever believeth in Him should not perish, but have everlasting life." This knowledge of salvation through a crucified Saviour must come, not only to the outward ear, and be read by the natural eye, but must, by God's grace, be received into the heart, and have an abiding-place there, so that we may say, not with hypocritical cant and self-delusion, but in sober thoughtfulness—" He loved me, and gave Himself for me."

Let us give ourselves to Christ and His salvation, and our fears to the wind. When we came into this world

there were loving hearts and tender hands to minister to
our helplessness, and to enfold us in their bosom ; and
when our eyes are closed in death, and we cease to recog-
nize the dear familiar faces that gather around our bed,
and are unable to return the gentle pressure of the trembling hand that holds ours, and hear no longer the melody
of voices we have long loved, then shall angel-hands bear
our freed and ransomed spirit from all the trammels of
earth "through the portals of praise, to the temple of
light," and there, before the eternal throne, at our Father's
feet cast our blood-bought crowns of victory, and, as the
waving palm-branch is given to us, hear in soft and thrilling accents, from the lips of Him who once was crucified,
the welcome and transporting words—" Well done, good
and faithful servant, enter thou into the joy of thy Lord."

These, gentle reader, are my concluding thoughts ; and
yet when I gaze around me upon the fair and beautiful
face of nature, and think of those I love, I weep—

> " Tears, idle tears, I know not what they mean,
> Tears from the depth of some divine despair
> Rise in the heart and gather to the eyes.
> In looking on the happy autumn fields,
> And thinking of the days that are no more."

In parting with my book, and with my readers, I am
reminded of other partings. Natural partings are painful
and tear asunder our hearts, but spiritual partings are far
more distressing. The writer of these pages was once
witness to a scene on the platform of one of our railways
that he will never forget. It was early morning, and there
was all the bustle going on of the necessary preparations
for the departure of a train. Aside from the crowd stood a
little group consisting of a father and mother, and a young
girl of about nineteen, who was leaving her native land
with two friends, who were returning to one of our distant
colonies. The time for the train to start had expired, and
this little group moved towards the carriage that was to bear
away a first-born darling child to the ship—

"That sinks with all we love below the western wave."

Oh, what a parting was that, where the lines were verified with terrible faithfulness—

> " When eyes are beaming,
>   What never tongue might tell ;
> When tears are streaming
>   From their crystal cell;
> When hands are link'd, that dread to part,
>   And heart is press'd to throbbing heart;
> Oh ! bitter—bitter is the smart,
>   Of those that say farewell !"

Never shall I forget that mother's countenance, and the
dumb agonized look of the father, who struggled to master
the strong emotions that made him stagger like a drunken
man, as the train moved slowly out of the station, and they
stood silently gazing up the line, long after the carriages
were out of sight.

This was a scene that will long be remembered ; but
there are spiritual partings that are even more solemn and
affecting. To take leave of those we have talked with
upon the great matter of the soul's salvation, and whom
we have tenderly and affectionately warned " to flee from
the wrath to come," is intensely painful, and is also fraught
with consequences of the greatest possible moment. Oh !
that I could hope and believe that some who have read my
humble pages, and who have hitherto neglected their eternal welfare, have been led by anything I have written to
moral thoughtfulness, and to yield themselves to God, our
Father. If so, let the following beautiful lines of one of
the " sweetest singers of Israel " be the expression of your
heart—

> " O God, mine inmost soul convert,
> And deeply on my thoughtful heart
>   Eternal things impress ;
> Give me to feel their solemn weight,
> And tremble on the brink of fate,
>   And wake to righteousness.

Before me place, in dread array,
The pomp of that tremendous day,
   When Thou with clouds shalt come
To judge the nations at Thy bar;
And tell me, Lord, shall I be there,
   To meet a joyful doom?

Be this my one great business here,
With serious industry and fear,
   Eternal bliss to ensure;
Thine utmost counsel to fulfil,
And suffer all Thy righteous will,
   And to the end endure.

Then, Saviour, then my soul receive,
Transported from this vale, to live
   And reign with Thee above;
Where faith is sweetly lost in sight,
And hope in full supreme delight,
   And everlasting love."

We must now separate, my kind and patient reader, you to take upon yourself the responsibility of having heard again and again the offer made to you from God's Word of pardon, sanctification, and eternal life, through Jesus Christ our Lord and Saviour, and I to render an account of what I have written. We shall meet again. May it be in heaven!

As I take a parting glance at these pages I say from my heart—

" Go forth, O book! baptized with tears;
Tremble no more with modest fears;
   With love thou shalt be blest.
If any greet thee with disdain,
Suffer, but not parade thy pain,
   And meekly do thy best.

O book! if any show thee slight,
Thou knowest with pain and with delight
   Thou of the heart wast born;
Hast in thee life of shade and shower,
Of sunny and of starry hour,
   Of evening and of dawn.

A little while and he who writes,
With silent voice and pen laid down,
    In quiet earth shall lie.

*   *   *   *   *

Inspiring Saviour, unto Thee
My work I give in fealty,—
    Thy life I have, and seek :
Accept this sacrifice, O Lord ;
Weak am I,—but if therefore strong,
    O keep me ever weak !"

One more word, and I have done.   I hope I have not written a line in these pages that shall leave a stain behind, or shall be a matter of regret in my last hours.   I have put my pen through many a passage which, though true, too true, might nevertheless lead many a youth to do what I would fain have him avoid.   And, finally, let me remind all who have glanced over these brief reminiscences of my chequered and eventful life, that—

" We live in deeds, not years ; in thoughts, not breaths ;
In feelings, not in figures on a dial.
We should count time by heart-throbs.   He most lives
Who thinks most—feels the noblest—ACTS THE BEST."

INDEX.

LIST OF SUBSCRIBERS.

THE ROYAL LIBRARY, Windsor Castle.
The Queen's Private Library.
H. R. H. Albert Edward, Prince of
Wales.
His Grace the Lord Archbishop of Canterbury.

Adams, H. G. Esq. Rochester.
Anthony, Charles, Esq. Hereford.
Baber, Rev. H. H. Streatham, Cambridgeshire. *Two copies.*
Baines, Frederick, Esq. Leeds.
Barnard, Miss, Richmond, Surrey.
Bascomb, G. H. Esq. Chiselhurst.
Bellamy, Edward, Esq. London. *Two copies.*
Binney, Rev. T. London.
Benham, Fred. Esq. London.
Bohn, Henry G. Esq. London.
Bonthron, R. Esq. London.
Boone, Thomas, Esq. London.
Bosworth, Rev. J., D.D., F.R.S., F.S.A., &c. Christ Church, Oxford; and Trinity College, Cambridge.
Bowser, J. C. Esq. London.
Brackett, Wm. Esq. Tunbridge Wells.
Breton, H. Esq. Southampton.
Bridges, Sir Brook W. Bart. M.P. Godnestone Park, Kent.
Bright, John, Esq. M.P. Rochdale.
Brock, Rev. W., D.D. London.
Burden, Stephen, Esq. London. *Three copies.*
Burden, Thomas, Esq. London.
Callard, T. K. Esq. London.

CALLARD, D. J. Esq. London.
CALLARD, DANIEL, Esq. London.
CANNON, CHARLES, Esq. Assistant, British Museum.
CARLESS, JOSEPH, Esq. Hereford.
CARR, E. Esq. Forest Hill. *Two copies.*
CARTER, C. P. Esq. Kennington Hall, Ashford.
CHICK, WM. Esq. Hereford.
CHOWNE, REV. J. P. Bradford.
CHRISTOPHERSON, REV. H. London.
CLARKE, R. H. Esq. London.
COBB, CHARLES, Esq. Strood.
COBDEN, MRS. RICHARD, Midhurst.
COLLICOTT, MISS, Tunbridge Wells.
COOKE, H. A. Esq. Hampstead.
COOPER, THOMAS, Esq. Thannington House, Canterbury.
COUTTS, MISS BURDETT, London.
COWTAN, CAPTAIN, Hereford.
COWTAN, MAWER, Esq. Kensington.
COXETER, JAMES, Esq. London.
CULYER, MISS, Blakeney.
CUNNINGTON, MISS ISABEL, Devizes.
CUNNINGTON, WILLIAM, Esq. Devizes.
DAVIDSON, WM. Esq. Haggerston.
DAVIES, THOS. Esq. Blackheath.
DALE, MRS. Hampstead.
DAY, A. GREGORY, Esq. Dorking.
DELMAR, WM. Esq. Canterbury.
DICKENS, CHARLES, Esq. Gads Hill.
DUNNING, MRS. Throwleigh.
EDEN, REV. A. Ticehurst.
EDMONSTON AND DOUGLAS, MESSRS. Edinburgh.
EDWARDS, CHARLES, Esq. London.
EIVES, JOHN, Esq. Forest Hill.
ELPHINSTONE, JOHN, Esq. London.
ENGALL, THOMAS, Esq. M.R.C.S. London.
EWART, WILLIAM, Esq. M.P. Broadlease, Devizes.
FAULDING, F. H. Esq. Glen Osmond, Adelaide, South
    Australia.

FAULDING, J. ESQ. London.
FILMER, THE DOWAGER LADY, London.
FLOWER, MISS, London.
FURLEY, GEORGE, ESQ. Canterbury.
GARNETT, RICHARD, ESQ. Assistant, British Museum.
GOODE, C. H. ESQ. M.P. Adelaide, South Australia.
    Fifty copies.
GORDON, MRS. ALEXANDER, Hampstead.
GORE, FRED. ESQ. R. N. Chislett.
GORE, REV. JOHN, Vicar of Shalbourne, Hungerford.
GORE, MISS, Chislett.
GRANT AND SONS, MESSRS. Edinburgh. *Four copies.*
GRAY, MRS. JOHN EDWARD, British Museum.
GREENHILL, JOSEPH, ESQ. Stationers' Hall.
GRIFFITHS, C. DARBY, ESQ. M.P. Padworth House,
    Reading.
GUMBLETON, MISS, London..
HABERSHON, W. G. ESQ. Belvedere, Kent.
HALDANE, ROBERT, ESQ. Edinburgh.
HALDANE, MRS. Edinburgh.
HAMILTON, REV. J., D.D., F.L.S. London.
HARVEY, JAMES, ESQ. Hampstead.
HAWKINS, EDWARD, ESQ. F.R.S., F.S.A., F.L.S. London.
HENDERSON, H. ESQ. London.
HIDER, MISS, Rochester.
HOPE, A. J. B. ESQ. M.P., F.S.A. Bedgebury Park,
    Kent.
HUMPHREYS, T. ESQ. Weobley.
JARVIS, JACOB, ESQ. Houghton Hall.
JOBBINS, C. ESQ. London.
KENNETT, F. ESQ. Canterbury.
KENRICK, MISS, Canterbury.
KEMP, JOHN, ESQ. Copyright Office, British Museum.
KING, EDWARD, ESQ. London.
KING, MISS HARRIETT, Hampstead.
KNIGHT, J. C. ESQ. Assistant, British Museum.
KNIGHT, REV. R., A.M. North Marsden.
LANDELS, REV. W. London.

LONGMAN, WM. ESQ. London.
LOWELL, WM. ESQ. London.
LUSH, SIR ROBERT, London.
LUSH, LADY, London.
MACLAREN, J. ESQ. Edinburgh.
MAJOR, R. H. ESQ. F.S.A., F.R.G.S., &c. Assistant,
    British Museum.
MARSHALL, J. D. ESQ. Edinburgh.
MARTIN, C. WYKEHAM, ESQ. M.P. Leeds Castle, Kent.
MASTERS, MR. ALDERMAN, Canterbury.
MAYS, MRS. WM. East Rudham.
MESHAM, REV. A. B. Canterbury.
METIVIER, J. ESQ. Assistant, British Museum.
MIALL, EDWARD, ESQ. Welland House, Forest Hill.
MILLARD, MRS. EDWARD, Hampstead.
MILNES, WM. ESQ. Bradford.
MOORE, GEORGE, ESQ. M.D. Hastings.
NELSON AND SONS, MESSRS. Edinburgh.
NEWENHAM, MRS. London.
NORTON, JOHN, ESQ. Raynham.
OSMOND, A. ESQ. London. *Five copies.*
OWEN, RICHARD, ESQ. M.D., D.C.L., LL.D., F.R.S.,
    Superintendent of the Natural History Departments,
    British Museum, &c., Sheen Lodge, Richmond Park.
PETO, SIR S. MORTON, BART., M.P. Sevenoaks.
PLAYER, J. ESQ. Birmingham.
PORTER, G. W. ESQ. Assistant, British Museum.
PRIEGGEN, MRS. WILHELM, London.
PRYCE, REV. R. VAUGHAN, M.A., LL.B. Brighton.
PULLAR, JOHN, ESQ. Perth.
PULLAR, LAURENCE, ESQ. Perth.
RATHBORN, EDWARD, ESQ. West Rudham.
RAWLINGS, DANIEL, ESQ. London.
RAWLINGS, WM. ESQ. London.
REED, HENRY, ESQ. Tunbridge Wells.
RIDGWAY, MRS. London. *Two copies.*
RIDGWAY, MISS, London.
ROTHWELL, PETER, ESQ. London.

ROUCH, REV. F. Canterbury.

RYE, W. B. ESQ. Assistant-Keeper, Department of Printed Books, British Museum.

SAMPSON, MARMADUKE B. ESQ. Consulate General of the Argentine Republic, London.

SANDERSON, DR. BURDON, London.

SANDERSON, MISS BURDON, Hampstead.

SANDERSON, MISS J. C. BURDON, Hampstead.

SANKEY, ROBERT, ESQ. Canterbury.

SEATON, S. ESQ. Chatham.

SEYMOUR, MISS, Hampstead.

SEYMOUR, MRS. BENJAMIN, Hackney.

SHIPTON, W. E. ESQ. Secretary Young Men's Christian Association, London.

SIBREE, PRIESTLY, ESQ. Cobham Park, Bristol.

SIMONS, N. W. ESQ. Assistant, British Museum.

SIMPSON, PROFESSOR J. Y., M.D., F.R.C.P.E. &c. Edinburgh University.

SLADEN, REV. E. H. M. Alton Barnes.

SLOPER, G. E. ESQ. Devizes.

SMITH, F. ESQ. Canterbury.

SMITH, THOMAS, ESQ. East Rudham.

STENT, MRS. WARBURTON, London.

STEPHENS, HORATIO, ESQ. Tunbridge Wells. *Three copies.*

STEPHENS, EDWARD, ESQ. Tunbridge Wells.

STEVENS, HENRY, ESQ. London.

STRATTEN, A. C. ESQ. London.

STRATTEN, REV. JAMES, London.

THOMPSON, JOHN, ESQ. London.

THOMPSON, LIEUT.-GEN. PERRONET, Eliot Vale, Blackheath.

THORLEY AND BECKLEY, MESSRS. Tunbridge Wells.

TUPPER, M. F. ESQ. Albury.

TURMAINE, GEORGE, ESQ. Canterbury.

TYSSEN, J. R. D. ESQ. F.S.A. Brighton.

USHER, JAMES, ESQ. Clifton.

WACHER, JOSEPH, ESQ. Chislett Court.

WALKER, J. ESQ. London.

WASE, MRS. Richmond, Surrey.

WATTS, THOMAS, ESQ. Assistant-Keeper, Department of Printed Books, British Museum.

WAY, T. B. ESQ. London.

WELCH, MISS, Tunbridge Wells.

WESTON, MRS. EDWARD, London.

WHITE, ADAM, ESQ. F.L.S. &c. Edinburgh.

WICKS, J. SENR. ESQ. Colchester.

WIGAN, MISS, Clare House, Maidstone.

WILKINSON, J. J. GARTH, ESQ. M.R.C.S., L.S.A., &c. London.

WILKINSON, T. ESQ. Canterbury.

WILKS, JOS. ESQ. London.

WILSON, JOSHUA, ESQ. Tunbridge Wells.

WILSON, SIR THOMAS MARYON, BART.

WOOD, JOHN, ESQ. Chatham.

If any names are omitted in the above list, they were received too late for insertion.

CHISWICK PRESS:—PRINTED BY WHITTINGHAM AND WILKINS, TOOKS COURT, CHANCERY LANE.

BY THE SAME AUTHOR.

Preparing for immediate publication, printed by
Whittingham and Wilkins, in 8vo.
Price 12s 6d.

A CENTURY OF GLEANINGS FROM

KENTISH NEWSPAPERS.

HISTORICAL, BIOGRAPHICAL, ANECDOTAL,

POLITICAL, AND DOMESTIC.

RELATING TO THE COUNTY OF KENT.

1736—1836.

" Kent, in the Commentaries Cæsar writ,
Is term'd the civil'st place of all this Isle.
Sweet is the country, because full of riches;
The people liberal, valiant, active, wealthy."
SHAKESPEARE.

EDITED BY

REGINALD FITZ-ROY STANLEY, M.A.

As only a limited number of copies will be printed, those desirous of obtaining them will please communicate with the editor, 3, Bickerton-terrace, Maitland-park, London, N.W.